The Gifts We Keep

The

Gifts

We

Keep

KATIE GRINDELAND

OOLIGAN PRESS | PORTLAND, OREGON

Library Writers Project

Ooligan Press and Multnomah County Library have created a unique partnership celebrating the Portland area's local authors. Each fall since 2015, Multnomah County Library has solicited submissions of self-published works of fiction by local authors to be added to its Library Writers Project ebook collection. Multnomah County Library and Ooligan Press have partnered to bring these previously ebook-only works to print. *The Gifts We Keep* is the first of a planned annual series of Library Writers Project books to be published by Ooligan Press.

The Gifts We Keep
© 2019 Katie Grindeland

ISBN13: 978-1-947845-06-0

Ooligan Press
Portland State University
Post Office Box 751, Portland, Oregon 97207
503-725-9748
ooligan@ooliganpress.pdx.edu
http://ooligan.pdx.edu

Library of Congress Cataloging-in-Publication Data
Names: Grindeland, Katie, author.
Title: The gifts we keep / by Katie Grindeland.
Description: Portland, Oregon: Ooligan Press, Portland State University, [2019]
Identifiers: LCCN 2018043433 | ISBN 9781947845060 (pbk.)
Subjects: LCSH: Domestic fiction.
Classification: LCC PS3607.R5665 G54 2019 | DDC 813/.6—dc23

Cover design by Kristen Ludwigsen
Interior design by Bryn Kristi

References to website URLs were accurate at the time of writing. Neither the author nor Ooligan Press is responsible for URLs that have changed or expired since the manuscript was prepared.

Printed in the United States of America

Contents

ꙮ

For my bright and beautiful children.
And for you. If you are reading this, then this is for you, too.

One

Henry begins

We are turning spring beds in the garden when Tillie tells me
Emerson is coming home. My shovel blade slips and strikes stone,
jarring my calloused hands and corkscrewing away.

"Forget your herb garden, Tillie. You're better off growing
stones." I drop to my knees and begin to dig with dirt-creased
fingers, trying to free the rock. It is blue-sky mid-May, and warm
enough to make me wish I hadn't worn boots. The dirt plants a
thorn in my hand that my broad, grubby fingers can't retrieve. I
lean toward Tillie and she pulls the thorn delicately.

"Did you hear me, Henry? Emerson's coming back from the
city. I thought you'd like to know."

I haul a fist-sized stone from the half-turned bed and chuck it
toward the blue wheelbarrow. The one Will bought to replace the
broken wooden one just before he died. I wipe the sweat from
my eyes with the back of my hand and look at Tillie. Where she
sits she looks planted, like a small tree, and flushed from the sun,

brown and gray hair fraying from a loose braid. She wears a faded denim shirt that used to be mine, although she probably doesn't know it, and cut-off shorts that end raggedly where her legs end, just north of the knee. Where her knees used to be she wears beige body socks—to protect her legs from all the flinging around, she says. She holds a red-handled trowel mid-air, caught in the question of her unknowable sister.

I throw another rock into the wheelbarrow with a satisfying clang. "There should be a Farmer's Olympics for shit like this," I say. "They could televise it. John Deere could buy air time. Guys in overalls hucking rocks, racing combines, speed-milking cows." I know it pisses her off that I say guys, as if all farmers are guys, as if all those Friday night beer-on-the-porch feminist sermons have yielded nothing. I yank another stone from between my knees and heave it toward the blue metal wheelbarrow. It clanks dismally against the outside and falls dull to the ground. I shake my head and climb to my feet.

"Henry?" Tillie is concerned, and I admit I like it. Let her wonder. Henry the rock. The solid. The standing stone. Henry the weary. I dig into the bed again and turn a shovelful of thick earth. Barring the stones, this soil is rich and healthy, good for growing.

"Emerson, sure," I say lightly. "That's good. It's her place, she should live here. She hasn't been over since, what? Christmas?"

Tillie nods, still looking at me carefully, squinting against the bright afternoon sky. Her hazel eyes are almost green in the sunshine, and smile lines fan deeply toward her temples. "She's coming to stay, for a while at least. Mother spoke to her last night on the phone."

I can't tell her I dreamt Emerson just two nights past. Both of them, actually, sisters side by side, but young again, in their twenties, as if I'd known them then. In the dream, Tillie is in her wheelchair at a crowded gallery opening where we're both showing artwork, but the sun is too bright to see anything and too many people are in the way. Then Emerson is there, tall and beautiful and purposeful and alone, and I think she is the true work of art, the real reason we are all gathered. Then she falls to her knees and begins to cry, and I can do nothing to help her.

I kick at the soil to nudge a rock. "So, all of you here together? I'm surprised she'd want that. She's not booting you out, is she?"

Tillie's laugh is like a boat you want to sail away on, the kind that makes you want to jump on board. She laughs now, and I know she isn't worried. "We're kind of a lot to move, Mother and me."

I stop to drink water from her Nalgene bottle and watch her tan arms spade the earth tenaciously. For the hundredth time I wonder what she was like before she lost her legs, when the boys flocked around her. I imagine her teenage-rock-climber strong, with that buoyant laugh and her talented, artistic hands. Maybe a jealous god thought she got too much, had to lop off just a little to make her more like the rest of us. She unearths a stone and tosses it over her shoulder toward the wheelbarrow, where it lands clean among its wayward brothers.

I cheer madly and make crowd sounds, startling the crows overhead. "And the American wins the gold, ladies and gentlemen, in the garden-full-of-rocks event! Let's go in for an interview." I drop to my knees to be Tillie-height and thrust the shovel handle her way.

"Thank you so much, it's just been an honor." She makes a show of brushing her hair back from her face, girl-style, and speaks into the microphone. "First, I'd like to thank the competition, for being so lousy…" I nod slightly. "And secondly, I guess I'll have to thank Mother Nature for depositing so many rocks in my sister's field."

She drops the shovel and frowns. "Something weird is going on, don't you think? Why would she be coming back?"

I shrug. "Maybe it's about Will. Maybe she wants to…" *make amends*, I think but don't say. I sigh heavily. "I don't know."

After Will died twelve years ago, Emerson was like a wraith, floating around the autumn house. From next door I watched her walking the traces of the property, down from gabled country house, past the decorative barn, and up to Looking Lake Road—then back again, past the house, past the manicured garden and all the way down to the edge of the lake. She would not use the garden gate to my yard, not even look that way, and soon the rhododendrons grew and obscured the little stone path. And now, from this side, the gate doesn't seem to be there at all.

"And the weirdest part, Henry? She's bringing someone with her. Can you imagine?"

I step too hard into my shovel, my boot hits the dirt, and my chest hits the wooden handle like a stab to the heart.

"Who knows? She's your sister." The words catch in my throat, and Tillie glances up from where she's planted in the earth. "Maybe it's a boyfriend," I say, and my voice is too loud for my own ears. "Hell, maybe she remarried and didn't get around to telling anybody."

Beautiful Tillie laughs lightly at the sky. "Can you imagine?" she says again. "Can you even imagine? Emerson falling in love again?"

Tillie begins

Four o'clock light spills through the kitchen window, and I can see the African violet needs a dusting. My arms are tired and the wings of my lower back ache. A working-the-body ache, a still-alive-and-humming ache. I imagine it's the ache a cedar trunk feels after a December storm. I can see myself, tall and red—I always wanted to be a redhead—and swaying with the wind over everyone's head. The kitchen light spills from the window to the dusty leaves to the burnt-orange tiled counter and onto the blond hickory floor. I sip ginger tea and watch the light and remember when Emmy and Will were converting the old farmhouse, the fun they had arguing over the floors. Brazilian teak and white oak and other hard woods for Tillie's wheelchair, and no loose rugs, no high lips between rooms, nothing to impede me from free movement, on the first floor, at least. The wheelchair ramps, the extra rooms. We didn't say the words out loud, but we all knew we were graphing Mother's death, planning the eventual. And it's true; I looked forward to the country house, imagined myself cruising from light-filled room to light-filled room, imagined my studio mid-beam, my easel bathing in good northern light. And we did not know, could not have known, how it would turn out. Maybe Will knew. I suppose he did.

I want to climb up to reach the African violet from the sill, give her a good dusting, but my arms are tired and the sunlight is on my face now and I just want to sit in the light and the quiet. Henry is upset but won't talk. He's in the garden still, though he said he was nearly done. I can see him in my mind, picking through his blue wheelbarrow, choosing rocks to salt away for his art or his landscaping or whatever. He is tall—to me, everyone is tall—and the youngest of all of us at forty-four, five years younger than me. Funny to think he's one of us; he's the neighbor, the caretaker, the sculptor, the brawny blond woodsman boy. His yard is finely crafted—a gift for Buddha, he says. Once, I found him sitting on the stone thinking bench in his rock garden. I wanted a ride, a trip to the store, just his company or something, but my wheels crunched the gravel, my breathing was too loud in the stillness, and it was cold enough to see our breath. Eyes closed, he was like a still dragon, like Buddha himself, sitting among the stones under his homemade cedar pergola. He was tan even in November and terribly handsome, blond hair casually pointing every which way. And I didn't want to interrupt, but I needed him, and needed him more for seeing how cold, how still, how alone he could be. I needed him, and I didn't know how to get to where he was, and then he opened his eyes and saw me, and I must have been crying. He sprang to me and wrapped strong, warm arms around me and knelt in the gravel beside my chair for the longest time on that cold, cold day, holding me and rocking me and not saying a word.

I hear Mother's car in the drive. She's been out most of the day, and I'm glad she's taken her anxiety elsewhere. Her feet pound on the porch, and she pushes through the kitchen door, forcing even the air out of her way. She is small-boned but hardly fragile, usually gentle, except when worry goads her to busyness, to hectic industry. She uses both arms to hug a bag of groceries from an upscale market and holds a large Starbucks cup in her hand. Her Guatemalan handbag dangles from the crook of her elbow, where it has slipped. She drops her groceries onto the counter, blocking the sunlight.

"Not a word about the Starbucks today, please, Tillie. I am not in the mood for an argument."

I raise my hand in abeyance and roll out of her way, next to the tall chairs at the breakfast bar we never use for breakfast. "How can I help?" I say, just as Henry steps in carrying two more grocery bags.

"That's the rest of it, I think, Eve." He sets the bags down and smiles faintly at me. My tea has grown cold, but I sip it anyway.

Mother takes a deep breath and laughs weakly. "I'm just scattered," she says. "I feel untethered."

"That's funny, Mother. Usually you like floating around in space."

"Oh, that's true, isn't it?" She takes fresh tomatoes and a carton of eggs out of the bag, then stops again. She reaches for Henry and puts a wrinkled hand on his cheek. "You're sweet for helping," she says, and I love to look at them together. Mother so small, Henry so tall. She loves him more than a son, I think, because you have to love your children, but she gets to choose to love Henry. "And you're filthy," she adds, patting his ratty shirt. "What on earth have you been up to today?"

"Think I'm bad, have a look at your daughter," he says, nodding at me, and I'm grateful to be included.

"Oh, you two," she chirrups, and I feel warm in her light. "You're like preschool chums, mucking about in the dirt." Her hands dance around while she talks, and that's how I know she's happy.

Henry opens the fridge and starts putting groceries away. "Is that what your girls were like? When they were young?"

"Oh no, nothing like that. Emmy would never have gotten dirty like that. Even when she was small, if the neighbor kids acted up and she didn't approve, she'd come inside."

Henry sets the lettuce in a colander in the sink while Mother floats out of his way, sipping her sweet coffee.

"Do you remember those Parker boys?" she says, stepping past me to put white sugar in the tin on the counter. "They used to have dirt clod fights at the end of the cul-de-sac one street over, where the new houses were being built. I swear, they were like wild savages, those boys, and Emmy would have nothing to do with them." Her hands wave like beautiful wings.

"I remember Aaron Parker trying to kiss me in the rocket ship at the park," I say fondly.

"Did you let him?" Henry asks.

"I did, because he smelled like Juicy Fruit. But Emmy found me and dragged me home. She was supposed to be watching me, and she ripped the strap on my Brownies jumper by accident."

Mother turns and frowns at me. "Why don't I remember that? We would have had to buy a new one. Your father must have been angry."

I look at her over the rim of my teacup, and she's so small and light, like a bit of fluff on the wind, trying to dip into everyone's lives then dance away before too much is expected. "Emmy sewed the jumper herself, before you got home from the Auxiliary." In my mind, I can see my sister punching the needle through the fabric while I hop foot-to-foot in my blouse and underpants. Her disapproval was oceans-deep but rolled off my delighted back like rain off a slicker. "She never told on me for disobeying."

Henry starts folding the bags while Mother stares out the kitchen window. "I can't imagine her telling on anyone," he says, trying to reel Mother back in. "Did she tell you about the Parker boys?"

"Goodness, no," Mother says, and I feel a pinprick of secret delight, as if for once I'm the good daughter. "Emerson wouldn't tell me anything. Didn't then, doesn't now."

"Then how did you know about dirt clod fights?" he asks, and I smile, knowing the punch line to this one.

"Why, because I was over there, for the Welcome Wagon, and those Parker boys set on me, the three of them from up on that pile of dirt. And now what boy would throw dirt at someone else's mother, I ask you? Little savages, they were, like wild Indians—can I say that, Tillie?"

I shrug. "You can say whatever you want, Mother."

She steps up close to Henry and puts her hand on his shoulder and he stops working and smiles down, as if she is a gift, a bird that's stopped mid-flight for him alone. "And do you know what I did? I charged up that hill, right where they were sitting, and I whooped and hollered and yelled like I was going to scalp them all. I scared those boys so badly, they up and ran, and I stood there in my good shoes and rose-print dress and threw dirt clods at their backs. I told Adam to expect a blustery phone call that night from their father, but it never came. I guess they never told."

"Eve, you amaze me."

Mother pats his arm in the light from the window while I sit quiet in the kitchen shadow. She reaches for the African violet on the sill while Henry begins to wash the lettuce in the sink. I watch her stroke the leaves absentmindedly, then put the plant on the kitchen table.

"Mother?" I ask, rolling toward her. "Do you know when Emmy's coming?"

She looks at me, her face like an open page in a book I've never read, as if she's surprised I'm there. "Oh, goodness. Well, she wouldn't tell me, now would she?" Thinking about Emerson seems to make her tense again, and she moves quickly to the drain board to put pans away. I wonder if maybe I've done that on purpose, pulled her back like that. Sometimes I hate watching her float away on her cloud.

"Oh, Tillie, I stopped at that little co-op you like." Her voice is sweet and teasing and I love her again. "Gavin was there. She asked about you, wanted to know how you're doing. She said she hasn't seen you in days."

I feel my neck flush, the way it does. "Mother, I really don't need your help with this." Henry turns from where he's washing lettuce and smiles at me with his eyes.

"I think maybe you should invite her over. Or to your next show, maybe. She's just charming, and so skinny and strong. I watched her unloading sacks of potatoes. And she seems *interested*." Mother doesn't finish clearing the drain board but walks over to me and bends down, smelling of lavender and caramel coffee. She kisses me on the cheek and whispers, "You deserve nice things."

"Yes, I do," I say, and maybe begin to mean it.

Mother turns to her favorite neighbor-son. "Thank you, Henry. You're a blessing, as always."

Henry doesn't turn from the sink but kisses the wet fingers of an open palm and raises his hand to the sky, a regular gesture for him. It looks like a benediction to the designer lighting overhead.

"I'm going to freshen up," Mother says. "And you two should consider doing the same."

Henry wipes his hands on a towel and turns. "Eve? Where did you want me to put the violet?"

"Oh, no, that's for Tillie. You wanted it, didn't you?"

"Um, yeah, I did." It is not unusual for Mother to sense my thoughts, but she always chooses funny things, never the really important ones. It's like she picks up part of a commercial when she's running down the radio dial but misses the emergency broadcast.

We are all anxious, coping as we may. Mother hummingbirds about. Henry works, and endears. I used to cope by making myself helpful, the way Henry does, but more and more I find myself just sitting back and watching the show, as Emerson would. I suppose when she comes I'll have to come up with a new way of coping so we don't occupy the same space. I roll to the table where the dusty plant sits, feeling covered in dust myself. Emerson is coming; my big sister is coming back to her own house. She is coming to stay, and we are all afraid she will dislodge us from our safe and tenuous home. She is untouchable, and Henry likes her best. Emerson is coming and she's bringing someone with her, someone who will probably resent all of us anyway, someone else to get in the way and block the warm afternoon light.

Eve begins

My daughter's master suite has two golden picture windows and a broad expanse of sky and a small veranda for lake and garden viewing, a widow's walk for her and me, both widows as we are. If I sit on the edge of the whirlpool tub, I can see the long gravel drive and the rustic horse fence for the horses we don't have and a small stretch of Looking Lake Road. My orbit takes me from the edge of the bed to the veranda to the picture frames on the vanity, then back to the tub, thinking I hear her car in the drive, thinking she may have really come. I lie on the chenille bedspread and think about the wrinkles I'm making in my linen pants and listen to the clock's *Tick, tick* on the mantel. Over the bed is a mobile of birds in flight. It is handmade, from India, a gift from Tillie. I like to watch the blues and yellows and reds in a gentle swing, as simple as fish in a daughter's fishbowl. It makes me think of the mobiles Tillie says hang over the tables at the ob-gyn. She laughs about it, as if something so silly could distract you from cold gloved hands and open, naked parts. When I had babies, I was alone in a room full of strangers and Adam was overseas and they told me not to scream. I don't tell Tillie this. Sometimes the gift we give our children is the luxury of not knowing.

Poor Tillie. When I told her Emerson was coming, she sagged like a sunflower in September. I'm glad she has Henry. He's never seemed awed or shadowed by Emmy, not like most everyone else. She's like a powerful tide, my eldest daughter, and that isn't always a good way to be.

The bedroom is warm from the spring afternoon, and my heart pings to think of giving it up. But of course it's Emerson's room, and I can move down the hall to the guest room. I stand from the bed and tighten the spread, thinking I'd like to get dinner started, maybe vacuum upstairs, but I don't like being barefoot on the hardwood floors when they need to be swept, and I don't want to put shoes back on, so I find myself back on the veranda, looking up at a jet trail in the blue, blue sky.

When Adam was alive, we both loved to fly. We had to add extra pages to our passports to accommodate all the stamps. I wish I'd taken the girls more places when they were young enough to enjoy it, but it was such a thrill to go away by ourselves. Business trips to London and Athens, pleasure trips to St. Moritz and Papeete. I used to love wandering the streets of a foreign city, getting lost just to hold a new taste in my mouth, just to photograph the Blessed Virgin in the courtyard of a hidden church, then a little bistro or a café for bread and cheese and wine, then a harrowing taxi ride back to the hotel, where we'd make love all afternoon while the breeze whispered the curtains free.

I walk to the bathroom again to watch the curling driveway. Emerson is so sad, so frozen; I can't imagine her throwing her clothes in a pile to lie naked in a soft golden field. I can't imagine her missing a flight because the landlady invites her for bratwurst and strudel. She is my eldest daughter, tall like a meadow reed, rigid and graceful, and my fondest wish is to take her hand and pull her with me into a mountain pool on a hot day, to watch her paddle and splash and float while dragonflies land nearby—free and easy.

And Tillie, my baby, I wish to see her grow and thrive. She sits in shadow, stunted, like her legs were the roots and now she cannot drink. When she was young, she galloped like a horse, her long brown hair like a mane streaming behind. I am proud to have daughters, but I worry at their sadness, their unwillingness to try. Did Adam and I do that to them? I can't imagine how.

And then I see a black Lexus pull into the drive, and my heart starts to pound like a sparrow caught in a screen. I can't see through the tinted windows, but I know it is her. As soon as I am able, I fling myself out of the room, down the stairs, and out to the front porch, ready to begin whatever comes next, ready to welcome with open arms.

Emerson begins

It feels like a failure to return here, but sometimes we have to admit that life is bigger than we can hold in our own two hands. I think of Robert Frost: "Home is the place where, when you have to go there, they have to take you in." So here are my hands, already full: my consulting business, and the City Club, two boards I like and a third I've just detached from, gourmet cooking classes on Thursday nights, and now Lily White's husband wants to collaborate on his wine book with me. And the Lake Oswego house is almost too much for one woman to keep up alone, but I hate to pay someone to do work I can do myself. Sometimes I feel so tired I want to curl up in a nest somewhere, someplace warm and sweet, but when I stop working, the gray clouds seep back inside and I feel lost in the darkness. I go to the MAC three times a week and cycle until my shirt sticks to my back, or run hills in well-appointed neighborhoods, and still I feel like a heavy, damp fog wants to pull me down and down and down.

I can see Mother on the porch, waving like a spirited puppy, and I have a swift memory of a birthday party—one I didn't want to have, with cartoon characters on the cake and Mother spinning from guest to guest like a tornado, gleefully trying to buoy us up. Tillie was cuter than me and won the prize at musical chairs even though Mother warned us she'd have our necks if we didn't let the other kids win.

I park the car and sigh. Beside me, Addie is stiff in her seat, looking down at her hands, and for a minute my heart aches. "Ready?" I ask.

She shrugs and I watch the end of her black braid scratch against her sweater. I reach over and put my hand on her shoulder, but the touch feels forced, uncomfortable for us both. I return my hand to my lap and watch her pale chin quiver. She is ten years old and the saddest child I've ever met.

"Well," I say. "Let's get this over with."

I step out of the car. Mother is down the porch steps, arms wide. I oblige her hug and feel how she's grown smaller, baby bird bones in an old woman wrapper. She reaches up to my face and I smile; I can't help but love her.

"It is good to see you," she says softly. "We've been waiting." She looks behind me, and I turn around to where Addie stands near the car.

"Mother," I say. "This is Adelaide. Addie Long. She's a friend of Michael's. She flew in from Anchorage yesterday, and she's going to be staying with us for a little while." I feel how tight my shoulders have become and force myself to drop them down.

Mother smiles broadly and walks to where Addie stares at the dirt. She's only a head or so taller than the girl. Her ivory linen pants are wrinkled, and she's exasperatingly barefoot. Her white hair is sparser than I remember, and wild, looking wind-whipped on this bright, warm, windless spring day. I feel that small sunburst of love again and wish it were easier for me to visit.

"Welcome, Addie! I'm Evelyn, but most everyone calls me Eve."

Addie does not raise her dark eyes from the ground, and she looks round and dismal in her thin plaid dress and blue cardigan.

I realize I will have to take her shopping and imagine standing at a clothes rack with her while leggy blond preteens prance around. *Do you like this one? How about this one?* And each time a shrug, never even raising her eyes to look.

"Addie, that's a beautiful necklace you're wearing."

The girl reaches up to touch the bone-white amulet and lifts her head. Her dark eyes are handsomely spaced, and her wide cheeks are a faint dusky red. Her full lips barely move as she says, "It's my mother's."

Mother takes Addie's free hand and squeezes it in her own. "Thank you for telling me," she whispers, then catches my eye to ask a thousand wordless questions. I turn away and Mother leads Addie past me, up the steps and into the house.

In the kitchen, I find Tillie in her chair. Her tan skin looks freshly washed, and her hair is damp in its braid. I notice the gray immediately and wonder what she would say if I offered to pay for a trip to my stylist. *Never,* she'd say, and with a smile. I go to her and feel a tiny diamond of happiness inside my own gray fog self. When I kiss her cheek, I'm reminded of grape jelly and Black Jack gum. Why is it our families always pull us back to our smallest selves? I've had many more adult years than childhood ones; why is it I always return to those youngest moments with her? She is beautiful, my sister, always was. A natural athlete, even without legs; she always looks like she just came back from a hike. As girls, we were both independent, but in different ways. Tillie was voracious for the world and bucking to go; I just wanted to separate, flow like a river away from its source. When did that change for her, I wonder? Was it after the accident? Was it that long ago?

Mother is making the introductions, and I am free to look about, discreetly. The house is nearly as it used to be, though now drenched in color: red wooden kitchen chairs, a colorful stained-glass window hanging next to the front windows, dishtowels in jewel tones—all courtesy of my boisterous mother. When Will and I lived here it was muted, more subtle. Our love of this country house was predicated by Will's fear of ever being seen as country, thus the style leaned heavily on clean, polished wood, natural light, and framed photos of natural elements. When I walked through the house twelve years ago, not a picture of a person could be found, only gray sand and round black rocks and white clouds on a black-and-white summer's day. In the hallway now is a gallery of mismatched frames: a legion of neatly grinning girls, Tillie and me, of course; Mother and Father in a rickshaw in Shanghai and on camels at Cheops; a wedding photo of Will and me, both of us so young and thin. A baby picture of Michael, the one where he's trying to cram an entire wooden block in his mouth and his cheeks glisten from earlier tears. And a recent one of him too, one I haven't seen before, crookedly set in a green, rustic-looking wood frame Mother no doubt bought on sale somewhere. He's wearing a beige winter cap over scruffy black hair, and bright yellow water-repellent overalls over a blue cable sweater. He is sitting on his fishing boat, unshaven, grinning terrifically, squinting in the bright sunlight. I run my finger over the glass before I realize I'm doing it, trying to touch the stubble on his chin. He must have sent her the picture. He didn't send one to me.

"Mother, where would you like us to sleep?" I call from the hallway.

"Well, you can have the master suite, and I'll move to the guest room. And we can put a bed up in the den for Addie, we'll just have to move the couch. That way you can have a TV of your own. Would you like that, dear?"

Addie shrugs, staring at the kitchen floor. I realize we are all bent toward her expectantly, Tillie leaning forward in her chair, Mother near the sink, as if Addie is an evening star and we're all waiting for her light to shine.

I feel impatience streak under my skin and I shake my head no, although no one has asked me anything. "Mother, you keep the bedroom. I'll take the guest room. I think Will's office would be better for Addie, no couches to move." I note the surprise in Mother's face but turn away before her eyes can catch mine.

Tillie reaches a hand out and places it gently on the girl's arm. "We'll be neighbors," she whispers. "My room is just on the other side of the bathroom."

"But we'll need to find Michael's old bed," I continue. "Is it in storage? In the basement?"

"Oh, Emmy, you would know, I surely don't. We can get Henry to help." Mother looks around with that freshly woken look she has. "Now where did he get off to? I'll call him, invite him to dinner—is his phone working, Tillie?—he loves my rosemary chicken. You'll like it too, dear," she says to Addie. "Do you like chicken?"

Addie nods limply. I want to be angry with her for being so forlorn, but of course that's ludicrous. She's a child far from home with people she doesn't know, and her mother is in a hospital in Anchorage for God knows what reason. Her long dark lashes blink as she stares at the floor, and I have to stop myself from sighing. Beside her I feel scraped bare and textureless.

Michael, my stormy son, called two days ago, and I wouldn't have agreed except I'd just been down to the lake at my other house in the dark, in the rain. I'd taken my headache there after a terrible day, and the sky and the lake grew grayer and grayer and the rain grew stronger and harder until I was standing on the dock in the darkness, still in my tweed jacket and black pumps, letting the wind and the rain blast me sideways, wishing I could be somewhere else, be someone else. But it felt like a punishment I needed, to stand in the elements and feel the pain inside. Lightning cracked across the lake and woke me from myself, and I flew from the dock, slipping on the muddy hillside, my drenched hair clinging to my cheeks and neck, my heart pounding as another crack of lightning lit the landscaped hill and my foolishness, if any neighbor should chance to look. I fell on the wet grass and ran up to the house, and by the time I came to where I'd dropped my bag on the landing, I was laughing and laughing, exhilarated beyond belief. I unlocked the door and then my cell was ringing and it was Michael, it was my son.

He said that he figured he had about ten years' worth of favors saved up, and he needed a big one now. A friend of his, a Native woman, was in the hospital in Anchorage. He found himself helping with her ten-year-old daughter, and did I have any ideas? Was there any way? Could I find it in my heart to? And of course, I have resources he doesn't have, and it would be good for the girl in the long run, and of course he would be down to visit, and of course it would be temporary.

And what about the rest of her family, Michael? If she's a Native girl, wouldn't she be better off with a Native family? Her tribe, or what have you? His answers were vague and turned to pleading, and my blood was up from the storm, and as I dripped on my Berber rug, pantyhose ruined, it felt portentous, a gift from a God who hasn't had much to say to me lately. And my headache was gone, washed clean by the rain like a new beginning. I said, *Yes, of course, of course.* And I said, *I miss you.* And I said, *Come home soon, okay?*

And now here I am with a stranger's child, a terribly sad one at that, and I don't know what I was thinking, how I thought I could help this girl. I don't want to think that maybe I agreed just to draw Michael home to me, because he's right, he has a lifetime of favors saved up. I would give him anything, everything.

She arrived midday yesterday with a small satchel of clothes and a backpack full of books and a very tired-looking, one-eyed doll. After six hours or so, I realized I would need reinforcements—big ones. And that's when I called Mother.

I haul the bags from the trunk of the Lexus, glad Henry's not around to do it for me. He has a heroic need I want to squash whenever possible, and I hate that I feel that way around him, as if I'm a rat nibbling away at someone else's cheese. Henry's goodness makes me think of Will and the life I thought we had.

Henry is like a granite pillar I just want to push over, once and for all. Easier to do it yourself than wait for it to crumble on its own.

I look up the driveway and see him coming around the front of the house. His blond hair needs to be combed, and his strides are long, as if everyone should have such strong, purposeful legs. His forearms are thick with muscle and his tanned face is lined and handsome. I begin to feel something thaw, something warm rise up inside and thrum my heart, just to see him again.

"Henry," I say, and turn away, a suitcase in each hand.

"Emerson," he says in return, and takes the luggage from me without a word, walking up the porch steps and into my house as if it were his own.

Addie begins

I have never felt this horrible in my life, here in this wherever place. Not even when I saw Mama on the floor, not even when I saw her in the hospital bed. The straight-backed woman said this is not Portland, it's next to Portland, and I have too many good manners to tell her I don't care, I don't care where it is, I shouldn't be here. I can't figure out if everyone here lives by lakes. Captain Mike's family is very blessed in the money department, I can tell. Mama and I are not so blessed in that way, but in other ways we are. Blessed in love and spirit, Mama says. Or used to say, before she got so all-the-time sad.

I also can't figure out how many grown-ups live in this house together, but it's warmer and nicer than the cold shadow house from last night. I could tell that the straight-backed woman was very uncomfortable with me being there. I didn't understand why Mike would send me to someone so chilly until I met the others. They are warmer people, but unhappy inside too.

This room I'm in is as big as the living room and kitchen in our apartment combined. It has a TV and big books on big shelves and a big window to look through. I can see the red barn like you'd see in a *National Geographic* magazine, and grass and bushes and sky. The tall, kind man put the bed together for me and didn't try and chat too much, which I appreciated. I can lie on the bed and stare out the big window at the growing-dark clouds in the sky. The tall man is sad and the woman with no legs is sad, but I probably would be too if I couldn't run anymore. Only the elder woman is not sad. She hops around like a chickadee, and it makes me smile a little inside. In third grade, our teacher Ms. Moore read a story about children younger than us getting chased on the tundra by a giant. And the children were saved by a chickadee. I don't know why so many grown-ups think giants want to eat children. Nobody writes stories about children wanting to eat giants, which is just as believable if you think about it.

My own sadness is like a heavy blanket that makes it hard to breathe. My eyes keep wanting to leak, but I won't let them. I want to be good and not be any trouble but I can't pretend I'm happy to be here. Mama tells me all the time to be a brave girl, but I think brave and sad can be in the same place at the same time, and she should know all about that. I can see her face like an empty coin on the hospital pillow and her dark eyes barely opening to see me. The doctors had lots to say, but not to me. I kept watching the grown-ups' faces, trying to figure out what was going on. I don't know why it all has to be such a secret, as if knowing something could be worse than this alone, not-knowing place.

Mama's best friend LuAnn—Auntie Lu—took me home with her. She's the one who called Captain Mike, and it was very lucky he was in town, not up with the salmon in Togiak. Mike brought me a cheeseburger from Wee B's, with only ketchup on mine and spicy peppers on his because we know each other well. And when Auntie Lu left to go back to be with Mama, Mike and I ate our burgers and watched not-very-funny TV shows and my stomach ached the whole time. *I don't like mean TV,* I told Mike. *Just because people in the audience laugh, that isn't going to convince me it's funny.* Mike laughed and called me *discerning,* as if that's bad news for me. I love Captain Mike. I've known him since I was born. I watched him smoke outside like a storm about to start, drinking Auntie Lu's beer. He gave me the rest of his Hot Tamales and then whispered with LuAnn on the phone. There were conversations, and him looking at me, and then him saying I would enjoy the plane ride, but I didn't know what he meant, and I really did not like the flight here, so he was wrong about that.

The plane was crowded and too loud. There wasn't enough air to breathe, and my stomach hurt the whole time. The skinny stewardess with the pink mouth gave me plastic gold wings to pin to my sweater and a Coke to drink, and I whispered to Mrs. Anderson not to be scared. Mrs. Anderson was scared anyway, and the people sitting beside us were very close and kept trying to chat, even though the other passengers pretended everyone else wasn't there. It was very weird. I hate when I know there are rules but I don't know what the rules are, and all the grown-ups seem to know already, without anyone telling them. Mrs. Anderson suggested I write a report on airplane trips, and I might, if I can walk to the library from here. I don't want to ask the straight-backed woman how to get there. She is frightening like a principal. When she got me at the airport, her eyes said she didn't like my gold wings or Mrs. Anderson's missing eye or me at all. The gold wings are in the pocket of my sweater now so she won't be mad. But I'd like to keep them.

When the tall man got the bed from the basement, he asked me to move a box out of his way, and I brought it up here. I didn't know what else to do with it. I wasn't sure what the rules are about where to put boxes when they are in the way. Now I am alone with the TV and Mrs. Anderson and trying not to be too sad. I keep looking at the skinny underfed moon out the window, wondering if Mama can see that moon from the hospital too. The straight-backed woman didn't want Mrs. Anderson to ride with us in the car, so I tucked her in my backpack with all her favorite books. But I let her sit with me at dinner and the woman with no legs asked her name. Because she whispered, I whispered to her, *Mrs. Anderson*. I didn't tell her that when I was little, my favorite book was *Are You There, Mrs. Anderson?* and that I made Mama read it to me over and over again. Mama wanted me to name her Ruthie after her little sister, who died in the earthquake in the orphanage in Seward a long time ago, but I prefer Mrs. Anderson. I didn't tell the woman with no legs any of this. I didn't tell her that the orphanage is empty now but haunted, and Mama sometimes dreams the ghosts of her orphan brothers and sisters. Maybe Mama is in the hospital dreaming ghosts right now.

I put on my nightshirt even though it's early and grab a big book from the bookshelf. It's an atlas, with pages full of colorful maps and magical names of places all over the world. How rich these people must be, to have all these beautiful extra books that no one is even looking at. I can tell no one has been in this room for a very long time. The quietness of the air tells me, like it's been stopped up too long by itself. The sheets on the bed are blue and soft and smell like a different kind of soap. Everyone's houses smell different, mostly due to soap and other cleaning products. My bed at home has yellow and pink sheets and Mrs. Anderson warm beside me and Mama singing softly as she does her beads. It always makes me think singing is a better, more beautiful language than the one we have, and why don't we just sing to each other all the time? Mama does her beads every night because she is an artist, and she makes the most marvelous pictures with just beads. It keeps her from going crazy working at the drugstore, she says.

Mama has long black hair and always smells clean and warm and is a very polite person. She taught me a few Yup'ik words even though we are not Yup'ik. The secret is that we are not what it says on our Alaska Native paperwork. Mama was at the orphanage, then a boarding school, and sometime someone just picked what she is, so that's what's written down. Mama says that we are more than what was assigned to us. Mama's friend Earl took us to his Yup'ik fish camp to be with his family last summer, and it was my favorite place ever—even better than libraries and school. We started learning to speak some Yup'ik, and I liked thinking about belonging there. Some of the elders wore clothes like they'd just found them on the side of the road, but it didn't matter because their hearts and their spirits were so big and open. I decided I wanted to be like that too, but I'm not sure how I'm doing these days.

At fish camp, the older boys had a running race and a girl won, even though she wasn't supposed to run, and all the grown-ups laughed and the boys decided to throw rocks instead with puffed up chests. I thought if I had the courage to run maybe I could win, but I was happy she beat the boys. I sat on the rocky beach with the women and tried to be quiet like the moon and the stars and just listen. Earl's family was very happy and jokey even if I didn't get all the jokes. They sang songs and taught us to dry fish on wooden racks and gather clams and other things, just like we learn about at school. That was last summer, and I thought for sure we'd be going back again this year, but then Earl stopped coming around and Mama stopped singing as much. Then she told me we weren't going to fish camp this year, and that's when her eyes began turning away from me all the time.

I hear *Tap, tap* on the door, and the white-haired lady comes in. She made a nice dinner and I took extras on a small plate, but she doesn't know. I'm afraid she'll be mad, so I hid it under the bed. She has a look of bright kindness in her eyes tonight, and I begin to feel less alone. She helps me get under the covers and rubs my back and I feel heavy sighs inside myself. She will be my friend like the chickadee and protect me like the children on the tundra. I think I should tell her to maybe protect the giant instead, protect him from the bad parts of me. My heart is squeezed up tight and my stomach hurts. I can watch the lean moon from my window, even lying down, but I want to go home and see the spring moon from my own window. The white-haired chickadee woman talks softly to me, but all I hear is Mama singing over her beads and Auntie Lu screaming for the 911 and the too-loud, stopped-up airplane sound in my ears. She rubs my back and my ear is wet from crying I don't even mean to do. All I can do is hold Mrs. Anderson tight and make quiet nighttime wishes at the skinny moon, praying for Mama to love me and want to be home with me again.

Two

Henry reads a sign

This morning I woke with a fever and a pounding chest, as if I'd run a fast mile, and now I'm bottled up, wanting to pace the house, stomp around. I want to go back to their house; I want Eve to need me, I want Tillie to want me, I want Emerson to have to see me.

I take my coffee into the workroom and sit—thick and sullen, achy-boned—on the tall three-legged stool. All my pent-up energy is making my blood run hot, but I feel heavy as stone, too tired to move. Usually in the mornings I sit zazen to meditate, but today I feel too lousy. I didn't sleep well. My mind kept returning to thoughts of Will, like an old song stuck in my head on repeat. In a lifetime full of regrets, he is by far my biggest. On the work-bench, I move a tube of wood glue and a utility knife and a pile of sandpaper to make room for my coffee. I've taken to making miniature Zen rock gardens lately, because they sell, and because I like making the tiny wooden rakes and picking the perfect stones. Tillie likes to drive with me to the coast to get the sand, and sift it with me, and sit on the beach, out of her chair, watching the waves and talking my ear off. Tillie. She is always good medicine for me.

The sky over the lake is smoky gray and closely packed with fat rain clouds. I stare west out the window as the rain starts and watch the steam rise like daydreams from my mug. It's a good Ethiopian blend from Starbucks that Eve scores for me, under Tillie's radar, but I wish she knew I like Stumptown better. It smells divine, but I feel too wrenched up inside to drink it. I feel dual, two-bodied, one of me wanting to run up the slope and into Emerson's kitchen, to grab her hands and shout, *Wake up! Come back! Come back to me!* and the other me wanting to sit like a boulder at the bottom of a slow stream, heavy as forever, letting the water decide everything for me, too deeply settled to move.

The rain is dismal on Looking Lake, and I remember my rowboat, *Daisy*, is only loosely secured. I know I should pull her beachward, but I can't bring myself to get up. From my seat I can see the wet stones in my meditation garden and the cedar pergola, dripping water onto the bench below. I made that pergola by hand when I designed the garden. The summer he died, Will came to watch in the evenings as I sawed and sanded and pounded the nailless dovetailed corners together. Strong as a tree, I bragged, doing a chin-up, showing off as he lit a Dunhill with his monogrammed lighter. And this, my own koan for him: *If you call this wood, you limit its reality. If you do not call it wood, you ignore the fact. Now, what should you call it?* And Will, hiding behind his summer-weight Italian suits and Ray-Bans, chewing on the ice cubes in his Jack and Coke, would answer: *Doesn't matter, chief. Call it an arbor, call it a fucking toothpick, don't call it anything. That wood doesn't care. Doesn't care what I call it or if I spit on it or lie dead as a squashed bug beneath it.* And smiling that Will Worthy smile, perfect capped teeth and years of good breeding designed to melt any adversary's resolve. I didn't think he could outmaneuver me. I thought he liked me because I cut through his bullshit. Eight years junior, I fatuously believed Will needed me, needed to learn something from me. But you can't out-shark a shark, especially if you're not a shark. Especially if you're me.

When Emerson and Will bought the Pilchard's old farm, I spent many days peeking around the fence at the progress of the new house. They parceled off much of the acreage, including the orchard on the other side of the barn, parlaying their investment into double what they paid, I imagine, and converting the old farmhouse into something they could stand. They kept some modest acres that Tillie is starting to diligently work now, and of course, the private lake access. The house dwarfs my little cabin, but it doesn't block my sun or my view of the lake, so what should I care? I did enjoy wandering the tall fields before they came and plucking around in the abandoned outbuildings, and was sorry to lose my dominion of the place. The solid fence that once separated my father's cabin and the Pilchard's farm— that now partitions me from them—does not run plumb from lake to road. It begins ten paces up from the coarse beach and extends most-ways up the drive, like a lady's dressing screen. One can easily walk to the other property either beach-way or drive-way, and once upon a time there was gate-way too, but no longer.

That was the way Will and Emmy used to come, but never together. Down from their house and past the trimmed rhododendrons and Oregon grape, through the arched wooden gate and along the path to my budding rock garden, before the thinking bench was there. Sometimes I would come home and find one or the other sitting on a deck chair disconsolately, waiting for me. But the stone bench outside is bare now, like negative space, and dripping rainwater onto the wet white pebbles below.

My cheeks are still hot, but I feel cold where I'm sitting, watching the rain and the fading coffee steam. I cannot reach the throw from the couch without getting up, but I have a stack of good thick towels under my workbench. I set one on my lap and wrap one on my shoulders and huddle around my coffee mug. Will called me *obstinate* as a sign of affection, just as he could call Emerson *dry* and make her smile. A natural talent of the charming, framing stabs to the heart with sweet, sweet honey.

I remember a black-tie party they had that summer to raise money for some charity or another. I wasn't interested in going to their amusing little ball, let alone jamming my feet into rented shoes. Will came over to pick my clothes, boyishly charming me into wearing something casual, chinos and a faded button-up, I think. He said I'd look stifled in starch. After that, Emerson came over to iron for me and fuss over my stubbly chin and pick my belt. She didn't know Will had been there before, and he didn't know she'd been there after, and we all kept our secrets close to our chests. Emerson and I drank vodka lemonades in my bedroom while I showered and dressed and it was easy to be friends with her then. She told me what a drag it was hosting Will's old alums and was so grateful I'd be there. *Yeah,* I said, *just a diamond in the rough.* And Emerson said, tapping my bedroom door before she left, *That's the best kind of diamond, Henry.* At the party, they both smiled conspiratorially at me, and they were right, I was a hit with their rich friends in a droll, outdoorsy, pool boy sort of way. Because *artist* means "unambitious" and *landscaper* means "hired help," and both are amusing when the man in question is handsome and easily swayed. The way the Worthys smiled at me that night made the ground under my feet feel rocky and unsteady, and nothing seemed very clear.

I see a black shape roll by outside the window and am startled enough to thunk down my cooling cup of coffee. Tillie is haranguing with the door, then inside and dripping wet on the work room floor.

"Like my bags? Emmy was appalled I was going out like this but I couldn't find my raincoat." Tillie looks thrilled to be out in the morning storm under black plastic garbage sacks, irritating her sister. She runs a hand over her braid and rainwater whips around over her shoulder. "Are you okay, Henry?"

I shake my head no. "Thinking old thoughts today."

She peels off her garbage bags and rolls over to where I'm lumped on my stool. "I like the towels. You look good in paisley." She puts a hand on my forehead, then my cheek. "Henry, you're burning up. You're sick. Why didn't you call me? Is your phone turned off again? Why aren't you in bed? C'mon, big guy, up you go."

I walk to the couch and lie down so I can look out the window at the rain. Tillie glides over to cover me with the throw, then brings me Tylenol and a glass of water.

"Stay for a while, please," I say. "Just talk to me, okay?"

"You sure you wouldn't rather be in bed?" she asks, rubbing a kind hand on my head. "You know, most people's living rooms have thick rugs for me to get stuck on and tables to navigate around, but not you. The only rug you have is that ugly braided thing by the other door. You have a concrete floor and a work-bench full of crap and a wobbly stool. No chairs to offer me."

"But you bring your own chair wherever you go," I say. "Besides, I'll share the couch if you want. Doc Holloway gave it to me—remember?—for helping him build that toolshed. Watched me like a hawk the whole time."

"How's his wife?" she asks, knowing the answer full well.

My head is pounding, but the thought of Missy Holloway's light touch makes me close my eyes and smile.

"My point, Henry, is that you're terribly spare."

"Usually you say I'm terribly fucking spare."

"Well, you're sick. You can't defend yourself."

I close my eyes. "Yes, I can. I like spare."

"I know," Tillie says. "And Buddha likes spare too. Except work benches. Buddha doesn't care about messy work benches."

I kiss the fingers on my right hand and raise it to the sky, eyes still closed. It's my *Right on, brother* to God.

"Can we talk about my sister now? Can you believe her? That poor child. How did she get stuck with Emmy? I'm so glad she brought her to us, to help."

"It's Michael, right? I mean, she's Michael's kid, you think?"

"What a surprise that would be! A granddaughter. I don't know, I don't think so. Then again, must be pretty extreme circumstances for him to send someone to Emmy. She raised him, he knows what she's like."

"She wasn't always like she is now," I say. "I remember when she was happy."

"We must be talking about a different woman." Tillie reaches for my forehead again and I sit up fast.

"But really," I say, "do you think she could be? Wouldn't that be wild for your sister to have a grandchild all of a sudden?"

"I know!" Tillie's face is round-cheeked and happy today. "And the kid's cool; I like her. This morning, she got up early, ate her Cheerios, put on her backpack, and announced to the breakfast table that she's ready and could one of us take her to her new school please? I swear, I thought Emmy was going to spit coffee all over herself. She told her that since there's only a little bit left in the year, she isn't going to enroll her here. Apparently, her school in Anchorage gets out in May, so she's nearly done."

"Wow, she must really like school."

Tillie has a light in her eyes that's different from the usual sparkle. She seems invigorated by her life's sudden change in the program. When I brush some mud splatter from her forearm, her earthen skin feels warm and vital.

"And last night at dinner," she continues, "wasn't that all so strange? Nobody talking about anything real? I guess it's always that way when she's around."

I try to think, but my head is fuzzy. Is she talking about Emerson again? I can see the kid—Addie, I mean—at the dinner table, sitting quietly between the two sisters, head down, eating steadily and silently. "Does she know why she's here? Does anybody?"

"All Emmy said was that her mom is in the hospital and Michael begged for a favor and will be coming down from Anchorage soon."

"Well, that's a big deal," I say, "if he has to leave his boat. I bet she's his kid. What a mess." I lie back down on the couch and stare at the bare ceiling.

"So Mother offered to take her clothes shopping and to get a library card today, because she absolutely loves the library. Isn't that cool? Wish I could take her. That would be fun."

"You can take her," I say. Eve got Tillie a big Chrysler with hand controls a few years back, but she refuses to use it. She is so strong and independent in some ways and so childlike in others.

"I don't like to drive, Henry, you know that. I was going to ask you to take me to my appointment this afternoon in Sellwood, since Mother will be busy, but I can't now."

"Why? I'll take you."

"You're sick. You're not going anywhere."

I cover my face with my hand, feeling floaty and heavy-hearted again. *"Daisy* is going to float away." Maybe Tillie could climb in my soggy rowboat and ride streams all the way to the Willamette River and her appointment in Sellwood.

Tillie leans over me and rests her hand on my chest. "I'll take care of it. I'll make Emmy go down. What else is wrong?"

"I've been thinking of Will today."

"It wasn't your fault, Henry."

Yes, I think it was. I can't tell her this, even if she is my best friend. There are pieces of ourselves too ugly to share, too ugly to be loved, even by those who claim to love us regardless.

"It's only because Emerson's back," she says.

"I know," I say, nodding, still covering my eyes. But I've seen her nearly every Christmas for the last ten years or so, and it's never been like this. I don't think of Will in my garden just because his widow ignores me over the dinner table again.

"It's a sign," I say, uncovering my eyes to stare her dead in the face. "She's his granddaughter. I just know it."

"A granddaughter he wasn't alive to meet. And if she is then she's my grandniece, and Mother's—Lord—great-grandchild."

"It isn't because of Emerson, it's because of the girl, Addie. She must've brought him back with her."

"Who, Will? You're not making any sense, Henry. You're sick. You have a fever. You rest now. I'm going to bring the phone over here to the couch, and you call me if you need anything. Okay? Will you? Is your phone working?"

I nod and watch her bustle and wheel away. Addie brought Will back to me. Tillie smiles at me as she puts her black Hefty bags back over her shoulders and tucked around her legs. I love Tillie, but I don't think she can understand. I don't think she can understand how deep some feelings, some knowings, can run. The rain on the window is insistent, and I close my eyes to rest, imagining my boat floating away with Tillie content to ride and Will majestic in my garden and his granddaughter's handsome eyes and raven hair, absolving me, washing me blessedly clean.

Tillie reads a sign

I woke this morning feeling energized, and even Emmy's sour face can't take this feeling away. The traffic is prolonging the trip to Portland, but her Lexus is terribly comfortable, and all the brake lights look pretty in the rain. Emmy is punching radio buttons from one news station to another and anxiously rubbing the small, old scar at her temple. Her hair is just past chin-length, expensively dyed in honeys and caramels, and I briefly imagine her rubber-capped and blue-smocked vulnerable in her stylist's leather chair. I have a sudden urge to paint her as she is now, aging in the gray light of noon, the muted light dripping reflected rain-drops down her distracted pale-butter cheeks. She would never acquiesce, I know. She's the only beautiful person I know who doesn't like having her picture taken.

"You're sure you don't need to stop at the Lake Oswego house? I don't mind, I'm sure you need a few things."

"No, Tillie, I'm sure. I have everything I need."

"But you only brought a couple bags…"

Emmy makes a swift lane change, and we're heading toward the Sellwood Bridge and across the Willamette River. "I'm sure," she says again.

Watching her jaw set so tight, it occurs to me that she doesn't need more of anything because she isn't planning on staying with us. She's going to leave Addie with Mother and me. I feel a streak of sudden anger. Not that she would impose on us (we are, after all, living in her house) but that she would, could, abandon the child, the grandchild. I can already feel a tenderness growing in me for her; not mother arms like Mother has, but an auntie willow's circling branches of protection. She has a slow, fluid way of moving that I admire; a conservation of movement that reminds me of Emmy and Michael both. And she speaks so carefully, as if every word were a coin chosen from an ancient purse.

We pull up to the blue house and find street parking right in front. Emmy leans over me to look out the window and shakes her head.

"Don't like psychics?" I ask with a laugh.

"No, it's all those stairs I'm looking at. It's too wet for you to climb." She sighs and I feel like a child again. "No, we'll have to carry you. Stay here while I get help."

She leaves me to sit in the car while she puts on her Eddie Bauer raincoat, and I feel my happy, excited feeling whoosh away like air from a quick-closed bag. By the time she has my chair from the trunk and a tight-smiling woman from the shop at her side, I am staring at my hands, clenched tight in my lap. It's that hospital feeling, that can't-do-for-yourself feeling, that ugly, small feeling. I'm sure Emmy's never felt anything like it in her life.

I hoist myself into my chair, and Emmy hands me her umbrella since I didn't wear any garbage bags this time. She forces the wheels over the rutted sidewalk and up to the steps as rain splatters madly around us. The other woman's saffron dress is darkening in the rain flurry, and her grin begins to turn down at the corners as she bends to lift one side of me and the chair. I stare straight ahead, *thinking light thoughts*, as I often tell Henry, clenching the black umbrella over my head and feeling foolish. I cannot reach the umbrella high enough or wide enough to guard anyone else from the rain. The woman's foot slips on the wet stairs, and she whispers, "Oh shit" as my chair yaws sideways, threatening to pitch me out of my cushioned seat. *Please let them drop me*, I think wildly. *Please let them not have to do this*. Emmy heaves up, strong sister that she is, and the woman catches herself and evens me up again, and then we are at the top, under the covered porch, and a Hispanic woman of uncertain age with coal-black hair and a broad chest full of clunky gold jewelry is opening the door and beaming at me like sunlight, and when I see her wrinkled, animated smile, something unloosens inside and I feel softly better.

I exhale and she says, "Just leave that at the door, *mi hija*."

"Oh, of course," I say, closing the umbrella and bending down to lean it on the porch.

"And the umbrella too," she says. "We'll let the bad feeling blow away with the rain, but the umbrella you may want later. *Gracias*, Stella," she says to the woman who helped us, as she brushes by. "And you, too," she says to Emmy. "You are welcome here, daughter."

Emerson is polished as she gives the woman a grocery-store smile and presses me inside the over-warm, narrow-winged shop. I take my wet handgrips and push myself forward, my elbows bumping racks of cards and knitted scarves and tall seashore-scented candles, and once my wheel catches the corner of a buff-colored bookshelf that seizes me up short. Emmy steps back in close to push me again, and I lean back gratefully. The Hispanic woman is waiting for us to follow her to the rear of the shop, where she has a small round table and two folding metal chairs. Stella has returned to the register at the front of the shop, and I hear her greeting another customer who has come in from the rain. I turn to see a middle-aged man with long hair in a pony-tail and silver rings in his ears and a blue fleece vest and tattooed forearms. He looks like a cooler version of an L.L.Bean model, and the woman brightens to see him. It is a nice tableau, and I try to imprint the picture in my mind, her yellow dress, his navy vest, the dark wood door frame, the hanging chimes, the Chinese characters on a scroll over the door, the smile she gives him, and the dimple on his chin. I imagine it is the first time they've met, that it's the moment they fall in love. I close my eyes and smile, already seeing phthalo blue and cadmium yellow on my white bristle brush. Emmy clears her throat and I turn to see both her and the Hispanic woman waiting for me. Emmy has draped her raincoat over the back of her folding chair, and I watch water run down and drip onto the floor. Watching her, I think she could be that very rain herself, my older sister, that numbly persistent, that coldly certain.

The psychic's table is covered by an intricately designed scarf in gold and black and blue and I'm not surprised to see the blue and yellow again. On the scarf sits a Thoth tarot deck and a purple velvet pouch.

"I'm Floramaria," the woman says, rolling her *r*'s beautifully. She has a round face and a round body and sparkly, happy eyes that reach deeply into my own. I shake my head slightly at the tarot, and the woman reaches over to touch my hand. "You don't care for this deck then? I have another you might prefer." She sweeps the Thoth tarot off the table and reaches under the gold and blue table to offer me a different deck.

"Moon Garden?" I ask. Emmy chokes a laugh and covers with a small cough. "Should you maybe wait in the car?" I ask her.

"Fabulous idea," Emmy says. "Take your time."

"No, stay, *por favor*," Floramaria says.

Outside, the rain lashes the window and a roll of thunder sounds nearby. The shop is well lit, but gray light filters through the cold windows, making me shiver. Despite Floramaria's bright benevolence, I feel a sharp seed of doubt that maybe I shouldn't have come. I made the appointment without overthinking it, because a gallery owner told me what a tremendous experience she'd had, but the truth is, I'm afraid of what's happening to me. Lately, I've found the landscape inside myself to be growing deeper and swampier, and without my consent, I keep sliding down steep banks of bleakness, ugliness, deficiency. I feel left behind somehow, all of a sudden, as if the people I love have all turned a corner, and I'm not allowed to follow. I tell myself it is because Mother is aging, and we all fear change, but that doesn't help me feel less stuck, or more valuable in my own life.

"I am very fond of this deck," Floramaria is saying, "because it is so gentle." Emmy shifts beside me but stays in her seat. I can hear the murmur of voices behind me in the shop, and the sound of distant thunder outside. When I look over, I see the window light up with the afternoon lightning. It reminds me of grammar school, when the Oregon rain kept us all inside and we felt cozied up against the storm outside. But now I don't feel cozy, just cold.

Floramaria hands me the deck. "Hold this and think about your question. Do you know what kind of a spread you would like?"

I shake my head, letting the slick, brightly-colored cards slip through my palms. "They're very colorful," I say.

"It's a playful deck. I've been told the artist envisioned La Luna, the moon, as the Garden of Eden," she says.

I glance at Emmy who is glancing at me. When we were younger, we were always sensitive to Eden references, having secular parents named Adam and Eve, although now it's become something you tell strangers at gallery receptions to make a joke. Will used to love making Cain and Abel allusions about us sisters—Emmy, of course, being the wicked one.

"Please shuffle with your left hand. Then choose two cards and place them face down in front of you."

Emmy looks interested for the first time. The rain is beating hard enough on the roof now that we all three glance up at the ceiling. I'm glad I didn't plant in the herb garden yesterday; I'm afraid all the starts I've been growing in my studio would have washed away. I lay two cards down and put my hands in my lap.

Floramaria leans forward. "The first card represents you right now." She taps the left card and I turn it over. "Knight of Pentacles," she says. "This card is about growth and fertility. *Mira*, his horse is heavy and slow, a workhorse, for doing in the field. The Knight is easy and relaxed. With his projects, he is very responsible, maybe even predictable. He is of the earth and gentle with spirit. This is a very nice card for you."

I want to say, *I don't feel very easy right now.* I pat the side of my wheelchair, my heavy horse.

"But maybe you are a little stuck? You have some growing to do, perhaps? Let's see the other. This one will be the direction you go." I flip the card. "Ah," she says, smiling broadly, "El Sol. *Muy importante* to my culture." She taps the gold design on the table scarf beside the card, and I see a stylized pre-Columbian design of the sun. I run my fingers on the cool scarf, tracing the design.

"The Sun," she continues. "Major Arcana. He always returns to rainy Portland, does he not? This card is about summer and radiant light and unlimited *felicidad*, happiness. It is good health, a refreshed soul, protection from negative things. Señor Sun, he reminds us there are no limits to the good in our lives and the good in the world all around."

I clear my throat, meaning to speak but not sure what to say. I feel anything but radiant now on this stormy spring day, and her optimism feels like a hollow trinket from a seasoned peddler. I want to believe it, but I don't.

"*Escucha*, you are unsatisfied. You do not feel these things in your life at this time. Maybe there is a piece missing still." She lifts the purple velvet pouch to me and I reach my hand inside. I pull out a green rune with the letter *r* on it. "The Jade indicates love, relationships. This rune is Raido, *la rueda*, the wheel. It is sacred to the Norse god Thor, god of thunder. In Mayan culture, the god of thunder is Chaac. He brings life by weeping rain, and he will teach any farmer that asks him how to do it."

Floramaria stops to listen to the storm outside and I find myself biting my lip. "The wheel is a personal journey for you, physical or spiritual, and in the end, a choice. Because this is all a choice, is it not? This too is a positive indicator." Her eyes tighten in concern. "Do you have questions?"

I shake my head, turning the small green tile in my hands. A choice. A journey. Tears falling from a kind god's eyes. Floramaria holds the bag forward, and I drop the piece inside with the others. "And now you," she says, turning to Emmy.

"Oh no thank you, I'm just here with her. And if we're finished…"

The black-haired woman holds the tarot deck out to Emmy and her necklaces clank softly together on her large chest. "Now you," she says again.

Emmy stares at it for a moment then takes the deck—I didn't think she would—and holds it tentatively in her hand. "I don't have any questions," she says.

Floramaria waves her hand lightly in the air. "Pretend this is a parlor game. Pretend we are at a little function and you just finished at the roulette table. *No importa, si?*"

Emmy's lips faintly smile as her left hand, deliberate and firm, slowly cuts the deck. I hear the door chime again, and the deep rumble of a man's voice makes me think of gold coins falling.

Floramaria leans forward, toward me, and whispers for us both to hear, "Because it really does matter. *Es muy importa*. And sometimes we have to sneak up on these things so we don't scare them away."

Emmy lays two cards down carefully as the thunder rolls. I see her staring at the backs of those cards, the curiously bending trees, and her hands are tight in her lap, so white, and that is when the lights go out. It is not full darkness, we still have the gray light from the windows, but it is sudden enough and strange enough that we all make little startled sounds. I hear voices from others in the shop behind us, and one woman's light laughter. Emmy looks still as ice beside me, but in the dim light I can see a quiver in her jaw.

Floramaria chuckles and leans forward, placing both hands on the table and covering Emmy's cards. "I think someone is trying to tell you something," she says.

"Yes, that we should go."

"No, it's only the storm, we will have lights again. Stella?" Floramaria rises and disappears behind us.

"Let's go," Emmy says fiercely.

"No way," I say, laying a hand on her cool forearm. "This is too good to miss."

Floramaria returns with a tall lit candle and a bright smile. "The whole street is without power. It will be back on soon." When she sits, her gold necklaces glow in the light, and I close my eyes to hold the picture. When I open them again, Emmy has turned her first card. She is as curious as I am.

"The Queen of Swords. You are divorced? Widowed, perhaps? You are a very strong woman, independent. And sensitive too, but most people don't see that gift, *es verdad*? You are intelligent. People are uncomfortable with you. Because you see truth when others are blind."

Wordlessly, Emmy turns the second card.

"La Estrella, The Star, how lovely to have that with her bright sun. Your futures are connected by that. You are *familia, no?* The Star is also a Major Arcana. It is about reconnecting your soul and freely being your true self. You do not need to hide any longer. When you let go of the control, you will see that you do have great purpose, despite your doubts. Do not be of despair. Look for the Divine in your life every day, whichever god you would like that to be."

She holds up the purple velvet bag, and Emmy pulls out a white, almost clear tile with an etched x. "The Ice rune indicates conflict or struggle, sometimes achievement. This rune has a sacred mark for the gods, perhaps to help them find you, if you are in hiding. It is about generosity and love and relationships, giving gifts, though not necessarily material gifts. And it is about meeting someone peacefully, letting the old dry hurt fall away. Forgiveness. This will be very good for you."

Emmy's fingers tremble as she tumbles the rune back into the bag. Floramaria is looking at her closely in the candlelight. I remember watching her at Will's graveside service. She looked terribly thin and pale in her black silk dress, her eyes absent, so guarded, so afraid to show the weakness of emotion. I did not see her cry then. I do not remember the last time I saw her cry. Candlelight dances on her chin, her contoured cheekbones, her stern, even nose and damp ocean-blue eyes. Her eyes are sad and wet with tears but none fall. I reach a hand to her arm, but she stands up abruptly and turns.

"How much does she owe you?" she asks with her back to Floramaria. She fumbles in her pocketbook and hands me some twenties.

"It doesn't, it's not..." I begin.

"Thirty-five for half an hour," the psychic says gently. "I didn't spend that long on you combined."

I hand her two twenties and turn my wheelchair to follow Emmy through the darkened shop. I run into a card carousel just as the lights come back on and greeting cards flutter down onto me and the floor. Flustered by the bright light, I try to grab the ones still in the air as they rain to the ground. Emmy bends down quickly to pick cards from the floor, and the blue-vested, handsome man squats down to help.

"Are you Mrs. Worthy?" he asks. We both stop to look at him. He is tanned and smiling, the dragons on his forearms dancing as he gathers cards. His ponytail is held back with a small blue band, and he wears an expensive-looking gold watch on his wrist. His hint of cologne is pleasant and clean, like warm cedar. "I'm Robert Lyall. My daughter Sarah loved your American Lit class at Bayles."

Emmy stands quickly and smiles at the model-handsome man. When he stands they are the same height. "I remember Sarah. She had a low tolerance for slow American fiction. I quite agreed, actually. She went to one of the Sisters, didn't she?"

"Wellesley, yeah. Took a break but now she's studying law at NYU, settled down a bit, thank God. Engaged to a boy I don't care for, the usual."

"Mr. Lyall, most fathers don't like the men their daughters take to bed."

They both laugh and I realize I'm staring. In the once again well-lit shop, my sister looks perfect and polished again, unflappable. Whatever coarse emotion she'd been battling is now stuffed down, back into that interior darkness. Her eyes are warmly lit and brightly smiling, a saleswoman's smile.

"Call me Robert, please," he says. "Mr. Lyall is what the junior architects call me."

"And this is my sister, Mathilda."

"It's Tillie." I've never gone by Mathilda a day in my life, and she knows it. He extends a calloused hiker's hand to me and we shake, but his attention quickly returns to Emmy's smile.

"You're not at Bayles anymore, are you? Are you still teaching?"

"I left a few years after my husband's death. I do some financial consulting now. It was the right move for me."

"Well, I'm sure you're eager to get back in that rain, but I'd love to grab a cup of coffee with you sometime."

I hear the deep baritone gold-coin voice up front again, laughing. Like a newscaster's voice, it makes me think of new shag carpeting, Mother watching the nightly news when we were teenagers. I look toward the front of the store, but the deep voice has left to face the storm outside.

Emmy nods and smiles. "That would be lovely." She hands him her stack of greeting cards and he puts them back on the carousel carefully, one per vacancy. Emmy takes a business card from her pocketbook and hands it to him. "My cell is on there. Good to see you, give your daughter my best."

He nods and smiles and she steps behind me to push me through the shop. The same saffron-dressed woman helps us down the stairs, but the rain has settled to a light mist and the thunder has moved on. I think it is strange that Emmy didn't ask Robert Lyall to help, but maybe it's too intimate to show an acquaintance—look, here's my fucked-up sister, and here's what we have to do for her.

We bump down the stairs and gather ourselves into the car. When she sits beside me in the driver's seat, she looks me in the eyes—the first time in hours, it seems—and says, "Don't tell Mother."

Which part? I wonder. *That I'm a knight on a heavy horse? That she's an icy queen? That a former student's dad asked her out? That she almost cried?* The sky is deep gray as we drive home, full as it is with the thunder god's benevolent tears, and I think it's a sign. I want to tell Emerson that he will teach her to cry, if she wants, that she can water the earth and return life to us all. But I say nothing, because I know it doesn't matter; my words will fall into that deep, terrible void between us and wash away with the tide.

Eve reads a sign

I woke early, so excited to start today, and now I feel warmly satisfied with our productive morning. Addie is across the small table from me, chewing slowly on her hot dog and sipping from her soda. She looks at me and smiles occasionally, but her eyes are busy, taking everything in. I nurse my caramel macchiato to make it last longer and stretch my short legs around the shopping bags at my feet. The food court is more than half-empty, but I can feel the buzz of life around me, like a flock of cedar waxwings hidden in a leafy tree.

Addie watches two teenage boys walk by—shouldn't they be in school? It's early afternoon yet—and looks back at me. "Aren't you hungry, Ms. Eve?"

I shake my head and smile. "Oh, to me coffee is better than food. Don't get me wrong, I love to cook for my family, and so enjoy trying new foods in new places, like Indian subji or African peanut soup—"

"Soup made from peanuts?" she asks around her straw.

"It's good! Surprising, isn't it? But, day-to-day, I just sometimes don't feel like eating. My husband, Adam, used to say I live on air." I shrug and raise my eyebrows. "Have you ever heard of such a thing?"

"My mom says we should eat what's in front of us, that not everyone's so lucky." Her brown eyes drop to her ketchup-stained paper hot dog tray, and her moon-round face is heavy and sad.

"Are you thinking of your mother? I don't even know her name."

"Leah Long. Our last name is what the orphanage gave her; Mom says it's because it was a long time ago. Get it? A long time?" Her lips hint at a smile, and I smile and nod. "The orphanage was in Seward. Her sister was there too, my Aunt Ruth, but she died in the earthquake."

"Oh dear, when was this?"

"Oh, ages ago. In the 1960s." Addie picks up her hot dog again and dips it in the ketchup. I don't tell her I was a mother of teens in the sixties. "Can we call her, do you think?"

"Sure, I don't see why not."

Absently, she reaches to the bone amulet at her neck, a white totemic bear, and rubs it while she eats. "I was scared when I found her," she says after a bit. "I was at school, but I had a stomachache, so they sent me home. I had to walk because no one answered at home, and Auntie Lu didn't answer either. I told them at the school she was picking me up, but then I left without being signed out. She was at the laundromat."

"Your mother was?"

"Auntie Lu was."

"Is that your mother's other sister, then?"

"No, she's Mom's best friend, I just call her that."

"And then you found your mother when you came home?"

"I should have known when she gave me her necklace," Addie says and looks me in the eyes. "I should have known." She looks away, sips her drink, chews thoughtfully. "She was on the floor. She wouldn't wake up. I ran to Auntie Lu and she called the ambulance."

I reach my hand over the table to squeeze her wrist. "Oh, my dear, that must have been so frightening. I'm so sorry."

"I ran as fast as I could," she says quietly.

"Oh, I bet you did. I just bet you did." I try to guess what happened to her mother. Heart attack? Embolism? At my age, the list of deadly culprits is long and intimate, but Addie's mother is probably younger than my daughters even. And who gives a necklace away before a heart attack? The thought makes my cheeks warm with quick anger.

I imagine Addie bent down at her mother's side, tugging on her hand, touching her face, shaking her shoulders in frustration and fear, saying *Mama! Mama! Wake up!* then up and running, jacket hanging half-off, flying out the door and down the apartment steps and running, running—how far?—to find her Auntie at the laundromat, because she is only ten and doesn't think to try the apartment next door first or call for help herself. It makes my heart clench to imagine it, and I want to wrap warm strong wings around the child.

The Gap bag falls over at my feet, and I bend down to retrieve a pearl-pink hoodie from the floor with a sigh. So far, we've braved Macy's, American Eagle, Eddie Bauer, and The Gap. I'm not an avid shopper, not like some women, but I really don't mind doing anything, especially if it's something new and might be an adventure. And shopping with Addie has been a bit of an adventure. She didn't know her sizes, of course, and the first few times in the dressing room seemed to take forever. In Macy's I had to knock on the door several times to get her to answer, and when she finally let me in she looked so anguished in the tight wrap-around skirt that I almost laughed. *Oh, honey, it's okay, you won't love everything. That's why we try it on.* She looked down at her legs, up at me, and said, *Do I unwrap it to use the bathroom?* I laughed and said, *I honestly don't know. Can't you just shimmy it up, or something?* And that made her laugh, which seemed to make it all better somehow. When she determined I wouldn't be mad, she let me come in the stalls with her, and we laughed and laughed at some of the silly clothes made for girls these days. After three hours, we ended up with two pairs of jeans—one with sparkles and one with a pink sash belt—three T-shirts, two pairs of shorts, one hoodie, six pairs of underwear with sayings like "Sweetie" and "Cutie Pie" on them, no skirts, and two summer dresses. At each cash register she turned pale and fidgety, but I assured her I was fully prepared to spend thirty dollars on a pair of jeans.

I set the bag upright at my feet and see that Addie is sliding over to the garbage, skating with her feet on the slick tiled floor. Watching her gives me a great idea, and my face breaks into a big smile. She wrangles with the swinging door on the garbage can and drops in her empty hot dog stick and crumpled Pepsi cup. She looks at me and makes a face.

"I need to wash my hands, to discourage germs."

Oh, how she makes me smile, this child. "Well, we'll find the ladies' room and discourage germs together."

When we finally leave the downtown mall, the rain is hammering down, and I feel light as a feather dashing across the wet street to the parking garage.

"My goodness! You are a fast runner!" I holler, as she beams and wipes the rain from her face. We didn't bring jackets—I'm forever forgetting things like that—but the heater in the Mercedes dries us quickly. When I look in the mirror, my ivory hair is dampened down, but my cheeks are a lively pink. I tell her I want to show her something, and we can go to the library after. We drive from the parking garage across the Willamette to the east side of town and she stares out the window at the busy rain.

"That's a nice-looking river," she says.

"Nice to look at, maybe, but not so great for swimming. It used to be polluted, but the city's trying to clean it up."

"No fish, then?"

"Oh, people still fish in there. Steelhead, I think, maybe Chinook salmon. And sometimes you can see kayakers or dragon boats."

"Dragon boats?"

I laugh in her direction. "Isn't that a funny name? Teams of people paddle around in big boats with dragon heads. It's Chinese, I think."

"Are there lots of Chinese people here?"

I look over at her round cheeks and fine black-lashed eyes. She's like a single constellation in the night sky, much too far from her fellow stars.

"Not lots, but some. Portland has all kinds of people."

"Oh," she says kindly, and looks out at the rain. I could never be that contained, not ever. I have too much to say at all times, too many places my body wants to go. She lets me chatter on as we drive, listening quietly, letting me lead her wherever I may.

We park in a covered lot and I lead her into another mall. "But this time," I say, "we aren't going to shop." I take her to a railing on the second level and watch her face brighten as she looks below.

"Oh," she says softly. "Ice skaters."

Below us is an indoor skating rink, mostly empty, but with a few young girls in figure-skating dresses in a class, and some half-talented adults skating backward around the middle of the rink. I read the sign by the entrance below: "Skating for Fun and Pleasure! Open Skate 11 to 5! $4.50 per person plus cost of rental!"

"I wasn't sure if we could! Do you want to?" I say. I'm so suddenly excited, I can feel my legs trembling. I love anything that makes me feel like flying, and I was a good skater as a girl. Thoughts of arthritis or broken ankles or cracked hips are far from my mind, and my greatest desire at this moment is to *Skate, skate, skate.*

"I can't. I never have…" she starts. She pulls her cardigan closer around her round belly and takes a step back from the edge.

I pull her hand, lead her to the escalator. "Now, I haven't in years," I say, "but wouldn't it be fun? I think it'll be fun. Please?"

She shrugs and her black braid bobs. I figure that's as much enthusiasm as I'm going to get, and I suddenly remember my daughters at that age, so unwilling to make fools of themselves. *It's good for you,* I used to say. *It's good to make a fool of yourself, from time to time.* And then my girls, *But Mom, you don't understand!*

"I do understand; it'll be good for you," I answer them, and Addie looks confused. I pull her to the counter and pay for us, enjoying my senior discount, then sit to yank off my shoes. She does the same, slowly, and I can see how I could grow seriously impatient with her tedious nature. I get this pressing feeling, a pushing inside, like if I don't go now, do now, *jump now,* the moment will be gone, and something tremendously important will be missed. Adam understood that feeling. That spontaneity kept us vital and young together for many years. Although his impatience often led to brisk anger, it also sharpened his business acumen, and he used to tell me often: *Waiting is wasting, in my opinion.*

"You can walk on the edges of the skates, like this," I say, and wobble across the carpet to the boards. I look back to see her sitting, small and round, on the wooden bench. Her face is creased and frightened, and I kick myself for my haste. I wobble back and sit beside her on the bench. We are the same height sitting. I take both of her hands in mine and say, "You don't have to do anything you don't want to do, honey. I didn't mean to scare you. Can you try? Do you want to try?"

She swallows and nods, and I help her to her feet. She walks slowly to the side and looks at the scratched ice. I step out and glide forward. "Whew!" I yell. "Whoo-hoo! Look at me! Look at meeee!" I lift my feet, one at a time, and my speed builds. I steer back toward the wall and lean close to grab on, breathing hard and laughing like it's Christmas morning. When I look back at Addie, she is standing on the ice, holding onto the edge of the rink. She is very still and her eyes are closed and she's almost smiling.

"Addie, honey? Are you okay?"

"The ice," she says. "It smells like something special is happening. Like a good possibility."

I push myself back to where she stands. "It does, doesn't it?"

I take her hand, and we begin to work our way around the rink, one ten-year-old, black-haired child, and one seventy-something, white-haired grandmother, and I don't know which of us smiles more, or which of us feels more joy blossoming inside, but nothing else matters, nothing but holding her hand and feeling her pulse as the fear cracks away and her eyes light like torches in the wild Alaskan night. She laughs and I laugh and she falls several times, but I don't, as we skate slowly past the white-costumed blond girls in their class, past the teenagers laughing from the balcony and the frail white-hairs watching from the benches, past whatever anguish nags in our minds, past the point of feeling foolish or anything less than wonderful. This Addie child is beautiful and bright and strong and brave and I whisper these things as we wobble together on the ice and tell her without words that I will be steadfast for her, and fly with her, and honor her strong like a night bird honors the distant winter moon.

Emerson reads a sign

I woke today with a headache that has given me no relief. Tillie's amusing outing just seemed to make it worse, and now, driving her home after other errands, I feel tightly bound, my temple throbbing. She has been unusually silent since we left her psychic, and I turn the radio up to encourage her quiet. Today feels wasted, as did yesterday. My to-do list is growing longer, but my mind feels scattered, windblown. I've already cancelled my appointments for the rest of the week, but I need to get to the gym, need to pick up my dry cleaning, need to make pasta in my own kitchen and steam up my own shower. Both houses are legally mine, but the Looking Lake house feels foreign to me. When I visit, I get an unkind feeling, like the neighborhood mice have moved in, and I'd just as soon leave them the place. That house hasn't felt like home since Michael surprised us from Stanford and found Will at Henry's place. Last night, Henry kept peeking at me over Mother's rosemary chicken, and I wanted to scream at him to stop it, stop trying to make some kind of connection with me. What does he think I'm going to do? Fall into his arms and cry on his shoulder? He's in the same place that I left him, more than a decade ago. He looks older—finally looks like an adult now that he's in his forties—but otherwise he seems to be exactly the same as when I left. He is my canyon wall and I am his river and I don't like people I can carve that easily.

The rain is Portland gray today and traffic is heavy. Heading west is always a nightmare in the afternoon, but today it's abysmal. We are stuck in a construction zone, waiting for the flagger to let us through. A TriMet bus is trying to merge without a signal, and a wet man with a cardboard sign is staring from the sidewalk. I make sure the doors are locked and glance at Tillie. She is running her hands down her black pants, up and down, up and down. Her face looks pinched and her hair is coming loose from her braid. She usually looks so healthy and outdoorsy, it's unusual to see her vitality sapped.

"You're losing the braid," I say.

"I know," she says quietly. She pulls the hair band out and uses her fingers to unbraid her long hair. I let the TriMet bus merge in front of me as we inch forward.

"Okay, what is it? What's wrong?" With Tillie I always feel stern, like our father was, as if I need to jump into the fixing of things quickly and efficiently. I think she is going to rehash the psychic's folderol, but she surprises me.

"Do you miss teaching, Emmy?"

"Well, some days I do. Why do you ask?"

"Because you were good at it. The girls liked you, didn't they?" She means the students at Winston Bayles, the private school I would have sent Michael to, had he been lucky enough to have been born a girl. "Sarah Lyall liked you, right?"

"I suppose she did. I'm happy with what I'm doing now."

"No, you're not."

Her words are sharp as branches, and I step on the brake hard to keep from hitting the bus. "You don't know what I am," I say.

"Well, neither do you, then," Tillie says. Her hands have stopped their sliding up and down her foreshortened legs and are twisted together in her lap.

"When we were children," I say, moving forward again, sliding around the bus and past the road construction, "you used to try and pick fights with me, do you remember? Do you know why you did that?"

Her wet clay cheeks have color in them now, high on her cheekbones. "I'll tell you why," I continue. "You used to fight with me when you didn't have anyone else to talk to. You didn't know how to have a regular conversation with me. And you still don't."

Tillie raises both hands in surprise as if I've just pushed her in the back. I feel wet prickles inside my chest, like ice sleeting down.

"God, you are such an ass, Emerson, you know that? We all act so afraid of you, why? And why does Henry stick up for you all the time?"

I look at her, but she is staring out the window at the rainy streets, shaking her head. I retrace what I said—it wasn't emotional, it wasn't irrational, it was simply astute observation, the kind of thing Will would have said as a matter of course. But when he made observations, people called him witty and wise. It's different for women. Call someone on her bullshit and she calls you an ass. What did that Floramaria person say? *You see truth when others are blind.* Well, generally speaking, the blind don't want to know what they're missing.

I'm just merging onto the Sunset Highway when my cell rings—a regular phone ring, not "Chariots of Fire" or any such nonsense—and when I check the caller ID, I am deeply grateful it's not a 215 area code. An old boyfriend has been trying to contact me lately, and my patience is growing thin. His persistence is beginning to border on infatuation.

"You're calling me," I say, handing the phone to Tillie. She doesn't even look at me, and on the fourth ring, my voicemail answers. I make an exasperated sound in her direction and dial my voicemail to listen to the message. "Mother says that she took your phone by accident. She says Gavin just called for you, to tell you your nettle came in, and that I'm to take you there and also get potatoes and an onion. And where exactly are we to find Gavin and his nettle?"

"Her nettle," Tillie says. "My nettle. The co-op. Take the first exit before the Lake Road exit, and you'll see the sign."

We drive in silence to the exit and she points me to the gravel parking lot, where I park near a rusting red pickup and a Subaru covered in left coast bumper stickers. I retrieve her wheelchair from the trunk, grateful that the rain has tapered off so much, and hold it for her by the car door. Tillie lifts herself swiftly into the seat, and I step back to shut the door.

"How often does Henry stick up for me?" I ask, trying to make her smile.

"Ask him yourself," she says, and pushes hard to wheel around me. I stand back and watch as she rolls herself to the wooden wheelchair ramp and up into the store. Her hair is still pleated from the braid and wavy down her back. She looks strong and determined and the feeling comes sharply that I do not know her, my little sister, my always-needing-attending-to sister. I realize

I don't know the difference between who she is and what she became—what I made her into—or if they're one and the same. I look around the mostly empty parking lot, in a place I've never been before, hands in the pockets of my raincoat, letting the mist collect on my face. The damp smells clean and green and I hear low thunder in the west, a warning the rain is coming back. I turn my collar up, push my hair behind one ear, and walk up the steps beside the wheelchair ramp into Gavin's co-op, expecting nothing.

The co-op is concrete floor and plastic bins and metal shelving; a study in economical furnishing. The ceiling is low and feels claustrophobic to me, but the walls are brightly covered with conference posters, yoga pamphlets, framed art. I am surprised to find one of Tillie's paintings next to the dairy case. It is one I haven't seen before, but her style is distinctive; even without the small title card, I know it's her work. It's titled *Preamble*, a large framed canvas in oils: in the foreground is a small group of what appears to be migrant workers in a field watching a brilliant sunrise in the distance. There are small black crosses—grave markers, I assume—a silhouetted barrier between the workers and the bright sky. The migrant workers are created entirely in a blue palette of lights and darks, although the sun and sky are multicolored and heavenly. At the bottom of the painting is faint black text, a quote I can't place right off. Truncated fore and aft by the confines of the canvas, it reads: *"disregard and contempt for human rights have resulted in barbarous…outraged the conscience of mankind, and the advent of…human beings shall enjoy freedom of speech and belief…freedom from fear and want has been proclaimed as the highest aspiration…"* It is a gorgeous painting and could easily command several thousand dollars. I'm quite sure she donated the painting to the co-op to make some sort of statement; that's the sort of thing Tillie does all the time. I wonder why she doesn't just sell the painting and donate the profits to her favorite charity for the tax write-off. I decide to ask her later, when she's feeling less peckish toward me.

I look over to see Tillie in the produce section, parked in front of a short-haired woman in a dark-green apron. The woman is sitting on an upright wooden box at Tillie's height, talking animatedly and sporting a wicked grin. She is lean and wiry and boyish, with almost-black spiky hair and too many earrings and a thin white T-shirt and jeans under her cloth grocer's apron. I sigh and walk over to where they are parked.

Tillie introduces me, and the woman—Gavin—reaches up to shake my hand firmly. Her eyes evaluate me and I feel lacking in some measure, although she's easily fifteen years younger. I have a sudden urge to whip out my portfolio, mention my Lexus, invite her to one of my houses, or in any other way step on her toes. But I pride myself on having grace under pressure and say nothing untoward. Tillie asks me to pick out some potatoes and onions for mother, and I'm pleased to have a project.

I look over the produce and watch Tillie with her fiery friend, watch the way her fingers dance toward her neckline, the way her head tilts, the way her eyes glance down, then up again. Gavin reaches out and puts a hand on Tillie's knee just for a moment, just to emphasize whatever story she's telling, and Tillie's own hand wanders unconsciously down to rest on the spot she's touched. Surprise jumps like a tiger into my throat and I drop my potatoes onto the concrete floor. Both of them look at me, then back at each other. I hurry to pick the white potatoes off the floor and peek at them from my knees, suddenly eager to read the signs. I was not expecting this. I did not have this definition for my sister. Makes me wonder what else I've been missing.

It's true it's been years since she had a steady man in her life, only one since her divorce from that fragile poet, Stan, but I chalked that up to age, to menopause, to routine, figured she had discreet encounters, same as I. I'm a little embarrassed to watch—at my need to watch—but it's exciting too, like flipping through the channels and pausing on one you don't normally see. There are several other customers in the co-op, and a man behind the counter, but no one is watching me watch them. I walk to the other side of the produce island and pretend to examine organic peaches.

Gavin says something and Tillie laughs, brushing her hair back. She looks so much younger, happier than I've seen her in ages, and my heart opens a little to see her diamond shine. I think of young green trees by a sweet little creek, bending to reach the morning sun. I close my eyes and smile a secret smile. When I look again, Tillie is heading toward a door marked "Unisex Restroom," and I carry my potatoes to the small counter.

Gavin is behind the register now and smiles at me. "Would you like to become a member of the co-op?"

"Oh no, no thank you," I say. "I'll just wait for Tillie, then. Did she remember her nettle?"

"It's right here." She puts a large plastic bag of chopped green leaves on the counter. "Have you had nettle tea before?"

"Not that I remember," I say, arching my eyebrows. "Does it sting?"

Gavin smiles a charmingly crooked smile and shakes her head. She follows me as I walk toward Tillie's painting.

"What do you think of your sister's work?" she asks.

"I think she's gifted. I also think she's overly generous."

Gavin laughs. Standing beside me she barely comes to my shoulder and she smells sweet, like honey or sweet talcum. I realize I'm a little afraid of her, as I'm afraid of the mentally ill, because I don't know what to expect.

"I don't think there is such a thing as overly generous," she says. Her voice is even and she sounds well educated. I have the impression she would love an argument with me. "I think the world needs more generous, in fact. What do you think of her statement?"

Does she mean the figurative statement or the literal text on the canvas or something else entirely? I don't want to match wits with her or argue ideology. She is reminding me of Will, and I don't appreciate it. I was young when I met Will, and energetic enough to enjoy the battles, the arguments, the tempestuous, smart foreplay. Now the thought of a political debate makes me weary.

"Why don't you tell me what you think?" I say. We are standing like guardians in front of the oil painting, arms crossed defensively across both of our chests. I notice this and clasp my hands at my waist instead.

"It's a portion of the preamble to the UN's Declaration of Human Rights," Gavin says. "All member nations were asked to teach the declaration in their schools, among other things. That was 1948. Do you remember being taught the Human Rights Declaration in school?"

I shake my head no, slowly.

"It's worth reading, if you haven't," she says. "Article 13 states that everyone shall have the freedom of movement within their own state or country, and the right to both leave and return to any country, including his or her own. Pretty subversive shit, actually."

Tillie joins us from the bathroom and I raise my eyebrows to show I'm more than ready to leave. Gavin nods her over to the counter, and I stand blessedly alone while she pays for her things. I watch Gavin lean over the counter on her elbows, raise her eyes to me, then say something low to Tillie. Tillie laughs, and I decide to wait outside. The parking lot is cool and empty in the late afternoon. I lean against the car and rub my head with my hand. I'm just searching in my bag for Excedrin when Tillie comes out of the co-op and rolls down the wheelchair ramp.

"Your friend is—" The look in Tillie's eyes stops me from saying whatever joke I was going to make. "She didn't like me," I say, "Not that I'm surprised. What did she say about me that was so funny?" Tillie tips her head and I stammer a little. "At the counter, you laughed like you were embarrassed. I'm sorry if I embarrass you."

"God, you're vain," she says. She rolls to the passenger door, and I hold it open for her while she lifts herself to the seat. I collapse the wheelchair and stow it in the trunk, then sit beside her in the Lexus. My hands are cold, so I pull my black leather driving gloves from the glove box.

"She asked if I like dinner," Tillie says. "And of course, I stupidly said, *Dinner?* And then she said, *Because I like dinner, and I'd like to like dinner with you sometime.* And then she said she made great gazpacho, and would I come over this weekend, and then she said, *Your sister doesn't like me.*"

I turn to look at Tillie. "She said that?" Past Tillie, I can see the porch of the co-op, where Gavin now stands calm in her garish green apron. Tillie turns to look through the window and raises a hand to wave. Gavin waves to Tillie, then waves big at me; I barely raise a hand back, feeling perturbed.

"So, we're pretty sure we don't like each other," I say. "Wonderful."

Tillie sighs. "I told Gavin that you're difficult—" This makes me laugh out loud. "And I told her that you don't like anyone—"

"Which isn't true," I say, pulling out of the parking lot.

"And I told her that you're just jealous and I'd love to have gazpacho with her this weekend—"

"And so now you're dating women?"

Tillie gets quiet and bites her lip. "I'm not any different than I was. Not an hour ago, or a week ago, or twenty years ago, I don't think."

"Then you've always been gay? You'd think it would have come up before now."

Tillie's voice softens, and I feel some small contrition. "I don't know if there's a name for what I am. I don't expect you to understand."

"Is this something you do ... often?"

"Never have before, and I'd appreciate if you'd just shut up about it."

"I thought she was electrifying, actually," I say, truthfully. "I didn't want to take my eyes off her. I imagine there are a lot of married women that do their shopping there just to have her look them in the eyes the way she does."

Tillie looks shocked, and I open my eyes wide. "I'm completely serious," I say. "She probably has her pick. Although I found her to be . . . I felt like she was trying to intimidate me."

"Yeah," Tillie says, "you two are just peas in a pod . . ."

I look at Tillie and smile. I like her best when she's standing up for herself. She smiles back and looks out the window. Despite what she may believe, I have great interest in her well-being, and not just because she keeps Mother out of my hair. I'm glad I met her Gavin before she pitched headfirst into something I can only imagine will end badly. And then she'll have to find a new place to grocery shop, and we'll have to litigate to get her painting back. And now I'm driving her to the Looking Lake house, where I will tell Mother I cannot possibly stay, where I will avoid Henry's stare, and give little Addie a quick hug on my way out the door. I will return to my own house, alone, and to my own life, such as it is, where no one expects anything from me, and if they have something to tell me they do so carefully and respectfully. My family drains me with their upfrontedness, their joviality, their for-ever-coursing insecurity and gladness. Give me distant neighbors, give me colleagues, give me acquaintances, give me leave of these hungry people, these ones who want me bare and open-handed, these muddy, needy people who think they know me best.

Addie reads a sign

Today with Ms. Eve was an adventure. She has more energy than I even know what to do with. I didn't know she would buy me so many things, and now I'm worried in my stomach because we can't pay it back. When we came back here, I went to my room and stacked all the new clothes and sat and looked at them. And then I took the big bag and stacked all the library books and looked at them too. The library was very grand, with marble floors and echoey staircases, and Ms. Eve let me look outside the children's section too. I wanted books about airplanes to write a report, but mostly what I found was Wright brothers at Kitty Hawk and military airplanes. I just wanted some books about a girl who rode on an airplane and about what it was like. When I grow up, I am going to write all the books that are missing, so the kids who look will be able to find themselves there if they need to.

Ms. Eve calls me from my room and when I go to the kitchen the tall, blond-headed Henry is there. He is sitting on a stool and looking a little tipsy, but Ms. Eve says he is only sick, not drinking.

Henry laughs, but not a mean laugh, and so I laugh a little too. He asks how I know what tipsy looks like, but Ms. Eve shushes him from her chopping carrots. Then she says she'd like to see the fashion show, and would I oblige, she says. Then with a big bustle in comes the straight-backed woman named Mrs. Worthy and her sister with no legs named Tillie and their eyes are busy like a lot has happened. I have to back up to get out of the way, and I find myself next to Henry, and he smiles at me, and he is very nice. We watch the three white women together, and boy, do they have a lot to say to each other, always, like starlings.

Ms. Eve says, "How was your appointment?"

And Tillie says, "It was very strange."

And Mrs. Worthy says, "Traffic was a nightmare."

And Ms. Eve says, "Did you get your message Gavin called?"

And Mrs. Worthy says, "How are you Addie?"

And Tillie says, "Henry, what are you doing out of bed?"

And Ms. Eve says, "We were just going to have a fashion show," and that's when everyone looks at me. I feel my cheeks get hot and I look at the floor—it needs a sweeping—and then I feel the kind man's hand on my shoulder and it is warm and strong, like Mama's or Captain Mike's, and then I feel a lump in my throat and I don't want to talk.

"It's okay," he whispers. "You do what you want."

I shake my head, and look up at Ms. Eve, my chickadee friend. "Can we call my mom tonight?"

She looks at Mrs. Worthy and their eyes get big like a secret and then she says, "I don't see why not? Let's try. Now, before supper." She wipes her hands on a towel and hands Tillie the carrot chopping. "Girls, did you get my potatoes?"

I like Ms. Eve. She is what Mama calls a straight-shooter, though she is easily distracted. Sometimes today she would start to tell a story and forget in the middle what she was even saying. Sometimes I'd remind her and sometimes not. I remember the elders' stories at fish camp. Never would they forget to finish a story, because stories are sacred. And everyone listened like it mattered. In regular life, people act like stories don't really matter, but I think they do. I think we could all be a little more careful.

Ms. Eve takes me to the big room she calls the great room, and we sit down on a soft brown couch.

"Well," she says. "Let's start by calling Michael, shall we? Maybe he can give us some news."

She unsnaps a book with pictures of cartoon kids on the front, like a girl my age would have if she had nice things, and looks for the phone number. She dials the number and holds my warm hand in hers.

"Michael, honey? It's Grandma." I watch her smile. She has a beautiful smile. We are about the same size, but she's skinny. I had fun ice skating, although I was scared to fall. I was more scared that Ms. Eve would fall but she didn't. I was afraid she'd break in half. "I have Addie here. Yes, we've been having a wonderful time. Yes, she is a lovely girl. We're becoming good friends. How is—?"

There is a long pause, and I can hear the women in the kitchen arguing about whether or not to peel the potatoes. My throat feels scratchy and nervous and my eyes are burning but I sit very still. When I was little, I knew that Mama liked it best when I held still and now I'm very good at not fidgeting. I overheard two white teachers talking at school once about how they liked the Native kids better because they don't fidget as much and they respect their elders. I was proud to be a Native kid then.

"Oh, I see. Well, that's positive. And her friend is able to—? Yes, of course. Well, could we—? Will you get a message to her then, give them this number? We'd love to have you, whenever you can make it down. Just tell me and I'll buy the ticket myself."

She hands me the phone. "He'd like to say hello, dear."

I hold the phone with two hands, pressed close to my ear. Captain Mike. I love Mike. He has tough eyes except when he looks at me, then he is gentle. He's Mama's friend and he's my friend too and he's known me forever. We have pictures of him holding me when I was a baby all wrapped up in a blanket. He loves red hot candy and always has some in his pocket that he shares with me, and he gives me quarters too.

"Hey kiddo, how are you? Are you having fun? Grandma Eve is a handful, careful she doesn't wear you out." His voice is scratchy from smoking cigarettes. I like listening to him. It's like wearing a big warm wool sweater. "Listen, your mom is out of the hospital, okay? That's good news. She's going to stay with LuAnn for a while, and she's going to be seeing some folks that can help her."

"Auntie Lu," I whisper. "I know the number."

"Yeah, but . . . your mom is still sick, okay? She needs some time to rest, so why don't you give her a few days before you call her."

"But she needs me," I say. "She needs to hear from me."

"Honey, she's on some medication right now that might make it tough. She really just needs to rest, and then she'll be able to talk to you, right? Hey, I wanted to tell you, a buddy of mine went down to BC last week on a fishing trip, and he saw a spirit bear. Do you know what that is?"

I shake my head no and he keeps talking.

"It's a special kind of black bear that's totally white. They're not polar bears and they're not albinos. They're really special. He told me about the legend. See, in the beginning, when Raven descended from the night sky, he wanted to remind the people of the ice and whiteness that came before." Captain Mike is smoking a cigarette now. I can hear the difference in breathing when he talks. "So, in this one special place, Raven went through and he made every tenth bear white. That way everyone would remember what we are and where we've come from. Raven said these special bears would live in peace and harmony forever."

There is quiet on the phone for a minute, but I don't mind being quiet with Captain Mike. "That's a good story," I say.

"Yeah," he says. "It made me think of you. Is my family taking good care of you?"

"Yes, thank you," I say. We say goodbye, and Ms. Eve sits with me on the couch for a while.

"Are you okay?" she asks, looking into my eyes.

"I feel a little tired," I say. My eyes are really scratchy now and I feel sleepy. "I don't feel very good."

"Yes, I think you should go lie down." She puts her hand on my forehead and I close my eyes. "Oh! You're so warm. Let's get you into bed." She helps me stand from the couch and together we walk to my room. "Henry!" she yells as we pass by the kitchen, I guess for getting me sick. He makes a look like, *What'd I do?* but Ms. Eve doesn't say anything else. She helps me into bed and I close my eyes and she brings me some mashed-up medicine in a spoon since I can't swallow the pills. I listen to the family sounds of dishes and laughing and quiet talk, and outside the rain again, saying *Pitter, pat, pat* and then I must have fallen asleep.

When I wake up it is very dark outside and I have to pee. I remember my dreams were very fast and too hot. I pull the covers back and my legs feel shaky. I have to walk slowly to the bathroom and when I get there I sit for a long time on the toilet because it's too hard to get up. I try to stand but my legs don't want to hold me up and I crumple down. The tile in the bathroom is cold and smooth on my cheek and I lie still, feeling coolness on my legs and through my nightshirt. I look up and I can see out the window to the far-off moon. She is smaller tonight than last night, that means she's waning, just a narrow bitty thing. I raise my hand up to try and touch her, but she is too far away. I can only pretend. I love her because she is the same as she was at home and she came all this way to be with me. She is watching over me, for Mama. I can read the sign. All the best Yup'iks can read signs. I will have to tell Mama thank you for sending the moon to me. I feel my body shaking, and I'm both very hot and very cold now. I try to sit up, but my head swims and I start to cry. My tears are cool on my cheeks and my fingers trace the white spring moon through the window.

I imagine Mama sitting with me, looking up at the dark sky.

Why do you cry, little one? she says, softly petting my hair.

Because I'm sick and you're sick and we don't have anyone else.

We have more than you know, baby. More than you know.

"Addie? Is that you?"

I look at the bathroom door and see Tillie moving toward me in the dark, out of her wheelchair. She is smiling a little but her eyes look worried.

"Honey, are you okay?"

"I can't walk," I say, crying even harder. "I'm stuck. I don't want to be here."

"I know, honey, I know." She laughs and says, "I can't walk either." She pulls my head into her lap and whispers to me, "It's okay, it'll be okay," over and over again. She strokes my head like Mama did and I let my tears fall onto her soft pajama shorts. I close my eyes and feel for Mama's good amulet around my neck. It was her most special thing, and when she gave it to me I should have known to be suspicious. It is like Captain Mike said, a white bear. Mama has always worn it. She said my dad gave it to her before he died. I don't know my dad. All I have is Mama's bear, his bear.

"I'm nobody's spirit bear," I say. "I don't even want to be."

Tillie laughs and rubs my forehead. "Then what do you want to be?"

"I want to write down the things that matter. I want to be a great storyteller. I want to be like the moon."

"That's lovely. You can be that if you want."

I kiss the bone amulet, like I've seen Mama do, and sit up. "Will you help me to bed?" I ask quietly. "I'm done looking at her for now."

Tillie puts her hand on my cheek and smiles, but her eyes are sad. We crawl together across the bathroom floor to the hallway, then rest before we go to my room. She lies beside me until I fall asleep. She feels nice, even through her sadness. I don't know what Mama meant when she said we have more than we know. I will have to ask her when I call and ask if she remembers me sick on the bathroom floor because she helped from far away with the moon. I bet she'll remember. I bet she needed to see me too.

Three

Henry shares a secret

The morning sky is sweetly blue after several days of off and on spring rain. I'm up early after two days flat with fever. My body feels wrung out but fresh, as if something difficult and wonderful has happened inside. I thought I was better the night Addie got sick, but after dinner my head felt heavy as stone, and Eve sent Emerson to walk me home in the rain.

She gripped my elbow and steered me slowly through the cold and the dark, holding her black umbrella steady over our heads in silence. I thought of a thousand things to say, but they all seemed eager or greedy.

When we got to my cabin she said, *I forgot you don't lock your door.*

And I said, *That's so all the neighbors can come as they please.* I rested my tired head against the wooden door frame so she wouldn't leave. The landing blocked the rain, but she kept her umbrella open, twirling it slowly on her shoulder.

She looked ice-sculpture perfect in her tasteful, understated way, as she said, *You mean all the neighbor's wives, don't you?*

I felt a rush of warmth and shivered. *I'm glad you're back, Emerson*, I said.

Her eyes showed momentary surprise that she covered by glancing down. *Goodnight, Henry*, she said, turning away.

The early morning clouds are slow, and I can see a pair of red-tailed hawks circling in the distance. It isn't warm yet, but it's going to be a fine day. I have a thermos of coffee and a ripe orange and a cheese sandwich and a bag of Eve's oatmeal chocolate chip cookies, and, thankfully, a rowboat that didn't float away. She bobs now, the *HMS Daisy*, tied to the Worthy's dock instead of my single shore-bound wooden peg. I smile to think of Emerson down by the lake that wet morning, tying my boat up and cursing me, I'm sure.

You mean all the neighbor's wives, don't you?

And my foolishness: *I'm glad you're back.* Even if it's true, I shouldn't have said it. Maybe she's turning it over in her own mind, or did yesterday, while I dozed fitfully, sweaty and exhausted from breaking the fever. Maybe she's in bed thinking of me right now.

I turn from the lakeshore to look at her house and make a sharp sound of surprise. Addie stands quietly by the Worthy boathouse, not fifteen paces away. The breaking sun gives her black hair a faint corona.

"Good morning," I say, shielding my eyes from the brightness. "You startled me."

"I don't like to interrupt," she says slowly, so matter-of-fact. "You were busy looking at the sky." She is wearing a new pair of jeans and tennis shoes, but has her old blue sweater buttoned up tight. Her black hair is in two braids now, one behind each shoulder, and she's holding her one-eyed doll loosely at her side. She is a familiar child to me now, although we haven't spoken much. I like her stillness, her roundness, her seeming patience with all things.

"You feeling better? You want to come out on the lake with me?"

She nods and smiles and her face lights up like sunlight. "Mrs. Anderson would like that too." She holds up her doll so I know who Mrs. Anderson is.

"When I was a kid, I had a plastic cowboy named Blackjack. He was pretty awesome. I accidentally dropped him in the ocean on a fishing trip with my dad."

I walk over to the boathouse and creak open the rusty door. "There are some old life jackets in here, although I don't think we'll find one small enough for Mrs. Anderson." Addie ducks her head and smiles, squeezing her doll's ragged arm. Inside, Will's old MasterCraft is riding dry on a chocked boat trailer. An old milk crate sits on the plank floor, along with a dented tin can I use sometimes for an ashtray. Dusty life jackets hang from chest-high pegs, and I pick a smallish one for Addie. Outside, I cinch her in tight and she looks happily pinched in the blue foam.

"That's too bad," she says. "About Blackjack. Maybe it was just time for a new adventure."

"I bet you're right," I say, and the idea makes me smile. "Hey, can you swim?" I ask, helping her into my rowboat.

"I took lessons at the YMCA," she says, stepping carefully in the rocking boat. She sits on the wooden bench seat and looks at me expectantly. "But I didn't bring my suit."

I laugh, and she realizes she's made a joke. I push us off and hop in.

"It's just in case," I say. "I haven't had a casualty yet, but I'd like to know in advance who's saving who."

"Okay," she says, and pats an approving hand on the gunwale. "Why is she named *Daisy*?"

"After my mother," I say. "She passed away when I was a teenager. Daisies were her favorite. One of the things I remember."

She nods seriously and is quiet. The lake is calm in the early morning light. The sun is still low in the east, the lake neighbors asleep in their warm family homes. I row gently through the shallows and pull up the collar on my flannel shirt. Addie sits facing me in the boat, silent, but her face animated with delight. I point behind her, and she turns to see a great blue heron fly low over the water. A fish jumps beside us and she squeaks in joy.

"Can you fish here?" she whispers.

"Oh yeah. We've got trout and some bass. If Eve weren't around, that's all I'd be eating, probably. Next time we can bring the poles, if you want."

She nods and smiles, hugging her knees and looking around at the water. Looking Lake is big enough for my rich neighbors to boat on, pulling tan sons and daughters in elliptical waterski or wakeboard circles, but small enough to keep it undernoticed and unremarkable. Just over twenty years ago when my father moved back East to live with his sister, he deeded me his little lot and tiny cabin. The surrounding lakeshore still mostly belonged to the trees and the farmers. Back then, I'd drive from the university in Corvallis with a friend or two, and we'd get so naked and stoned and full of ourselves we'd forget to go back to school for a week. The cold lake was mine then, before the rich and the unfulfilled flocked to her lapping, gravel-strewn edges. I could spend whole days floating peaceably on her lulling mother's belly.

"You don't have to go to work today?" she asks, and I shake my head.

"I used to have a real job, doing construction. I hated it. I mean, I don't mind *work*, I think it's good for you, but it wore me out. I drank too much and watched too much TV. I wasn't doing anything I loved and I hated it. But I figured out I don't need much to live on, really. I help Eve around the house and she feeds me."

She listens carefully, as if everything I'm saying matters. "That's a nice arrangement," she says. I smile, and she smiles back.

I row us across the lake's narrowest waist to a shallow stand of reeds that anchor us in place. A kingfisher calls, and Addie and I watch as he glides like Christmas swag from tree to tree.

"This is wonderful," she says softly.

I open my sack lunch and we share the oatmeal cookies while I start peeling the orange. "This is my favorite place, this lake. But too many people live here now, with their power boats and WaveRunners. Kind of ruins it, I think."

"Like the Worthys?" she asks.

"Only Emerson is a Worthy. And Michael. You know, Captain Mike. Eve and Tillie are Fosters. They don't ruin anything. They're good people. Tillie and Eve, they try and take care of things. They try and take care of me, anyway."

I make a neat pile of orange peels in the bottom of the boat and hand a section to Addie. The water laps the boat softly and the oars gently rise and fall in the oarlocks. It's quiet still, with just a small breeze over the top of the lake, swaying the reeds around us.

"I wish I could stay here," Addie says. "Mama would like it here. She likes peaceful places. She hasn't been happy for a long time."

"What does she do, your mom?" In my mind I can see Eve shushing me, Emerson giving me a look. They have a well-mannered way of not talking about anything important sometimes that feels stifling. I'd rather not talk at all than make idle chat.

"She works in a pharmacy, but she doesn't like it. She makes beads. I mean…" Her hand waves around with her orange slice as she tries to explain. She sits wide-kneed, stuffed in her blue life vest, feet together sole to sole. "I mean, pictures with beads. They're beautiful. One was a fox; one was a bear. They take a long time to make."

"So she's an artist," I say. "Like me and Tillie. It's hard to make a living, even if you're very good. I bet your mom's good, right?"

Addie nods and I hand her another piece of orange.

"And I know you miss her. How's she doing, do you know?"

She drops her eyes and her shoulders slump. She shrugs. I lean back to look at the golden blue sky, and we sit in silence. I hear Addie's feet scrape on the bottom of the boat and glance her way.

"She doesn't want me anymore," she says.

I gather my spare jacket in a wad behind my head and put my feet up on the edge of the boat. "I'm sure that's not true," I say. "You're a great kid. You're smart, you're funny, and you know how to be quiet and not chase the birds away." That sad heaviness has returned to her pale face, and I feel a weight settle in, a comfortable boulder of responsibility for her. "Did your mom say that to you? That she doesn't want you?"

"Not with words," she says, "with her feelings."

The sun is starting to warm me, and I peel off my thick flannel shirt to the T-shirt beneath. "Here, use this for your head. Like this." I wad it up and she tries to put it behind her head and lie down.

"I can't..." She tries to lean back, then sits dejectedly in her bulky life vest.

"Just take it off, kiddo. There isn't anyone around." I lean forward and release the yellow buckles. She takes a deep breath. We lie down together, feet to feet in my small boat, and stare at the white clouds and busy swallows overhead.

"Do you know what *autonomy* means?" I ask her.

"No. Do you know what *caciitua* means?"

"No," I laugh. "It means freedom to be your own person, whatever you want to be, with or without a life jacket. What does your word mean?"

"In Yup'ik, it means I have no idea what I'm doing. I used it a lot at fish camp."

"Do you speak Yup'ik?"

"Just a little," she says. "I'm learning."

"Is that your people?"

"I don't know which my people are. Mama and Aunt Ruth were orphans, and nobody ever told them."

We float quietly together, and I have a great feeling of warmth, like a celestial blanket is being pulled over the top of me. I want to tell her that I don't know my people either. That most people, in fact, don't know their people, but it seems superfluous to say. Dismissive, even.

"A long time ago, I went to the university in Corvallis," I say. "On a wrestling scholarship." I watch a pair of jets fly high overhead, leaving two long white trails across the bowl of royal-blue sky. "Before that, I wrestled in high school and my squad was the best in the state. I had a friend named Hutch; he was this small Asian guy, wrestled in the smallest weight class. His mom was Vietnamese and his dad was white, but he didn't know his dad. His mom never came to watch, except this one time."

I look to the other end of the boat. Addie is lying on her side, head on her makeshift pillow, curled like a backwards *s*, watching me speak. She doesn't look away from me like she does with Emerson, and that makes me happy. Her skin tone is a creamy yellow, with dusky rose on her cheeks, her smart eyes thick-lashed and beautiful.

"Hutch was a pretty quiet dude, kind of like you, but he told me his mom was coming to this one match. We were undefeated, playing to a full house. Lots of screaming girls, I remember." I smile, thinking of what all those girls meant to me. "Hutch was first up, but before we started he showed me where his mom was sitting in the bleachers. She looked so small and worried sitting there." I take a deep breath and sigh. "He was crazy good that night. He just kept shooting at the guy. He used a body-lock with an outside step, but the other guy was getting tired and his trailing leg twisted and he tore his ACL. That's a ligament in your knee."

I remember the darkened gym, the silence in the room, it was always silent during the matches, and watching the guy's knee twist wrong and then that sound—*Pop!*—and screaming, screaming. The guy went limp and fell to the ground, just rolling and screaming. The coaches and trainers were on the mat in a flash, and the rest of us just sat and watched without saying a word while the ambulance came and took the kid away.

"Well, then the ref took Hutch into the middle of the mat and raised his arm in victory. He looked awful, like he was going to throw up, and a few people clapped. And then his mom stood up with a sob, and ran past all the people in the bleachers and out of the room. You would've thought Hutch had been the one hurt the way she carried on. Hutch turned to me and he said: *Which is worse, watching your kid get hurt, or watching your kid hurt someone else?*

"His mom didn't come to any more matches, but that didn't mean she didn't love him, or that she wasn't proud of him. Sometimes our parents have feelings that are *around* us but aren't *because* of us. She just had her own thing about it, and I think Hutch thought it was about him. And maybe it was and maybe it wasn't. But what could he do? Just keep wrestling, you know?"

"At fish camp, Robert Soo pushed me into a puddle and I cut my lip. His mom hugged me and she helped me wash my mouth. She said mothers love all children, even the ones their sons push into puddles."

I laugh and say, "What's that word again? I think everyone should say it every day."

"Caciitua."

"Caciitua," I say, letting the sounds tumble in my mouth. "Caciitua." I have no idea what I'm doing."

"Henry!"

Addie and I look at each other, holding very still.

"Henry Oliver! I can see your boat there! Hiding in my reeds, are you spying?"

I sit up and look. Twenty yards away is the shore opposite my home, and standing on the gravel is Missy Holloway, Doc's wife. She is wearing a sky-blue down vest and a white turtleneck, perfectly put together like a gift wrapped in luxurious paper. Both her blond spaniel and Irish setter are wet to the haunches.

"Missy," I say, as if I didn't know where I'd parked my own boat.

"Good morning!" she yells, too loudly. "No, Buddy! Stay! Heel!"

Addie sits up and turns around and we all three watch as her white-muzzled Irish setter starts paddling out to little *Daisy*. I shake my head and open my thermos to pour myself a cup of coffee. Missy is slapping her thighs and calling as her spaniel barks relentlessly, but Buddy paddles on, swimming toward us with a doggy smile on his wet face.

"Addie, meet Buddy. Buddy, Addie." The setter is at the side of the boat, treading water and panting, trying to find purchase in the bed of tall reeds. I screw the top back on my thermos and reach down, one-handed, to help the dog into the boat. Buddy slips and the boat rocks; I raise my eyebrows at Addie, who laughs. I hand her my coffee and watch her take a sip.

"Leave me some," I say, and use both hands to haul Buddy into the rowboat. I pull him in and fall backward in the boat. He stands between us and shakes his red coat extravagantly, making the boat sway. The spaniel continues to bark, and Addie giggles as Buddy turns around and tries to lick her face.

"Missy, you need to call off your hounds," I say, settling the oars back into the water. I try paddling backward to get out of the reeds, but Buddy seems to think we're going for a ride. "No boy, going back home."

"Hi there!" Missy calls. "You must be the new girl staying with the Worthys! My husband and I are big collectors of American Indian art. I'd like to find a real totem pole next."

"She's beautiful," I whisper, tapping my temple, my back to Missy. "But the attic's a little bare, if you know what I mean."

Addie nods and her expression changes from dismay to concern, as if she's looking at one with an affliction. I paddle close enough to the shore that Buddy can jump out and he does, leaping wildly to the gravel and splashing us on his way back to his barking brother. "Nice visiting with you, Buddy," I say, and Addie giggles again. I could grow seriously attached to that sound.

"Henry, I've missed you." Missy has long blond hair and cheekbones that go on forever and a husband who loves his university department more than he loves his wife.

"Well, we both had the flu. I got poor Addie sick. But you don't hold it against me, right?" I watch Addie's eyes flash as she smiles and drinks my coffee. "Hey, give that back."

"Henry? I could use some help with my still lifes. Can I bring my paints over later?" Missy asks.

I watch her two dogs dance around, watch her shift her weight foot to foot, watch the screen door open on the porch above and behind her. I raise my unshaved chin as her husband steps out into the sun, sipping from a steaming mug.

"Morning, Doc," I call. Addie hands me my coffee cup and turns again to watch this new development.

"Morning, Henry. She really does need help with her painting." Doc is overweight and fully bearded, but behind his glasses his eyes are sharp and hawkish. Next to his gossamer wife, he looks like a Russian diplomat accustomed to luxurious bribes.

"Doc Holloway is head of the anthropology department at Portland State," I say casually to Addie, shifting in my seat on the boat. "His name isn't really Doc. That's just a nickname from an old TV show."

"I know artists can't afford to work for free," Doc calls from the porch overhead. "You help her with her painting and I'll pay you for your time. What say you, sir?" Missy looks disquieted, but I feel rock-solid calm inside.

"That would be fine," I say, looking calmly at Missy on the gravel shore. "Anytime this afternoon."

Missy waves delicate fingers at me and I hand the coffee back to Addie. I dip the oars in the water and paddle us away.

"Why doesn't Tillie give the painting lessons?" Addie asks. "Isn't she the painter?"

I look at Addie and she looks at me. "Do you know what discretion means? Can we maybe keep this a secret?" I say, paddling through the warm morning light, across the lake and back to our homes.

"Keep what a secret? That she likes you?"

"Yeah, maybe."

"But she's married," Addie says.

"I know, kiddo. I didn't say I like her back."

"Then why doesn't Tillie give the painting lessons?" she asks again.

"That's a good question," I say. "Caciitua."

Addie laughs and the real answers tumble through my mind. Because I'm stuck. Because I'm obligated. I think of Hutch watching his mother run from the gym. Why do you break your mother's heart? Because you can, because you have to. And why do I sleep with my neighbor's wife? Because when she runs her hair on my arm or lays her cheek on my chest, I feel all of my doubts wash away, and it doesn't matter if we have nothing to talk about, it doesn't matter if she's rich and married and slumming with me, it doesn't matter that we don't love each other. I remember watching Tillie eat Betty Crocker chocolate frosting one time, from a can. We were talking and she just kept dipping her finger in and eating and eating. And when I asked her if she liked it she said no, and when I asked her why she kept eating it she said, *I don't know. I guess I just feel like I have to.* And I watched her eat it and eat it until I felt sick inside, but still I could understand that she had to, she just had to.

Tillie shares a secret

We are outside, all of us except Emmy. The late morning sun is warm on my hair and the soil graciously welcomes my seedlings. I will miss the sprouting trays in my studio, but I'm happy to get them planted. I remember Floramaria's Knight of Pentacles: *Of the earth*, she said, *relaxed and easy*. I love the feel of soft earth in my hands. It makes me think of green and ancient lives, growing and ebbing like moon tides. I imagine women and men before me, Native and strong, living and dying and becoming deep, thick, brown earth. It blossoms my heart to think of returning to soil myself someday, although I wouldn't tell my family that—Emerson would sink into black thoughts and Henry would look stung that I could ever leave him and Mother wouldn't hear me, most likely. And Addie? Do I call that child family?

She is an arm's length away from me, on her knees, laying seedlings gently into the tilled soil. She's in a new pair of shorts and a T-shirt and wearing a crimson Stanford baseball cap that she found in a box in Will's office. The cap is closed on its smallest setting and still almost too big for her head, but it keeps the sun from her eyes. I look up and see Mother's floppy sunhat as her back rises and falls, attacking the weeds around her perennials. She is chatting with Henry as he pushes his blue wheelbarrow this way and that, filled with bags of soil and his wood-handled shovel. Addie doesn't mind dirty hands, I'm noticing. If I told her I longed to return to the earth, she would probably understand.

Henry walks closer to us, and I smile to see him. He is handsome as a dream, my mighty friend, blond hair longer than he likes and smile lines growing deeper every day. His brown T-shirt has sustained a long tear down the side and flaps as he walks in the bright sunshine.

"Your mother cracks me up, Till," he says, and smiles. He drops to his knees and starts to poke small holes for my seedlings. He does this without asking or being told—he has an amazing capacity for seeing the need and filling it. Henry's mother died when he was teenager-young, and he told me once that his best skill as a child was the ability to be anything that was required.

"She said I visited her in the night last night. Sounds sexy, right? But no, in her dream she told me I have arms like a milkman, which is what they used to say about guys when she was younger, or something, and it wasn't always a compliment to have such strong arms. So I got angry and picked her up and threw her, and she flew across the sky and just kept flying. She said she enjoyed the trip."

"Mother's always happy for the chance to fly," I say.

"Addie, what are you guys planting there?" he asks.

She looks at me. "Which is which again?"

"Rosemary," I say, pointing. "Lemon balm. Dill. Basil."

Addie smiles at me from under her white and crimson cap, and then goes back to her work, mouthing the names of the herbs as she plants them. Henry sits back on his heels and looks at her. "Hey, do you know any good songs?"

Mother stands and stretches her back. "I know lots of good songs," she says, plopping down beside Addie. "Oh my, these knees just aren't what they used to be." She sits sideways, as if she were lounging on a loveseat. "Might be I'm getting old," she says, laughing.

"Never, Eve," Henry says.

"Wear it with pride, Mother," I say.

"And thank you for my new music, Henry," she says. "He downloaded all sorts of new songs for me on the computer. The Andrews Sisters, Dean Martin, Lawrence Welk... *Telegram my handsome soldier, tell him rosy spring has come, tell him sweetly please come home,*" she sings.

"Pirated, I'm sure." We all look up to see Emerson walking toward our little planting party.

"No, I paid for them," Henry says. His brown eyes darken like he's plotting something or bracing for a slap.

"*You* paid for them?" she says as if it isn't a question.

"*Don't you know the lilac's bloomed, the skies are blue, the swans, my dear, are on the pond, the only thing missing is you.*" Mother's voice is light and airy, and I have a quick memory of lullabies in moonlit rooms, her White Fire perfume clinging to the fur collar on her coat as she bends to kiss me before going out with Father. "*The only thing missing is you...*"

"Want to pull up a spade, Emmy?" I ask.

"No, I just need to talk to Addie." She squats down in her week-end casual slacks and three-quarter length sleeve shirt. I feel dirty and baggy next to her in my white T-shirt and cut-off jeans. I tried wearing knee pads once, but they kept sliding off, getting in the way. If I had my wish, I'd just garden naked.

"My good friend Lily White's granddaughter is having a birth-day party this afternoon, and I told her you would love to come."

Addie's eyes have grown big, staring up and away from Emerson.

"So we'll have to get you cleaned up. You have a few hours. I have an afternoon appointment, so I'll drop you off at the Whites' and pick you up again this evening."

Henry rises from his feet as Emerson does the same. "Does she have to go?"

Emmy's voice falls low but I can hear her still, "Don't instigate, Henry. There's nothing wrong with a little social life."

Mother reaches over to pat Addie, "You'll do fine, my dear. You are as charming as they come. Now what's the next verse?"

Emerson stops from turning away and her body grows stiff. "Addie? Where did you find that hat?"

We all stop to look at the crimson cap. "It was in a box in the office," I say. "I told her it was okay. I assumed it was Michael's."

"No," she says softly. "It belonged to Will. It was a gift from Michael."

"Well the box is in my studio now, if you want it," I say, and my voice seems too loud, like we've all been caught doing some-thing wrong.

Emmy nods, distractedly, and wipes her hands together, as if she could've possibly gotten dirty. "Well, it looks good on you," she says to Addie. "You have until two o'clock." She turns and walks quickly to the house, and I'm suddenly surprised that she's still here, with us. She hates us. Why would she stay?

Mother rests a hand on Addie's shoulder. "It's okay, dear. Let's go put together some lunch. Will you help?"

Addie nods somberly, looking anything but okay, and takes Mother's hand to help her to her feet. Henry reaches for Mother's elbow and they all look so lovely together I feel a lump in my throat. How does it happen, these people we draw to us? These family members or not-family-members that orbit around us, that sustain us like the roots of a tree. And who do we sustain, whether we know it or not? Who become our leaves, our branches, our deep shelter? I feel quietly mawkish and blame it on menopause.

"Chorus again, ready?" Mother says as she and Addie walk away. *"Tell my handsome soldier the only thing missing is you dear, the only thing missing is you."*

"I love your family, kid," Henry says. "It's just that sister of yours that needs work."

"Don't I know it," I say. He smiles at me, just turning away, when I reach a hand out to his jeans and stop him. "Henry?"

He must see the emotion in my face, because I'm terrible at hiding such things. In an instant he is beside me, eye to eye. "What is it, Till?"

In the sun, his hair is blonder, his brown eyes more golden, his face brighter than usual. A long time ago, I wondered if maybe I should fall in love with him, as if we can make such easy choices. But he's much more valuable to me as a friend, and I know that other road would only lead to heartache.

"I'm afraid," I say. "And I can't tell anybody else, it's a secret, and I feel stupid even saying so."

"God, what is it?"

"It's stupid," I say.

"You don't have a stupid bone in your body, Tillie. What's wrong?"

"Well I have that . . . I'm going to Gavin's house tonight . . ."

"And you're going to sleep with her."

"God, no! That's not it. Oh my God, were you just going to tell me—?" I cover my face with my hands and laugh. My fingers suddenly itch to hold a paintbrush, just to have that comfort. "No, I'm not going to sleep with her."

"So say you now, but you don't know what's going to happen, you don't know how you're going to feel." Henry has leaned back, away from his earnest concern, and is sitting butt-down in the middle of my unplanted row. Oh, how I love him. Life is so fucking absurd sometimes.

"I don't want advice," I say. "I don't need a tutorial."

"Sometimes they cry," he says.

"What?"

"Sometimes women cry, when it really means something. I don't know why, they just do, like something deep happens inside, so then you just have to hold them and tell them everything you love about them. But wait, you're a woman, maybe you already know that."

"Goddamn, Henry, will you just be quiet a minute?" He bites his lip and smiles, giving me contrite eyes, and I feel hugely stupid again. I look down, trace my finger in the dirt. "The problem is that I'll be driving myself there."

"That's great! Of course you are."

"And I'm scared. I'm scared to do it."

He reaches over to where my hands are patting the earth and lays his big tan hand on mine. "Let's go practice," he says. "Right now. And we won't tell anyone, and we won't make a big thing about it, let's just go do it."

"Really?"

"Hell yeah. Here, climb on board." He turns to offer his back to me and I grab on around his neck, piggyback style. He pushes up from the earth as if I weigh nothing and lifts me to the sky. He wheels my empty chair over the rutted grass and around the house to the driveway while I hang on tight and laugh in his ear. He is marble-strong, and I feel safe in the shelter of his shadow. When we reach my car he drops me softly into my chair and sneaks toward the house to find the keys. But then I have to pee, and change my dirty clothes, and anyway he's forgotten my bag with my wallet, so in I go, and I tell Mother we're going out, and she gives me a shopping list, and I grab granola bars and a juice box for each of us and meet him at the car.

"So here's the part I hate," I say, staring at the door of the big maroon Chrysler.

"Just try," he says and we both glance at the house, as if we are doing something surreptitious, which, I suppose, we are.

I open the big door and steer close to the driver's seat. It isn't hard for me to pull my body into the leather seat—I'm well-accustomed to lifting myself with my arms—but once I'm there, I can't figure out what to do with the chair.

"Okay, fold it," he says.

"Well, obviously," I say with effort as I bend awkwardly at the waist. I fold the wheelchair—ultralight, thank God, one of Mother's better gifts—but can't maneuver it over my body into the car. "Dammit!"

"Wait, wait," Henry says. He's standing beside the open door of the car, holding my maroon bag comfortably on his shoulder. He leans down to adjust the driver's seat. "Here, if we push this all the way back..." He runs around to the passenger's door, and I have to unlock it so he can get in. He leans in and adjusts the front passenger seat all the way forward.

"Now we can accommodate one very tall driver and one very short passenger, and thank you very much for your help," I tell him.

He laughs. "Just try it, you doubter."

Miraculously, the folded chair passes over me and fits behind the passenger seat. "You're a genius, Henry Oliver!"

He climbs into the shortened passenger seat and sits crumpled up, looking pleased with himself. "Onward, Jeeves," he says, poking a straw into his juice box. I lift my chair again and practice moving it back and forth, bumping his shoulder in the process. It isn't easy or comfortable, but it's possible, and sometimes that's the best we can get in this world.

I start the car, and we sit together as the Chrysler idles. Funny that Mother got me such a tank of a car; how little I think she knows me sometimes. I have to remind her often that I don't like walnuts in my brownies, that I don't like the hospital smell of bleach cleaner, that I love flaxseed in my oatmeal. My husband, Stan, was the same way so many years ago, and I thought that was just the domain of men until I returned to Mother's house. So I guess it is the domain of people, to be so forgetful. We all want to be known, every wonderful part of us—down to our tastes and hungers and fears—and yet even the best someones aren't able to know us that much. But then Mother surprises me sometimes, like when she brought home rubber cement for my watercolors, which I really wanted, or the time she walked right into the bathroom to hand me a new roll of toilet paper from under the sink, which I really needed.

I laugh and Henry smiles. "Ready?" I ask.

"Ready," he says.

I put my hand on the central control—what looks like a gear shift between our two seats—and look at him. "I don't remember what to do," I whisper.

"First, shift into drive, then pull back to accelerate, and forward to brake," he whispers back, motioning with his hand. "And here's the brake latch, so you don't have to hold it forward if you're stopped at a light."

I pull the hand control backward and the big Chrysler takes off, spitting gravel, heading right toward the front porch.

"Brake," Henry says.

I panic. I can't remember what to do. I yank on the wheel and pull back on the control and the car speeds up. "Shit, oh shit!"

"Brake! Brake!" Henry yells. He stomps his brake foot into the passenger floor mat, then reaches for my hand on the control. I hear the terrible scrape of branches on the bumper, the underbody. He pushes my hand forward, hard, and the tires bounce. We both lurch forward in our seatbelts as the car stops. My heart is pounding madly and tears spring to my eyes. We are less than two feet from the white outside wall of my sister's kitchen, and if I opened my window, I could reach out and touch the porch. And, of course, we are on top of the shrubbery.

"That boxwood will never be the same," I say casually, wiping my eyes.

"I know the feeling," Henry says, lifting his leaking juice box from the floor. He reaches a hand to my shoulder, and I turn to him. "Shift to reverse," he says quietly. "Then back to accelerate, forward to brake."

"No, fuck no. I can't do this. You drive, please."

"Shift to reverse, then nice and easy…" His fingers are warm on my shoulder, and I can feel his strength, his steadiness.

I take a deep breath and put the Chrysler in reverse. Very gently, I pull the control back, and we scrape and heave off of the ornamental shrubbery and beauty bark. I back far into the gravel driveway before shifting to park. We survey the damage. One boxwood is down for sure, and its sister has a definite wind-blown look. Beauty bark is scattered everywhere, and two wheel tracks drive through the ground cover, right up to the side of the house.

"Do you think anyone'll notice?" I say quietly.

"I don't know," he says. "We can rake over the bark, I guess. And I'll take out that boxwood."

"I never liked driving. Even before the accident, I made Emmy drive me everywhere in that little Ford Falcon of hers." He's still resting his hand on my shoulder, and I wonder how anyone can survive without a good touch like that around. "Am I a warm hand to you?" I ask suddenly.

"What?" he says.

"You always help me. Always, in every way. Do I help you? Am I a warm hand to you?" My voice is shaking, and I raise my hands to cover my mouth.

We are stopped in the middle of the driveway, in the middle of the day, in the middle of our lives, and suddenly I feel cast far from solid ground and drifting.

"Tillie, you help me more than I could ever say." He moves his hand from my shoulder to the back of my neck and pulls me near. Gently, he leans his head against my head and we sit in a sideways hug. "There was a bad time, do you remember me telling you?" he says. "After Will died. Your sister and I were … friends. I was confused. And then the Worthy house—this beautiful house—was empty, and I'd walk through the yards, all alone, stoned out of my gourd, watching it all go to shit. And then you came with your mother, and it was like the clouds parted." He laughs and leans back in his seat to look at me. "You saved me, Tillie, the two of you. I know you've never understood that. I don't think you've ever believed me, have you?"

I shake my head, watching his serious eyes. I remember his sadness when we first became neighbors, his quietude. And his drugs, Lord! I've never minded loose friends, but Henry smoked and snorted and dropped like it was his true vocation. His friend Lyman from Eugene would sprawl on his couch for days, and the two of them would try and rouse themselves for me, having barely-coherent conversations and laughing like they were having a good time, trying to get me to stay at their party.

"I know you were unhappy," I say softly. "I'm glad you're not that person anymore."

He looks away, at the green grass and Mother's perennials. "I don't think I'm anyone *but* that person. I think what you are is what you are, then and now and forever onward." Henry is far away, beside me, and his voice sounds low and reverent. "We don't change, not really, not the parts of us that matter."

"Then God, what's the point?" I say, trying to sound funny, trying to catch his attention again. "That's so hopeless. I, at least, need to think I'm evolving."

"Well, we get better at being ourselves. I think the point is learning to love what you are. What you really are." He reaches his hand for mine and squeezes and the light is back in his eyes. "Believe me, I need you as much as I've ever needed anyone. Probably more."

He kisses his fingers and points at the sky, just as the front door opens and we see Mother on the porch. I glance at the bent shrubs, the thick tracks through the brown bark, then back at her open face. Slowly, Henry opens his passenger window and we both give her grim smiles.

"Oh, I'm glad you're still here! I forgot milk. Half a gallon of 2 percent, please!" She is little and smiling, still wearing her sunhat.

"Okay, Mother! See you soon!" I call over Henry's lap. She waves at us as I shift into drive and turn the wheel grandly. I pull back slowly, and we cruise sedately down the drive, as if I do this every day, as if I agree with Henry's theories, as if nothing in the world could ever go wrong.

Eve shares a secret

Tillie just had a bit of an accident, but I'm pleased to see she's driving herself. The house is cooler than outside, and my garden clogs make a satisfying *Clump! clump!* on the kitchen floor. I sent Addie to the bath with a book, poor child, upset as she is by Emerson's invitation. From the kitchen window, I can see brilliant blue sky and swallows with their pointy wings flying errands around the garden. I'm glad Tillie is planting more this year. Every year she grows a little bolder with Emerson's land, as if perhaps she has the courage to really tear it up this time. It's been an unspoken arrangement for so long that it's almost as if we dare not be noticed here.

Oh, in the beginning it was temporary. It was Emmy needing guardians for the place, Emmy worrying the value would plummet without tenants to care for the house, Emmy preferring the Lake Oswego house with its grim, gray corners and cold lake views and better memories of her husband than the ones she had here. I remember how steady she was when she called me that night; she needed someone to be with Michael. He was home from Stanford, a surprise visit. And he found his own father, hanging in Henry's garden. If ever I could curse Will Worthy, I would, for doing that to his son, never mind the rest of his family. And where was Emmy when Michael found Will? Where was Henry that warm summer night if not in his beloved stone garden?

I hear footsteps in the hall and greet Emerson before I turn around. She has that self-important look on her face, but her arms are crossed at her waist defensively.

"Mother, I need to talk to you." She steps forward and takes the sunhat from my head. I'd completely forgotten about that.

"You know I love talking to you, anytime," I say, wanting to calm her down. Both of my daughters get so worked up over little things sometimes; it's always been my job to make their mountains into molehills.

"Addie said she loved your trip to the library. And ice skating, too, was it?"

"We went to the Central Library downtown, and she stood there just breathing it in, all those books. The children's room has that stony sculpture of a tree, and she stared at it so long, I thought she'd climb to the top then and there. She said it was almost as good as the one in Anchorage. That child loves books, just like you did when you were a girl."

"Mother, please don't make assumptions. If Michael doesn't call tonight, then I will call him. We need to know what's going on. I think we've all been very patient."

"And I'm sure you're concerned about her mother's health, too," I say. My daughter has some glaring blind spots when it comes to general compassion.

"I have less patience than I used to with people who take their own lives," she says. "Or who try to, anyway."

"That's not what I'd expect. I'd think you'd have more patience than most, honey." I turn back to the sink where I have three plates to soak. I'd noticed the small salad plates were disappearing and found them, as I thought I might, in Addie's room.

I hold one up. "Rosemary chicken," I say, and point to another. "Sweet potato pie. Spareribs. Cheese biscuits, hard as concrete."

"What's this?"

"I found these under her bed. She's been hiding food."

Emerson's face flashes worry for a moment, and then she sighs. "Food insecurity, maybe? I'll talk to her. She should know there's plenty here for her."

I shake my head, "Please, let's keep this a secret for now. I have an idea I want to try first. What did you need to talk to me about?" I ask, even though I know. She wants to leave; she wants to leave Addie with us, in our safekeeping. She wants to wipe her hands—one, two—because she's wise enough to see the direction it's heading. We're all becoming emotionally involved, whether we like it or not.

"I won't be able to stay," she says, seeming terribly downhearted about it. "I have so many commitments in the city, and the Lake Oswego house really needs looking after, there's just so much…"

"Well, that's too bad. I've so enjoyed having Addie here, but I'm sure she'll like your other house too."

"Oh no, Mother, I meant—"

"I know what you meant, dear." I walk toward her and take her hands in mine. She's so tall and thin; she reminds me of the icicles that used to hang from the eaves of chalets in Switzerland. Her skin isn't cold, as I would've guessed, but warm and strong. When I look into her ocean-blue eyes, I can see that, in a minute way, she's afraid of me. Afraid of connecting with me.

I squeeze her hands and smile gently. "Emmy, I love you. I want rich happiness for you. I want the sun to shine on you and keep you warm and well-loved. But you need to accept this responsibility as your own. This child came to you. For whatever reason, she's yours. But if you stay here, we'll help you."

She pulls away, pulls her hands away, looks away. "What sort of coercion is this? If I stay, you'll help me? This is my house, for God's sake. Who is doing whom the favor here?"

She turns away, hands on her hips, trying to overpower me like Adam used to do. Oh, they are so alike, that father and this daughter.

"And on that subject," I say. "We need to have a conversation about this house. Your sister walks on eggshells around you—"

"Figuratively speaking?"

"And I know I don't bring it up, but we can't live like we're going to be kicked out of a place. So let's either draw up an agreement, or I'll buy the property from you outright." I don't tell her that the family lawyer has been pressuring me for years to solidify the arrangement, but he's a sanctimonious boob and I only take his advice when I have to.

The color has risen high in her cheeks, and her eyes look like she's about to bolt. "Do you have any idea what this place is worth?" she asks, her voice rising an octave.

"Do you have any idea how much money your father left me?" I say back. My hands are on my own hips now too, and I can feel my own cheeks growing red. Oh, to be so impudent, so hungry for power you need to try and grab it from your own mother! I have to bite my tongue to keep from saying anything rude.

I take a deep breath, needing not to fight with her. "Your father took great care to ensure we'd be fine, and you already know this. We love it here, honey, and we love it even more when you're here with us." Emerson has turned away from me, and I'm speaking to a poker-straight, white-shirted back. "We can talk about all of this another time. Just think about it. Tillie and Henry and I have enjoyed having the both of you for a visit."

I dry my hands on a dish towel and walk down the hall to the bathroom Addie and Tillie share. I knock on the door to check on her, and Addie says she's fine, she doesn't need anything. I walk the rest of the way down the hall to the back-porch door and out into the sunshine. The deck is golden in the spring sunshine, and I wish I'd kept my sunhat on my head. I crank open the umbrella over the glass table and pull a chaise into the shade. Here I will sit and look at the sky and dream of other places I could be.

Henry asked me once why I don't travel anymore, and I didn't have a good answer. I told him it just wasn't the same after my windswept husband passed away. Adam and I used to love being able to up and leave whenever we wanted, close the door on whatever was bothering us and find a sitter for the girls. When we stepped on a plane, we could be anyone we wanted to be, and nothing could touch us, nothing expected us or needed us. Every time we left, we were alone and free of everything.

Emerson shares a secret

Mother makes me furious with her flapping about, the arguments she refuses to finish. Sometimes I just want to have it out with her—with all of them—but no one will stay to fight. Sometimes I think that's why Will left: he refused to stay and finish the fight.

Mother's kitchen is clean and bright, though I'm noticing the corners of this house are starting to collect dust. It won't be too many more years before she and Tillie will need live-in help, and of course I'll have to fight them for that too. I walk down the hallway and stop outside the bathroom door. I almost knock, but reconsider—I'm not ever sure what to say to that child. If she is my granddaughter, why would Michael wait ten years to tell me? My son is like a storm on the horizon—powerful and holy and terribly angry with me. Part of me is grateful that he stays so far away.

The door to Tillie's studio is ajar, and I push it open, silently. The room is wide and full of sunlight, with art supplies and canvases heaped all about. Tillie has two places she likes to paint. One is a futon couch on the floor with a shortened easel Henry made for her. The other is a tall stool she climbs onto near the window, where she has a half-finished canvas. I walk quietly toward the painting, afraid to disturb even the dust in the air. I sit on her stool and look at the horizontal canvas. A group of women stand in the arc of an unfinished circle, heads bowed, the sky twilight-dark although their faces are richly lit. Some of them hold hands, all of them reverently acknowledging something in the middle of the circle that hasn't been painted yet. It reminds me of *The Last Supper*, whether or not it's meant to.

I step away from the painting and toward an open box on the floor, the one Addie found. She must've dragged it in here to ask Tillie about the hat. I kneel down and open the flaps, wondering if perhaps it's a box I filled myself a decade before when I was cleaning up, tossing things away. A black T-shirt with a white raven silk-screened on the front, Michael's, I'm sure; a glass paperweight; a small box with a Cross pen set inside, a gift from someone with average taste; a brown wool scarf; a Thomas Pynchon and a Mark Twain, neither a first edition; and a tan Arturo Fuente cigar box.

I open the box to a neat line of cigars and a pair of round, silver cigar scissors and a lovely deep smell of tobacco. I have a sudden memory of touching Will's jaw, his five-o'clock shadow, in one of the rare moments he held completely still for me, hearing the ice clink in his Glenlivet, that faint scent of tobacco and cologne, and standing on the balls of my feet to kiss him on the lips, so lightly, so perfectly. He loved me. He is the only person in my life who I know truly loved me.

I close the cigar box and tuck it close to my body. Tillie's empty studio is like a drug for me, which I always forget until I'm here again. Something about the warm, soft air tamps down my wicked parts and leads me quietly to peace, for a time. I think of Tillie's half-painted women—reverent for a gift just given, one they don't understand enough to see yet. I'll have to tell her I prefer it undone.

I leave the studio and quietly close the door. I walk out onto the back porch and into the sunlight of a perfect Northwest spring day with a smile on my face like a cool drink of water. Mother is asleep on the porch, under a green shade umbrella. I walk past her airy little snores, down the porch stairs, past the upturned earth of Tillie's doing and the manicured lawn that is slowly being replaced by patches of garden. I walk the long paces down to the pebbled beach and rippling lake, past the sleeping boathouse and around the hedges and the fence.

Standing on Henry's beach, I look up to his cabin and I'm struck again by the beautiful order of the place. He's not a put-together man, generally speaking, and yet his yard, his stone garden and meditative paths, are striking in their perfection. I walk up his path, past giant stones he planted as mysteriously as *moai* heads on a Pacific island, past small lush topiaries, past the heavy cedar pergola to the rear door of his cabin. I knock quietly, holding my cigar box tightly, then let myself in. I feel entitled; I am a neighbor, was once a neighbor's wife.

"Henry," I call. I can hear the shower running behind the moody ripple of a Henry kind of song on the stereo and a man singing *"…you did what you could and it wasn't enough, just a face in her crowd…"* I can see he hasn't lost his adolescent taste in music. I walk into his bedroom and call his name again.

"Be right out!" he says.

"Abandoned illusions, you're just her black cloud," the stereo in the bathroom plays pensively.

I slip off my sandals and lean his pillows up, just right, and sit comfortably on his bed, where I often sat so many years before, now holding my box on my lap like an offering. The bathroom door is slightly open, and warm steam tumbles out with the music. I feel wonderfully dazed, and not sure why I'm here.

He opens the door abruptly and stands before me, naked and wet and richly tan. On his head is a black winter hat with the stitched letters "BFF."

"Look!" he yells happily. "Look what came for me today!"

It is a pleasure to watch his face register such deep surprise. I am not the woman he was expecting to find on his bed. His body is perfect, like a sculpture if sculptures had soft spots, and I wonder how any woman could want a twenty-year-old when older men are so much more handsome. He pulls the hat from his head and covers himself, like soccer players do.

"Nice hat," I say. "Nice and big." I can feel my face growing warm.

He gives me a toothy photo booth smile and says, "I'll be right back." Stepping back into the bathroom, he closes the door and I hear the music soften, then stop, before he emerges wrapped discreetly in a towel. "Might want to close your eyes," he says, "unless you want the rest of the show."

I laugh and cover my eyes, peeking through as he gets dressed. Henry has always made me feel so beautiful, so wanted. He is unabashed, without pretense, as if he's incapable of hiding his attraction—whether that's true or not, that's always how he makes me feel.

"But do you like my hat?" he asks, pulling on pinstriped boxers and a pair of jeans. "Your sister got it for me. It came in the mail today."

"'Best Friends Forever?' That's cute."

"Blond From Fargo," he says, stretching a T-shirt over his blond head, then replacing the hat. "It's a band."

"And it's always good to have a snow hat this time of year," I say. "You never know."

"That's right, you never know," he says with a grin, lying down at the foot of the bed, crosswise to where I sit. "What've you got there?"

I look down at the tan box, then open it and pass it toward him. "Remember these?"

He leans toward the perfect line of cigars and breathes in deeply. "He used to get so mad at me," Henry says, propped on one elbow. "I didn't like his scotch. I preferred a warm Guinness with my cigar."

"That sounds like a punishment." I make a face, remembering Henry and Will in deck chairs under the stars, the tips of their cigars glowing red. "Will was very taken with you, you know. He said he'd never met anyone like you." I shut the cigar box and run my hand gently over the tan lid.

Henry's face is inscrutable. "That was a long time ago," he says, clearing his throat. "Twelve years, this summer." He is beautiful lying by my outstretched legs. I feel his hand gently on my bare foot, and his eyes watching me as if nothing else in the world exists, as if he's waiting for me and isn't afraid.

"We were close once too," he says softly, and I feel my throat catch.

"Oh, that made Will so angry. Do you remember that night with the bonfire?"

Henry laughs his deep laugh and his brown eyes sparkle. "My God, of course I do. I thought he was going to kill me."

Will had been in LA on business, and I'd opted not to go. He was a successful man, always, and Tate & Bookhammer was a successful firm, but an old Beta brother suggested a more lucrative move to entertainment law. That appealed to his vanity, of course, and he flew down to test-drive the lifestyle for a few days. He came home half a day early to find Henry and me at a makeshift bonfire on our beach near the lake shore. A balmy night under perfect stars.

"I'd never seen him like that," Henry says. "I'm sure you were used to it."

"We'd been married almost twenty years by then," I murmur.

Henry once likened Will to a speed freak after he'd been up for two days painting and repainting the bathroom. He was like wildfire tearing through wilderness, having to be everywhere at once, and the next morning socked in by fog, rolled up in the blankets, as gray as wet ash. Will was medicated, and of course he self-medicated, and we coped. When he wasn't tangled up in his depression, he was phenomenal: wickedly smart, highly driven, terribly entertaining, a covetous lover, a witty friend. Will had never hurt me before, never raised a hand to me, never twisted my arm or pinched me too hard.

He'd flown in early from LA that night and saw us together, sitting by the lake. Will stood, tall-suited, dark hair tufted from travel, cheeks ash-gray with pain, believing I was cheating on him, loving another man. Henry had used his old wooden wheelbarrow to haul firewood over to the beach and it camped nearby, casting shadows in the summer dark, with only a few sticks of wood and the axe inside. Without a word, Will kicked over the wheelbarrow and picked up the axe. I remember Henry leaping from his chair like a sprung toy, but I felt frozen, stuck in place. It happened fast. Henry reached his hands up and Will raised the heavy axe to his shoulder. Then he spun, yelling, and plunged the axe into the thick wood of the side-stranded wheelbarrow, wood splintering as the axe head stuck. Working it free, he raised it and struck again, and again, and again—yelling, the axe head biting. I watched in the firelight; watched my husband's face shine damply, his color high, lit from within as he was with his own terrible fire. His wordlessness was as frightening as anything. Finished, the wheelbarrow splintered into pieces around the metal frame, he gave me a diamond-sharp look, dropped the axe onto the grass, and walked back up to the house in the evening dark, his gray suit jacket swung casually over his shoulder like a pilot who's finished his flight.

"Do you know what I remember?" Henry says, and I shake my head slowly. His brown eyes, so strong and kind, are like a quiet riverbank I could nap on. He makes me think of who I used to be, when Will and I had a son away at college and a new house and so many hopes for how our lives could be different.

Henry squeezes my foot, gently. "I remember how you didn't even react. You didn't scream or cry or jump up and down or run away. You were always so calm. Too calm. Still are."

His words make my throat tighten and I look down at my tightened hands. Why is it that men think if a woman isn't hysterical she isn't reacting? I close my eyes to keep from snapping at him and take a deep breath, feeling my body strung tight as a bow.

"Can I tell you a secret?" I say softly, with measure, and watch his snow hat make a slow bob. "I hated you for a long time, Henry. It wasn't an accident that he hung himself in your garden."

"Emmy," he says, and stops.

"But then I stopped hating you. I just decided it would be wiser not to consider you at all."

I raise my chin and watch Henry's face bloom with color, transparently wounded. I'm not sure why though; it's not something he doesn't already know. He opens his mouth to say something when we hear a delicate woman's voice at his cabin door. I slip my sandals on quickly, as if we'd been planning something untoward, and stand up in a hurry. Henry reaches for me, but I turn, remembering the never-used front door. I slip from his bedroom to his kitchen, down a dirty hallway, tripping on the ugly rag rug there, and spill out the rusty-hinged front door into the sunshine of Saturday afternoon.

I don't want to see who he was waiting for, what woman is so blindly captivated by him. Henry is too young, even in his forties, and any feelings I may think I have for him are the same ones every woman has. There's a reason he's so popular with my sister, with my mother, with whoever he was expecting to find on his bed this afternoon. It's cultivated, his appeal, and he'll never be able to choose one woman because he'll never be able to turn it off or turn others away. His need is no different than anyone else's; it's just wrapped in a more likable package.

I stomp my way home, past the woman's Jetta parked by his cabin, up his gravel drive and down my own, making a giant circle from the way I'd originally come. It isn't until I'm on my own white porch steps that I realize I've left Will's cigar box behind, stranded and forgotten on Henry's wide and welcoming bed.

Addie shares a secret

I've been to birthday parties before. Mrs. Worthy seems to think I won't know how to behave, or that maybe I'll do something embarrassing. She's driving and talking and keeps looking over at me with squinting eyes. When Ms. Eve drives and talks, she mostly watches the road. Well, at least she doesn't squeeze her eyes at me. On my lap, I have a big blue-papered present with a soft, white bow that Mrs. Worthy handed me. My fingers keep wandering over to rub the fuzzy bow. It's the most beautiful package I've ever seen; I'm giving a present to someone I've never met, and I don't even know what's inside.

Mrs. Worthy is dressed importantly, like always, but she seems more distracted. I've been trying to figure some things out, and one thing I've figured out is that she's a *pushing* sort of person, always rushing like a river. It must be tiring. I wonder when she gets to rest. It makes me think of Mama trying to rest, trying to get better. Ms. Eve says the plan is to call LuAnn tonight and talk to Mama, so I have that to look forward to, at least. We drive on the freeway and then on steep, steep roads with houses close together and then park outside a big house. I feel shaky inside again. I almost wish Mrs. Worthy was a hand-holder, but that might make me more nervous. I left Mrs. Anderson at home because Mrs. Worthy's eyes insisted. Her eyes said, *Please don't bring that doll!* So I didn't.

We walk into the house without knocking and down a tiled-floor hall to a big kitchen with a sliding glass door. There's a big wooden deck with some white grown-ups and a swimming pool full of white kids mostly older than me. Mrs. Worthy introduces me to Mrs. White, the grandmother here. Her body moves like she's very busy, but her eyes lock onto me and I hand her the giant blue present. My fingers hold Mama's bear amulet tight. She calls for "Whitney! Whitney!" and a blond girl in a bikini swimsuit runs up the stairs to meet me. She's the granddaughter who is turning thirteen. She's nice; she says "Hey" to me and leads me to a plastic chair where I sit in the sun by the pool. When I turn around next, I see Mrs. Worthy leaving without even saying goodbye.

My pool chair is blue and white plastic woven together, and it can tip back if I want to lie down, but right now I am sitting up.

On the green and white plastic chair beside me is an older boy, like an eighth grader, sitting in wet swim trunks and talking on a cell phone. He has wet brown hair and brown eyes and freckles on his nose and he is very good looking. He smiles a little at me and keeps talking on his phone saying things like "Yeah," and "No doubt." I am wearing my new jeans with the pink sash for a belt and a pullover shirt with a collar and my blue sweater, and of course I'm too hot, so I take my sweater off. The girl Whitney brings me a can of Coke and sits on the edge of my plastic chair.

"Did you bring a suit? Do you want to borrow one of mine? I have tons. Grandma's always buying me shit I don't need." Her face is wide open and nice; she looks like a commercial, even saying a bad word.

The boy beside me laughs and says, "Wash your mouth out, girl." He's done with his phone call. He must be rich to have his own phone.

The girl Whitney keeps smiling at me, so I say, "No, thank you. I don't feel like swimming." Her grandmother, Mrs. White, calls for her, and she pats my leg before she stands up and walks away. It is a nice pat.

The sun is squinty-bright bouncing off the water, and the kids are splashing loudly. They remind me of too many sea lions crowded on a rock. I wish I'd brought the too-big red baseball hat for my eyes. The pop is good, and the can is cold and wet in my hand. The boy beside me is drinking a Coke too, and I keep peeking sideways at him. He has muscles in his arms, and his chest looks strong. He makes me think of a bull moose, like he could just walk down the middle of the highway if he felt like it. His swim shorts are blue and green swirled together, like ugly wallpaper, but it doesn't look ugly on him, which makes me start to wonder what ugly actually means.

"Hey, where're you from?" a boy yells from across the pool. He's in up to his chest, and holding another boy under the water. The other boy is kicking him, then pops up like a seal and tries to dunk him. The first boy swims away, over to the side of the pool near me and hangs on to the edge like a man overboard. "I said, hey, where're you from?"

"Anchorage," I say. "It's in Alaska." Lots of kids have stopped what they're doing to look at me. I really wish I had that baseball hat.

"Well, what're you doing in Portland?" he says, and I shrug. He has the weaselly kind of eyes that say, *watch out*.

"Just visiting," I say. He has brown-blond hair and braces and is wearing a wristwatch in the water. "You forgot to take off your watch," I say, pointing at him. "It's getting wet."

He looks at his arm and laughs. "Oh, snap!" he says. "It's the twenty-first century! Watches can go underwater! And we have computers and cell phones and indoor plumbing too!" He says another word I can't understand, calls me a name, I think, before diving back underwater. Some of the other boys are laughing, and some of the girls too. The boy beside me isn't laughing. He leans toward me a little in his chair.

"That's Bryce. Total loser. His parents are getting a divorce, and you know how most parents fight over who gets the kids? Well, in his family, his folks are fighting over who doesn't get the kids. They don't want him, and that's the truth. I know because my dad is his dad's lawyer. His dad's an asshole too. I'm Carson, by the way."

"Nice to meet you," I say. My clenched up chest feels a little better, just by sitting beside him.

"Dude, catch!" Bryce yells.

"No, forget it, I don't want to play," Carson says, but the weasel boy throws a soft, wet, red football and it hits Carson in the chest, spraying both of us with water.

Bryce laughs until Carson jumps out of his chair, chest puffed out like he could just knock anything down. He takes the wet football over to the other side of the pool and the weasel Bryce is yelling and laughing. Carson is angry. His ears are red and the girls are giggling. Bryce is underwater and Carson waits until he comes up for air, then throws the football as hard as he can at Bryce's head. It's a soft football, so it doesn't hurt him, but it must've made Carson feel better. He throws his arms up into the air like the boys do when they score a touchdown and smiles. He walks slowly back to his seat, and everyone can see that he isn't that tall, but he's handsome and popular. He's like the sun in the sky, almost too bright to look at.

When he sits back down he says, "Sorry about that. We're animals. Welcome to the zoo." That makes me laugh. "So really," he says. "What're you doing here?"

It sounds different when Carson asks. "Well, my mom is sick. She just needs to rest for a little while."

"How old are you?" he asks.

"Ten and a half," I say. "I'm going into fifth."

"Is it weird being away from your mom? Or is it cool?"

I find myself shrugging again. "I miss her a lot. But I'm staying with a nice family."

He pulls his knees up to his chest and I can see light hair on his legs. It's nice hair. "Yeah," he says. "My mom was gone for a while too when I was your age. She found out she had breast cancer and she, like, took off with this guy instead of doing her chemo, but then she got really sick, and the guy sent her back. Or something like that. Your mom have cancer?"

"No," I say, and sip my Coke. He doesn't ask more questions, we just sit together quietly and watch the splashing. Whitney brings us each a paper plate with a hot dog and some chips and we eat fast. I think she shouldn't be doing so much work on her own birthday, but maybe she wants to, maybe she likes to help. Bryce sits on the concrete near Carson with his hot dog plate and asks me questions I don't answer, like, *Do you live in an igloo?* and *Have you eaten a hot dog before?* until Carson says he's going to beat his ass if he doesn't shut the bleep up. Bryce gives him the middle finger and cannonballs back into the pool. Carson smiles at me sympathetically.

"Not cancer," I say to those nice brown eyes. "She took too much Tylenol. She left work at lunchtime and took nearly the whole bottle. I came home early from school and found her on the floor. She almost died."

"Boy, that sucks," he says softly. "What about your dad? Where's he?"

"He was a fisherman. He died a long time ago, when I was a baby. I don't remember him." I can tell by Carson's eyes that he's wandering away. He's looking at a girl that's appeared by the side of the pool.

"Can I tell you a secret?" I say. I want to tell him that I think he's lovely, but I know better.

He looks back at me and smiles. "Sure."

"I've never been in an igloo but I've eaten hot dogs tons of times."

I want to say, *And Bryce can believe whatever he wants about me,* but I don't, I just think it. That way I can keep the truth of me safe inside. That's the best way with mean people. It's like when you throw a gull the heel of your bread so you can keep the rest of your sandwich to yourself. It's like that.

"That's cool," he says. I watch Carson's head move like a hungry dog, and his smile grows as the new girl walks over. "Hey babe," he says. "This is Addie from Anchorage."

"Hi," she says. "I'm Kyra, from West Linn." She's tall with long arms and legs and long brown hair. She looks like a teenager model, like she should be in a magazine. Her nose is little and upturned, and she has glittery earrings and painted nails. She's wearing a bikini swimsuit and something like a long scarf around her waist and she's developing already, upstairs.

"Sorry I'm so late," she says to Carson. "I had to go shopping with my lame sister." She puts her hands on her hips and looks around. "There's nowhere left to sit." She looks sharply at me and I fold and unfold my legs on the plastic chair. I think maybe she wants me to give her my seat, but I don't want to. I don't think she likes me very much.

"Well, sit here, there's room," Carson says. He scoots a little in the chair, and Kyra sits down snugly beside him. He puts his arm around her, and I listen to them talk about nothing. He doesn't have anything to say to me now. He even forgets to look at me. I drink my almost-empty Coke and think about my friends from school, about what they're doing now that it's officially summer break. I should be at day camp at the YMCA instead of here. If I were there, I would swim.

I look up at the warm, blue sky. I can faintly see the moon, and it makes me feel a little better, but my stomach hurts from the hot dog. I scrunch my knees up to my chest and watch the little moon so far away, and make a hundred big sky wishes I don't even have the words for, as if wishing could do me any good at all.

Four

Henry makes a discovery

Emerson leaves fast when Missy calls from the back door, and I remember again my afternoon's engagement. I find her standing inside by the door, demurely holding her paints and canvas, head tilted with a little smile. She's changed from this morning; now she's wearing short pants and a tight pink T-shirt. As I watch she reaches up, unloosens something, and lets her blond hair stream down to her shoulders like silk. I don't smile; women sometimes like it better when I don't smile. I step to her, and it's easy to reach my hand to her cheek, easy to pull her toward me and kiss her lipstick mouth. Last year it was a big, soft redhead named Laura from the other side of the lake, and before that, a regular brunette named Wendy who reminded me of a horse, in a nice way, and before that, I'd have to think a little to remember. And now it's Missy. She was a cheerleader in college, and her personality is paper thin. She's never finished any of her husband's books, but she hikes like mad with those dogs of hers and she has a mean tennis serve. Sometimes she brings leftover hors d'oeuvres from luncheons, but today she's just brought herself.

They all like something different, and the married ones are quick to tell you what that is. Missy likes to feel overpowered. Not in a dangerous-man-in-the-alley way (though I've had that request before), but in a protective, I-am-a-mountain-that-will-not-be-moved way. Maybe she has a daddy thing; being married to Doc, it certainly looks like it.

I steer her to a wall and push her against it, kissing her hard. My body is pinning her body, and her hands on the back of my neck move like little pebbles falling down a hillside. I feel warm inside and strong and terribly wanted. I imagine it is Emerson I'm pinning down and that she likes it. Missy makes little mewing sounds when I kiss her neck, and my arm around her waist squeezes tighter. I carry her to my bedroom and lay her on my bed and she reaches for the buttons on my jeans. I yank the hat from my head—my new snowcap from my BFF Tillie—and throw it over my shoulder. From the corner of my eye, I see the tan box, Emerson's cigar box, abandoned on the comforter, and for just a second I stop moving, stop kissing, stop attending to my work. I reach up gently while Missy watches with big, soft eyes, hair fanned gently on the spread, and move the box to the bedside table. There it sits for the rest of the afternoon, accusing me, trying to distract, trying to remind me I'm making love to the wrong woman.

Afterwards, I take a drowsy nap while Missy blotches paint onto her canvas, laughing and talking regardless of whether I listen or not. It is a peculiar talent of women like her, taking up all the air in the room with their words as if we'd just suffocate without them, when really it's the other way around. She's in my front room, talking through the open bedroom door, and although nothing is required of me, I feel imposed upon. Buddha likes quietude, as do I.

I use the bathroom, pull on shorts, find my new black BFF hat, and yank it on over my ears. Still Missy talks, something about two women arguing at the tennis club. I sit down on the bed again and pull the cigar box into my lap. The fact that Emerson brought it to me speaks more than any argument she could make. I think of her lying on my bed where I am now. My hand on her perfect, pedicured foot. The turn of her slim ankle, her lean runner's muscles peeking from beneath pressed cotton. I love her best before the arguments start, when I can see in her shrouded blue eyes that I've hit bone, deep inside, and for just that moment, we are honest and true with each other.

I remember the first time I met the Worthys. They were together walking the paces of the place, and I was sunning nude on my little pebble beach. It was February, true, but the sun had been out for two days, and when the wind was down it was warm to the skin. Back then my hair was longer, maybe I was thinner, but the world was mine to enjoy, poor as I was. Today I'm still poor, and the world, while still mine, finds me huddled in the cold more often than naked in the sun. Missy laughs at her own joke from the other room, and I can hear enthusiastic splashing from her paintbrush in the water cup. She doesn't care whether I listen or not, and suddenly I realize her husband also doesn't care whether I listen or not, because at least that means he doesn't have to.

So I lay naked in the February sun on an old pool lounge by the lake. I could feel coolness around me and sunshine warming my skin, and then from nearby the sound of someone respectable clearing their throat. I looked up to see a tall, thin, very handsome couple standing with hooked arms on the Pilchard farm lakeshore not ten feet away. I was reading a romance novel, left at the house by a girlfriend, or a friend's girlfriend, so out of politeness, I put it down.

"Hey," I said, motioning with my finger. "Are you thinking of buying the place?"

"Already bought it," the man said. He had short, almost black hair, a classically handsome jaw, and fire-bright eyes like the very ambitious have.

"Well, welcome neighbor. I'm Henry." I extended my hand for a shake but neither stepped forward in their REI boots. I crossed one bare leg over the other and the woman tightened her scarf. She was beautiful in that well-cultured way, that sharp, disapproving way, and I had to laugh.

"It takes all kinds, doesn't it?" I said, and that made both of them laugh a tiny, uptight laugh because they thought I meant *me*, when really I meant *them*. And I picked up my romance novel because it was just getting to the good part and that's when Will introduced himself and his wife, and I pretended to care.

Missy comes into the bedroom, carrying her wet canvas. It looks like a child's pointillist version of an egg and an orange and a cup. She's laughing, admiring her own work, leaning down to kiss me, whether I want her to or not. She asks if I've seen the latest *Portland Monthly* magazine, says that Emerson Worthy's picture from some charity function is in it. It gives me pause to hear her say Emmy's name, but Missy keeps talking. She barely knows the Worthys, never even met Will, doesn't know how forceful he could be.

I didn't expect to have such a strong reaction to Will. He stopped in occasionally when they were building the house, and at first, I think I just fascinated him. He liked to discuss anything with me. He said he enjoyed my proletarian point of view. I said, *Fuck ideology, all uprisings are merely the boiling point of hungry people*. Will said we were the two extremes of modern man: the successful, soul-impaired capitalist versus the starving, soulful romanticist. I said, *Not socialist? Not communist? Romanticist?* Will said art and nature were the true enemies of capitalism, and did I have any more of Lyman's homebrew? That was Will and me, in the beginning.

Missy is putting her paint away. Her face looks freshly washed and energetically bright. It's hard to believe we've been to the same event, we feel so differently about it. But she's blessedly oblivious in her tissue-thin way. Score one for Missy. I carry the tan cigar box to the door to see her out and watch as she walks around the cabin to the Jetta I know is parked in my driveway.

I'm still in just my shorts, but it's warm enough out. I walk to the cedar pergola, the one Will watched me make. The one he strung a ready rope across just a few months later. I jump up to one of the strong crossbeams and do a pull-up in the afternoon sun. I showed off for him when I built it, showing him how strong it was, or I was. My feet reach for the stone bench, and I let myself down, then sit. I put the bench in after he hanged himself, my grief lying shallow in the shadows by my feet. In my mind I thought, *If I'd done it earlier, he couldn't have killed himself.* His feet would have skidded the air for purchase and found the heavy unkickable bench, for the body wants to live, always wants to live, even when the mind screams *Die, die!* But that evening there was no stone bench, just a wooden sawhorse he dragged over and a rope he must have had ready for a good, long time.

I sit on the bench with Will's cigar box on my lap. The view is not of the lake, not of the cabin, not of anything but the tall fence between our properties and the overgrown, unused gate between our homes. I've expanded the stone garden over the years, using muscle and ancient ingenuity to transport rocks large and small to my little, unassuming home. The stones are like friends to me now, and when I sit with them I feel surrounded by kindness and stillness. They remind me of Buddha, of the best ways I want to be.

I sit cross-legged on the bench and open the hinged box. I wonder if the cigars would be stale by now or better with age. I was never enough of a connoisseur to know, but always willing to smoke whatever was handed to me. I lift one out, raise it to my nose, and close my eyes. I can see Will shirtless, on his MasterCraft, leaning back, smoking a cigar. When I open my eyes again, I see a patch of white in the bottom of the box. I pull out four cigars at once, enough to discover the long envelope hiding underneath. I look up at the perfect afternoon, look around, for anyone, but I'm alone with my silent stones. The envelope is heavyweight, pearl white, and made from expensive paper. There is no writing on the outside, no name or markings. It isn't sealed. My fingers shake as I ease it open, and pull out a heavy, folded sheet of handwritten paper. It is Will's perfect script, the kind that always looks polite, even when he's not. It reads, "You can see nothing else when you look in my face; I will look you in the eye and I will never lie."

My chest feels like it's been pounded and I exhale fast. I read it again and again. I want to crumple it up, I want to throw it away, I want this note to have never been found. I want to stand up and yell, but I don't, I don't. I fold the paper as carefully as I can, back into the envelope, not sure what to do. I seal it shut—I don't know why—and put it back into the box, bury it again with old cigars. He might have just written my name on the page a hundred times, he might have just telegraphed a message to Emerson: *It was Henry's fault, it was Henry's fault.*

Because in the end, it was my fault, I did betray him. I betrayed him by never loving him the way he loved me. When he raised that axe in fiery fury, it was me he was punishing, me he meant to destroy. With Will I shared my body, but not my heart. With Emerson, my heart, but not my body. He saw this, and he knew. And when she finds this note she will know too, and hate us both. She'll hate us both, and in the end, that's what we deserve, I guess.

Tillie makes a discovery

I drive slowly on Looking Lake Road because it's long and curvy and because I can. Traffic is light and the sun is bright and I'm driving—driving!—through wide countryside, past old brown barns and new gabled houses, past a mud-colored yard full of penned goats and geese, past a hand-lettered sign selling dill pickles and fresh flowers. I practice slowing and accelerating, and I can almost remember which is which every time. Teenagers in a Jeep pass me, and I smile and wave at their mirrored sunglasses, and miraculously, they wave back. I dropped Henry back at his cabin for his afternoon nap, and here I am, alone and driving. It feels perfectly natural to head to the co-op after I've circumnavigated the whole lake. Mother gave me a list, after all, which is excuse enough to go see Gavin, even though we have a dinner date tonight.

A date tonight. Every time I think about it, my stomach does flip-flops of terrible nervousness, and then my head says, *But she's a woman, we're just becoming friends,* and then my stomach does its thing again. One spring evening a few years ago, Henry took Mother and me to a pond nearby, and we all three lay in the grass by the reeds and listened to the bullfrogs' mighty calls and the other frogs' smaller peeps. The bullfrogs sounded like lowing cows, and I said, *How can something so small be so loud?* And Henry laughed, and Mother said, *It's true for me, sometimes how I feel is bigger than what I am. Bigger than my whole body even!* And that's how I feel right now every time I think about Gavin.

I pull into the parking lot. It's full today (Oregon is a blue state, after all), but I have the handicap spots to park in. I have to ease in slowly, and it takes full concentration. After I park, it's easy to get my chair from behind the passenger seat, outside the door of the Chrysler, and up the wheelchair ramp. The co-op is filled with bodies, and I have to speak up once or twice to get past handbags and conversations. I fill my lap with produce, looking for Gavin without trying to be too obvious, and see a man looking at my blue migrant worker painting. He seems familiar to me, from behind and to the side. Maybe another artist I know? I wheel over toward the dairy case to get a better look and a green-aproned worker greets me by name. The man turns quickly and smiles down at me, and I realize in an instant my ex-husband is back in Portland.

"Tillie," he says sweetly, as if my name is a beautiful flower instead of just a name. "I knew this was your work even before I saw the tag. I knew from across the room."

"Stan," I say. "What a surprise. What are you doing here?"

"I'm, uh, out at the coast now. Living in a, well, a hovel really, but with an incredible view. I'm writing the most amazing poetry these days. God, it's good to see you. You look great."

I have to admit, in this moment I *feel* great, like I've been transplanted away from the shady side of the house and the sunlight on my face is helping me shine.

"You look good too, Stanley." His hair is thinner on top, but he isn't as skinny as he was, and his color is good like he's been getting fresh ocean air. When Stan and I divorced, there weren't fireworks, or big fights, or even little ones really. We just stopped being good for each other.

He walks me to the register and talks to me while I pay for my produce. I tell him I'm living with Mother at a place near Looking Lake. He tells me about his brother and his brother's wife and the property they have outside Newport where he's thriving, and the phenomenal community of openness he's found on the coast—all sorts of people living with intention and generosity. I take that to mean he's being fed well at vegan potlucks and helping his neighbors with their solar panels. We go outside and still he talks and I remember the spell he used to weave that I just wanted so badly to believe, that he doesn't need to be gainfully employed because the universe will provide for him and others too, if only they believe. With a little more charisma, he could be a storefront preacher; with a little less kindness, he could be a Manson cultist. But Stanley means it all, he believes it, and with a puppy dog likability he is taken care of, and thus proven right. I took care of him for a long time; see now, I just bought his peach smoothie for him, without even thinking about it.

We stop by my car and he smiles a loopy grin. "It is so good to see you, Tillie. Boy, it's been a long time. Do you want to go have a cup of tea or something? Or lunch, maybe?"

Behind Stan, I can see someone wheeling a bike down the wheelchair ramp and before I can think, *Gavin!* my stomach tumbles and I feel warm and scared inside. She smiles at me, and I look back at Stan.

"I really can't right now," I say. "But it has been good to see you." He looks startled and I reach up to hug him goodbye. "And you do look great, Stan. Give your family my best."

Gavin wheels her bike over toward me, and I roll over to unlock the massive trunk. "Throw it in the back," I say, boldly, "and I'll give you a ride." I would never have planned that, never have done that, but my ex-husband's expression of stupefaction inspires me.

"Who's this?" he says, lifting a thumb at Gavin, and under his friendly tone of voice is a hardness that's foreign to me. I realize I don't want to see him, I don't want to be friends with him, I don't want to talk about the good old days. He isn't bad, he's just stuck, still in that same place I left him, and I don't want to be there anymore.

I lift myself into my seat and pull my chair across my lap expertly. I smile up at his expectant face, those narrowed eyes. "She's my date," I say, and close my door. Gavin waves her fingers at him, then slips in beside me and laughs. I reverse and drive away, and still he stands there like I just threw a bucket of seawater on his sandcastle.

"Sorry about that," I say, and she laughs again.

"No, no, that was great," she says, and I realize Gavin is seated beside me in my car and I have no idea where I'm driving, I just know she looks strong and happy and smells like growing things. "This is a cool setup," she says. "You're driving without feet."

That makes me laugh. "I've been living a whole life without feet. Since I was seventeen. Where am I driving us, then?"

"My place? I have an important dinner to make. I just hope my date isn't early," she says. I think she's the kind of person that, if I weren't very smart, her jokes wouldn't be very funny. Is that what's meant by a dry sense of humor? Emerson's dry, but she isn't usually funny to me, just unkind.

Gavin points the way to go and I want to apologize for calling her my date, but then I think she'll say, *But you are my date*, and then I'll feel scared again, so I don't say anything about it. I've known her, known of her, for months and months, but only in the last few weeks have I had the nerve to stop and really talk to her. She's smart, she has a master's in social work, and she teaches ESL classes when she isn't at the co-op. She has two roommates and a car they all share, a cat, an expensive bike, an appreciation for photography, and a record collection of artists I've never heard of.

When we get to her house, I eyeball the small set of outside stairs, and she says, "Yeah, that's the only bad part. But the rest of the house is level. I was afraid if I told you, you wouldn't come."

"I don't mind. I like a challenge." Because really, if we're going to be spending any amount of time together, she's going to have to see me crawl.

We clamber out with her bike and my chair, and after a bit of work on my part and several trips on hers, we are all inside and I'm free to explore. The living room is smallish but full of light and green leafy plants. One wall is covered with bookcases, and I wheel over to admire the range of authorship. Besides the sea of books, there is a fireplace, a big fluffy couch, a coffee table, a bean bag chair, and no TV. There is a stereo, and Gavin pops a CD from its case to play. Women's voices swell softly as she invites me into the kitchen, a clean, white-cabineted place, with a worn-in honey-colored table and matching chairs, and I begin to think that if I had my own home again, it would look quite a bit like this.

"This is home," she says. "My roommates are gone this weekend, at a retreat at Breitenbush." She unpacks her backpack and smiles down at me and her crooked front teeth charm me again. She makes me a cup of tea, leaving me to sit in the living room while she showers and changes the music again. I pick a book from her shelf, something I've never heard of, but it's written by a woman and has a pretty cover. I transfer myself to her couch and lean back into big cushions and sip my tea with the book on my chest. The open windows let in warm air and the sounds of kids playing down the street, and I feel relaxed and easy and excited all at the same time. The kind of happy where you know something good is waiting, but you can't remember what. I open my eyes when I feel Gavin sit beside me and she is close and wet-haired and dark-eyed, and I have to close my eyes again for a moment.

"You have a beautiful house," I say. "It feels—it just feels wonderful."

"We're lucky," she says. "We're blessed. And you have a houseful these days too. How's Ms. Addie?"

"This morning she helped me plant in the garden, and she rowed with Henry in his boat and drank his coffee, he said. And she vexes my horrible sister."

"Horrible?"

"Sometimes horrible. Addie won't look her in the eye and Emmy gets so exasperated."

"That sounds like a cultural difference to me," Gavin says, sipping her tea.

"My sister, the authority figure. I'm sure you're right. Addie's smart. She reads everything, and she's very observant, I think she has good instincts about people, but she isn't very worldly. In some ways she seems older than her age, and sometimes she seems younger. Maybe that's just what ten is like. I don't know, I don't really remember." I play my fingers along the back of the couch in the sunlight, thinking about my black-haired girl. "I do like her very much."

Gavin's hand travels near mine on the top of the couch. "When your mom brought her into the co-op, we talked about the northern lights. Only lucky people get to see the red ones. Most people only see the green, she said."

"I bet she's lucky people, isn't she?" I say and Gavin nods. Her fingers are long and quick, and the nails are cut short. When I tap-tap my fingers on the couch, she does the same, and I try to hide my smile.

"She wrote a report; did I tell you?"

She shakes her head no and puts her hand on top of mine. It is gentle but not tentative. I quaver a little at her confidence. "It was about the plane ride. Her first. She wants to be a writer when she grows up." Gavin's hand moves slowly on the back of mine. When I turn my hand palm up, she takes it in hers, and we touch softly in the sunlight. I think, *I'm holding hands with a woman!* and feel panicky again.

Gavin pulls my hand into her lap. She is sitting very close to me on the couch. "What happened when you were seventeen?" she asks softly.

I raise my eyes to see if I heard right and realize I've been avoiding her strong gaze. She has a short cute nose and long lashes and if she had pointy ears she would look a little like an elf. She has wrinkles around her eyes, like I do—what is she, fifteen years younger?—and soft, wide lips, and her dark-brown eyes are strong and wicked smart and I realize she probably doesn't miss much.

"Seventeen?" I say dumbly, and she laughs. "Oh, that." I pull my hand from hers and gesture to my jeans, empty from the knees down. "We had a car accident, Emmy and I. Let's see, it was raining, a terrible storm actually. I needed a ride home from a friend's house, we were here in Portland, and our parents were in New York." I recite the facts as I have before, as if I were telling someone else's story and I'm not very attached to the ending. "It was dark, she was driving, probably going too fast, we missed a turn in the rain and rolled down a hillside. I had a bad concussion and my legs were crushed. Emmy was relatively unhurt. She had to crawl out of a broken window to go find help for us. She had to run to a farmer's house in the dark, in the rain. That's it."

"That must have been awful," Gavin says. "For both of you." I roll my shoulders and press my lips into a smile.

"I think I would be very angry," she says, "if it were me."

"I was angry a long time ago, not anymore," I say, dropping my chin and glancing out the window. "Life happens." I want the conversation to change. Part of me wants to leave. Part of me wants my hand to find its way into hers again. "My friend Henry said something funny to me earlier today. He said people don't change, not really. I think he means the vital elements of us, what we are."

"You mean a zebra without stripes is still a zebra?" she asks.

"I guess. What do you think? Do you think people can change what they are?"

Gavin laughs and stretches her arms toward the ceiling. "All the best people do. Change is what makes us interesting. Who wants to go back in time to that person they were?"

With or without legs? I think.

"Who wants to be stuck?" she continues. "But I see his point, too. You, beautiful Tillie, would pull someone out of a burning building if you had to. That would never change."

"Would I? I'm not sure. And what if the person was a horrible dictator, like Pinochet or Pol Pot? Then it isn't so good to be the building-puller-outer, to have that be my unchangeable nature."

"Even when you save the wicked," she says, "even then, it's good."

And she leans over, without my even expecting it, and kisses me so softly on the lips that all I can do is say, "Oh!" Her hand is on the back of my head and she tastes like strawberry toothpaste and her kiss is gentle, like sliding into a big soft bed. My hand, up for a moment in a *Wait!* gesture, is resting on the strong part of her chest, and I can feel her heart beating under her skin. Tears spring to my shut eyes and still she kisses me, even as she wipes the wet from my cheeks with a stray hand. I forget to think, *I'm kissing a woman!* because as I kiss her and I cry, I discover something breaking open inside like a long-planted seed, and sadness spills out to mix with the happiness, and I feel marvelous and lost as I think, *This is the most wonderful thing that's ever happened to me.* And it's true, and it is.

Eve makes a discovery

I have the house to myself this afternoon now that the girls are gone. When they were children, I loved the moments after they first left the house each morning for school. The air would still hang with whatever argument they were having, or whatever slight one was feeling, so there was still that whooshing buzz of life, but slowly, slowly, it would be replaced by a stillness that I could feel to my very wings. I could dance and twirl if I wished, or lie on the couch, or bake brownies and eat them all myself, or go for a drive. Adam was never one of those windbags who believed women shouldn't drive. Some days he would leave the car for me, and I would spend hours tooling around with my scarf pinned to my hair so it wouldn't fly through the open car window. Many times I wouldn't be home when the girls came home from school, and when I did finally come in, their eyes would shoot angry little daggers my way from over their schoolbooks and Ovaltine.

I wander upstairs to my big bedroom and lie on the bed to dream about Adam for a while. He was a wonderful man, and I've never stopped loving him. Soon after we married, he went into the service, and I remember evenings spent with other wives, listening to the radio for news from South Korea. When he came home, he was angry I'd named our firstborn after a writer, but surely he wouldn't make me change it, and he didn't.

He was the only man I've ever been with, and I have no regrets about that. I do enjoy having the whole big bed to myself, but when I think of him, I imagine his long arms and legs wrapping over mine. Adam was so warm and strong, and I always felt young and beautiful with him. I touch the skin on my stomach—not as flat as it once was, my skin is loose everywhere and not as soft— and imagine his cheek on my belly. *Oh, my Adam! How we danced together into the sky!*

The phone rings downstairs and I open my eyes, not wiping away the tears. The sun is bright through the windows, now reaching toward late afternoon, and I think perhaps I will take myself to the movies. Adam named Tillie after his dear mother, but of course neither of us could bring ourselves to call that bright-eyed baby "Mathilda." It's good that Emerson came first, or else we'd have had the younger tending to the older; she was always so attentive, clucking like a hen, mopping up every mess like a child born to duty. And Tillie, born to run, to flop on the earth, brown hair full of leaves and twigs and pudding stains on her shirts. Sometimes I think if I could combine them, then halve them, I would have two perfectly-made daughters, just the right balance of happy and able. I imagine someone else adding onto me, filling my rucksack with a healthy dose of ambition or respectability. How boring! I laugh at the empty room and sit up on the bed, put my shoes back on.

I remember I wanted to check on the bluebirds. We have a family that returns each year to the same too-tall, pole-bound box. Some conservation group put the nest in years ago, then diligently checked it for some years after. But last year no one came, and this year again. I guess the bluebirds and I are on our own.

I wander downstairs and outside into the June sunshine. My perennials are exuberant this year, and I open my arms wide with joy just to see them. It makes Emmy's catalog-looking house a little less perfect, a little more livable. The flower perfume is strong, and one of the neighbors is mowing their lawn—I can smell that too. The sun is nice on my thinning hair—Adam would laugh if he were still alive, because not just the hair on my head is thin now!—but I don't want to trouble with going inside for my hat because I'm sure to be distracted if I do.

The birdhouse is up past the barn about half the distance to Looking Lake Road. There is a little bit of cover for the birds, a willow and some old walnut trees, and when the bird people came, they used to hop the old horse fence from our driveway to the box and bring homegrown worms for the fledglings. On my way to the barn to get the ladder, I see swallows, sparrows, chickadees, and nearby I can hear the summery whistle and response of red-winged blackbirds. I find the old wooden ladder where Henry has left it, leaning against the inside of the barn, and drag it behind me through the tall grass. Our landscaper has been occupied with other things lately, and I think to chide him next time he's over. The next time he's wiping my dishes or piggybacking Tillie or rowing Addie or mooning over Emmy, I'll say, *The horse pasture is near about out of control, Henry.* And he'll make a joke, and the next morning it will be sheared short as a springtime sheep.

I'm sweaty by the time I get the ladder to the box and set upright. The ground is mushy soft and the wooden legs sink right in. The ladder looks tipsy, and for a moment I reconsider. The day is too bright, really, without a hat, and the sun is beginning to give me a headache. I watch a car speed by too fast on the lake road, and I begin to climb the ladder. I have to rest after each step and hold on tight, but then, near the top, I hear a sound. It's a little chippery sound, like only the smallest among us could make, and I try to still my pounding heart to be sure I can hear it again. And there it is, from the plain wooden skyward box, a baby bird sound, and I pull myself to the highest rung and look inside to discover four miniature, wide-open beaks surrounded by scruffy, wet-looking feathers. I hold my breath, but still they fear me, and answer with silence. Baby bluebirds! I have baby birds! I must leave them quickly so as not to scare the parents away. It is a slow trip down my creaky ladder, and an even slower trip to drag the ladder a respectable distance away. I lay the ladder down and sit on the grass beside and shield my eyes from the afternoon sun. If I wait long enough, the parents will come.

Soon I can hear the babies, and nothing else matters. Not my too-long grass or too-thin hair or fractured children, not even my hatless head. I try to think like the bird people. I think, *I must feed them!* I plan to shop for worms first thing tomorrow, and I get excited to think I can show everyone, and then I get more excited to think I can show no one and keep their precarious little lives a secret. Sometimes it feels like the more fragile a thing is, the more you have to protect it from even being known. Our most beautiful selves, our biggest wishes, our sad, sad hearts, we gloss them all, smother them in our desire to keep them safe. I make a pledge of well-being to the baby birds, and lay my own bird-self back in the grass, to watch the land and sky for trouble, and keep their new and secret selves safely in my heart.

Emerson makes a discovery

I am late getting to NW 23rd Avenue, but that is fine with me. Addie was big-eyed to be left with Lily, but what am I to do? She needs to socialize, and certainly I cannot be expected to tend to her all day. Traffic on 23rd is thick and slow, and the sidewalks are full of shoppers and coffee drinkers enjoying this warm Saturday. I have to buzz around the blocks several times before a spot opens up on a side street, and I wave gratefully at the woman leaving. I pull down the mirror to check my face, and feel suddenly less light, less grateful. I look tired, even to me, and tense around the eyes. I dab on more concealer and a spot of gloss on my thin lips. I've considered having work done—surely it is commonplace these days—but I can't help thinking that cosmetic surgery is somehow a plot against women. God forbid Tillie or her green-aproned woman friend should hear me say such a thing, but I recently read of a podiatrist—a woman, no less!—advocating for cosmetic surgery of the feet in order to make high heels more wearable. I say, accommodate the women, not the shoes. Then again, some days I think a little brow lift would be nice.

I step out of the Lexus and cross the street. I'm meeting Robert Lyall at a little bistro he likes, and by now I'm late enough for him to think I've reconsidered. I see him in the window and smile just as he looks up. He is handsome, although I wish he'd cut his hair. It's pulled back in that same ponytail, and for a minute I imagine taking him to bed, and having his long hair accidentally drape into my face—ugh. Otherwise, he looks wonderfully smart and rich, save for the tattoos on his arms. And people with tattoos you can see usually have tattoos you can't see too. That thought makes me smile.

The bistro is full, and Robert stands at his window table for two as I walk over, gushing apologies. He's red in the face like someone lost on a trail, a little flustered from worry, I think, but he's quick to kiss my cheek, to tell me how beautiful I look, to help me with my chair. I order a regional cabernet and it comes quickly—apparently the waiter is glad I've arrived too—and I enjoy the deep color against the crisp white table linens. Yes, this is the sort of place I like, and yes, this is the sort of man I like, except for some of the aesthetic details.

Robert is easy to talk to and the conversation sweeps gracefully along. Some people are so awkward it takes extra effort to keep things moving, but this man doesn't need any hand-holding. We discuss his daughter, Sarah, and her summer internship at a law firm. We discuss whether to order the jicama and seared tuna or the fresh mozzarella appetizer. We discuss city politics, the tumultuous cost of local real estate, vacations we're planning, and places we've been. I only think of Henry once or twice and almost spill my water glass when I remember his warm hand on my foot.

After our salads have come, Robert looks up swiftly and says, "Oh, I nearly forgot. I met an old friend of yours. Karl Henley?"

I have to put my wine glass down to be sure I heard right. I smile at Robert, so he'll continue.

"He saw me talking to you at that shop in Sellwood. He showed me your picture in *Portland Monthly*. He says you've known each other for years, since you were in school together."

My cheeks feel stiff, but I force the smile to continue. "Knew each other, yes. He went by Butch back then. I wore his ring, did he tell you that? He mentioned he was back in town." I can feel my heart beat faster, but try to mask my irritation. Emails that have become more frequent. Annoyingly persistent phone calls. I am realizing, for the first time really realizing, the problem of him may actually *be* a problem. Has he been following me? How else would he have seen me in Sellwood?

Robert nods, "He said he moved from Philadelphia recently, said he had some old business to take care of here."

"I'm starting to worry I'm that old business," I say, around the rim of my cabernet.

His eyes are wiser than before. "Can't take a hint, huh?"

I nod. "I find him... off-putting. I think he's decided I'm the answer to an old question or something. I have no interest."

Robert's phone rings and he pulls it from his pocket. He looks down, looks up, looks down again, looks at me. "Is it him?" I ask and he nods.

"I'm sorry," he says, not answering the phone. "If I'd known, I would never have..."

I lift my hand to still his apology. "Of course, of course, I know."

Our salad plates are taken away and our entrees delivered. I lean my head on my hand, look out the window at the busy street. Everyone is moving one way or another, except across the street, one man stands. He is tall and broad like the athlete he once was, face long and strong, like a weightlifter, his quick eyes hidden by silver-rimmed sunglasses. I assume they're still overpowering and quick to sting. He's still holding his cell phone, leaning against the brick, drinking from a paper coffee cup, dark glasses staring into me from across the busy street. I remember taking Michael to the zoo in Seattle once when the lions were out, years ago. I watched a lioness on a hill watch my little son run back and forth, back and forth, and then she looked at me, dead straight in the eyes, and even though we were behind a moat and a fence, I felt threatened, prey to the predator, and grabbed my son with cold arms and dragged him away. I have that feeling again now, that ice in my spine, realizing he's been watching me, he's been following me.

I reach for Robert's hand across the table, and we both stare out the window at the man staring at me. "Karl was planning on joining my father's business after school, although no one called him Karl then, just Butch. His family was not wealthy, but he was incredibly ambitious. He was at school on scholarship. My father courted Butch as much as Butch courted me. My father had a soft spot for ingenuity and hard work, and he believed the Henleys needed a leg up. I ruined that for him, for both of them."

We watch as Butch puts his cell phone in his pocket and ambles down the street out of our view. I remember the night of the accident with Tillie. I remember the blood on my temple, the viciousness of his eyes. Our parents were in New York with his parents, and when I called their hotel in the middle of the East Coast night, they didn't believe me, didn't believe the seriousness of the accident, because of the steadiness of my voice. The duty nurse tried to explain to my just-woken father, and it wasn't until the police officer got on the line that he believed any part of the story.

I poke at the salmon and risotto on my plate, eat some asparagus. Robert looks concerned, but I smile to put him at ease. "And on another note, what were you doing in that little Sellwood shop anyway?" I ask.

"I took up meditation after the divorce." He smiles a sweet smile, and I feel protective of him. "Our counselor suggested that even the toughest of guys could meditate the blues away. And this is a good town for that sort of thing. I needed some new music. Wind chimes, bubbling brook, whale song, you know. How about you?"

"My sister wanted her tea leaves read. I was merely the escort."

"And was she compelled by the prognostication? Does she know which Lotto numbers to pick?"

"I think a day in the sun for Tillie is better than a jackpot. As long as she's scrabbling around in the dirt, in the garden, playing with her friends, she's happy. I have to admit, I'm a little jealous. She makes it seem so simple. She just *lives*, without worrying what anyone else thinks of her. When we were children, I used to think of her like a pet sometimes. A pet I was responsible for. Isn't that awful?"

"I love your honesty," he says. He's almost finished his lemon chicken, and he's eyeing my risotto. I pass my plate over and he laughs. "And how about you? Were you handed any pearls of wisdom?"

I remember the thunderstorm outside the little shop, the lights going out. The cards spread before me and the ice-cold rune in my hand. *Hide no longer*, she said. *You are marked by the gods*, or something. *Let loose the control, be of forgiveness.*

That sort of powerlessness is ugly to me. I look out the window, trying to see the man who once sucked my power away with my father's complicity, but he is gone, or at least out of sight.

I smile at Robert, which I've been doing a lot. "The only wisdom I had when I left was the same as when I walked in. But it was a good show nonetheless. And that was worth paying for." There are some things that should not be forgiven no matter how much time has passed, no matter how much water under the bridge.

Robert pays for lunch, and I walk him to his car. He wants to hike the avenue for a bit, maybe find a gift for his daughter, but I beg out. I tell him I have someone waiting for me, that I really must go. He is sweet and respectful, very Portland. I let him kiss me, a gentle kiss, and I do not tell him that he kisses like a friend. I think of Henry again. He would not kiss me like a friend. We make plans to see each other again, and I walk lightly to my car. I am thinking of men. Wonderful men and not so wonderful men, and I feel surrounded by them. For years I have felt as if I have a bubble around me, and that no matter how hard I try to touch someone, our hands just won't meet. I stop by my car in the sunshine. The air is clean in my throat and my eyes feel bright and clear and I suddenly feel as if that barrier is gone. I could feel Robert's kiss, I could feel Henry's hand, I could feel Butch Henley's stare, and I can feel Will too, if I try, inside of me, like a small lit fire, keeping me warm. I touch my hands to my cheeks and smile and look down at my marvelous self, my runner's body and expensive shoes, and that is when I discover the sagging curb-side tire of my Lexus, flattened, my luxury car wounded and stuck like an abandoned ship in the mud.

Addie makes a discovery

I am back at the big house and worn out from my day. If I were back home, I wouldn't have to go to a stranger's party. Mama would never make me do something like that. It's funny that we don't think about the good stuff we have until it changes. I didn't even know my life was so good, I thought it was just regular. Whitney was nice, but mostly nobody wanted me there, especially me. I would have rather stayed here and helped in the garden or read a book or helped Henry with a job. I am waiting for it to be time to call Mama, and I think about how everything I do now is just waiting. Waiting to find out. Waiting to get to go home. I sit on the couch in the darkish great room and listen to Ms. Eve talk-talk in the kitchen with Mrs. Worthy. Tillie came home and took a shower, and I can hear her wheelchair rolling back and forth, a soft rumble-rumble, between her bedroom and her art room. I tiptoe down the hall and hear Tillie singing softly, like a happy breeze in the leaves. I tap on the door and she calls me in. The sun is going down over the lake, I can see through the windows, and the sky looks painted red and pink and light blue. It makes me feel like crying.

Tillie says, "Are you okay?" and I don't have any words to give back. She pats the big futon mattress and I sit down beside her. I scoot back so I can lean against a cabinet and turn my head so I can see the sad twilight colors in the sky. Tillie is pulling old bent tubes of paint out of a fishing tackle box, and throwing some into a garbage can beside her. She has a nice warmness tonight that feels good to be around.

"How was your party?" she asks. Her wet hair is in one long braid, like mine, and the outside light seems to make it sparkle. I don't imagine I have any sparkle myself. I pull my knees up to my chest, trying to ball up. My stomach stopped hurting, but now it's hurting again. I don't know why it does that.

I shrug in response, and Tillie leans against the cabinet beside me. "Let me guess," she says. "A bunch of rich kids saying mean things about other kids? Watching the creepy magician that the dad hired? One or two cute boys that would probably be nice if they were by themselves? Wishing you could just leave?"

"There wasn't a magician," I say, and sigh. "And the boy was nice until his girlfriend came." I remember what that girl looked like, all long and thin and perfect. I shake my head. "I don't know how someone who looks like that can feel so unhappy." My voice sounds quiet to me and I have to clear my throat to be heard. "If I had that perfectness, I would be happy."

Tillie smiles down at me and she is beautiful, even the lines around her mouth are beautiful. "I used to look at my sister and think that," she says. "After I lost my legs, I used to watch her, so jealous, and think if I just had what she had, then I could be happy. What do you think? If I traded with Emerson, would I be happy?"

"No, no, you're wonderful." I feel my words having to come out fast. "You have sparkles that she doesn't. You're warm and she's not. She should be trading with you."

"What if this?" she says. "What if no one traded with anyone? What if we were all perfect just as we are?"

"But I'm not perfect," I whisper. "Boys like Carson only talk to me until girls like Kyra show up."

"But you are perfect," Tillie whispers back. She wraps her arm around my shoulders and pulls me close and I was right, she is warm. "Consider this—is the earth jealous of the rivers that flow on by? Do you think that trees are jealous of the moon? Look at that sunset." We both turn our heads to the fading sky colors over the lake. "Are you jealous of that sunset?"

Her question is funny to me and I laugh. "No, how can I be? But I do think it's beautiful."

Tillie squeezes my shoulders in a hug. "And you are beautiful too, my dear, in ways you don't even know about yet. Perfect in your own way. When you walk past, the grass in the field watches you and thinks, *Look at that marvelous girl!*"

I start crying, I don't know why, and Tillie holds me in her arms, sitting on a mattress on the floor, in a room that's growing dark, and she whispers, "Believe it, believe it," and she is crying too.

Someone knocks on the door and then Ms. Eve walks in and turns on the light. We are startled like animals by the light, and Tillie laughs. Ms. Eve is holding the phone out to me and smiling. I take a deep breath and stand up, and when I put the phone to my ear and say hello, I hear Mama saying my name over and over again.

I walk to the hallway where it's quiet, and say, "I'm here, I'm here," until she believes me.

She says, "Baby, I miss you," and her voice sounds hollow and far away.

"When can I come home, Mama?"

"Soon, baby, soon. When I get better, when I'm better."

"Did we lose the apartment?" I ask this because she's always worried we'll lose the apartment, as if it weren't such a great big thing, but I know what she means when she says it.

"No, no, that's taken care of. Mike has been such a big help…" Her voice wanders away and I can't understand what she's saying.

"Mom? Are you there?"

"… LuAnn says she misses the dickens out of you, those are her words, and when you come home, she'll make that sweet bread you like."

"When, Mama?" I'm holding the bear amulet around my neck, rubbing it with my thumb. "When?"

"Are they treating you well there, baby?"

"I was sick and I was on the bathroom floor and watching the moon and I pretended you were there with me." I'm crying again, but I won't let it stop me talking. "And you could see the moon too, from where you were. Did Mike tell you about the spirit bear?"

"I'm so tired baby, I need to go…"

"And the library here is big and I've been helping with the garden and Tillie doesn't have any legs and—"

"Addie, honey? It's LuAnn." Her voice is clean and fresh and reminds me of the smell of lemon cleaner, like she uses at her house.

"Auntie Lu," I say. "Is Mama okay?"

"She's on some medication, honey. Her head isn't working right just now. But she's getting better. She talks about you every day. And she has some good doctors. We'll talk again soon, hon."

"Can I tell her goodbye?"

"I'll tell her for you. We love you. Be good for those people, okay?"

"Okay. Tell Mama I love her." I hold the phone in my hand for a long time and look at the pictures in the hallway. I don't know why some people are born into families that have a lot and some people are born into families that don't have a lot, and it's hard not to take it personally either way. My mom is sick. She can't take care of me right now. I think of her voice on the line, so different from her normal voice that it's a little scary. For the first time, I think, I'm grateful to Captain Mike for sending me to his people. I look at a picture of him when he was a little boy with his mom—Mrs. Worthy—and I guess his dad. They are dressed in nice clothes and they look like a family that has a lot of good things. Mrs. Worthy looks happy in the picture.

I go back into Tillie's art room because I'm not sure where else to go, and she and Ms. Eve are talking and stop when they see me. They both have questions in their eyes, so I say, "That was my mom. She needs some rest now."

They both nod and Tillie motions me over to a short stool and a table covered in little paint pots. I set myself onto the seat and look at the big white paper on the easel in front of me. I give Ms. Eve the phone and she kisses me on the head and leaves and Tillie presses a long, fat paintbrush into my hand.

"I was hoping you'd keep me company," she says. She puts a CD into a small, paint-dripped-on player, and soft music comes out, like the symphony orchestra we saw on a field trip. After my second grade class went to that, I begged and begged Mama to take me again, and she did, once. We went on a Saturday afternoon and sat in a row to the side, all to ourselves, and every time I looked at her, she had her eyes closed, but twittery, and I thought her beautiful eyelashes were keeping time with the music. She smiled the whole time. That was before Earl, or at least before I knew about Earl. He was a nice man and I miss him, but Mama misses him more.

The room looks different now that the ceiling lights are on, and it's getting dark outside. I know Tillie won't care what sort of picture I make, but I worry for a minute about wasting her supplies because at school we don't get to use very much. Mama talks sometimes about school when she was a girl. After the earthquake at the Seward school and her little sister Ruth dying, they were all sent to boarding schools. She says that the boarding schools tried to make Native kids hate being Native and for punishment they would get sprayed by hoses and everybody had a number instead of a name. I feel bad inside when she tells me, but she says it's important that people know, especially Native people, so I accept the bad feelings as a tradeoff for knowing.

I can't decide what sort of picture to make, and I'm feeling very nervous. I glance over at Tillie who is glancing at me, and she laughs. "It doesn't have to be anything," she says. "Just put some color up, wherever it feels good. Don't overthink it, honey."

I can't not think it, I am all the time thinking. If I didn't think so much, I wouldn't have anything. When we were at fish camp, I would watch Robert Soo in the front of his father's little boat and think, *That boy is wild but he's going to be somebody special someday.* And when I watched the elder women laugh I thought, *They are happy and sad at the same time, like sweet and sour candy.* I don't know why I have so many thoughts, I just do.

I plant the paintbrush in the red paint, then softly lay it on the paper. If I don't lift my hand, I can make a slow, smooth line right across the top, like the spot where the sun comes up every morning. I don't know what I'm making, but it doesn't matter. I clean the brush and dip it in yellow and make another thick line across the page. I do this with every color and then go back and start again, and it is like a sea of colored lines, like layers of sand in a place like the Grand Canyon, like a little girl looking through window blinds. I pretend I can fit even smaller lines in between my lines and find a smaller brush and paint and paint and paint and listen to the violins and flutes and then I realize I'm not thinking and it's sort of wonderful for a minute.

When I go to bed, it is full dark outside, and my picture is drying on the easel. Tillie told me she loved it. She said it was like lying down in warm clean sheets from a spring catalog of expensive things. I like when she talks like that. I crawl into my bed in the dark, but I don't feel tired. I think about the party and think about the phone call and think about thinking too much and fall asleep before I even know it.

When I wake in the night, it is late and the moon is up. I use the bathroom and brush my teeth, because I forgot before bed, and go back to my room and leave the lights off. I have big windows for looking at the yard, and the moon is brighter than it has been. I look under the bed to see my stash, but it's gone. I had some plates and some bowls with extra good food, but it's gone. I feel a sudden stab of bad feeling in my stomach, like I've been caught doing something wrong, and my heart beats faster under my nightgown. Under the bed now is a dim something that is new. I lie on the mattress, upside down, and pull out a flattened basket. Inside are all kinds of snacks, like maybe a hotel room would have. Fruit snacks in silvery cellophane bags and miniature cookies and juice in boxes and peanuts in a little can. Ms. Eve must have cleaned up. It makes me feel like crying to see it. It makes the darkness in my stomach feel not so bad, not so tight and small. I don't think she's mad, or else she wouldn't have left me so many treats. I don't think she's mad at all. I open the peanuts and walk to the window and stare out and snack a little. In the moonlight, I can see bushes, grass, shadowy clouds. It all looks very beautiful and clean and I think maybe it's calling my name. I hold my amulet while I slip on my sandals and quietly leave my room and walk down the hall to the back door.

Outside, I stand on the porch in the darkness and it is lovely and not too cold on my skin under my nightgown. I can feel the house sleeping behind me, and when I slip out of my sandals and go down the porch steps, the grass is cool and damp under my feet. The clouds aren't moving in the dark sky, and everything feels hushed and still, waiting for me. I hear a bird call down by the lake, but then all is quiet again. The moon is lovely, a fat crescent in the sky. She makes me think of Mama, of the parts of her I like best, like when she smiles and hums and pets my head. I whisper, "Hello, moon," and my own voice is too loud for the sweet and quiet night. Her small light spills onto the big bushes with fat pink and white flowers by the Henry fence and the big grass there. It is the only part of the yard that is allowed to grow so wild, and I wonder why. The fence is long and too tall for a tall person to see over and the bushes are bigger in one spot than in any other and that is where the moonlight falls, so that is where I go.

I don't know the names of all these plants but that doesn't mean I don't know them. I put my hand on the thick, strong bush and smell the waxy, wet-looking flowers. I pick one in the night's dark with quiet all around, and her stalk is sticky in my fingers, and then I think I'd like to drink from her white petals like a cup. I pretend to drink, and it makes me smile, and the grass feels lovely under my feet and so does the nighttime air on my face. I reach for another flower, and that is when I see a handle in the fence, a big metal door handle. I have to sneak my body to get behind the tall, strong flower bushes, but when I get to the fence, I have room to stand. There is a gate. I have found a gate in the fence. What sort of grown-ups forget about a gate, especially when they go back and forth to each other's houses so much? I put the hand not holding the flower cup onto the big metal handle, and it is black and cold to the touch. I press the button down with my thumb, and I have to push hard, but it clicks and the door swings a little toward me. The hinges make an awful squeak and I hold still for just a heartbeat or two, afraid I may have woken a sleeper. The door can't be opened very much because of the giant flower bushes, but if someone were to clear the way and oil the hinges, this gate could be wonderful. I think of books where girls find good secrets behind hidden gates, and even though I know what's on the other side of the fence—just Henry's house—I feel excited at my discovery. If this were a kid's house, I would think this were either a secret or a thing forgotten, because that is how kids are, but I don't know if grown-ups have more reasons than that. I can't open the gate far enough to peek through, so I close it as quietly as I can. I have to fight my way back out of the bushes and I can feel sticky flower parts on my nightgown and in my hair, but I am happy and excited inside. What a find! And in the moonlight!

I stop in the grass to stare at the sky again, but it is different now. The wind has come up and is blowing toward the lake and the clouds are moving faster in the sky and the moon winks in and out. I shiver and for the first time feel afraid to be outside after midnight. A long way off, I hear a neighbor's dog barking. Then I hear a sound like a stick breaking and look in the direction of the house toward the shadows, toward a bad feeling I suddenly have, so full in my body I feel like a pillow stuffed full with it. I reach for my amulet at my neck, my mama bear, so scared my legs feel stuck. I stand in the cold—for now it is cold—and try to see into the dark, and just when I've convinced myself it's just my imagination, or a raccoon, or nothing, I smell cigarette smoke in the air, and that is what makes my legs finally move. My perfect, white-petalled flower cup drops from my hands and my toes curl into the damp grass and I run back to the house as fast as I can. My feet pound, pound on the wooden boards of the porch, and I reach the back door, breathing fast, and turn to look, but there is no one there. Just the moon and the clouds and the deep, deep night. I lock the door and shiver my way back to my bedroom and lie awake for a long, long time.

Five

Henry slips

My old Ford Bronco has a bent license plate and rust like dappled paint on its dented frame as if some teenager painted it by chucking stones, and as I walk toward her, I think I ought to clean it out a little, maybe later today. I keep all kinds of tools in the back, but other junk has gathered too, and sometimes it feels like I'm carrying someone's cluttered dreams or memories around with me and they're getting in the way of my own, and maybe if I just open things up, air it out a little in the sun, maybe I can scour those feelings away.

The truck is creaky, and I idle in the driveway to warm the engine up. The Sunday morning is stony gray and damp and cool. Yesterday I spent most of the afternoon under a dark cloud and today feel granite despair settled deeply in my chest. After Missy Holloway packed up her good cheer and left, I shivered in the rock garden all the sunny afternoon with Will's cigar box heavy on my lap. And all night too, I lay awake, the cigar box once again beside the bed, in my mind a glowing ember I couldn't help but watch. The note is inside still, nestled safely in its hiding place where it wasn't meant to be found right off, I have to think. Never could Will have thought that Emmy and I would light up together to remember him, our fine old fellow, like an Oxford don. I try to remember each word of the little poem, but I can't: *All you can see is my face; I will look you in the eye and never lie.* Is that his last dispatch to us? There wasn't a suicide note, or at least one ever found or divulged. Emerson packed up most of his things, and while she let me wrap my arms around her once or twice, she was impenetrable: she never cried and she barely spoke and she kept whatever secrets they had clutched tightly between them.

I drive up my driveway and stop at the end of the fence, well before the road. Eve is out in her robe and plastic curlers, standing and waiting for me. She crosses in front of the Bronco with a smile on her morning bedroom face and a gift in each hand. I lean out the window and feel a small ray of light inside.

"Good morning, Henry!" she says. "You look like you haven't slept!" She hands me a travel mug steaming with coffee and a bagel sandwich wrapped in a paper napkin. "I'm glad you're still here. I was afraid I'd missed you."

"I'm headed to the Vincents' this morning, across the lake. Matt wants help painting a couple rooms while the family's gone for the day. We should be able to slap it out pretty quick."

"Good, because you're invited to a picnic this afternoon with Addie and me, and you must be prompt because I have an important job for you after, regarding some rhododendrons." Eve is so short she has to reach up to lay her forearms on the deck of my open window. I take a bite of my egg sandwich and sip my coffee and try to remember when my own mother was so kind.

"Thank you, Eve. This hits the spot." Her robe has come untied, and her soft white nightgown shimmers in the damp gray light. "Is that silk?" I ask, smiling.

"Oh, this!" Eve laughs, and her own brightness shimmers too. "I was thinking of Adam last night. I miss him so! He loved me in silk." She winks at me and I laugh too. So unexpected she is, always.

"Well he was a lucky man, your Adam. I'm sorry I didn't know him. Tell Addie I look forward to our picnic."

She tells me to drive safely around the lake, and I remind her it is Sunday morning and most wise people are sleeping in, and she reminds me that tardy churchgoers can be dangerous in their single-mindedness. And I blow her a kiss as I drive away, and isn't it amazing how one little thing can make everything else feel okay, for a little while at least?

I've only worked for the Vincents a few times, but I remember Matt as kind, a little preoccupied, a salt-of-the-earth kind of guy. They are only one house up from Doc and Missy, and I'm a little tense at the thought of seeing either one. Matt Vincent has coffee on when I come and he refills my travel mug for me. He's friendlier than I remember, and jokes a lot, and when he shows me the three rooms, I think we'll be lucky to be done by noon, but everything's already set up, the outlets are taped, and both of us are quick with a roller. He turns the music up and I can work in peace.

I dreamt of Will last night, no surprise, between bouts of sleeplessness. It started with us in a fight, and the sky so bright it felt shattered. Will was so angry I couldn't even look in his eyes. He jumped off the side of his boat and swam to shore, and when I caught up he was happy again and doing pull-ups in my stone garden. And then he jumped down and walked to the closed gate between our properties and tried to open it, but he couldn't. And then I was back in my childhood home and Mom was in her room, dying all over again, and my heart felt scattered, like the best of me had been thrown like ashes to the wind, leaving me hollow inside.

The bedroom we are painting upstairs is getting a light peachy pink, and I think there's no way in hell Matt Vincent picked this color himself.

"Craft room?" I ask, over the loud retro rock.

"Wife's office," he answers. "Her mother isn't doing well, so she's moving into the spare room downstairs, and Julia's moving her office up here. So here we go. My mother-in-law's bringing her cats." He makes a face and opens one of the big clean windows to let some air in, and I have a swift vision of this regular guy, this suit-and-tie guy, with his freckled arms around his weeping wife, whispering, *Yes, of course she can come. I'll fix up the spare room*, while her salty tears drip down his arm and the weight of burden doubles on his back. Sometimes regular people are fucking amazing to me.

Out in the yard, the Vincents' old pug barks once, twice, then stops, then starts again slowly.

Matt sighs and says, "That old bastard. I'd better go see what's up."

I turn the music down after he leaves and paint with even pressure, up and down, up and down, then dip the roller and repeat. The rhythm is meditative, a soothing cadence. Dreaming of my mother's death has brought it close to the surface this morning. She died when I was fourteen, from a tumor in her stomach that spread, doubling, quadrupling itself until it had infected her everything, the X-rays showing flat organs riddled with sinister black spots, or so I imagined. After she died, Dad began spending more time at his Looking Lake fishing cabin than he did at home, and I was mostly left to my own devices. I was reckless but likable, and was coached and carried by well-meaning adults through high school and into a wrestling scholarship at the rougher of the two state schools. What I remember are long, lonely, teenage days at home, wandering from kitchen to black-and-white TV to bedroom to garage weight bench, hair fashionably long, shorts fashionably short, waiting, just waiting, for the next person to arrive in my life. I spent whole Saturdays in the garage with my dad's *Playboys* and the radio on the AM burnout station and what was left of the resinous ounce I'd scored from my friend's uncle, dreaming of hot girls and Jacuzzis and the muscle car I planned to own when I was old enough to get out of that place, and still just waiting. How much of my life has been spent like that? Waiting for Mom to die, waiting for Dad to leave again or come back, waiting for whichever girl, waiting for college, waiting for the score, waiting for Will to sneak over, waiting for Emerson to catch us or decide she loves me. And here I am, waiting again, waiting for Will's note to be found, waiting for *me* to be found.

I have a sudden memory of Mom's funeral—it was spring, and her too-thin face in the silk-lined casket was white clay, cold as marble, even with the awful makeup they'd put on. I stood beside the first pew in a dark brown Lutheran church with my hair falling into my face and my big, modish collar itching my neck while fat church ladies heaved their bosoms against me and Dad in smothering hugs and I thought I'd breathe their old-woman perfume forever, and I looked at Dad beside me, but he didn't look at me, and he wouldn't and he wouldn't and he wouldn't.

Anger makes my teeth clench, and I drop the paint roller—or it slips from my hand—and it clangs and splatters as I drop to my knees on the plastic-covered floor. The weight of my stony heart is pulling me down, and I think of Will in my kitchen, in my strong arms, his forehead on my shoulder, his salty skin always warm to the touch. And lying in my big bed, after, his dark eyes soft and warm. *I will look you in the eye and I will never lie,* he wrote. It aches inside to have loved him, in my way, and know it wasn't enough for him.

I hear dogs barking outside and sit on my heels, lifting my head from the plastic floor. Tillie always says there aren't enough words for all the different kinds of love in this world, and why is it my love for Will and my love for my father, wildly different as they are, lead me to the same lonely place? I look up and around at the half-painted room. This is not my house, not even what I ever wanted. So what is it, again, I wanted?

On my knees still, I crawl to the open window and lean my arms and head on the sill. The sun is breaking gently through the gray morning, and my head is filled with the smell of peachy-pink paint, and my shoulder muscles feel warm from the up-and-down with the roller, and even though my eyes sting and my chest feels wrapped tight, I just make myself breathe, in and out, listening to the sound of Matt Vincent's voice outside and barking dogs. In that moment, that tiny little moment, I feel something tight inside let go. I watch the patches of blue sky grow, and think that how I am in the world is not what I'd actually like to be, and how is it, then, that we get stuck in places? I think of Emerson, and her perfect, untouchable, still-water sadness. I will give her the note. I will drop a stone into her pond. I will tell her everything; the pain of her knowing could not be worse than the pain of no one knowing, I think.

Chin in hand, I smile a small smile at the sky just as Matt Vincent comes into view from around the house with his pug, and Missy with her Irish setter, Buddy. Buddy is off-leash and bouncing around, and Matt's pug is straining to join in and barking protest to Matt, who is pulling him across the yard and talking with Missy at the same time. My first instinct is to pull my head back and in, but I tamp the urge and stay put. I watch her laugh at something Matt has said and put her hand on his arm. I watch the way she brushes her hair back from her eyes, the way her face opens to him like a paperwhite to the sun. "I didn't know," I whisper to the air above their heads, "you're as bad off as the rest of us."

By the time Matt returns, after tying his pug up out of Buddy's sight, I'm back to rolling paint onto the walls.

"That was Missy Holloway," Matt says, then smiles and blushes a little.

"Nice neighbor, huh?" I say.

Matt climbs his little ladder to edge the corners and paint drips on his arm. "The other day Doc told me she's seeing someone. Having an affair, you know? Damn, she's the kind of woman that could make me that kind of man."

My heart stops for a minute when he says it, but then I think, *Well, of course her husband knows.* "No way," I say, "Despite temptation, you don't want to be that kind of guy."

He looks at me and shrugs and says, "Not that I'd ever actually cheat on my wife or anything, she's my best friend. But it's nice to have a beautiful woman flirt a little, you know?"

"When Doc told you," I ask, "was he pretty mad?"

"That guy's hard to read," Matt says. "Honestly, if anybody I know were to go postal, it'd be him, I've got him pegged. So mad, no, but close to the edge? Maybe."

Should I be scared of Doc? I'm not. Should I be scared of Missy? I think of her hand on Matt's arm, how deep her need must be. She wants something I don't even have inside to give. But then I think about Eve with her curlers and morning gifts. I think about Addie with her round face and her calm. I think about Tillie and her girl-date and the details I can't wait to hear. And of course, I think of Emmy, when she softens, when she smiles. I have something inside for them, some deep kindness for each of them, and even to consider it makes me feel more whole than I have for ages.

Matt's just about to turn the music up when I put my roller down. "I'm him," I say. "I'm the guy. Missy's guy. Or at least I was. Not anymore."

Matt just stares at me as I dip the roller into the paint and go back about my business. I smile at the wall for having said it, for having said out loud, *I'm done,* even if I've said it to the wrong person. It feels as if I've finally pushed a large boulder down a hill. As if I'm Sisyphus and just said, *Screw this,* and let a lifetime of punishment go.

Tillie slips

I woke to sprouting happiness this morning, and I find myself humming endlessly as I roll back and forth in the kitchen, making a late breakfast. Mother keeps glancing smiles my way as if she's waiting for me to tell her about Gavin, and I want to, but I'm not sure how. *She kissed me, like a thousand times I'm pretty sure, and it was the most incredible thing, ever.* But we can't put the most incredible things into words, at least I can't, not sufficiently. How do you say, *It changed me?* How do you say, *I understand something now?* How do you say, *I felt the best of God inside me,* and have that be understood and honored and carried tenderly forever? You can't, I can't, so instead I just have to let my happiness be what it is, and not try to explain a thing.

Mother seems spacier than usual, leaving wet rings from her coffee mug on the table and her slippers on the bamboo-topped island, and she keeps talking about Dad. Funny how someone you love can see a person so differently than you can. I got along with Dad okay, better after I lost my legs. Emmy was his little angel until just before the accident, when they had some big blowout. She stopped speaking to him for a time, and it never got much better after that. Dad was tough; he loved Mother and gave her the world, but he could be ruthless too. He had only one opinion of a person and that was the first. A fine example of someone's best qualities being their worst as well. But to Mother, he was a shining knight and a gentleman, and what good does it do a person to try and snatch their best memories away?

I watch as Addie finally comes to the kitchen after an unusually late sleep-in, and Mother wraps her tiny arms around her and holds and holds. Addie is happy, bright-eyed and excited, her loose black hair in wild orbit around her head, and she asks Mother about the fence and the gate between the two properties.

"Have you been night-walking?" Mother asks, and it startles me. I almost drop my tea. "The moon *was* lovely last night."

What does Mother know that I don't? Addie outside in the night? She just beams and nods to Mother and I think how much she's changed since the evening before, when we cried together in the twilit dark.

I roll to my art room, tea balanced carefully in my lap. Addie's painting is the first thing I see, and it is strong and purposeful, horizontal lines of infinite color, some fat, some thin, all beginning and ending somewhere beyond the edge of the canvas. In her ten-year-old knowing, she intuitively grasped something it took me four years of art school to really get: what's on the canvas is only part of the story, and our wisest selves know we aren't seeing all there is to see. I'm reminded of a summer internship with an art program for the developmentally disabled before its funding was cut. I spent hot afternoons in open-windowed rooms, watching men and women who couldn't tie their own shoes painting and sculpting and writing as born artists, as insightful and discerning as anyone, lacking only the sophistication and censorship of the internal critic. They made fabulously awkward and beautiful art, simple and deeply satisfying. It was a marvelously humbling experience, and looking at Addie's painting makes me feel similarly. Maybe I should be teaching art to kids again. I've grown so insular with my work; it would be good to be recharged with new perspectives.

I roll my wheelchair to the window and look out at the backyard and the lake beyond. I try to imagine Addie out there in the moonlight, her white nightgown flapping at her ankles, her bare toes snug in the grass. I wonder if she is Emerson's granddaughter, if my nephew is her father. Why else would Michael have sent her to us? It is a conversation I wish I could have with my sister, but Lord knows it would be challenging.

Is everyone broken? I asked Gavin last night, trying to catch my breath. *Yeah,* she said. *I think everyone is.* Then she flexed her strong little arm and her bicep popped up from under her T-shirt. *See how broken I am?* she said. *New muscle's just a result of little tears healing in the old one. So maybe broken is just what has to happen first.*

I close my eyes for a moment and think of Gavin's fingers in mine, her breath in my ear, her mouth on my neck, the smell of her cinnamon skin. I did not sleep with Gavin, nor did I get to taste her gazpacho. We spent the whole of the afternoon on her couch, and when I got too scared or too turned on, I stopped her and we talked and then she'd start kissing me all over again. I never thought I could let another woman do that, thought maybe I was just being contentious to consider it, but when I leaned into her soft, strong arms it felt like something terribly important was happening, and I could either resist and be safe, or fall and be saved. And then, too, I thought of what Emmy said. Do all the housewives have crushes on Gavin? Is there a waiting list, a revolving door for the sexually frustrated? And, worst thought of all, am I just another project for her social responsibility? It is so easy to derail our own best feelings sometimes, isn't it?

I can see blue patches burning through the stony sky and think of Henry. I sort of thought he would be hanging around last night waiting for me to come home, waiting to get the scoop. A little disappointing that he had someplace else to be. I try to plan my day, think about what work I'd like to get done. I do have that show at the end of the month, which I'm mostly ready for. But every time I try to concentrate, I remember Gavin's house and the sunlight on her couch, on my hand, then my shoulder, then on my cheek, until it was too bright to see, and my eyelids glowed red from the outside while we kissed and kissed.

I hear light footsteps in the hall that pause by the door, then a hesitant knock on my studio door. I say, "Yes," expecting to see Addie, but it is my older sister who tentatively opens the door and steps inside. She's in her running gear and her cheeks are red and her short, damp hair is pushed back and she holds a Nike water bottle in her hand and she looks beaten down and I think, *What is it you want from me?*

"Can I come in?" she says, and it's like she's softened, put her chisel down.

"Of course," I say. "Did you have a nice run?"

She doesn't say anything; she steps lightly across the room to my half-finished painting of women-in-circle, then wanders back, wiping the sweat from the back of her neck. Her face is flushed red, and the white scar on her right temple stands out like a beacon. She drinks water from her bottle, puts her hands on her hips, then says, "Fuck," and slides down the wall onto the floor.

"I'm getting old, Tillie," she says, sitting like a teenager on the wood floor.

"Yeah," I say, sipping my tea, "You are. But Addie told me that fifty is the new thirty, so you might have a few good years left."

"Where'd she get that, TV?"

I laugh and roll a little closer to where Emmy's sitting. I can't help but be cautious, even as I feel the wild, childish urge to be close to her.

"I can't be a grandmother," she says. "I'm not even a very good mother. I think there's been a mistake." She laughs, and I can see how beautiful she is, my marvelous, talented, able-bodied sister.

"Do you know who I saw yesterday? Butch Henley, remember him?" Her laugh is flatter this time, with less humor.

"Of course I do, oh my God," I say. "I thought he was amazing, just golden. I had such a crush on him! I got so mad he called me kiddo that one time that I threw my clog at him and hit Mom's lamp and scuffed the wall, remember? He used to fight me for the TV when you guys stayed in. He'd pin me down until I let him change *Sonny & Cher*. We all thought you were going to marry him. I kind of thought it was my fault you didn't, actually."

Emerson's eyes are like starbursts, like cut crystal, when she reaches for the arm of my chair. "Don't think that. Don't ever think that," she says.

"After the accident, everything was different." I look down at my calloused finger, tracing the rim of my hand-thrown mug. Something sharp catches inside my chest and my throat feels tight, such a swift reaction I feel quiet and small. "You spent so much time with me, I guess because I needed so much—"

"No, no, no, no," she says and she's on her feet, dragging a metal stool over to my side. She sits close and puts her hands on the armrest of my chair. I feel cool even as the morning brightens outside, and still ever so small. My finger rubs the rim of the mug and I remember the hospital smell, the starched nurses caps, seeing Mother's blanched face over mine, the feeling of floating, being untethered, and not in a good way. And Emmy, always Emmy, nearby, eyes swollen from tears I never saw, bruises on her face, ugly stitches in her temple, her lips a thin tight line never broken with words.

"That isn't why," she says to me now. "You didn't end it. He wasn't good, Tillie, and I didn't realize until…" She drops her head and her short damp hair flips onto her face. When she raises her head and pushes her hair free from her eyes, she looks almost like her old self, her model-handsome face restored to order. "Listen, he was a narcissistic prick. I'm glad I found out when I did, and I'm infinitely glad I didn't marry him. I don't know why he's trying to get in touch with me now." Emmy laughs and I laugh too but she's sitting so close; it's hard to let someone be false with you when they're sitting so close.

"Did you talk to him?"

She leans back on the stool and stretches her hands over her head. "No, I think he's following me. I have no idea why. I've stopped answering his calls." She stands and carries the metal stool back to where she'd found it.

I sip my tea and watch her back as she looks out the big bay windows. "Should you be worried?" I ask. She shakes her head slowly, as if she barely heard the question. But she's telling me, which means she is worried.

Emmy turns and grins. "How was your dinner last night?" she asks.

I think of Gavin's couch and the ginger smell of her house and the warm sun on her cheek and feel the corners of my mouth turn up in the smallest of smiles.

"Divine," I say. "We didn't eat. I don't think I've been less hungry in my life."

"So now you've done it, hopped the fence." She gestures to my legs. "So to speak."

I smile and shrug. "It doesn't change me. I'm just—don't you think it's possible to fall for a person just because you do? Even if they don't fit the script you thought you had for yourself? She's just so...I don't know. I don't think I've ever felt this way before." Emmy's watching me carefully, and I'm suddenly aware of how surprised I always am when she so completely listens to me. I feel a stammer inside and drop my chin back toward the earthen mug in my lap. The tea inside is cold. "I can't explain it, I guess."

She nods and watches me for a minute. "I get it. I think we all have a list in our minds of what we think would be best for us, and then we meet someone who just tosses the list out the window, maybe even without our permission."

"Like Henry?" I ask, and she shakes her head, smiling.

"I'm going to go take my shower," she says.

"Emmy?" I call, the words slipping out even though I know better. "Do you remember that night very well? The night of the accident?"

"Of course I do, I remember every bit of it." She sets her jaw, puts her hands on her hips, and I can tell I've sprung up against that wall again. "One of the two worst nights of my life, why wouldn't I remember it? Don't you think I wish I could forget about it? But I can't. Every time I look at you, I'm reminded of what I did to you. Don't you know that I carry that everywhere with me?" She stops herself, rubs a hand up to her temple, taps at the scar for me to see before she leaves, closing the door too hard.

I don't think she heard me, not really. She didn't hear my next question at all, the one that didn't even get past my lips. *Because I don't remember so well. Can you tell me?* What was I thinking, expecting Emerson to stay genuine with me? I rub my hands on my legs, my hateful legs. I do that a lot, I know, like a tongue searching for a missing tooth. You don't mean to keep going there, you just can't help yourself. I've lived more of my life without half my legs than I ever lived with them, and yet I still feel like it's some sort of trial, a temporary condition. I miss them terribly: those calves of mine, lean and strong, those shins, often bruised, those loose and agile ankles, those over-arched feet, those sandal-perfect, polished toes. Those parts I lost, how much of my self, my spirit, left with them?

After the accident, Butch Henley came to the house. I don't know if Emmy even knows that, that he came to see Dad. They were broken up, and Dad was pretty mad about it; he'd planned on Butch coming to work for him after he had his accounting degree, and now his plans were supposed to change because of his daughter's romantic failure? At least that's how he put it to Mother when I overheard. When Butch was leaving, he came to my bedroom. I was sitting by the open window in the heavy wheelchair I had at the time. It was summer by then, and hot, and I sat that afternoon sweating in my shorts, listening to the same Joni Mitchell album on the record player over and over again, staring at my ugly legs, at how roughly, how rudely, they stopped, just above where my knees used to be. He tapped at the door and came into my room, which he'd never done before. *Don't do it*, he said, in that golden baritone of his, *Don't jump*. And I turned my head, just so he could see the tightness of my jaw. *Why the fuck not?* I said, so seventeen. He sat in the window seat and looked me in the eyes until I looked at him. It was so sweaty hot, and the maple's wilting leaves outside my window fluttered, but I couldn't feel a breeze. Karl Henley was perfect, even with a stupid nick-name, tall and football broad, his blond hair combed sideways, his blue eyes like precious metal, his white shirt buttoned, so uncool for 1974. *I won't be seeing you again*, he said. *Your sister...* he shook his head. *She's turned everything against me. The university, my scholarship, your father. She doesn't know how hard I've worked, how much I deserve this. She doesn't understand*. And all I could think was how handsome he was, how perfect, but with an edge, a sharp edge. Those eyes that could turn stormy in a flash, the times when our wrestling felt a little scary to me, and how even that was a turn on. And here I sat, with my ugly, sawed-off legs, and not even a blanket to hide under. And that was when he reached forward, his hand on my face, he lifted my jaw and he kissed me. I was startled but good, but when I tried to pull back, he grabbed my wrist, just for a second, he grabbed me, he took something from me, just the tiniest something in that moment when the kiss lasted longer than I wanted. I was scared, and later felt a deep gut understanding of what horrible things men can do, if they choose, and that was just a kiss. *Maybe I picked the wrong sister*, he said. When he left, the record started again, and I cried and cried and cried.

I turn in my wheelchair and roll toward my paints in the corner by the north window. There is no reason to tell Emmy about that kiss, and yet I'm tempted. I told Stanley once, early in our marriage when the bedroom darkness felt safe and deep, and he said, *That guy's just got a different life lesson than you, that's all*, and I remember pulling the blanket closer, left alone as I was in the cold.

Eve slips

It's a perfect blue-sky June afternoon, and I'm distracted by the swallows outside. They fly like guardsmen in self-important loops and I'm reminded of visiting the wall in Berlin when Adam had business there. Adam told me the wall wasn't actually halfway between, and when I scraped my hand on the graffitied side, I was actually standing in East Berlin. I felt like a renegade, an arrow standing straight up for freedom in my linen dress and walking shoes. I would have made a good emancipator, I know, or a freedom fighter, if Adam had let me.

I'm in the kitchen making picnic sandwiches—two for Henry, one and a half for Addie and me—while the curtains dance over the sink and the breeze blows in the smell of warm grass and sunshine. I have more annuals sitting in flats in the shade, but they can stand to wait until after lunch. I have fresh Bing cherries, cucumber spears with salt, iced tea, and my homemade chocolate chip cookies. I have an oversized plaid blanket with black tassels nearly worn off the edges, my sunhat, and a basket big enough to hold it all. Adam used to pretend he had little patience for such trifles, but the truth was he loved my excursions, my distractions, my suggestion to miss the last ferry just to spend an extra night on a foreign island with only the clothes on our backs and no toothbrush in sight. He was such a staid and orderly businessman; he needed to be led off the path from time to time.

I'm cutting the crust from Addie's sandwich and watching squirrels play outside when the knife slips and I hear myself make a soft sound like "Oh!" I watch my finger bleed onto the wheat bread, and there is that moment when there is no pain, only interest, surprise at what our bodies can do, what strangeness we have inside. Then, sharp pain, and I'm running my finger under cold tap water and watching blood drip into the bleached white sink. I will not die well, this I know. I think one should be entirely present at such an important moment, and I know I will be distracted. I could be run over in the street or gunned down by a gangster, and still I will notice the ants running errands on the sidewalk beside me or the rain on my face or the sound of an ice cream truck on the next block.

I hear footsteps behind me and turn to see Addie's face looking pale and pinched. She watches the blood from my finger drip into the sink, making perfect red food-coloring puddles against the white.

"Oh honey," I say, "It's nothing. It's a scratch." I grab a dish towel and squeeze it to my hand and turn to her with a smile. I see something in her eyes, like a flash of starlight from a quickly closing door, and take a step toward her just as she steps toward me. She wraps her soft arms around my waist as her shoulder fits under my arm; she buries her face against my chest, nearly pushing me over with the force of her hug. I feel her body move in a heavy, shaking sigh, but I cannot tell if there are tears on her cheeks. I lean my cheek against the top of her head—her black hair smelling rich and warm with sunshine—and hold her breastbone close, wishing just the force of me could be protection enough.

"It's okay, it's okay…" I whisper to her shut eyes and sing, *"Don't you know the lilac's bloomed, the skies are blue, the swans, my dear, are on the pond, the only thing missing is you…"* I take her cool-palmed hand in mine—her left to my right; my other hand I raise skyward, like one of Henry's gestures, and keep the compress tight. I swing her arm one-handed and sing to her gently tear-spotted face, *"Tell my handsome soldier the only thing missing is you dear, the only thing missing is you…"* She sings quietly with me the parts she remembers.

"I like that song," she says, when I finish. "I never heard it before you."

"Are you ready for our picnic? Will you run get Henry?"

She nods and hustles out, and in my mind's eye I can see her running down the back porch, past the new plantings, over to the tall, wooden fence separating the two properties and down past, all the way past the boathouse—Henry's old haunt—and to the pebbled beach and then back up, through Henry's stone garden and to his ever-open back door. Will she pause, I wonder, at the place in the fence where the hidden gate is overgrown and rusted shut? That is the gate that Emerson used to visit Henry every day when she and Will lived here together. That is the gate that her son Michael walked through when he found his father, blue lipped and loose limbed, a foot off the ground. That is the gate she cursed, in her cold and silent way, as if it were the passage to be hated, instead of the destination. Perhaps Addie will pause, remembering her moonlit walking dream that I saw from my widow's walk, and look carefully from Henry's side at the unused gate and wonder at the inefficiencies of these grown-up people who are supposed to be managing the world.

The bleeding has stopped, but a loose flap of skin gapes at the tip of my index finger. I find a waterproof Band-Aid, then gather up the picnic things and make my way outside, under the darting swallows and bright noon sun to the tall grass of the front horse pasture where I intend us to lunch. I spread the black-tasseled blanket, plant my rear firmly on one corner, and lean back, arms cupped behind my head for a pillow, the blue sky and still clouds a benediction, a blanket for my sun-happy soul.

"Eve! Eve!" I sit up to see Henry calling for me by the old empty barn and wave my arms over my head.

"Over here!" I yell, startling a red-winged blackbird in the middle of his song.

"Damn, this grass is long," he says. "Why didn't you tell me it was this bad up here? Makes me feel like I'm neglecting you." He tramps forward, his blond hair corkscrewing up like frosting peaks in a mixer. He looks to Addie beside him and says, "This is bad, right? Needs a mowing, right?" and she nods emphatically.

"Henry, your hair looks like meringue," I say. "Did you know that?"

He laughs and shakes his head and drops himself down to the blanket beside me just as Addie does the same. He's holding something, a small tan box of some sort. I lean over, kiss his cheek and ruffle his hair, and he ducks his chin like a favored pet. He looks happier than he did this morning and I tell him so.

"A little work, you know, it's good for the soul," he says. "Do you ever find that to be true, Addie?"

She bobs her head up and down. "Sometimes when I'm doing the chores, I can think of stories easier. I can imagine what people are doing. But then I sometimes forget to write them down."

"Ain't that the truth?" Henry says, and I laugh. The sun is really too bright for all of this, but if my children—my surrogates—are willing to carry this daydream along, then I am too. Funny to me that my earthly children, the ones of my blood, are not anywhere to be found, nor, truthfully, invited. They wear me down, my girls. It is much easier to mother other people's children, I've found, because there is less muck to wade through, less implied by every gesture. These two here, they love me—they love me. I start handing food around and smile to watch them begin so eagerly.

"What did you bring?" I ask, nudging Henry's box gently.

"Found these old cigars. Emmy brought them to me. They used to be Will's."

"Who's that?" Addie asks, around a mouthful of sandwich.

"Emerson's husband. He died before you were born," Henry says through his own mouthful.

"Will," she says softly. "Mrs. Worthy and Will. How did he die?"

Henry looks at me and I reach for Addie's hand. "He was unhappy, honey. He was so unhappy it made him sick."

"Oh," she says, "Like cancer?"

"Like cancer of the soul. Like a hurting heart that just won't stop hurting."

Addie nods and says, "Like my mom."

I squeeze her fingers. "Look up," I say. "Look at that."

All three of us lean back on our corners of the blanket, surrounded as we are by overly tall green grass, and raise our faces to the perfect blue sky. Above our heads, fluffs of cotton fly by, carried by a sweet and gentle breeze. Thanks be that I don't have allergies, I think, as I watch the white puffs sail past.

"They're like fairies," Addie says. "They're all going to the same place, look!"

"Oh, Henry," I say, remembering. "Before you mow this field, will you trim back the white rhodie by the fence? The one by the gate?"

He looks at me, chewing his cucumber thoughtfully. Addie drinks tea from her mason jar and loses some onto her shirt, unfazed. "Are you sure," he says, "that your daughter would want that?"

"It's time," I say, watching Addie watch the cottonwood over-head. "Besides, my legs are too old to keep taking the long way around. I need a shortcut to your place."

"Eve," he says, laughing, "you're not close to old. I'll let you know when you start to even look old."

"That reminds me, I have something to show you. Stay here!" I climb to my feet and brush my skirt clean. My cheeks feel warm from the sun and my cut finger is throbbing and I feel flushed with love for my company. And Adam too, he's felt close again lately in a way he hasn't for years. Maybe it's the coming of Addie, his great-grandchild. Maybe he's been lingering to get a glimpse. I hurry to the barn and drag the ladder back through the grass.

"Oh, damn, Eve, let me help you..."

"No, no, no. Just watch steady now!"

Both of them watch me intently as I drag the ladder to the birdbox pole. One of the adult bluebirds flies away just as I get near, and the hatchlings get suddenly quiet and still. "Don't you know?" I whisper. "Just me, just me..." I set up the ladder and look over my shoulder at the picnic blanket where the two lie, heads propped on arms, a carbon-copy if you can overlook color and size. I smile and lift a hand in a small wave, then turn back and begin to climb. It is a warm day and now all the birds are still. I look up to see a red-tailed hawk circling high over the road, and all around me cotton fluff flying past, lightly, steadily traveling to wherever it's supposed to go. I reach a hand over to the birdbox stoop to see if the worms I brought this morning are gone. I hear one tiny, reassuring *Peep!* from inside, and then the ladder is leaning, the world is tipping. I reach for the birdbox but too late, and my mind knows only blue sky overhead, like a fledging bird—or a falling bird—would know. I am falling backward, I don't make a sound, the sun is warm on my face, cotton sails by, and I hear a shout from Henry. When I hit the ground, my breath is pushed right out of my body, my head slams the sunbaked ground, and then warm, warm blackness.

Emerson slips

It's a hot afternoon at the Lake Oswego house, and I open long-closed windows, letting in air to banish the stale stillness. Dust has settled in the corners, and I feel a little forgotten walking through the quiet carpet hall. I don't love this house. I've never loved this house, with its well-appointed views and high-end zip code, but I feel I belong here. I feel it is a perfect, appropriate match for me in a way the Looking Lake house has never been. When I'm there, I feel like a child at someone else's Christmas party, where there are no presents for me. It is better to be alone by choice than left alone in a group of others.

It wasn't always like that. When Will and I found the place, I had such magnificent visions—we both did—of the kind of vibrant life we could live, as if even the land itself was breathing new hope into our skin. It was needed; Michael was soon to be off at school, our marriage had grown heavy with obligation and resentment, as all of them do, made worse by the depression he mostly refused to manage. We worked so hard to build the Looking Lake house into our renaissance—we planned, we crafted, we hired, we gossiped, we hosted, we were liked and wanted. And then, of course, there was Henry. Meeting him was like walking through a new part of the city, when you realize that people live and thrive in ways magnificently different from your own. He was the first male friend I ever had that didn't have a job with stock options or a retirement plan. He was so warm, so solid; I felt safe with him in a way I never felt with Will. Will who was likely to burn like fever all night, pacing the hall like a tiger while I begged him to take his medication. Will who fired a friend during an argument over a lunch tab. Will who charmed me into taking overnight trips with him, only to abandon me in a hotel suite in a strange city while he crept the streets all night as I watched dawn paint the ceiling and waited for him to find his way back to me.

But Henry was granite. I was never physical with him, but I forever wanted to slide my body against his chest, lean in, and tumble like waves into his safe, strong cove. The attraction was secondary—I'd be lying if I said it wasn't there—but it was secondary to my desire to be loved by him, protected by him, stock options or no, patched jeans or no.

After Will died, I returned to the Lake Oswego house because it was easier, because I could be alone. The long shadows and dark corners don't frighten me, the cool summers and insulated winters help keep me numb, because the truth is that love of husband, of neighbor, of sunlit country home, leads only to the unsettling of things, only to pain. And nothingness is frankly better.

After my run this morning, I showered and dressed and checked that Mother had an eye on Addie and came back here to this house. I had to collect the bag of mail from my neighbors across the way and throw some food away, and now here I find myself alone. I try to think of Robert and our nice afternoon date yesterday, but I keep coming back to Henry. As I watched the young round tow truck driver from AAA change the flat tire on my Lexus, I kept thinking, *Henry could do this part himself, and faster too, and with better jokes.* The greasy-shirted man kept saying, *Someone sure did a number on this one, yep, someone wasn't messing around,* until I finally offered him five dollars to shut up, only I said it nicer, said, *A bit of quiet so I can think, please?* which he obliged.

I pull a bottle of flavored water from the fridge and stand in my immaculate kitchen. I walk to the window over the sink to look out at the sun sparkles on the cold lake, thinking I need to reschedule a Monday meeting, thinking I need to tell Jack White once and for all that his wine book is a bad idea, thinking that I need to call Michael to find out when he plans on collecting the child. The raspberry water is flat—tastes old—and I see my sour face reflected in the fixtures as I start to pour the rest into the sink. My hand jumps—*Oh my God!*—and I splash pink water on my shirt like a frightful baptism. In the bottom of the sink is a boot print, a muddy boot print pointing at my now-wet chest, the edges blurring as it's swept away by the red-tinged water. I grab the edge of the counter and spin around, one hand clamped hard to my mouth, listening so hard it hurts. Nothing, nothing, the tick of the mantle clock, the bark of a neighbor's dog, the quiet of sunlight spilling into my deserted house. *Breached*, I keep thinking, *breached house*. I look back at the sink, to the counters, to the high-polished floor, not another mark anywhere. The window over the sink is large and slides open to the upper deck, and the latch—I can see now—is broken, hanging half-free. My skin prickles; the hair raises on the back of my neck, and I feel a noise rise in my throat that I have to cram back down. I dive for my purse on the counter and scramble for my phone inside.

"911."

"There's someone in my house," I whisper. "Please, there's someone here."

Stupidly, the woman has to tell me to get out, get to a neighbor's, if I can do so safely, and I sneak down the entry to the front door, the sound of gravel burning my ears as I run to my Lexus parked in the drive. I dive in, and my breath is loud in the hot afternoon quiet, the sound of my interior door lock a very reassuring *Thunk!* to my highly-tuned ears. From my driver's seat, I survey the exterior of the house, the potted plants and pruned decorative trees, the empty bird-feeder, the neighbor's red-painted wooden duck spinning gaily in a breeze. We never had an alarm on the house, either house; Will said he'd never bow to such pedestrian fears. Now I'm kicking myself, my own high-born stupidity. The world feels deserted; I'm the only survivor. I wonder if Henry is alone right now, or if he's screwing one of his women in his father's tiny cabin when he should be here with me. I remember him suddenly at one of our parties, pushed casually against the porch rail by an overly-friendly woman—a close talker, one of those—and catching his eye in the twilight dark, lit by torches and the ends of men's cigars, and his wink, his slow and easy smile like a secret we shared, even as Will kissed the back of my neck.

Two cruisers glide down the drive, and I leap from the Lexus to meet the officers, one a K-9 unit. Two officers and the K-9 walk the house and return shortly, telling me it's empty now. A female officer with smart eyes takes my statement, "Do you have any idea…? Is anything missing…? Do you know who did this…?"

"No and no and no," I say.

I jump when my cell rings and hesitate when I don't recognize the number. But the blond officer is watching me, so I turn aside and answer. It's Henry, calling from a courtesy phone at the hospital.

"Eve's fallen," he says, and I want to laugh; it sounds like the preamble to one of the Adam and Eve jokes. "Emerson? Your mother's had an accident," he says, and again I clamp my hand to my mouth to stop any sound from escaping. I take a deep breath, close my eyes, open them again to interior calm, like a stage curtain closing inside. "Can you come?" he says. "Can you?"

I tell Henry I'm ten minutes away. "How bad is she?" I ask importantly, and I feel removed, as if I'm tending to an injured pet, or someone else's crisis.

"She was unconscious," he says, as if that's an answer. The officer has my statement, another offers an escort to the hospital, which I decline. I leave them there, in my rearview mirror, as I brush my hair back and pull my sunglasses down. I pull my cell out, but I'm not sure who to call. Well, Tillie, of course, but I hate to do so until I have the facts, and Henry's probably done so already. The family lawyer? One of Mother's canasta friends? I don't even know the name of her doctor these days.

I drive distractedly to the freeway, then to the hospital. What could have happened? Perhaps she fell in the bathroom? In the kitchen? But what made her fall? She's a spry woman still; a stroke perhaps? An embolism? The list grows frightfully long in my mind as I consider the effects of age and feel the sudden heavy weight of responsibility. Surely Tillie isn't equipped for this, and Henry either; really, I'm all they have.

I feel surreal driving into the parking garage, patiently circling higher floors for a spot. How many goddamn people are in a hospital that they need parking garages these days? I dash to the emergency entrance, my purse banging on my hip, my hair falling into my eyes. I scan quickly, my pulse pounding, and see Henry against the white wall, sitting in a molded plastic chair, one hand on Addie's stiff shoulder beside him. They both look cookie-cutter still, and even in that moment—that moment of fear, of terror—he is beautiful to me.

"Where is she?" I ask fiercely. "Where is she?"

His eyes flash vulnerable and bright as he stands and says, "They're transferring her, she's on her way upstairs. She's conscious now, but we can't see her yet. We waited here for you."

I look at his face, then down to Addie's anguished eyes, and drop to my knees in front of her, onto the hard cold tile. I put my hand on her cheek, so soft, and pull her close to me. She's warm in my arms, a humming, living thing, and I can feel her tremble as she pushes her face into my neck.

"I'm here," I whisper. "It's okay, I'm here, I'm here."

I hold her close, so tight, this beautiful child I'm afraid of, and look up into Henry's wrenched and weary eyes. My throat is closed tight, my lips shake, the tears slip from my eyes. I reach my hand for his, and his fingers cover mine.

"I'm sorry," I whisper. "I'm so sorry."

He shakes his head, *No, no,* and then someone is saying Mother's name, and I stand, trying quickly to assemble my fractured self, to appear self-assured. *Yes, yes, I'm her daughter, I'm the one to speak with.* I follow the woman down the hall to the elevator and look back once to see Henry with his arms around Addie, his face pressed into her hair.

In the elevator, I'm trying to listen, trying to comprehend, "A stroke caused by a small blood clot, followed by a mild concussion from the fall, she's conscious now, resting, needs to be kept under observation, there may be another." The nurse is young and serious as she leads me to Mother's room. I pause in the door-way and the nurse stops to look at me, her eyes on my face like she's seeing me for the first time.

"Your mother was lucky," she says softly. "She wasn't alone. We got her quickly." I look at the nurse as if she's speaking a for-eign language, and then I look over to the hospital bed. Mother is small in the white bed, sleeping like a child in a cocoon of IV and oxygen tubes.

"Damn it," I whisper. "Goddamn it." I walk to her bedside and take her hand in mine, her white skin paper-thin. "I'm not ready for this," I whisper. "Not for this, not with you."

The doctor walks in and starts talking quickly and I can't hear him, even as I nod in response, biting my lip. He does something to the clipboard by the foot of her bed and I pull up a chair, still holding her weightless hand. A stroke, my distracted, tenacious mother. She looks like a miniature version of herself, as if some-one's projected an image of her, shrunk by degrees. My chest feels heavy and dark, and I feel nineteen again, sitting at Tillie's bedside in her fluorescent, antiseptic hospital room. *Why in God's name do we go through the work of loving each other? Why do we allow ourselves to be punished by so much goddamned pain?*

"I'm not ready to lose you yet," I tell her, stroking her thin white hair. "I'm not fucking ready. Do you hear me?"

I don't know how long I sit there before Tillie comes; she rolls up beside me, her face looking pasty and punched, interrupted. I let go of Mother's hand and fold my arms around her in a tight hug as the wet springs to my cheeks again. We sit together and cling, and I feel glacially cold and wordless.

I want to ask her why we bother to love anyone, but I can't, I can't. My hip is crushing into her hateful metal chair—the one I put her in, my vibrant, capable baby sister—and I welcome the pain of it, the sharp discomfort an outlet, a punishment. Tillie's voice is steady and low, like a swaying in the wind, and I feel myself calming by degrees as I slowly warm in her sun-baked arms. *When did you get so strong?* I think. *When did you arrive at this?* She's telling me I should go, that I should be with Addie, that we'll work in shifts to stay by Mother's bedside.

"I won't leave you here," I say, feeling sea-swept. "I won't leave Mother here."

Tillie's hand is light on my cheek, and her eyes are strong. "Right now, Addie needs you more. And I think probably Henry needs you too. I'll be here, it's okay. We'll take turns."

I'm scattered as I try to stand from my chair, and I realize the afternoon has turned to evening outside. I raise my shoulders up and try to breathe as another nurse checks Mother yet again. She's stirring more in her sleep, and I think perhaps she'll wake up soon, but Tillie assures me she'll call when that happens.

"Okay, okay," is all I can think to say. I look down at my beautiful, clear-eyed sister and squeeze her shoulder. "Thank you," I say quietly and kiss the top of her head.

She nods. "You too," she says.

When I leave the hospital, it is nearly full dark, and I drive to the Looking Lake house on autopilot. Henry's Bronco is in our drive, which I've never seen before, and it looks like all the lights in the house are on. I remember, for a minute, the Lake Oswego house and the footprint in my sink, but it seems so far away, so unimportant, like a movie whose ending I just don't care to see. I park by Mother's Mercedes and let myself in, quietly. Henry's at the kitchen table playing solitaire, and when he looks up at me, I feel my heart catch in my throat to be seen so clearly, to be so deeply and suddenly known.

"Addie?" I say.

"She's in the bath. I made us dinner, but she didn't eat much. How's Eve?"

"Stable," I say, my voice shaking around the word. "Tillie will call. We'll take shifts."

He stands so quickly he knocks the red wooden chair over behind him and crosses to me like a flood. His arms wrap around me, marble strong, and hold me and hold me. I press my cheek against his white cotton T-shirt, feeling his heart beat like a talisman, the pulse of his life: his strength, my protection. The muscles in his back are rock-strong beneath my hands and I cannot hold him tightly enough. We stand together, and I can feel him, my chest to his chest, my blood matched to his blood, and the force of it frightens me, but I do not pull away.

"Emmy," he says, "Emmy." He steps back to look me in the eye and I'm suddenly afraid he's going to kiss me. *Not now*, I think. *I cannot do that now.*

"I have to talk to you," he says. "I have to talk to you."

I cover my face with my hands as my chest tightens, and all I can think is that more pain is coming, that more of this life is rushing in my face whether I like it or not, that more will be expected of me and that I'll be lacking, that I cannot possibly handle the force of it, this life of pain and regret.

Addie slips

I wake to sunlight on the wall and remember that something is wrong again. I remember that feeling from Auntie Lu's—sleeping on her lumpy hide-a-bed couch that made my nose itch, waking to that hurt-stomach feeling of *Mama, Mama!* and the smell of cigarettes and breakfast frying in a strange place. Now it's Ms. Eve and a big empty house and no smells of breakfast at all. I tiptoe into the hall and try to listen for whatever news the silence may tell, but the wood floor carries no one else's footsteps. I didn't go walking last night; I didn't think it was a good idea, even though I wanted to. I wanted to go sit by the lake and watch the moon and have prayer-thoughts for my loved ones. Instead, I laid in bed with Mrs. Anderson and a pile of books, so I wouldn't be any trouble, and stared at the walls, the big wooden desk, the bookends that for some reason are on different shelves, the rich and fabulous things forgotten by everyone else in the dark. I don't think I like this house anymore. Not without Ms. Eve in it.

In the kitchen is a note from Mrs. Worthy that she's gone back to the hospital, and I don't think Tillie came home at all. I feel small in the cool and the quiet, like a marble that's been kicked away and forgotten. Someone has left cereal out for me and a bowl and a spoon. Henry's big truck is still in the driveway, so I know he's still here somewhere. And they wouldn't have really left me alone, I don't think. I don't feel very hungry, but the Carnation Instant Breakfast is out, so I make myself a cup. Mama is maybe-dying, and Ms. Eve is maybe-dying, and even though I guess we all are maybe-dying, all the time, it doesn't make me feel any better. It's hard to swallow, and I feel suddenly shy in my nightdress, that maybe if someone comes they will need to take me somewhere, and quickly, like to the hospital, or back to the airport. I don't know what's going to happen. I hurry to dress and take Mrs. Anderson outside.

It's chilly out even though the sun is up, and it will probably be hot again later. The house blocks the sun from getting to the porch in the morning and the shadows are cold. I walk down to the lake, like I would have in the dark if I'd gone, and drag my shoes in the grass because I like the feel of it. No one is around. I don't know where Henry is, but I'm feeling a little worried. *Doesn't anyone want to check on me?*

The lake is glossy and delicious-looking in the slanting morning sun, and I wish I could take a big mouthful. There aren't any boats yet, and I like it best when it's peaceful. I hunker down on the gravel next to the boat house, Mrs. Anderson hunkering with me, and watch a blue heron stand like a statue in the shallow water nearby. The morning breeze pushes my unbraided hair around, and I squeeze my legs with my arms and bite my knee, holding on tight like a small planet trying to keep its place among all these bigger stars. I don't want to be here. I don't want to be anywhere. I rock in the tiny wind and let myself cry onto the gravel.

I hear a wooden *Smack!* and my shoulders jump. I turn to see Henry stumble out of the boathouse behind me, wearing the same clothes from last night. He squints at the brightness and something is wrong with his eyes, like he can't see well. He looks at me like I'm a polar bear that just showed up on his beach and he's not sure what to do about it. He walks around the backside of the boathouse and I can hear him peeing like a little boy would do. I guess he slept in there, and I guess he has to pee, but it makes me feel like I'm the grown-up here and he's the kid. He comes back around the boathouse and leans up against the wood. His blond hair looks like he slept in a windstorm, and his white T-shirt isn't looking so white anymore. His legs slide down until he's sitting on the ground and I watch him yank a pack of cigarettes from his jeans pocket and light one.

"That's bad," I say.

"Yeah," he says. "Well, so am I." He isn't like the person I know, the Henry I know. He's cold like a teenager, and I'm suddenly mad that they left me here with him.

"What's wrong with you?" I say, and I know I sound angry.

Henry smokes his cigarette and I watch smoke come out his nose. He puts one hand over his red eyes and raises his other hand to me, as if to say, *Don't.*

I stand up and throw a rock in the water. It makes a satisfying *Plunk!* so I put Mrs. Anderson down and pick up a whole handful and throw them in. I want to ask him if Ms. Eve is even still alive, if he even knows. I throw another handful of rocks, and the blue heron raises her wings and flies away, and I'm glad. I hear crows crying far off, and that is how I feel inside. I throw another handful of rocks and Henry says, "Can't you just stop already?"

I feel my chest get big with breathing, and my face is warm even though the rest of me is still cold, and I pick up a big rock, I do, and I turn and throw it at him, as hard as I can, at his closed-eyes, crumpled self. It hits his shoulder and he startles, his red eyes big and hurt and then angry.

"What the hell—!" he yells, and I turn and run up the grass slope toward the house. I don't know if he's following me, so I keep running without looking back. My stomach hurts and I run past the place where the gate is hidden in the fence, past the big white house with nobody inside, past Henry's truck parked slant-wise. I run all the way to the too-tall grass in the front meadow, past where the picnic blanket still lies damply from yesterday, all the way to Eve's birdhouse on a pole. I drop down to the grass and curl up, clutching my stomach that hurts so bad, listening for the sound of Henry chasing me. All I can hear is my fast heartbeat and the sound of my own heavy breathing. I roll over so I can look at the sky, the growing blue sky, and the faint morning moon. She's growing fat, on her way to full, my moon. I hold Mama's bear amulet in my hand and make quick prayers, but the only word I can think to whisper is *Please, please.* I don't know where I am supposed to be, but it isn't here, it isn't in this far-away place, it isn't so deeply away from Mama. Even if she were with me, she'd be far away. I don't think children are supposed to feel these feelings, these lonely in the wet grass, stomach-hurt feelings of alone and rock-throwing and people-dying. I know I'm in trouble with Henry; I know I did a really bad thing. Maybe they will send me back for that reason. But where will they send me back to? The wet leaks out of my eyes and runs down into my ear and my heart aches and aches for Ms. Eve and Mama both.

I watch wispy clouds form and separate, and I think that would be a good way to be. Ms. Eve is like that, those clouds. My breathing calms down, and I can hear again outside of myself, and then comes a tiny pipping sound from just overhead. *The baby birds! Ms. Eve's birds!* The ladder is nearby, and I think to set it up but then I remember the image of Ms. Eve on the step and the wooden ladder tipping, like in slow motion, and her falling to the ground. I stand up, and the babies are quiet at my loudness. I want to whisper that I'm good and won't hurt them, but then I remember hitting Henry and wonder that maybe I'm not so good after all. Don't have to tell the birds that. I stand quietly holding the pole, not caring that Henry can see me now over the tall grass, if he's even looking. I glance over my shoulder, but no one is at the house. I hear an engine on the quiet road, and watch a dark blue car drive slowly past. Funny because most people seem to drive really fast on that road.

After a minute, the car comes back from the other way and slows down across the street from the house. It's far from me still—I couldn't throw a rock that far if I tried—but the driver rolls the window down and waves and calls something to me. I walk through the tall grass all the way to the road and lean up against the wooden fence to see him. He's on the other side of the road, smiling and leaning part-way out his window. Mama always says not to talk to strangers, but everyone here is a stranger, so what am I supposed to do?

"Hello there!" he says.

He is old—old like Tillie, not like Ms. Eve—and has blue eyes like something expensive and tan arms and a fancy silver watch. He looks like the tourists look in Anchorage—not the Japanese ones, the white ones. I expect him to tell me he's lost and then I will say I don't know my way around and anyway, he's supposed to ask a grown-up, not a kid, because people will think he's trying to trick kids into his car.

"Is Emerson home?" he asks, and his voice has a nice music to it, a rich sound like a radio announcer.

I shake my head no. "She's at the hospital."

"Oh no!" he says, covering his mouth with his hand like worried people do. "Is she hurt? Which hospital?"

"No," I say. "It was Ms. Eve—"

A pickup truck filled with watermelons drives between us on the road, and he shakes his head and squints his eyes. He motions me with his arm, and I climb between the two wooden parts of the fence. I have to wait for another car to pass by fast before I can cross over to where his car's idling, pulled off to the side. I have to stand close to his arm to stay out of the road, and I can smell the rich red-jewel smell of his cologne and under it, the faint smell of smoked cigarettes. He is very handsome, like an actor.

"No, it was Ms. Eve. She fell. She had a stroke, they said."

"Oh no, oh my God. Emmy must be devastated. Which hospital, do you know?"

I shake my head slowly. His words are the right words, but his eyes look like they're trying to figure out mine. I take a step backward, and he grabs my sleeve just as a big SUV drives past with Jet Skis behind.

"Watch out now," he says in his musical voice and smiles.

"You can call her," I say. "I don't know anything."

He reaches up to my hair and gently pulls a piece of grass away. "Been playing this morning, have you?" he says. "I like your necklace."

"I think you should just call her," I say.

"Here," he says, offering me a pack of green mint gum. Beside him on the seat, I can see a map and a bag and a silver lighter. "Here, have one." He shakes one stick out and smiles his handsome smile, and I get that pit-of-my-stomach feeling all of a sudden, but my stupid hand reaches forward to get the gum anyway. His other hand clamps my wrist and pulls me to the car door and I drop my gum just as another car drives past.

"Hey! Hey!" I hear big feet slap the pavement and then Henry is there, grabbing me hard. He pulls me back and behind him as he steps up to the door of the man's car. He slams his hands against the window frame and then reaches in to grab the guy's shirt.

The man raises his hands, like *I give*. "What are you gonna do here, pull me out? Assault me? I was just asking questions."

Henry's hands loosen but his whole body is tense. His face is red, and the veins in his neck are sticking out.

"Just a little lost, my friend. Your girl here was helping me."

"Get the fuck out of here."

"Will do, brother. No harm, no foul." He leans around Henry and looks at me. "Tell her I said hi, okay?"

I nod dumbly as he smiles and winks, then drives off fast, leaving tracks in the grass at the edge of the road. Henry watches him drive away and then looks at me and shakes his head, panting. "Addie, damn."

I step backwards away from him as the fear breaks open in me and I start to shake. I back all the way across the road into the wooden fence and I'm crying, I can feel the man's big hand on my wrist, I can hardly see Henry at all, and my legs won't hold me. But then he's there, and he's not mad, he's hugging me, his arms around me like something safe, and I shake and shake, and he holds me. He's on the grass, we're both on the grass, our backs against the fence, and my face is half-buried against his safe chest, and all I can say is, "I'm sorry, I'm sorry," and I can see the green-wrapped mint gum on the ground across the road.

He just says, "It's okay, it's okay," over and over again.

When I look up, the sun is higher, the day is starting to grow into its warmth, and Henry has ahold of me like a father would do, I think. His eyes are still red-rimmed, but I can see him again, like he's back inside himself, almost like he never left.

"I'm sorry," I say. "The rock. It slipped."

He pulls the collar of his T-shirt over and motions down with his chin, and we both look at his shoulder, at the red welt there.

"I know, kid," he says. "We both slipped."

Six

Henry deals

The morning sun has baked me out of my T-shirt, and my sweat smells like Will's single malt scotch, stinging blood-shot eyes as I squint in the glare. I am tackling the head-high rhodie by the garden gate, and the handsaw keeps slipping from my dumb, calloused hands. Sticky white petals are everywhere, stuck to my boots like packed snowfall, like a final dispatch home from the bush I'm murdering. If Tillie were here, she'd say a prayer; all I have is a litany of *goddamns* and *sons of bitches*. My head pounds and I feel like a fucking idiot; Addie hovering on Emmy's lawn behind me just serves to further remind me my failings. I keep seeing her by the guy's car on the other side of the street and the tremendous distance I had to cross to reach her there. How do we let our people venture out into the world at all? Fucking terrible parent I would be; I want to scream at them all for leaving me in charge. But Eve is stable, Emmy says, awake and making groggy jokes. Tillie should be coming home soon, I think.

The rhodie branches are heavy as stones, falling to my feet. I saw most-ways through the biggest branch and kick at it violently, punching it down and down and down. I remember Emerson in my arms last night, me holding tight like a drowning man, breathing in the sweet smell of her in her mother's kitchen, my heart thrumming against hers. I said, *We need to talk*, and she said, *No and no and no*. Will's cigar box sitting behind me on the table and the words I could not say, the words she would not hear.

I'll have to get the shovel to dig out the big taproot, but the bush is gone, suddenly there is a wide open breathing space of room, the garden gate exposed and vulnerable.

"Addie, kid. Can you run to my house? I've got some WD-40 on my workbench, okay?"

She runs off down toward the lake, and I watch her small and perfectly round form in the sun, stuck deeply as I am in my own stony self. I toss the branches into the wheelbarrow, and then she's back, breathing hard, the blue can in her hand and my new black snowcap in the other hand. "Here," she says. "I got your hat."

Her eyes are open and forgiving, and I feel like an asshole again, the bruised skin on my shoulder a reminder of my own ugliness. "You're the best," I say, pulling the black BFF cap over my sweaty hair. I step over the protruding root to oil the hinges on the gate, then put my hand on the cool metal latch. The sweat on my bare back is suddenly cool too, and I shiver at the cold touch, a memory of pain so swift and deep it hurts even to breathe.

"Henry? Aren't you going to open it?" she asks, and her wide cheeks look soft and worried in the sunlight.

I close my eyes and depress the latch, then swing the gate open toward us both. When I open my eyes, I see my own stone garden, the cedar pergola like a beacon in the center, and I swear I can smell his cologne. We stand together, she and I, and I cannot tell her what it was like to hear the scream, Michael's scream, and run from the boathouse with Emerson by my side in the twilight, what it was like to come to the open gate and see Will hanging by his neck in my yard. Self-assured Michael, swaggering, brilliant Michael, so like his father and mother both, standing and staring, a raging storm frozen before its torrential burst. And Will Worthy hanging from a rope, barefoot, his silk tie on the ground, his ivory-buttoned shirt open at the chest, his dead eyes open and vacant. I ran to him, I pushed Michael aside, I lifted him with all I had, I held the weight of him in my arms, like I had so many times before, in my bed, in my kitchen, in my shower. I yelled for help, my chest felt torn apart, I yelled and pleaded, and Emerson was there, arms around his legs and together we lifted and held, until Michael broke from his shock and stood the sawhorse upright. I climbed up, but it was no use, it was no use, and the sun kept setting and Will was still warm in my arms, and when the ambulance came, I fell to my knees on the hard stone pavers and part of me thinks I just never stood up again.

Addie's hand slips into mine and I look down, into her moon-bright, sun-lit concern. "Did you hurt yourself?" she asks.

"Yeah," I say. "Long time ago."

She holds my hand and leads me through, and it's just my house, just my garden, lit with spring sunshine and the bloom of accidental flowers. "It's good," Addie says. "It's really good. Thank you for fixing it. Now we can get back and forth so easy."

"So easy," I say, trying to breathe, trying to stand and breathe. I hear a car in my driveway on the other side of my cabin, and we both turn to look. There is a light step on the gravel, and Missy walks around the side of the house, toward the lake-side door that everyone uses.

"There you are," she says, her voice high as a pop song. "You've been a pain to get ahold of. Hi there again," she says to Addie.

"Now isn't a good time, Missy," I say, still holding Addie's hand as if her child-self can somehow keep me in orbit.

Missy shakes her blond hair in the sunlight and puts her fists on her hips. "Well, when will be?"

"I don't know," I say. "I don't know when I can."

She ducks her chin and her blue eyes show quick hurt. "You're an idiot, Henry. You don't even know how good you've got it." She turns her tennis-perfect body and waggles her fingers at me in goodbye. "It's a stupid hat, Henry!" she tosses at me, "White-bread wannabe gangsta hat!"

Addie squeezes my fingers, and I look down at her. "It's not a stupid hat," she whispers. "You don't look like a gangster."

"Thank you," I whisper back, and feel a tiny bit of warm inside. We close the gate and practice opening it from my side a few times. I'll have to trim back some bushes and dig out the rhododendron root, but otherwise it feels quite fine. Eve was right, I guess; it's time.

We hear Tillie calling for Addie and turn back through the gate. She's rolling her chair through the short grass toward us, and her face is bright with surprise at the garden gate.

"Look at you two!" she says, and I feel a boyish rush of pride. "Nice hat, Henry. I'm glad it came."

"How's Eve?"

"She's okay, she says she's just really tired. The doctors sound positive." Tillie opens her arms wide, and Addie hugs her, nearly climbing into her lap. "I brought home burgers for lunch," she says. "Ketchup only for you, young lady. Just how you like it. They're on the table inside." Addie hustles on up toward the house and Tillie reaches a hand for my face.

I drop to my knees on the grass beside her wheelchair, still shirtless and sweaty. She looks bright-eyed and blessed by the sun. "You opened the gate," she says, holding my cheek in the palm of her hand.

I drop my forehead onto her arm and she puts her hand on the back of my neck. "It hurts," I say. "It all still hurts."

"Henry, my Henry. It wasn't your fault, you know that. Don't you?"

I can't lift my eyes to look at hers, I just bury my face deeper into her earth-soft skin. I can feel the sun on my bare back and her hat on my head, the gift like a talisman, and her soft, strong hand on the back of my neck. I can feel her breathing.

"You don't know," I say finally. "You don't know what happened between us. I have to tell her."

She's so quiet for a minute, I think maybe she hasn't heard me. "What happened? Can you tell me?"

My breath hitches in my throat when I raise my head up, and the concern in her eyes makes my heart feel like breaking all over again. On my knees, at her side, I think, *Why does she love me, as I am?*

"Tillie, I think you're the only friend I have that I've never slept with. Well, except Lyman, and your mother. Why is that?"

Her eyes sparkle when she says, "Well, he's an old hippie, for one."

"Why not us? Not ever? Not once?"

"Is this a proposition?" she jokes, and my chest closes tight to not be heard. She reaches her hand to my shoulder and leaves it there until I'll look her in the eye again. "I could fall in love with you every day. Every day, I could. But would it matter? Would it change anything?" Her eyes are wide and damp and so strong I almost want to look away. "I love you, Henry. I couldn't love you more, I don't think." She smiles grandly, and I can see how tired she is. I feel suddenly guilty for doing this to her. "There aren't enough words," she says, "for all the kinds of love in this world."

"Me and Will…" I say, but don't know how to finish.

She nods and rubs my arm. "Then yes," she says, "you should tell Emmy."

"Damn. I knew you were going to say that."

"But here's something else, Henry. Whatever we think we know, or believe, about the things that happened to us? It isn't the whole story, sometimes it's not even the right story. She may need your story as much as you need hers. But if all you're looking for is absolution? Well then you may not be able to hear so well."

"I'm not sure I can deal with any of this," I hear myself say.

"Welcome to life, brother. It's bigger than all of us sometimes."

The back door opens, and Addie pads onto the porch, happy as a bear cub. "Well, are you going to eat or leave it all for me?"

Tillie laughs and says, "Be right in!"

"I'll catch up," I say, and she nods.

"I adore you Henry. You're my best friend." She rubs a hand across my black snow hat. "Don't kick your own ass too hard, okay? And lay off the scotch."

She turns in her chair and wheels away, back toward the house and the porch ramp. I sit on the grass so I can look at the lake, a perfect June blue today. My body feels beat up from my night in the boathouse and my throat burns from smoking again and my whole chest aches, like someone kicked in my heart. Tillie loves me and I never had to sleep with her for it. I think of Missy, Doc's wife, driving around the lake to her soulless castle, and feel so completely done with her that I don't know if she'll ever forgive me.

I don't know if Emmy will forgive me either. The first time she came to my cabin alone she was looking for Will, but he wasn't there. It was early spring and still cool, and as she stood in my little austere room, arms crossed for protection, I thought, *Damn, loosen up! I could teach you so much!* We ended up drinking lemonade—without the vodka—in my kitchen while I made us tuna melts. And the first time with Will—not the first visit, but the first *time*—we were in that same kitchen of mine, but instead of slicing cheese, I was weighing dime bags of pot, and he was smoking his Canadian cigarettes extravagantly, like a sultan in an old movie.

"You get much from dealing?" he asked, stubbing out his smoke.

"Not as much as lawyering'll get you, but a little."

"Fuck the man and all, is that it?"

"It's not a rebellion, dude. It's spreading the love—the earth is generous, you know. It fills us all. We're just some elements flung together ourselves, anyway." And I must have smiled too big or something, because he stepped across my tiny kitchen, put his hand on my shoulder, pushed my body upright and close to his.

"It's a crutch," he said. "It dulls a man, makes him weak. I don't like weak." Will Worthy didn't kiss me then—not until much later did he ever kiss me—but he pulled my tank top from my waistband and held me tight with his eyes while he unbuttoned my jeans. Every muscle in my body flexed in surprise, but I didn't turn away, didn't run from his challenge, didn't want to be that weakness he despised. He dropped to his knees on my dirty linoleum and his mouth was warm and my fingers found the back of his black hair, his strong hands on my hips, and I felt animal-strong and heavily-built, like I could bust rock with my bare hands, and together we did, we did, we did.

"Henry?" I hear Addie call from the porch.

I rub my itchy eyes with my hands and my heart aches, looking at the blue dream of sky above us all. It's never enough, what we get. The wanting just always seems bigger than the getting, and meanwhile we're all of us dying, just trying to hold on.

Tillie deals

The sun is really too warm to be out here, but it feels good to work my body. My spade is quick and true, and each seedling seems to whisper a thank you from its white packed roots to my dirt-soaked hand. I've put Addie to work with the garden hose, and she seems easy and happy. We are waiting to hear from Emmy at the hospital. I know I should be napping right now, like Henry, or worrying about Mother, but I'm just too amped and excited. Every muscle in my body is buzzing to think of Gavin. What that woman can do with her hands puts my years of marriage to shame! I think of my poor ex-husband, Stanley, mucking around on the beach with his poetry, and the waste of words always spilling from his side of the bed. All the things he wanted to do, was going to do, had plans to do, all the projects "in process" or "in dialogue" still, and which genius friend he'd met at which party, for which collaboration.

And his wanting of me, always like a private venture, as if I—the inside of me, the soul of me—was not even a participant. And I allowed it, because I didn't know it could be another way.

But Gavin, small and strong as a teenager, but soft, and slow, and deliberate. Yesterday, Sunday, I was at her house; I confess I was in her bed. She kissed my shoulder as if she'd never tasted one before. Her fingers on my cheek, her lips on my neck, she fed me ripe cherries—cherries!—and then kissed the sweet right out of my mouth, her fingers stained like sin. And all the time, her eyes, like sentinels, seeking mine, daring me to see her back. I was both afraid and unafraid, if such a thing can be true, and feeling her strong, perfect back, the downy warmth of the skin on her arm, it was as if I was returning bravely home to a place I'd never been before. And then Henry called, and called again, and on the third try I answered, sweating, and it was bad news, the worst news ever, and I scrambled back into my shirt, since that's all I'd lost so far, and watched Gavin's face as she knelt upright on the bed, eyes wide in black concern.

"It's Mother," I said, "My mother. She fell." And Gavin rushed to help me into my chair and wanted to come—almost begged to come—and I begged her not to. I called her from the hospital, and again this morning, and her sweet, throaty voice is lodged in my mind, in my chest, and all the way down to my most secret parts.

"Tillie? Is this enough?" Addie startles me into remembering the heat of the day, the work needing attending to. I nod at her, and she moves further down the garden, tripping lightly over her unruly green hose. My heart flips to watch her. My spade unearths a smallish stone and I toss it at the seat of my wheelchair, parked empty in the grass nearby. It clanks off the spokes of one tire and I think, *Where's Henry to throw rocks with me when I need him?* Henry. He's in such a bad place again; I haven't seen him this torn apart in years and years. We didn't know each other well before Will's suicide. I remember him from the parties. Their achingly handsome adoptee, their late-spring accessory. I remember not liking him much, truthfully, because how can someone be given that big a portion of handsome and likable and seem not to know it? I understand Henry better now, and I'm glad we never fell into bed together, glad his need and my need never coincided. Is that what happened with Will? That need?

I lift another stone, small and white, and it is tender and smooth in the palm of my hand. It's about the same size as the rune I chose that rainy afternoon with Emmy: *en espanol es la rueda, the wheel*. What else was it Floramaria said? I remember the Knight of Something, about growing things. And the Sun with his ever-returning happiness, for those who believe in such things. The June sunshine is warm on my coiled hair, on the back of my neck, and it isn't hard to imagine magic and healing in that. And the god of thunder, with a name I can't remember, bringing life by weeping rain. Both sun and rain necessary together, just like in my little hopeful garden.

My spade is quick without me. Addie is a pleasure to watch, so clean and easy in her perfect child's form. I meant what I said to her, that even the grass beneath her feet whispers sweet nothings when she passes by. It is so true, she seems to be exactly what she's supposed to be. As if the world felt the lack of her, and thus was she made. I spill dirt on my legs and swipe it away roughly. Why is it I feel so imperfectly made? It's been years since I felt the sense of my own body so keenly, as I did in Gavin's bed. I'm afraid to let her see me, my sawed-off legs, the ghosts I trail around behind me. Touching her makes my eyes leak, brings to life a deep and sullen ache I haven't felt in a long time. How can something that feels so good be so scary and full of pain at the same time?

I want her to touch me. I want her to want me more than I can even say. I'm afraid she will look at me, at the lack of me, and be repulsed. I do still dream my legs, although not as often as I did when I was younger. Mother used to be fascinated with my phantom itches, my true and utter belief I was kicking my legs, or cracking my ankles, or pointing my toes. The nerves that send those impulses from brain on down are still intact, it's just the receiving end that's absent. I'm accustomed to my body now; in truth, it's hard to remember looking different. I look at pictures of my young and beautiful self—who didn't even know it then!—and I think, *Hold onto that! Hold on!* The way Gavin looks at me makes me feel beautiful and giddy and funny and smart. I don't trust it, but I'd like to hold on, while I've got it.

Addie turns her hose off and lies down flat in the jade-green grass to stare at the sky. She's been unreadable since Mother's stroke, and I don't want her to shut down with me. I crawl my way to her and lie crosswise with her, my head on her belly. She giggles and I smile up at her smile.

"I saw this kind of Olympics on TV," she says, "and there were people without legs like you, but they had special things to help them run. Have you seen that before?"

"Prosthetics?"

"Yes, those. Have you considered them?"

I nod my head, still leaning against her stomach, and she reaches a hand down to pet my head a little. "Well, back when I had the accident, a long time ago, the options weren't all that good. They were big and bulky, and I found them uncomfortable. I know they've advanced so much since then, but I sort of feel like that ship has sailed for me already. Like I would have to learn a whole new way of being, and I'm not sure I could handle it."

"I think you could handle it," she says confidently. "But I also think you are good like this." She sighs and my head bobs. "How's Ms. Eve, do you think?"

"I don't know," I say. "She was doing really well when I left. She's talking and making jokes, thinks we're making such a fuss. She'll be home soon. Are you worried?"

Addie shrugs and I know she is. Her own mother swallowed nearly an entire bottle of Tylenol and can't even manage a phone call; she's been jettisoned down to our distant, overly-white city; she's living with strangers. And now Mother.

"Well you want to know how I'm dealing with it?" I ask, and see her nod, and then don't know what to say. Swallows are busy in the sky overhead, and in the distance I can hear a speedboat on Looking Lake. I can't say, *I don't know how we deal with anything, honestly.*

"I've been living for a good long while now, you know. Almost fifty years of summers and winters and all that." I take my head from her belly and hoist myself up beside her on my elbows, so I can see her open and worried face. "When I was young and looking forward into my life, I saw all these paths that took off in different directions, and I didn't know which way to go, or what would happen. But now, when I look back, all I see is one big, wide road that got me here. Does that make sense?"

She shrugs and looks away, and I'm afraid I've lost her interest. "Faith is a funny thing," I say. "I don't have much conventional faith, I don't think. But ask me if the sun will shine again, if the rain will fall again, and it isn't even a question to me." Addie nods, staring at the sky, and I reach over to take her hand, wondering if I should be saying any of this to a ten-year-old.

I put my head down into the grass, and it's cool and soft under my cheek. What's wrong with telling a child what you believe is true? The harm is probably bigger in keeping what we've learned to ourselves.

"Honey, I don't know what's going to happen to our mothers, or how long we get to keep them. But I will love while they are here, and I will love when they are gone, and I will keep faith in the cycles of this world because really that's the best we've got."

She squeezes my hand and I squeeze hers and together we lie in the spring loveliness with our sad and glorious hearts, and then my cell rings and it's Emmy and she says I need to come back to the hospital *right now*.

Eve deals

Oh, what is all this fuss still? I keep telling them I'm fine and more than ready to go home, and these tiny little girls in green cotton smile and go on fiddling with the tubes all around me. I've asked for Adam, but they won't let him in. So he sneaks in when the nurses chatter in the hall, and the daughters doze, one or the other, pale-faced, heavy-cheeked, and sad. *Evie, honey*, he says, *we're taking you home, screw these blustering quacks!*

He sneaks in and sits on the edge of my bed. He's so strong, my Adam, so unstoppable. He's the kind of man you can lean into against any stiff wind. Oh, he could be fierce, it's true, and he wasn't always the father the girls wish they'd had, but to me he was the most tremendous man I've ever known. I can feel him here at my side, with me now, even as Emmy clucks and whispers with the nurse over my lunch tray.

"Mother," she says, from a long way off. I turn my head to find her, and it's hard to focus, hard to see her, because she keeps moving just out of sight. It feels as if I'm wading slowly through heavy, invisible water. As if I'm trying to see these people, their self-righteous concern, through gauze, paper-thin.

"Mother? Did you get enough lunch?"

I nod and wave my hand at her, trying to get her to leave me be. "I ate," I say. "I ate it all. When can I go home?" Another nurse is fussing with my IV, and I swat her hand away. "Where's my daughter? Did she leave?"

"Right here, Mother, I'm here." She steps around the end of the bed, and I reach my hand out for her, suddenly so scared.

"Quit trying to trick me! Deal me out! I don't like these games! Take me home!" I feel the tears burst forth from my eyes and I'm so tired, so tired. I can feel Adam on the bed beside me, his arm next to my body, and I wish he'd hold me instead of just lying there.

Emmy looks up and says, "Tillie," and I close my eyes, hearing the quiet sound of my younger daughter's wheelchair. "Come to this side of the bed," she says quietly. "Mother can't see you over there."

"What do you mean? I can see, I can see!"

Tillie's face sags with pale concern, even as she tries to smile with her eyes. "How are you feeling?" she asks, and I want to slap away her kindness.

Emerson squeezes my hand to get my attention, but I won't look at her, I won't.

"Mother, your stroke was caused by a small blood clot, and you're going to have to remain on blood pressure medication. The medicine in your IV was able to dissolve the clot, and your prognosis looks very good, they're saying. There may be some physical changes, but they should resolve fairly quickly."

I feel her reach over and place my lunch tray back on my lap.

"I ate it," I say, and my voice sounds querulous, even to me. Breakfast had been more liquid than solid, and I'd been hungry for my lunch. I'd graduated, I suppose, because I'd been served lean turkey, unbuttered potatoes, limp green beans.

"Changes in vision are common, and slight paralysis too. In your case, both should be temporary," Emerson says, and I open my eyes. The lunch tray holds only my dirty fork and crumbs, until she rotates it, slowly. Then I see a full Jell-O, a small roll, and half a slice of turkey, jaggedly cut, since I'd only had one good hand to eat with.

"You're tricking me! Why are you doing this?" I feel small and lost and confused.

"Emmy?" my other daughter says, fright exposed like roots in her shaking voice, and I push the tray away, hard as I can, and it clatters over the side rail, spilling lunch scraps on my blanket—the lunch I ate, dear God in heaven!

"Leave me alone! Both of you, go away now!" I squeeze my eyes shut, feeling to see if Adam is with me still. His arm is lifeless at my side, and I toss over, turning away from their breathless, wordless worry the best I can. I open my weary eyes to the rough white sheets, the thin ochre blanket, and my own arm, only my own, caught underneath me now—the arm I couldn't see, the arm that belonged to someone else, my lovely Adam, only my own, and the terror is so deep the shriek clots my throat; stuck, bound, flightless.

Emerson deals

I don't realize how bone-weary tired I am until I'm driving back-streets away from the hospital. Yesterday's bright sun is gone, replaced by overcast gray and the threat of rain. Portland spring, fickle indeed, and a real fucking downer sometimes. I wear my sunglasses anyway because my head pounds, hungover without the pleasure of wine the night before. I think of who I can call, just in case I needed someone right now. I can rattle off a long list of acquaintances, community members, neighbors, old alums, but can't think of any I could lay my burden on—only Henry, of course. And what wisdom is there in that? An overgrown teen-ager, really, eyes always clamoring now for my own, seeking that intimacy, trying to ferret it out. As if a door, so long ago opened, could be his again if he just finds the right path through the weeds.

I pound my fist on the steering wheel just as the first fat raindrops hit the windshield. "Doors close, Henry!" I say out loud to no one. "Doors close!" And then tears like renegade soldiers course down my cheeks, and I have to pull to the shoul-der because I can't see to drive with all the goddamn water. Cars drive by fast as my shoulders heave, and I have enough ego left to wonder what kind of a fool I must look like to the suburban lacrosse moms whipping past, even as I wipe the snot from my face. After the biggest waves pass, I root around in the glove box for an ancient soft pack of Marlboro Lights I keep for occasional parties, when it's long past midnight and the case of shiraz is half-drunk. I light the cigarette and choke, barely inhal-ing, relishing the rake on my lungs. Sometimes it's good to hurt. Sometimes it's just what we need.

Mother is not coping well, but who can blame her? It does no good to say, *Oh, but you were so lucky!* even if it's true. I called a neurologist friend who explained, just as the too-young resident did, that the side effects will wane, and in just a few weeks most likely. She said left-side neglect is not uncommon, and we should expect mood swings as well, and some range of memory loss, maybe mild personality changes. And aren't we lucky there's no aphasia or slurred speech or spasticity? That hospital reminds me of my bout with breast cancer so many years ago, before it was de rigueur and drenched in pink. Just a lump, hadn't metastasized, and now I sport the tiniest of scars far east of my left nipple, almost to my armpit. The cosmic joke: we are given enough brain power to be keenly aware of our deteriorating bodies, but can do little to stop the mutiny. We know it will all end, and likely with agony.

The smoke is thick in the Lexus even with the window cracked, and I'm suddenly fiercely embarrassed with myself. I flick the burning stub out the window—Tillie would be appalled—just as my cell rings, a number I don't recognize. I answer anyway, thinking perhaps it's the hospital, or the consulting firm I contract with, or the Lake Oswego detective assigned to my dubious break-in for that matter. Amazing how quickly I can pull the curtain down, contain the mess inside. I answer with an alacritous, "Yes?"

"Emerson Foster! So glad to catch you, how is your mother doing then?" The deep golden voice catches me off-guard. He must have gotten a local number.

"Oh, for God's sake, Butch, leave me alone. I don't have anything for you. I don't have any answers." My words are steady even as I wonder how he knew about Mother; perhaps he is still following me.

"Hell, Emmy, no one's called me that name in years. It's Karl, please. Or Mr. Henley, if we're sticking to formalities." He sounds so damn pleased with himself it makes me ill. I glance around from where I'm parked on the side of the road, in the rain, to see if he's nearby, watching me. If he is, he's well hidden.

"I don't know what you want from me, Karl, but—"

"Lovely girl out at Looking Lake. When did you adopt? We connected, you could say, she and I."

My heart is thrumming so hard I can feel it in my throat like pounding hail. I'm scared now and plummeting into that panic I felt back at the house when I saw his boot print in my sink. *Henry's with Addie still, right?*

"Oh, Emmy. We could have been so good, don't you know?" I hear a crackle, and it sounds like he's chewing gum or cracking his jaw. "Do you ever have that feeling, when you look back at your life, that you got waylaid somehow? Pushed from the path? I've seen how drawn you are now, so full of your own mistakes, written like confession all over that perfect face of yours." I hear him laugh a little, and I know I should say something here, or yell, or take a swipe at him, but I feel frozen, ice-cold, and listening.

"Melinda left me, didn't think she even had it in her. And then she had the cojones to get a protection order from the judge? Do you know what that's like, Emmy? What that does to a man?"

I start the Lexus, listening hard. *Gather info*, I tell myself, *all you can.* "That must have been hard for you," I hear myself say as I whip a U-turn on the wet street, vaulting back toward the Looking Lake house.

"Hard? Unbelievable! She took the boys, the house, all my goddamn money. And then that Mark Merchant swiped the rug out from under me, told me Willy Row was downsizing—the best firm in Philly downsizing!—and offered me a part-time job-share with a fucking intern! And then when he tried to set me up with his boyfriend, I told him to go blow himself."

Willy Row? Date with his boyfriend? I cut off a slow-moving van and merge hard onto Highway 26, trying to think fast.

"Is that why you're back in town, Karl? To get a fresh start?" My voice sounds high-pitched and falsely cheerful against his low, metallic baritone. "How can I help, then? Money? Networking?"

I have no intention of helping him, I'm just trying to buy time, placate him.

The line is silent except for that jaw-cracking again. And then a low chuckle, as if I'm the stupidest woman in the world. "Always trying to close the deal, aren't you, girl? You don't have enough money to pay for what you did to me, how you fucked everything up." His voice is speeding up, and now he's rambling again, and I can't keep track of the disparate details.

Is he on something? My heart is whipping against my chest now, and I'm remembering Will at his worst: *decompensating* is the word that comes to mind.

"Karl, you need some serious help. Psychiatric help. I don't think you realize—" and I'm talking to dead air. The rain has slowed westbound traffic, and I feel suddenly suffocated by helplessness, by the feeling that it will not matter, I'm sure, whatever I do. I dial the number for the Looking Lake house, and the phone just rings and rings until Mother's answering machine picks up. Henry's cabin has a landline, which may or may not be disconnected, depending on his current finances. And no cell phone, of course, philistine that he is. I try the number again and again. Where could they have gone in the rain? "Next time I'm hiring a babysitter for you both!" I yell into the ringing phone.

The traffic in front of me has stopped, and I pound my fist into my thigh as tears of frustration spring to my eyes. I remember Butch at my parents' dinner table, so confident, singing a German lullaby, smoothly charming Mother. Bantering with Dad about long-run trade-offs and runaway inflation and OPEC's leverage. There's Butch's strong hand on the back of my neck, telling me how the future would be, planning it for us. There's him wrestling Tillie, and her delighted shrieks. Dangling his ID bracelet in front of me and smiling his perfect, white-bone smile. Freshman year, and I'm watching him walk through the quad— the laughing one from English Composition, the handsome blond—watching him kick autumn leaves away, his arm around a bronze Omega sister, making her giggle, boldly winking as he walks past my bench. The first time he spoke to me was when he hired me to tutor him, and I accepted although I didn't need a job and he didn't need a tutor. He was perfect, and I believed him. I believed him.

I find my exit and head to Looking Lake Road. Spring is wildly green on these backcountry roads, but I hardly see it, buried as I am in my soggy panic. I burn down the driveway to the house and park badly. The front door is unlocked and I run in, calling for Addie, for Henry, for anyone, run all the way through the house to the back porch, thinking I must check his cabin first, then the boathouse, then, I don't know what then, and slam out the back door, heels skidding on the wet cedar deck. There, in the steady rain, over by the fence and the gate that used to be and now—look! is again!—I see Henry pruning back rhodies and Addie walking armfuls of branches to the blue wheelbarrow. Both of them are in hats—Henry in his black BFF snowcap and Addie in Will's old Stanford baseball cap—and both of them stop and smile and wave a big hello at my shocked and silent self.

"Emmy?" Henry calls through the rain. "What's wrong? Your mom okay?"

I walk to the porch table, with its big green canopy still up, and slump down, leaning against my hands on the glass table. "I am buying you a goddamn cell phone," I say.

"Sure thing," he calls, and both of them turn back to their work, as if it's nothing to see me bent and torn in two, sodden, broken. I ease myself down into a not-too-damp deck chair and drop my head onto my hands, watching their brisk industry. I'm amazed to see the gate is open again.

I head back into the house, out of the rain, and pull my phone out, open my web browser and tap in "Willy Row Philadelphia." Nothing useful. Then I try "Wil Ro Philadelphia," and get a link for Wilson & Rowe, Financial Services. I dial the number, mentally adding hours to the East Coast. I tell the smooth receptionist,

"Mark Merchant, please," and am directed to another silk-throated woman, an executive assistant, most likely.

"He's not available right now. Would you like to leave a message?" she asks politely, just in case I'm assistant to the Queen of England, or something.

"My name is Emerson Worthy"—no point in lying there—"and I'm calling from the firm of … Addison Rhodes, here on the West Coast." I'm sure Addie, who I'm watching through a window carry a damp armful of rhododendron leaves, would be thrilled to be in on my fabrication. "Mr. Merchant was listed as a reference for…" I pause here, as if shuffling papers around. "Karl Henley." I give her my cell number, and I'm just trying to decide what to do with myself next when my phone rings. Philadelphia, of course.

"This is Mark Merchant, you just called my office?"

I give him my false facts again, and he laughs dryly in my ear. "I'm a little surprised he would use my name as a reference," he says. "Our parting was … less than auspicious, shall we say."

"Well," I answer, "we have had our questions. But he has an impressive résumé. You were his immediate supervisor, then?"

"Right, I was, I was. He's a fantastic CPA, no question about it." Mark Merchant clears his throat and I can almost see him loosening his tie. In my head I see a delicate and polished man, with wire-rimmed glasses and well-chosen Italian shoes. "But his behavior was becoming increasingly erratic. Missing work without explanation. Clients starting to complain. I know he had some personal issues that may have been affecting him."

"The divorce?" I ask. "He volunteered that in the interview," I add, as if I'm apologizing for having that information.

"Yes, that, and … look, I don't wish the guy ill. I tried to help him, over and over again. I suggested he see a friend of mine, a professional."

Your boyfriend, I guess. Butch was probably right about that.

"He did mention seeing a specialist," I say, trying to stay vague.

I'm watching little dribbles of rain fall off the edge of the green umbrella canopy outside. Faintly I can hear Henry singing.

"My, uh—he's a psychiatrist."

"Mr. Merchant," I say, pulling out my kindest, smoothest, wisest voice. "If I can be perfectly frank with you, I'm disinclined to hire him. On paper, he's an ideal candidate, but I just, there's just something... Now, my superiors would not be pleased to know I declined an applicant based solely on women's intuition, or what have you."

I can hear the smile in his voice when he says, "Well, you have good instincts, Ms. Worthy. Write down these words for my part: unreliable, mercurial, at times openly hostile, requires constant supervision."

"And if I put my pencil down, what else would you have to say?" I ask.

"Off the record, honestly, I became a little afraid of him. He was prone to aggressive outbursts, ended up threatening to black-mail me with personal information. My psychiatrist friend called him narcissistic, dissocial. Quite the package, truly."

"Well, I appreciate your time, Mr. Merchant. You've been very helpful." I hang up and watch my two charges diligently clearing away shrubbery. Addie looks happy. Henry looks like he overdid it last night, but maybe that's just stress. I need to ask if Butch has been around, but I don't want to just yet. Let them hold onto whatever peace they have at the moment, for surely it will not last.

Addie deals

It felt so good to work in the rain! Henry is still sad and upset, but he seemed to like the help I gave him. We are inside now, and it's getting warmer outside, even though it's late afternoon and gray. Henry says a storm is coming, says thunder and lightning are coming, and that makes me feel a little scared and a little excited at the same time. Mrs. Worthy didn't seem to mind the red baseball cap this time, even though it used to be her husband's, I guess. I think she's mad at him still for dying, or maybe she's just mad at everyone else for living. I don't know which.

The air is thick and warm, even inside. Henry and I are at the kitchen table, sitting on Ms. Eve's red wooden chairs, and he's teaching me and Mrs. Anderson to play cribbage, which I've watched tons but never played. I always thought it was a grown-up game: "fifteen-two, fifteen-four, fifteen-forty-four." But I guess kids can learn it too. I can't remember the order of things so he has to tell me what to do when, but I don't have to play open handed anymore. If I were younger, I'd whisper to Mrs. Anderson, who is sitting on the table beside me, and ask, *What should we do with this hand?* But I know Mrs. Worthy would give me that pinched, lines-in-her-forehead look if I did. She doesn't like my doll. She was probably a girl who didn't ever have dolls. I can't imagine her playing with anything, ever.

We are drinking lemonade when Tillie rolls in and says, "It's getting muggy, isn't it?" Then looking at Mrs. Worthy, "She sent me home. She's being difficult." So that's Ms. Eve, then, my chickadee friend. It's hard to imagine her ever being difficult. I don't like not knowing what's going on, but I realized today that the grown-ups don't really know what's going on either. Back home, I just thought they were keeping me in the dark, because that's what you do with kids, but here I understand they are all in the dark too. I shuffle the cards the best I can and deal them out, six each. I have to do this slowly, but Henry doesn't seem to mind. He is nice like that, never in a hurry. He's just like the big rocks in his garden, patient and waiting and knowing lots of information but not needing to share everything he knows.

Mrs. Worthy has started making dinner, but she seems stretched thin and distracted. Also, she looks like she hasn't been eating much lately. Tillie, on the other hand, looks very happy and tanned earth brown. She feels warm and kind just to be around. She rolls over behind me and puts a casual arm on my shoulder which feels really good.

"Better watch out, Henry, she's got five jacks over here."

"All diamonds too, I bet," he says, and that makes me laugh. He is also getting more relaxed now that Tillie is here. He won't even look at Mrs. Worthy really, or rather, every time he tries she won't look back. So, something is going on there.

The phone rings and Tillie answers, then hands it to Mrs. Worthy, who has a really pained look on her face, as if her stomach is hurting her. She turns her back and steps away from us, out of the kitchen, as if she's protecting us, or keeping a secret tight to herself. She reminds me of the ice rink Ms. Eve took me to. Thin and cold, and hard to fall onto.

"Oh, Michael," she says, and Henry and I both look up. Mrs. Worthy turns to see my face as she's talking to him, and I feel suddenly coiled up inside, like maybe I'm going to throw up. Captain Mike and Mama have been friends forever. They met a long time ago, when he and my dad worked on the same boat in Dutch Harbor and she worked at a bar called the Elbow Room. Back then, all three of them were friends. After my dad died, Captain Mike never stopped helping Mama. Which is a good thing, which is how I got here.

There are lots of "uh-huhs" and "goods" from Mrs. Worthy, but she's biting her lip, which makes me worry. When she hangs up, there is a smile on her lips that doesn't quite make it up to her eyes. She actually has really nice smile lines around her eyes, when she uses them.

"Addie, that was Michael. He's in Anchorage still, and he says he's found a place for you to stay." Her voice is dry and matter-of-fact and it hurts to hear; what a problem I must be to her! She will be glad to be rid of me. "He's flying down in a couple of days, and he's bringing someone for you to meet. And then you'll be going back."

I feel a buzzing in my ears, as if there's suddenly an ocean around me, and my stomach feels balled up and heavy. Mrs. Worthy must see something in my face because she looks to Henry, as if maybe he could help, and Tillie too, who comes to sit beside me again.

"This is good news," Tillie says softly, leaning her warm head against mine. "You're going home to Alaska."

"What about my mom?" I say, and my voice doesn't sound like my own voice. It sounds hard and sharp, like I don't really care. Like the bad kids sound when they talk.

"She may not be able to care for you for a while," Mrs. Worthy says.

And then Tillie says in a short voice, "Will you just stop, please? Emmy?"

I look around at all the grown-ups, at the lost looks in their faces. When did I ever think big people knew what they were doing? They're worse than kids because they know so much more, and they still act like they're lost.

I push my chair away and grab up Mrs. Anderson, then run down the back hall to the back door. All I can think is, *They don't want me, they don't want me anymore!* and the words are as clear in my head as if Mrs. Worthy had spoken them out loud. Because if they did want me, they would say so. They would tell Captain Mike. They would ask me to stay.

The porch is still wet from the rain and I slip, my feet flying out behind me. I land on top of Mrs. Anderson, and when I push myself up I see that now she is a no-eyed doll. The little black blip of plastic that was her one good eye is on the wooden porch, sitting in a puddle. I kick it with my foot and it falls down between the boards of the porch. In the distance I hear thunder rumble like God is playing ninepins, like Mama says. It's so warm out here I'm sweating, but it has started to rain again.

I run off the porch, through the wet grass, past the place where Henry and I worked all afternoon, all the way down to the gravel lakeshore. I hear the porch screen slam and hear a woman's voice calling my name. I'm by the boathouse, the place where Henry likes to hide, likes to smoke and drink, the way grown-ups like to do sometimes, even when they tell us it's bad. It must be something, because they keep doing it.

The calling of my name is getting closer, and I feel a desperate animal feeling of needing to get away, *Right now*. It is pressing me down, that feeling, and when I look around fast I see Henry's little rowboat named *Daisy* tied to the small dock. I run there and untie the heavy rope, even though my fingers are shaking. I throw Mrs. Anderson into the boat and step into the sway, pushing us away from the dock with my foot. I've never paddled alone before, but it doesn't look hard. I've seen men do it, both here and at fish camp.

Caciitua, I think. *I have no idea what I'm doing*. Just like everyone else. The rain is getting more furious now, and the thunder is coming more often. Out of the corner of my eye I see a flash of lightning, but when I turn my head, it's gone. I paddle deep strokes, and I'm surprised how quickly the little boat moves. It's satisfying. The lake is tossing a little in the rain, but I don't care. *They don't want me, and I don't want them*, I think. I miss my home so much and they almost never ask. Mama is a great artist, and she's smart and works hard and keeps our home together for us both. I can feel the bear amulet swaying against my chest as my body moves the oars back and forth. We are bound together, Mama and I, like the earth is bound to the moon. I'm not bound to these other people, these strangers.

On the shore now, Mrs. Worthy is calling my name and waving her arms. Henry is running down the grass slope behind her, pushing Tillie in her chair through the rain. Henry is serious faced, but Tillie is smiling a big smile, calling *Addie, Addie*, as if I'm a funny joke. I don't want to be their joke anymore. When I get far enough away, I put the oars down and float, just looking at them there, all three of them gathered on the gravel in the rain, hollering at me. If Ms. Eve were there too, she would laugh, and that would be okay because I would laugh with her. Ms. Eve would want me to stay. She's my friend. Thunder clangs again behind me, but I don't even move, I just stare at them with my angriest self.

I remember Mike's story on the phone about the spirit bear, when I was sick. One bear made special, to remind the people where they've come from. To bring peace and harmony, he said. And that makes him think of me? I haven't brought peace to these people; they are too full of themselves to have peace. I haven't done anything but interrupt. They have so much, and they don't even know it. I remember the story Mama told me about the arctic fox. So busy are they watching the burrow of their prey that a person could walk up behind them and yank their tail if they wanted to.

Mrs. Worthy is the worst. So why do I want her attention more than any of the others put together? I pull her husband's red hat from my head and throw it into the bottom of the boat, where it falls into some dirty water there. *Good*, I think. *You can send me away because I don't even want to stay. You hate Mrs. Anderson and you hate me.*

I look at the shore again. I'm far enough away now I could cover their bodies with my hand and they'd disappear. No one is calling now or waving their arms. Henry has his hand over his eyes, like you do when the sun is bright, and he's talking to Mrs. Worthy, I can tell. My heart feels like it's been wrenched open again and again and again. First Mama, then Ms. Eve, now this.

I start crying then, and it hurts so much I want to scratch my own face, or something, anything. I look down at Mrs. Anderson, my stupid, no-eyed doll, and pick her up by one loose arm. I lift my arm as far as I can behind my back and throw her as hard as I can, just like I threw that rock at Henry earlier. She sails away from the boat, tumbling head over feet, then splashes into the lake. I look up to see the shocked look on Mrs. Worthy's face. *Good*, I think. The rain is harder now, and the lightning flashes are all around me. I watch as her soft body floats on the surface, her eyeless face staring at the stormy sky. I want to scream; I want everyone I know to be dead. She must have filled with water because she begins to sink, slowly, and I cover my face with my hands, wanting myself to be dead too.

I hear Henry's voice and look up to see Mrs. Worthy emptying her pockets, removing her watch. She steps out of her shoes and walks into the lake, wearing all her clothes still. She wades to her waist and then dives in, looking so easy in the water—I had no idea! She is swimming toward me, smooth and sure, better than I can do even, her elbows raising, her head turning for breath. She looks like she should be in the Olympics! Raindrops fall into the lake like they are glad to make it home again, and Mrs. Worthy doesn't seem to notice or mind. I'm not sure if I should row toward her or away, so I do neither, just sit and slowly rock in little stormy *Daisy*.

When she gets close her head pops up like a harbor seal and she looks at me. She looks like a different person. Like she was sleeping and woke up. Like the ice rink, now unfrozen. "Here? Was it here?" she calls, and when I don't answer, she kicks her legs and dives down under the water.

What is she doing? Her head comes up, her short blond hair stuck to her cheeks, and she takes a big breath and down she goes again. This time she's down for a long time, and I'm starting to worry. I lean forward in my seat, watching the surface of the lake. What should I do? I look up at Henry's face, far off on the beach, and he looks just as worried as I feel.

Then she pops up again and starts to swim toward the boat. She's at my side before I realize she has Mrs. Anderson in her hand. She hangs her elbows into the boat, her eyes sparkly and triumphant, her cheeks red and bright. She flops Mrs. Anderson into the boat.

"Lose something?" she says, and I start crying again, I don't know why, and harder this time. "Can I get in?" she asks, and I nod, I can't even look up.

I feel the sway of the boat and she pulls herself in; I know you have to be strong to be able to do that. And I feel her sit on the little cross bench in front of me, fully wet and smelling coppery like the lake. "Addie? Honey?" she says, and that's it, that undoes me, because when I look up her eyes are so concerned, her hands on my elbows so strong and kind, her half-smile so true, I fall into her and she holds me tight.

I feel her rocking me, and she's singing a little. Now we are both soaking wet, but I don't care, don't even care about the storm or the rain or the sadness or the leaving. It feels so good to have her kindness wrapped all around me. She says, "You're mine," and "I will keep you safe, best I can," and "I'm here now, I'm here," and I close my eyes into all that good feeling, clinging to Mrs. Anderson as Mrs. Worthy clings to me.

Seven

Henry opens it up

I watch Emmy's soaked-self in the boat, my fingers tight on the handgrips of Tillie's chair, bare feet stabbed by gravel, and think: *If I thought I could hide from it before...* My stony-self is cracked open; I can feel the wild lightning strikes all the way to my sternum. All the women I've ever wanted, but never like this. I feel the wet on my cheeks, the rain in my hair. Emerson, perfect and distant, grips fiercely onto her maybe-granddaughter. Addie's beautiful, pain-struck face is barely visible over Emmy's arm, but I can feel the energy from here on the lakeshore.

"Emmy!" I shout into the growing dark. "Storm's moving! Time to haul it in!" and smile wide at the damp grin she sends me.

"Henry! Henry!" Tillie is saying, and I bend down to her marvelous face. She is beatific, wiping rainwater from her brow. "Henry!" she says again, grabbing my arm, and I kneel on the gravel with my hands on her hands as Emerson rows the boat to us. I love Tillie, and I love her sister too. I feel deeply found.

The thunder is thick and indeed growing closer, but nothing matters in the crackling wet. Nothing but my tossed-open, suddenly-joyful self.

I muster quick to the little dock when I see they're getting close, and grab the spiny rope. I tie them up and help Addie out, who's hugging a dripping-wet and eyeless Mrs. Anderson. When I take Emerson's hand, her eyes meet mine and she is incredible—bright eyed and strong. I want to grab her then, on the little dock, touch her cool china cheek, and hold her chin while I kiss her the kiss I've held fast for years. Her gaze moves houseward, and I step out of her way. She walks to Tillie and reaches a hand down to her sister, and for a moment, those two see eye to eye, so brave and lovely. I raise two quick fingers to my lips for a kiss, and just hint the hand skyward. My own private benediction as the thunder swells around us.

"Race you up," Emmy yells. Tillie hollers and Addie starts to run. I grab the wheelchair and heave us up the wet grass best I can. It's a pleasure to see Emmy run with the girl through the rain to the back porch and into the big, warm, lakeside house. I get Tillie up the porch ramp and inside, and it's all laughter and too-loud talking and towels for everyone while the storm washes over us all.

Then I'm sitting at the kitchen table with a cup of good coffee Emmy brewed after changing her clothes. She called to check on Eve again, and it sounds like she's coming home in the morning. Addie's in the tub—one of her favorite places, I guess—reading. Not upset anymore, not like she was. I guess what Emmy did out on the water is bigger than any words she got wrong. Tillie rubs my head with a towel before rolling off to her studio to call her new beau as I tease mercilessly.

And then Emmy is sitting with me and the house is still. The kitchen smells rich and the evening sweet around me, and I feel tall and strong in my skin. Will's cigar box is on the breakfast bar and I reach up to grab it. I push it to her and realize I'm holding my breath.

"Open it, Em," I say.

"Why am I suddenly reminded of cans of peanuts with snakes inside?" She brushes her damp dark-blond hair behind her ear, and her cheeks are red and glowing from the warmth. Only the white scar on her temple remains, like negative space. "You open it," she says, half smiling, half not. "Go on, open it up."

I tap the tan Arturo Fuente box twice, then lift the lid toward her as if I'm a salesman presenting an overpriced necklace.

"So are we smoking stale cigars now, Henry?" she asks over her crossed arms, her blue eyes sharp, as they always are when she's reminded of Will.

"Sure," I say. "Why not?" I push the box toward her and she's watching my face, trying to figure out the trick.

Emmy waves a hand at me, pushing the idea away, but when I don't move, she raises her hands in defeat. "Oh, screw you, Henry Oliver."

I smile as she leans toward me, her long, perfect fingers touching the dark-brown paper. "These weren't his best," she says. "But they were the ones I was willing to smoke with him. On our anniversary, usually. Isn't that a funny tradition?"

She lifts one out and leans away again, enough to make me think the note is lost—that I messed it up somehow.

"What's this?" she says, and stops.

I can hear my heart beating. I can hear Tillie's lilting telephone voice from across the house. The rain on Eve's kitchen window. Will's whisper in my ear.

Emmy pulls out the envelope, spilling cigars from the box, and only then do I let go of the cardboard lid and let it drop shut. Surely she recognizes the rich, heavy paper. She's looking at me, and for a swift moment, I have a memory of looking into a mirror-smooth lake at twilight over the edge of my father's anchored rowboat as a boy, seeing the reflection of myself and the sky behind.

"What's this, Henry? Do you know?"

She steps away from the table to find a knife and slits the creamy envelope open in a way I never could. I'm all rip, I guess. She sits with dreamy slowness and takes the paper from the envelope while I try to think of the words I will say: *He loved me; he touched me; I didn't mean for it to happen, it just did.* And the big winner: *I never meant to hurt you. Either of you.*

Emmy clears her throat purposefully, and smiles over the note. "It's from Will," she says. "Listen: 'You can see nothing else when you look in my face; I will look you in the eye and I will never lie.'"

The corners of her mouth have turned up into a smile, her eyes damp and bright. "Henry, look at this. It's from Will," she repeats. "I know what this is."

"He never left a suicide note, did he," I say, revving up my confession. "Never explained or—" Her eyes stop me short and I feel myself flinch. "Did he?"

She reaches a hand to me as Tillie's laughter spills from her studio. "Of course he did, Henry." She pulls her warm hand from my suddenly cool one to cover the growing smile on her face. "I know what this is," she says again, and my chest feels sharply punched.

I stand up fast, knocking over the wooden chair in my haste. Emerson is startled and holds the note to her breast as if I might steal it away. I bend to right the chair, my cheeks burning hot.

"You never told me he left a note," I say, and the bright anger feels good, it feels easy. "You never fucking told me." My fingers are tight on the back of the kitchen chair, my jaw tensed soundly.

Emerson's anger is quick too—of course it is—and I'm glad of it. Make her meet me where I'm at. "Was it really any of your business? We were neighbors—for what?—a year and a half? Was I supposed to coddle you too, along with everyone else?"

My chin drops. I can't help it. I can't bear to look at her, can't bear to feel the horrible feeling of not-mattering—can't bear to let her see it. I feel young again suddenly, mother dying, father disappearing—alone and unable. My voice is gravel low and punctuated. "You … have … no … idea."

I watch Emerson's eyes move, and I turn to find Tillie's wheelchair at the end of the hall, just inside the kitchen. "Henry?" she says, and I watch as the smile falls away from her face.

I shake my head at her, slowly. "I'm done. I'm done. I'm done."

"Till," Emerson says, and I feel as if I've stepped out of the room. I'm suddenly reminded that I'm in someone else's house. "It's from Will. It's my riddle. My anniversary riddle. Listen."

My ears are ringing as she reads it again, and I can feel Tillie watching me even as she listens to her sister. A fucking riddle? Is she serious? I do the only thing I can think of. I push in the chair. I walk to the hall, past Tillie, and to the back porch. I step out into the evening dark and the rain, but I can't feel any of it—not really. I slowly walk down the steps, through the garden gate, to the back door of my own empty cabin.

What's the use of confessing if no one cares enough to listen? How foolish am I to think that I mattered to him once? To any of them? The front room is dark and I leave it that way, moving to the couch, alone in the dim and the quiet. I stare at the ceiling in my damp shirt, heaviness lashing my heart while the rain lashes the window. No matter what I do, however I reach out, I am still and ever and yet alone. It isn't love that's hard. It's finding the people who will love you back. That's the impossible part.

I hear a knock at my door and think, *Tillie*, but don't get up. The knock again, and then Emerson is in my doorway. *Fuck you*, I think, *Go away*, and cover my eyes with my hands. I can feel her icy-blue presence in the stillness. I want to brick myself in—to build a stone wall between what I want from her and what little she's ever been willing to give. I want too much. I always have.

"Henry…" she says, and stops, as if she's waiting for me to speak, waiting for me to make this easy. I remember the boathouse with her on that warm evening, when one of us should have been with Will. My fingers gentle and slow on her arm, the smell of the wood around us, the openness of her gaze so tempting. When she spoke low and convincingly of the man she wanted to leave, of the marriage grown stifling, of the possibility of such beauty and happiness in her life, if only. I would have kissed her then, and I almost did. But Michael had screamed, and we had run to find her husband—our Will Worthy—so still and ashen and cold. Someone once told me that all suicides are an act of violence, but it wasn't until I found Will that I believed it.

"Henry," she says again, and I feel her sit on the edge of the couch. I pull my hand from my eyes just as she lays her cool palm on my other wrist. It is dark all around us, but I can still see her face. "You're right, you know," she says softly. "I should have told you. His letter was … mostly where to find accounts, things like that. I knew it all already. He wanted me to sell the other house and stay at Looking Lake."

"But you didn't."

She shrugs and turns her chin away, looking at the concrete floor. "I didn't want to be here anymore. You knew that."

"Yeah, I knew. But anyone could understand that. I didn't blame you."

"Henry, you found this note before I did? You read it?"

I nod slowly, and scrub a hand on my rough chin. "I did, right out there. On the bench. I thought it was meant for me, or was about me anyway."

Emmy's fingers are moving softly over the hair on my arm, and I'm not sure she even knows she's doing it. "Why would you think that? It's just a riddle, Henry. He used to do that for my birthday too, hiding my gift. I think you knew that, didn't you? Once it took me five months to find it. He could be so impossible sometimes!" Her hand stops moving, and I feel the muscle jump in my forearm. "I miss him, Henry."

I nod, not trusting myself to speak.

"And sometimes I don't, too," she says, and I hear my own heart beating in my chest. "Sometimes I'm glad he's gone. You were the other reason I couldn't stay here, you know. I just couldn't—"

"Emmy." I sit up on the couch and reach my hand to her through the dark. "Please just listen to me. I'm sorry if I fucked everything up, I'm so fucking sorry. I didn't want him the way he wanted me. I just—I couldn't stop thinking of you. But when I ended it, he was so mad. Lord…" The words spill out, but nothing is capturing what I mean, and I can't read her frozen eyes in the dark. "I just couldn't love him the way he wanted."

She shakes her head, so slightly. "None of us could."

"Are you hearing me? Do you understand?" My hands are on her arms now, pulling her close, making her hear. "He was cheating on you. With me, Emerson. And I broke it off, I…" My words trail off, and I'm not sure what to say next, what could possibly make any of it okay.

I watch her pull away, watch her face grow cold.

"Why do you think he did it here? In my garden? It was a punishment. It was the biggest *fuck you* he had. I live with it every goddamn day. And I didn't just lose him, I lost you too."

I expect her to yell, to cry, to say, *I know*, and surprise me. I'm prepared for questions. I expect she will want to know details: who started what, and how. Maybe she'll be better for knowing. Maybe it'll relieve us both somehow. But Emerson does none of those things, which is what I really should have expected.

She stands from the edge of the couch and steps back, away from me, almost tripping over the stool behind her. I wait for her to say something, anything, but she doesn't. She leaves. She doesn't even slam the door, just closes it gently behind her. I sit on the couch, alone again, and my chest aches, heavy as stone. I thought I would feel better for telling—unburdened somehow— but I don't. I only feel bruised and broken. I sit in the dark, weary and thick hearted, watching as the rain torments the windows of my small, battered home.

Tillie opens it up

Emmy's back but not talking much. When I mention going out, she's quiet and seems distracted. Something is happening with Henry, obviously, but she's not saying what, and I don't feel like jumping into it right now. Truly, I have other things on my mind. Gavin is home alone and wants me to come over. I'm still exhilarated from the lake, from watching Emmy dive in and swim. My sister can be so unexpected sometimes! But then again, everyone feels surprising to me right now, in all the best possible ways.

I maneuver through the rain to the car, and pull myself in expertly. Mother is coming home in the morning, and Emmy has already found a day nurse for her. In the back of my mind, I feel a pinch of worry, dark as soot, when I think of Mother, what has happened to her and what will happen now that her wings have been clipped. Feeling guilty, I shove the thought aside. The road is empty on the way to Gavin's house, and I have a mad desire to push the accelerator hard and really open it up. But the lake road is slick from the rain, and I contain myself, drumming excited fingers on the steering wheel in time to the music. Gavin opens the door as I pull up to her house as if she's been waiting, and we giggle our way up the stairs in the rain.

Her house is warm and comfortable and smells amazing. "Pecan rolls," she says. "I made them for you." She looks bright and happy, like a polished apple, and when I tell her this, she laughs and laughs. "That is the coolest thing I've ever heard," she says, and bends over to kiss me long and sweet.

I stop her when my heart feels like it's going to burst from my chest. I put my hand on her cheek and gently push so I can see her eyes.

"Gavin," I say, her name like a breath, but I don't know what to say next. She's so beautiful, this woman. Strong in a way I could never be, lovely as a song. When I'm with her, I want so badly just to let myself drop into all the big things I feel, but I'm scared. Scared of being too much or not enough. Scared of being too needy, too old, too awkward, too everything. She kneels next to me and lifts my hand to her cheek, to her mouth, gently kissing my palm.

"Let's keep each other safe," she says, and I see the fear in her eyes too—open and vulnerable. It surprises me, makes me reevaluate what Emmy said about her, about all the straight women falling for her. Gavin told me she's been single for a while, and I can see that it's true.

She turns, walks to her bedroom, and holds the door for me to follow. It's dark until she lights a row of candles on the bare windowsill. I watch her arm stretch to each one, so smooth in her skin that I feel like melting a little myself. The lit wicks reflect in the dark window like a mirror and draw seductive shadows on her forearm, her chin, her serious mouth. Before she can turn to watch me, I transfer myself to her tall, warm bed, feeling anything but sexy or graceful. There is a litany of ugliness in my head that I don't know how to shut up, and when she sits beside me and kisses me, I burst into sudden, terrible tears.

"I'm sorry," I say. "I'm sorry. I want this, I do. I just don't know what I'm doing here. You could have your pick."

"Tillie," she starts, and stops, licks her lips, looks worried. I want to hide my shameful face from her, stop pretending I could be whatever beautiful thing she thinks she sees when she looks at me.

"Tillie. I want to be with you in whatever way you'll let me. I don't want anyone else. I want you." Her voice is low, her dark eyes and elfin smile right there, close to mine. Even in the tears I feel a little swoony, like it's hard to think. What happens when someone says exactly what you want to hear? What you've been waiting to hear forever? What do you do then?

"Oh!" I say quick, and press my lips into hers. I can feel the breath of her surprise and her arm reaching behind me, pulling me closer.

She is slow and gentle. She is like lying naked and warm under perfect stars, feeling deeply loved by the whole night sky. Like swaying tree-strong and easy to the music of a breeze. She traces my outline with faint fingertips, with her red plum mouth, so sweet. I didn't even know I had the inside of elbow or just under jawline or just below breast until her smooth lips tell me so. And when her hand travels to my legs, to where I end, the tears spring loose again and I grab her short black hair to pull her face close to mine. She smiles, so sly, kisses my downy belly, and slides her hand down my thigh again.

"Emmy tells me my bootstraps must be easier to reach than most people's." I feel Gavin look up at me in surprise at the non sequitur, but I have to talk, have to distract. "Hovering as they must somewhere around where my knees used to be." I laugh at myself as Gavin's right hand travels down my left thigh, all the way to my rough-skinned stump. "Stanley used to leave the room when she made jokes like that. Made him uncomfortable." She drops her forehead onto my leg, and I could swear she's praying. Her hands are moving again, and I want to squiggle away. No one has ever touched the ends of my legs, save for doctors. No one's ever touched that part of my body, that part of me. Too intimate, too disturbing, too something.

"Gavin, did you know—"

"Hush, now," she says, and I do hush because she has a hand on each leg, cupping my hewn self, and when she puts her warm, soft mouth on me, on the core of me, all thoughts flee from my head, and I'm just a body springing to life, just a soul floating safely somewhere nearby, and she's loving on me, and I let her, I let her.

After, later, in the dark, curled into her body, I drift and doze while she murmurs sweet words. I think of art school, and the series of serious men I went through there. When I was young, I believed I didn't get what I wanted because of someone's deficit, usually my own. I'm old now—forty-nine years old and in another woman's bed!—and I have to think that I didn't find it because it didn't exist. Couldn't exist, until now. I'm not sure what to call myself. I don't feel any great desire to wheel after women on the street, but this woman, now, this woman!

Gavin gets up and I watch her muscular back as she walks to the door. The warm bed feels naked without her, and I smile into the pillow at this new earthly delight. Who can I share this with? I know a lot of people: artists, gallery owners, exes of exes, Stanley's hippie friends, women and their husbands from the relay team, childhood neighbors, brothers of girls I went to school with, the list goes on. But when it comes down to it, down to who I can talk to, I just have my Henry.

Gavin comes back with a pecan roll for us to share, and I want to tell her how amazing it was to have her touch my legs, but I don't feel like crying again so I just say, "Thank you, you're marvelous."

She feeds me sweet roll, then kisses my forehead, my nose, my lower lip, and I feel myself sigh. She laughs and nuzzles my neck, then props herself on an elbow to look at me, chewing brightly.

"In one of my ESL classes," she says, "I have an *abuelita*. She must be eighty, at least, and everyone calls her Dona, Dona Marguerita." Gavin's voice rolls like music over the *r*'s. "She's one of the loveliest women I've ever met. She wears thin dresses under old sweaters, and these dark, heavy shoes, but you wouldn't know it, everything else about her is so bright."

"Yes," I say, thinking of Floramaria with her tarot cards. "I love bright."

Gavin wrinkles her nose and laughs at me. "And when she looked at me this past week, she said—in Spanish, of course, because really she has no interest in English. In Guanajuato she was a poet, and both her sons are engineers. I'm pretty sure she just comes to class to bring me fresh tortillas and heckle her grandsons. So she said, *You have a new friend now, I can see it in your face*, and then she said, *It is good and right that your orchard is finally bearing fruit*. But of course I didn't know a word like *huerto*, orchard, I thought she was saying *huero*, which is how a six-year-old I know described the bananas he wouldn't eat. Abuelita laughed and laughed and sent me home with real tamales. See how blessed I am?"

She is so young looking and earnest in this moment that I put my hands on her cheeks and pull her close. "Thank you for touching my legs," I say.

Gavin's face grows serious, and she puts one hand gently on my chest, on the warm skin between my breasts. "Tillie, I have to tell you something. And I really don't want to mess this up, so you've got to tell me if I've overstepped, okay?"

I feel my face tighten, my ears get warm. "Okay," I say nonchalantly, inwardly preparing for the blow.

"So I did some research. Found an old article on microfiche about your accident. Since I knew how old you were, and you said it happened near Portland, I thought I'd take a look."

"They still have microfiche? Why'd you do that?"

"I was just curious, you know, and it seemed like something you weren't going to want to talk about, and I'm a person that needs information to feel safe. Facts, you know? I just wanted to know. I'm sorry. Are you mad?"

"I don't think so," I say. I'm not sure what I feel—mostly off-center, waiting to see which way the tipping deck will spill me into the ocean.

"And you told me it was raining that night, and that's why your sister drove you both off the road. But they interviewed the county deputy, and he said the roads were dry. He said the weather wasn't a factor."

I listen warily.

"Tillie," she says, and the room suddenly feels small and overheated, and my good, deep roots are itching for me to cut and run, just leave right now. "It was dry that night. Hadn't rained in two weeks. I checked with the National Weather Service. It started to rain later that night, so maybe that's what you remember? From the hospital?"

I close my eyes, and my ears are ringing from the heaving scrape of metal—now silenced. I know there is broken glass everywhere, so I lie as still as I can. Emmy was here, but now she is not. I can feel her absence like a living thing. There is the smell of warm grass in the darkness nearby, and after a while the crickets chirp again. My mind won't let me sort through the feelings in my body—the pain is suffocating and it's hard to breathe. I want to turn my stiffened neck but don't dare. Emmy's Ford Falcon is sideways and I'm crumpled inside and the world is upside down. I wonder if the wheels are still spinning, slowly, in the late spring night. I close my eyes when I think I'm going to throw up, and that's when I hear the raindrops start to patter on the metal overhead. It is a peaceful sound. I can feel glass in my hair, blood in my mouth, and, distantly, an ocean of pain near my kneecaps. I think this is dying. Dying alone.

"Tillie?" Gavin asks, and I push myself off her bed and fall on the floor, trying to get to my good, safe chair. "Till, wait!" I am grabbing my clothes and struggling to get into them and out her bedroom door at the same time. She doesn't follow me. Thank God she doesn't follow me. This is the closest I can come to running away, this bumping down the stairs in the night, this awkward roll to the car, half-dressed, this horrible, ugly feeling. Discovering something I believe to be true—fundamentally true, my origin story—is deeply, deeply wrong. Knowing a lie has been allowed, nurtured even, by the people who profess to love me most.

Eve opens it up

Oh, heavens and goddamn, I'm breaking out. *Did you hear that, Adam? We're going home.* Emerson brought me an ironed dress and decent flats, but I'd rather wear my slacks and sandals. I've been traveling the hall back and forth from the nurse's station to the janitor's closet, just for something to do. Walking isn't hard—my balance isn't too bad so long as I remind myself that I'm only seeing half the picture at any given time. The effect is most likely temporary; the stroke really was quite mild, and patients have been known to make a full recovery. The neurologist speaks to me as if I am a dim child, and so I quote Herodotus: "Of all miseries, the bitterest is to know much and control nothing." The doctor's eyes shine brightly and he nods in agreement.

"And the best medicine for me will be getting out of this place!" I waggle one finger at him and his eyebrows raise. "I may be half blind, but I know plenty of people that have traveled their lives fully blind without ever knowing it. No driving, no heavy machinery, no tractors, no factory work, right?" He's biting back his smile now, and I'm starting to feel as if I've returned from a brief but distant journey. "Plenty of rest, sunshine, la-di-da. Weekly checkups, OT, PT, iced tea, it's all the same to me, son. I have a nest of bluebirds to tend and a great-grandchild that needs me. That's all the rehab I need." I wave my hand extravagantly, and he takes my fingers in his own hand, squeezes them briefly, then turns to speak to my daughter—oh, I'd forgotten she was here!

"Did you bring my car?" I ask, and Emmy nods. She holds the wheelchair out for the trip downstairs—hospital protocol, she says—and I think, *Whee! I'm Tillie!*

"Yes, Mother. Henry's downstairs with it now. I don't know why you need a whole caravan. We could have done this just as easily in one car."

"Oh, pish, Emerson. No reason to spoil other people's fun." I wave at all the nurses as we pass them in the hall. "Bye dear, good luck with that boyfriend! Oh, that one has such a pretty face, if she would just lose a few pounds..."

"Mother!" Emmy hisses. "Don't be rude."

In the elevator, I swallow and look down at my hands in my lap. Rude? Me? My mind feels fuzzy, hard to hang on to. I'm subdued for the rest of the ride, but lighten when we get close to the automatic doors and the bright morning outside. I think, *When did hospitals start looking like hotels?* We aren't on the walk long before Henry pulls up in my Mercedes. I stand from the wheelchair and an attendant wheels it away. I have to stop myself from asking, *Where did he come from?* Clearly, I will have to stop being surprised at the quick entrances and exits happening around me.

"Eve, missed you, girl." Henry bends to kiss my cheek, but his eyes are shrouded, dark. He opens the passenger door for me and hands me my purse, then walks around to the other side. I wave at Emmy through the window and she waves back.

"You two aren't talking again?" I ask, and he shrugs and hands me my sunglasses.

"Oh, thank you, dear. Take the top down, would you? Open it up."

Henry laughs and looks at me. "You serious?"

"Serious as a stroke! Lord, I need some good coffee. That's the first stop. Then we just drive."

"What?"

"Starbucks first. Then we drive!"

He presses the button to open the convertible top, and I open the glove box to find my scarf but don't put it on. The wind feels good in my thin hair, the morning sun warm on my forehead. I close my eyes and lean back in my seat. Rude? Really? I've never been rude a day in my life. Fierce, maybe. Annoyed, certainly. But not mean, and definitely not rude. Henry stops the car, but I don't open my eyes. It feels too good to rest in the sun, and I'm so tired it's hard to think. He leaves, comes back, hands me my coffee.

"Decaf caramel macchiato, Eve. Just for now."

"Oh, no," I say, but still I'm pleased. He looks so darling and earnest and drawn. Something is wrong, but of course he's not saying. "How's Addie doing? Emmy tells me she's fine, fine, but I want to really know."

"I think she's okay," he says. "It's been a roller-coaster week for her. It'll help to have you home. Now, where am I driving?"

"Anywhere green, Henry. That's the medicine I need."

He drives and drives, and I doze under the shadow of green leaves and sunlight dappled on my cheeks, my hands. When I wake, we are on the lake road, nearly home. "Did you enjoy the tour, Eve?"

"Oh yes, very much," I say, and I do feel lovely, but groggy headed. Warm and windswept, like I'm just starting to spread back into my skin.

When we get home, everyone is there waiting. Emmy stands with hands on hips, Tillie stares at a spot on the ground, biting her lip, and Addie is holding the porch railing, squeezing, squeezing. When the car stops, she runs to me and nearly climbs into my lap. I take my sunglasses off so I can see her better, and we sit together in the passenger seat.

"Ms. Eve, Captain Mike's coming and he's bringing someone. He's going to take me back home, but not with Mama, with someone else, another family. I don't want to go. I missed you. Are you okay?"

I run my hand down her long black hair, loose today, and lean my nose close to hers. I want to tell her I'm scared. I want to tell her I feel wrong, undone. "I'm fine," I say. "Better for having a break. And this person my grandson is bringing better be fabulous, or else I'm not letting you go."

"Really?" Her dark eyes sparkle my way, and she looks older somehow, even after just a few days. "You can do that?"

"Don't worry," I say. "I have a fantastic lawyer."

Addie's smile is moon bright. She grabs her bear amulet in a friendly squeeze, and I hug her close, needing to feel her warmth. Emmy ushers us inside, tired of waiting, I suppose. I sit at the kitchen table with Addie while Emmy makes sandwiches for lunch. Henry is outside, washing my car, though I don't know why. Tillie is parked by a window in the living room behind me, and I can't remember ever seeing her so quiet. Instead of a warm hum of confusion, the house feels heavy and muted. Is that what happens to them without me?

"How's business, Emmy?" I ask, when I remember I like to chat, and her back stops moving for a second, as if she forgot she wasn't alone.

"It's fine, Mother."

"What do you do, Mrs. Worthy?" Addie asks, sipping her milk.

Emerson turns around in surprise and looks at the girl. "Oh, well, I'm a consultant. If a business isn't turning a big enough profit, I come in, look at the books, at the marketing, at the personnel, and make recommendations on how to streamline. Most people do stupid things with their money, I've discovered. It isn't difficult, really. I know people."

"I bet you're good at it," Addie says.

"I am."

I reach for Addie's glass, steal a sip of her milk. I say, "Sometimes it's easier for other people to sort out our problems for us. It's like having your nose so close to the pages of a book that you can't even read what it says."

"Well, why not just move the book so you can see it?" Addie asks.

"Exactly," Emerson says. "That's just what I do. Will you go tell Henry his lunch is ready?"

Addie runs to the front door, and Emerson clanks plates down on the table too hard. The sound hurts my aching head, makes me feel impatient. "Tillie, come on," she says.

Everyone sits and I look around. Pasty-faced, drawn, downcast. I bang my fork on the table and everyone stops moving, looks at me. "I'm gone for just a little while, and this is what happens?" My voice is angrier than I mean it to be.

Emerson starts stabbing at her salad again. "Whatever do you mean, Mother?"

"What's wrong with you people? Henry? Tillie? What is it?"

I turn my head to see Henry, because otherwise he's in my blind spot. He ducks his head, then says abruptly, "I'm going home," and stands, sandwich in hand. *Quitter*, I think. *Chicken*.

Addie looks up at him, mid-chew. "Do I still get to help you power wash?"

He looks at her as if he just woke up, then slowly nods, "Sure, come on." They take their lunch in hand and bang out the door, leaving the girls with me in silence. I'm tired. My head still hurts, and I'm seeing white spots. I've barely eaten but feel full already.

"Mother, we need to talk about arrangements. The day nurse is coming this afternoon. We can work in shifts at night, for now." Emerson speaks without emotion, and suddenly I feel like I'm someone's faltering business, and she's here to solve the problem of me.

"For now?" I ask, my voice quavering. "What sort of plans do you have for me?"

"Well, you need care, Mother. I don't think any of us are equipped for this. We can consider live-in care, or find a nice residential facility—"

"You wouldn't!" My hands are shaking. I feel baby-bird bare—damp and vulnerable. Swiftly, I realize how powerless I will become to my daughters as I age. Is this my punishment for Emerson's own unhappiness?

"It isn't necessarily a bad thing. You have to understand, someone has to be responsible for you—"

"I'm responsible for me!" I say, and my voice is loud.

Tillie has been silent beside me, up till now. "I'll do it," she says softly, firmly.

My eldest shakes her head. "No, Tillie, you won't. You—"

"Yes," she says, "I will. I will live here with Mother, and you can go back to your other house, any time now. I'm strong enough, I can take care of us both. If the stairs get too hard, Mother, we'll move you downstairs, and we'll keep a nurse during the day so I can paint, and so we don't get sick of each other. You won't have to leave. You can be as independent as you want, except you probably can't drive for a while."

Emmy puts her hand to her forehead, starts to say something, and stops. Tillie rolls her plate to the kitchen counter, and I startle as she sets it down hard. *My daughters and their bottled fury!* She wheels down the hall, toward her studio, silent again. I push my chair back, intending to walk to Addie's room for my nap, but Emerson's pinched face stuns me.

I move around the table just as her head drops into her arms. "Oh, Emmy, baby," I say, and wrap my arms around her, lean my cheek on her shoulder as I feel her begin to weep. "Oh, Emmy, you're trying to do right. You're just like Adam, trying so hard."

"Don't compare me to him," she says through her arms.

"He was a good man. He loved you. I don't know when you started hating him so."

She raises her head, stares at me. "Do you remember Karl Henley?"

"Of course I do," I say. I feel weary and heavily weighted, mushy headed, but I'm trying. "The Henleys were lovely. We took them to New York with us."

"Do you remember how Father was going to bring him on?"

"I know all this, dear," I say, brushing her hair back away from her bright, damp eyes. "But there was that business at the school, and you broke off the engagement."

"And do you remember that Vietnamese girl? That refugee? Oh, hell, Mother, I told you this thirty years ago. I caught him. I hit him with my bookbag. I just kept hitting him. I thought he was going to kill me."

Emerson's hand is cold and hard on mine, and my head is so heavy, so tired. I just want to go lie down.

"And I was the one that took her to the women's clinic at school. I was the one that convinced her to press charges. Her parents didn't want her to, Mother. Do you remember any of this? And I told him! I told your goddamn perfect Adam, and do you know what he said? He said, *Boys make mistakes.* He said, *I believe in second chances.*"

"Oh, Emmy," I say, and I want to cradle her heartache, hold her close, make it go away. "Of course I remember. Your father was doing the best he could. It doesn't mean he didn't love you less. Sometimes it's just easier to pretend that everything's okay until it *is* okay. He just thought if we waited it out... I'm so sorry it hurt you, Emmy. He never meant to."

She's quiet for a long time, then looks at me. "You must be tired."

I nod. "I was going to lie on Addie's bed, but I think I can make it upstairs." Emmy stands to help, but I wave her off. Everything inside of me feels tied up and wrong. I'm trying to remember what she's talking about and it's so familiar, but like a book I read a long time ago. My head is clamoring, my eyes are watering, my knees are shaking, but I don't let her see. She watches me walk toward the stairs and then I can't see her anymore and I think it's not so bad having a blind spot. Really not so bad at all.

Emerson opens it up

My breath feels heavy. Why do I try to talk to her? Why do I think I'll get anything from her? Something about being in this house makes me want things from people, and I don't like it. The girl's name was Phuong Lai and she worked as a housekeeper in the dorm and I'm probably the only one who remembers her. She was younger than us. I have no idea what happened to her. Maybe her parents made her quit, I don't know. Butch was in danger of losing his scholarship, Father and I fought, then Tillie lost her legs. Why all this old shit now? Because he's back. Yesterday I'd just about decided to call the Lake Oswego police to file a restraining order, but today it just seems useless.

I stand from the empty kitchen table and stretch my arms, wipe my hand over my damp eyes. My eyes have spilled more tears in the last month than in the last year or so, and I feel like kicking myself. What use is all this wasted water? I can hear soft music from Tillie's studio and start to walk that way, not sure if she would want to see me, or even I her.

I rap softly on her door, then open it up. Tillie sits in her chair, forlorn, staring out the big window at the summer afternoon, listening to something low and plaintive. That's how she was after the accident, for a long time after. I turn the radio off, and she doesn't even look up.

"Two things," I say. "No, three."

Still she doesn't look, but I can see her hands rubbing up and down her thighs, like she does.

"One. Henry told me he was sleeping with Will. Do you believe it?"

Tillie turns to look at me, and her lips are a tight, thin line. "Sit down somewhere, would you? When you stand like that, you're menacing."

I sit on the ground near her chair, back to the wall, head against the windowsill. "Did you know anything about that?" I ask, and she shrugs.

"He mentioned something the other day. Why would he lie?" Tillie reaches up and pulls her long hair out of its braid, slowly. Her skin is brown, deeply tanned, and even her sadness is beautiful to me. "It would explain some things, I guess. Did Will ever—I mean, did you ever have a sense?"

I hear how loud my sigh is, catch myself playing with my cuticles and stop. "He would leave sometimes, and I wouldn't know where he went. I thought it was other women."

Tillie is quiet, and I watch dust in the sun by where her ankles used to be. "Are you mad?" she asks, finally.

"No, just tired." The room is too warm, really, but it feels good to be still. "Mother says I'm just like Father."

"You are, Emmy."

I raise my middle finger at her and she laughs.

"You're fierce and strong and you don't suffer fools, and you're so crazy smart that everyone else *is* a fool, which means you're miserable all the time." She's still combing her fingers through her hair, and I suddenly remember she had a date last night with that Gavin. It must have gone badly, to have put her in such a funk.

"Tillie, when we were at school, Butch Henley sexually assaulted a girl—a housekeeper." My hand is on my forehead, keeping my hair from my eyes. "In my dorm room. She was Vietnamese, couldn't have been more than seventeen, hadn't been in the country very long. Her name was Phuong. I caught him. I hit his head over and over again with my bag, and screamed until someone came."

"Oh my God, Em," she says, and I feel like spitting. "I didn't know."

"His hand was on her mouth, he was covered in sweat, and her eyes, the way she looked at me. Do you think Butch remembers her name? I just reminded Mother that her beloved Adam wanted to hire him anyway."

Tillie nods, squints. "I remember it was something, but no one ever told me what. How horrible for her. What happened?"

"Well, I helped her best I could, but she stopped working at the school, so I don't know. No one kept me posted."

"No wonder you hated Butch so much," she says, and I think, *You have no idea.* "Why didn't you tell me?"

I ignore her question. How do I explain I was trying to protect her?

"And our sainted Mother is apologizing for him." For Father, I mean. My voice is starting to shake and I'm worried I'm going to cry again, goddamn it. "Butch and I didn't need to be married for him to inherit the family business. What stopped Father, Tillie, from bringing him on? I mean, if you're going to be an asshole, then you should really commit, don't you think?"

She looks down at me where I sit, and for just a second I feel like the younger sister, with all my anger, all my icy need.

"Mother did," she says. "She stopped him, didn't you know that? I remember that much. That long summer, all I did was sit in my room. I'd listen to them fight downstairs, night after night. I just sat there and stared at those ugly prosthetics I wouldn't wear and thought about all the different ways I could kill myself and listened."

"They fought about me?" I ask, and I'm surprised.

"Yeah. She told him she'd divorce him. She said that *he* didn't have to choose his own daughter over a stranger, but that she did and would. She told him he'd lose all of us. Close your mouth Emmy, you're gaping."

I close it fast. "You're not making this up, are you?"

"Oh, hell, when have I ever tried to please you? The only way I can talk to you is by arguing, remember?" Tillie looks at me sideways and I laugh.

"So Mother went to bat for me, huh? Would never have guessed it."

Tillie takes her dewdrop earrings out and tosses them at the windowsill. One falls to the ground, and I get it for her. She shakes her hair, leans back, closes her eyes. "If that was number one and two, I can't wait to hear number three."

I stand up and dust off the seat of my khakis. "Three," I say. "That was quite a number you pulled back there, with all that *I'll take care of Mother* crap."

She opens her eyes, looks at me. "I will."

"You can't even reach the high cabinets. You can't change a lightbulb. How the hell are you going to get her in and out of the bathtub, Tillie? How are you going to change her diapers, when it comes to that?" I walk over to where she sits, head still leaning back. I kiss her forehead, and she puts her hand on mine.

"So you're staying, then?" she says, and I nod.

"I'm staying." My sigh is so deep I can hear its echo. "I'm going to sell it, Tillie, the other house. Like Will wanted." I squeeze her hand gently and let go. "Can you stand to live with me?" I ask.

She shakes her head no, and I walk into the hall, letting the door click shut behind me. Despite everything—all the turmoil, all that I don't understand—I feel a lightness seeping into me. I feel like something has eased, like when I dove into the lake to swim to Addie, and a full layer of solemnity just sloughed right off. I will sell the other lake house. I will let its cold, empty corners leave my life, be a chill balm for someone else's heavy heart. I will move into this busy, needy house, and I will fight and I will laugh and I will be wanted and I will be known.

Addie opens it up

Henry said he would show me the power washer, and he did, and it was cool. He said the moss will eat his little cabin alive if he doesn't go after it, and this isn't usually the time of year he does it, but his friend had the washer for him to borrow, so we did it now.

Usually, I run back to the Worthy house from his cabin, but today I don't feel like running. I open the garden gate slowly. It's a big door, and it feels like something important is happening every time I use it. Maybe something important is happening, and I just don't know it. Captain Mike is bringing someone, and I'm not feeling very happy about that. I have my doubts. Mama tried to kill herself, and I probably won't be able to live with her again for a while. Maybe for the whole summer. I spent a good part of yesterday writing her a story about spirit bears and then I illustrated it, but I'm not as good at that part. I will mail it tomorrow.

I think about the kids I go to school with, and what they're doing in Anchorage right now. Swimming at the YMCA. Maybe going to fish camp, if they're lucky. I have some friends, but no real special friend. No special sleepover kind of friend. I'm too quiet. Most of my people are grown-ups. Auntie Lu, Captain Mike, Mrs. Richey, my teacher. Now Ms. Eve and them. I look at the big, white-cloud blue sky, and pray with my eyes open. I pray for everyone to be safe, and then I pray for more kid friends, and then I smell cigarette smoke so I turn all the way around, like an owl, but no one is there. I think Henry must be smoking again, but I'm not so sure, so I hustle inside, even though it's the daytime.

When I go inside, my eyes have a hard time adjusting, and I almost run into Mrs. Worthy in the hallway. She grabs my shoulder to steady me, then pulls me close for a surprise one-armed hug. She's holding a piece of nice paper in her hand, and her blue eyes are bright, like the sun on the lake, and her happy makes me happy.

"Do you want to help me, Addie?" she asks. "I'm on a treasure hunt."

"Sure," I say. "But the power washer hurt my hands a little."

"Oh no, did Henry make you work?"

"No, no, I wanted to try, but it was too hard. It hurt my hand and my wrist. Here," I show her, "and here. What's the treasure?"

"I don't know," Mrs. Worthy says. "It's a riddle. My husband, before he passed away, used to leave me clues like this. Once I had to tear the stuffing out of an old bolster in the attic. That one took awhile." I have no idea what a bolster is, but it doesn't seem like a good time to ask.

I can hear music coming from Tillie's art room, and I'm excited for whatever adventure this is. "But didn't he die a long time ago?"

"He did, but we just found this note, this riddle. 'You can see nothing else when you look in my face; I will look you in the eye and I will never lie.' Any idea what it means? I was looking at the pictures here in the hall. I thought maybe it meant a picture of his face, but then I remembered these pictures weren't even here ten years ago. Tell me, are there any pictures of Will in his old office?"

I close my eyes to think, then shake my head no. I would remember. "But we can go look anyway, if you'd like." I'm suddenly glad I made my bed this morning. I open the door, as if I'm the hostess and she's the guest.

"Oh!" she says, looking around at the dark wood and leather. "It reminds me of the way he used to smell."

"You can smell him?" I ask.

"No," she says, "it just makes me remember how he used to smell. Funny, isn't it?"

I'm reminded of the man in the blue car, and the rich, red smell of his cologne and the horrible panicky feeling in my stomach when he grabbed my arm.

"I have to tell you something," I say. She looks at me, clear in the eyes, and I swallow hard. She's so perfect looking, so in charge. I'm still scared of her, even though she's being nice.

I sit down on the edge of my bed and she does the same, then puts her hand on top of mine. "Addie, honey? You can tell me anything. It's okay."

"There was a man," I say. "Did Henry tell you?" She shakes her head, and I can see fear flash through her eyes. I tell her about going to the side of the road to meet him, even though I knew it was bad, and about the green-wrapped gum, and the map on his seat, and how he reminded me of expensive metal. Her hand tightens around mine, and I'm scared that she's mad at me. "I'm sorry," I say, and my voice is shaky. "I know it was wrong. I know I shouldn't have gotten close to him, but he said he knew you. Does he?"

"Yes, he does. But he isn't good, and he shouldn't be coming around. And he really shouldn't be talking to you. He's sick in the head. If you see his car again, you need to tell me pronto—super fast. Okay? Okay?"

I nod, and she wraps an arm around my shoulder, squeezes me tight. "You know, we can do this later," she says, holding up the note in her hand. "We don't have to do this now."

"No, I want to! Please let me help. I've never been on a treasure hunt before. But if it's from so long ago, maybe it isn't here anymore. Maybe it got moved or lost."

"Maybe," she says. She reminds me of that girl from the party, that Kyra girl—Carson's girlfriend. Except she isn't as sad, not today at least. I imagine what we must look like sitting next to each other, me in my wet, dirty T-shirt, her looking so rich and easy. And then I remember Tillie asking me if the trees are jealous of the sunset. That makes me smile, because I don't have to want to be what she is. I'm mostly good the way I am.

"What else looks you in the eye?" I ask. "A potato has eyes, that's a riddle I know. Or the eye of a needle."

"Eye of a hurricane," she says. "But what's the part that never lies?"

"Something that stands up, maybe?" Both of us scrunch up our faces in concentration, and then I remember something Auntie Lu says sometimes. "Mama's friend always says the mirror never lies. Except sometimes in department stores when they want to sell you something."

Mrs. Worthy looks at me, and her face changes, holds perfectly still for a minute. Then she smiles. "You're right, Addie. Mirrors don't lie."

She stands up and turns around in a slow, tight circle. She stops when her eyes land on the big wooden desk on the other side of my bed. "There," she says. "Back there."

We have to stand on the bed to get over it, which makes us giggle. When did this woman become so nice, like Ms. Eve and Tillie? Now I can see that maybe they really are family; I wasn't so sure before.

Behind the big desk are big wooden cabinet doors, and I never thought to wonder what was behind them. She opens them quickly, and there's a fancy mirror inside. "My husband certainly had his vanities," she says softly. We both stand and look at ourselves together. "Now what?" she asks.

"Is there something behind it?" I ask, and she tries to jiggle it, but it doesn't move. "No, and I don't think that's right. We're supposed to see something in it."

"Maybe it's like one of those old songs," I say. "Maybe the treasure is supposed to be something you are. Something inside yourself."

Mrs. Worthy looks down at me in surprise, as if she hadn't really seen me before. Then she bends down and kisses the top of my head. "I *love* how smart you are. I'm glad you came to us. Thank you."

"You're welcome," I say, even though I think maybe I should be thanking her. Our eyes move back to the mirror. I don't know what I'm supposed to be looking for, so I just watch her instead. Her eyes travel from our reflection to something farther back, and I watch as she scans the room behind her.

"Oh," she says, and I try to see what she sees, but can't. She's looking at the big bookcase on the other side of the room—the one I marveled at when I first got here, full of rich, old books. She turns and climbs over the bed again, and I follow. When I catch up, she is standing, looking at a pair of heavy-looking horsehead bookends. They are on different shelves, which I've wondered about before. "I bought these for Will in Italy. I told him they were just like us because one bookend is no good by itself—doesn't work without the other." She looks at me and laughs. "Sappy, huh? People in love say silly things sometimes. I wonder why they aren't together." She means on the same shelf, I guess.

She lifts one down and turns it over and around. Nothing. She puts it back, takes down the other, then stops. I watch as she reaches up, behind where the heavy bookend used to be, and takes out a small black jewelry box.

"Oh, that man," she says, but her eyes are wet and shiny. She puts the bookend back, and we sit on the bed together.

"Is that it?" I ask. "Did you find it? How did it last so many years?"

"Careless dusting," she says. "And no earthquakes." Then she laughs and covers her mouth because she's crying now. "And why do I keep crying?" she almost shouts at me.

"Mama says crying's good. Says it gets the hurt out." But Mama probably didn't do enough crying lately, since she had to get the hurt out in other ways. I don't say this because grown-ups don't like to hear kids think dark things like that.

"Your mama is right," Mrs. Worthy says, wiping her nose with a handkerchief from her pocket. "I'd like to meet her someday."

That makes me smile. "Well, are you going to open it?"

She hands it to me. "You do it."

"Oh no, it's your present. I couldn't do that."

"Please," she says. "I want to watch."

We sit on the bed together, and the room is afternoon warm. I can feel Mrs. Worthy beside me, without even looking. She feels safe to me, tall and smart, like she's a good person to have on your side. The little box is black and velvet soft. I think a prayer, even though I can't see the sky from where I sit. I think, *Good things.* Then I open it up.

Inside the box is a fat, black pearl on a chain, and a little square of paper jammed into the lid. The pearl is the biggest I've ever seen, and silky dark and beautiful. I hand Mrs. Worthy the box, and she takes it gently. She is breathing quietly and staring. Her face looks like important things are happening, but in a good direction, not a bad one. She plucks out the little folded scrap of paper and unfolds it.

"'Dearest Emerson,'" she reads, and her words are slow, like she's reading ahead before she speaks. "'Well done! This is a Tahitian black pearl, as rare and exceptional as you. They are formed, the story goes, when the deep ocean bravely meets the full moon, and the oysters rise and are filled with all the colors combined. See how perfect this is? You were always the brave one.'" Her voice breaks a little and she pauses. "'Happy Anniversary. Love you forever and always, Will. P.S. Don't move the bookend back. They work quite nicely on their own too, don't they?'"

I watch as she folds the paper in her lap and closes her eyes and smiles. It's as if she's watching a movie in her head, maybe one she used to star in. Then she sighs and opens her eyes and pulls me close.

"You are wonderful," she whispers. "Thank you, thank you, thank you."

And then the doorbell rings and we both jump at that unexpected sound.

Eight

Henry leaps

It's coming on close to twilight and my tiny cabin is brick-oven warm, even with both doors and all the windows flung open sky-wide. I am sitting at my work bench, laying smooth varnish down on long, sanded strips of white pine. When mitered, these will form the edges of my little rock gardens, which Lyman will sell at Saturday Market or in Eugene. Building Zen gardens is more zen for me than drawing pictures in pink sand with tiny rakes, although it is fun to move the tiny stones around. Working with my hands is my meditation, my tranquility, even when I don't sit Zazen. I think Buddha understands.

The early evening warmth is running sweat down my bare back, and the westing sun is filling my eyes with marvelous bright. My day feels long and well filled, and thoughts of Emerson Worthy have eased from anger to sorrow to something else, something calmer. It was only last night I told her about Will and watched her walk away so silently, and I feel as if I've traveled a great distance since then. Maybe that's the best we can hope for sometimes—just being brave enough to say what we need to say without knowing what will happen next. I feel strong and brave. I think of Tillie's warning: if all I'm looking for is absolution, then all I'll find is disappointment. Maybe what she didn't say is that the only clemency that does any good is the forgiveness we give ourselves. That part, at least, is in my own control.

I sit in just my jeans and my black BFF snowcap, bare toes curling on the heel rest of the stool, brushing the varnish from east to west, east to west, feeling a smile play on my lips. Feeling the long, warm stretch of my own lighter self.

"Hello, Henry." Emmy's sudden voice comes from my doorway and I flinch, my hand knocking into the gallon can of varnish. It rocks and I catch it before it tumbles, thank the gods. I glance up and she's watching me, biting her lip, leaning against the doorframe, looking so prep school polished it stings. Her white fitted shirt keeps reminding my eyes to notice the swell of breast, the rise of slim hip. I look away and cap the varnish carefully, suddenly feeling terribly self-conscious without my shirt. I start to clear the workbench, just for something to do.

"How do you breathe in here with that stuff?" She steps into the cabin anyway, and I step around her to carry the can to the back door.

"Is that better?" I ask, heading back to the cluttered bench. I make neat little piles and feel her watching my bare back move.

"The day nurse came. Mother's chatting her up nicely. Mostly talking about birds and poetry, from what I can tell. You should have seen Addie jump when the doorbell rang. She mentioned something about a man in a blue car offering her a stick of gum? She said you scared him off?"

I turn back and forth on the stool, feeling the sweat in the waistband of my jeans, and watch my fingers play with wooden dowels. "Who is he?" I ask. "You know him?"

"I do," she says. "I used to."

She leans against the work bench, close to my knee, and I squint upward in her direction. Her face is brightly lit by the setting sun through the window. "Did you go and get yourself a stalker?" I ask, trying to be light, and she laughs.

"Why do I attract the most unstable men?" she says, and I wonder if she means me.

"Because you seem so incredibly competent, is why," I reply.

"Seem being the operative word here," she says warmly.

"Have you called the police? Should you?"

"I will," she says, shaking her head. "Tomorrow." She pulls a black jewelry box from her pocket and hands it to me. "Look at this. It's from Will."

I open the lid calmly, dispassionately. Inside is a large black pearl attached to the slightest of silver chains. "It's nice. It's beautiful. You solved your riddle then?" I say, feeling my face flush.

"I'm sorry, you know," she says, and my breath hitches in surprise. "I'm sorry I couldn't hear you before. I'm not angry with you, not now. I'm—I don't know what I am. Surprised, I guess? I do want to know, whatever you feel like telling me." She stops and I watch her sun-bright face and all the emotions that dance through, just beneath the surface. I feel my chest clench, my cheeks grow heated. There's so much there for me to love.

"It made me realize I'm not the only one holding him in my heart, Henry. It's been so long. I always thought I was alone with that. I'm glad you think of him too. But I'm sorry for your—for the hurt. I thought I was the only one that felt responsible."

I watch her perfect hands twine together nervously like waterfalls, and think of all I've ever loved and lost. I think of my mother's marble-white face, my father's looking away; think of Will curled up and warm, whispering his day's triumphs into my neck.

"We're all so fucking selfish," I fire suddenly, my fingers running over the fine necklace chain. Her eyes shoot up quick, looking to be stung. "Well, we are. We all just think we're the only ones to feel anything. That we're the only ones that have horrible thoughts about ourselves. That we can't be known, deep down."

Emmy reaches over to where I sit. She pulls the snowcap from my head and runs her hand gently through my hair. She nods at the necklace in my hands. "Will you put it on me? I think it was meant to be worn."

I stand and she turns, bowing her neck. My bare chest brushes against the back of her shirt, and I stand close so she can feel me breathe. Her skin smells warm and freshly lotioned. My hands want to land on her small waist, pull her against my jeans. Instead, I undo the clasp, raise it gently to her neck. She lifts her hair, and for a second I can't move, so badly do I want to put my mouth on that downy neck. She feels my hesitation—surely she must—but doesn't move, neither toward nor away. My fingers struggle with the tiny clasp, and she turns her head so I can see the hint of a smile.

"Robert Plant is coming this summer," she says. "He's playing at the Edgefield. Would you go, if I bought the tickets? Would you go with me?"

With a snap, I clasp the necklace and step back. The absence of her body against mine is a cool emptiness rushing against my chest, and I want to turn away, find a shirt.

"What do I possibly have to offer you in return, Emerson Worthy?"

She turns to face me, and I notice how beautifully the necklace nestles in the hollow of her neck. *Such a simple thing, Will, and it's perfect.* Her blue eyes are hurt, but for once there's no anger spilling out. She raises her hand to my stony mouth, lets her fingers brush my lips. I drop my eyes, feel my jaw clench tight.

"Oh right, that," I say sharply, trying to step around her. She stops me, puts her hands on my arms to hold me still. And then her serious face falls, just dissolves, as she leans into my still-bare chest. I let my arms wrap around her as my bruised self softens.

"I get so much from you," she whispers. "I can't believe you don't know that. I wish I knew how to be what you are. So even, so calm. Always right there, inside."

"Only sometimes I am," I say, and let my lips barely touch the top of her forehead.

"You live like you mean it, Henry. I just rush around, doing things because I should, or think I should. Talking to people I rarely agree with, rarely even like. Kissing Robert Lyall...it just made me think of you."

She lifts her head from my chest, and her eyes, water-bright, latch onto mine. Her hand travels to the pearl at her neck in a move exactly like Addie's. "How long has this been waiting for me, and I didn't even know to go looking for it? What other gifts have I been missing, right in front of my face?"

So quickly I can't stop myself, I bend down to kiss her. Her mouth is warm, her lips are smooth, her breath catches, and for a soft minute we just breathe into each other, close, but barely touching. And then my hands cup her face and I pull her closer, kissing the kiss I've waited so many years to give, and it's long and sweet and leaves us breathless, while the sun paints hope and desire all over my leaky eyes, and I think, *My God, anything, ever, could be*, but even then I feel such terrible caution. My forehead is on hers, my palms strong on her jaw, and I cannot get her close enough, can't get enough of my body touching hers.

"Em," I say, and my voice is rougher than I mean, and she says, "Yes, yes," and I step with her to my bedroom, wondering if there will be punishment for me in this somewhere. But nothing about her feels false, and soon I forget all about looking for traps, soon I forget about everything but her.

Her hands squeeze my biceps as I unbutton her expensive shirt, and my eyes cling to hers as my fingers fumble. All the women's bodies I've known, and it's always been so easy, so smoothly, like a well-rehearsed speech, while my mind wanders and builds sculptures of stone around me. But this time, with her, this time—my hands tremble, the muscles in my thighs shake. Her skin is warm and damp beneath me, like skimming my hands over the top of still water. My feet reach under hers as I cover her body with my own. She is soft as a dream, sweet. Her hands travel over the muscles in my arms, my back, grab for my hips. I breathe her in, watch the light play into the black pearl at her throat. I want to know every salt-polished pore, every hidden scar, the caramel scent of her skin.

And when I cannot hold back any longer, she rises to me, and I feel strong in myself, powerful, every muscle tight. My chest opens to something that feels like light bursting forth and I feel her teeth in my shoulder and the pain is delicious and then, gloriously, thought ends.

The room is warm, the bedroom windows color purple with twilight, and Emerson is twined around me, her legs rubbing against mine. I hold her in my arms, her breath warm on my chest, and feel the rise and fall of her back under my calloused hand. Her fingers play lightly on my stomach, counting ribs, stroking tender skin.

"You're good, Henry," she says, and I chuckle.

"Years of practice," I say, and she slaps my stomach gently.

"No, I mean you're a good person."

She props her chin on my chest to look at me, and I marvel at the perfect softness of her breasts pressing into my flesh.

"I'm proud to know you." Her blue eyes are soft and open. "Will was very fond of you, you know. You were good for him too, I think. He said he felt calm around you."

She takes a deep breath and I count heartbeats, waiting.

"I will probably be angry with you later, you know. I'll have questions. But thank you. Thank you for being good to him. He needed it."

I nod, not trusting myself to speak around the lump in my throat, so close do I feel to her right now. She pulls herself up, lies on top of me, kisses me while I let my hands travel her curves.

I clear my throat, close my eyes, open them again. "I didn't feel like I was very good for him. I've been in love with you for a long time, you know."

"I know," she says softly.

The phone rings and we both flinch in the almost darkness. "Did you pay your phone bill?" she asks with a smile, and I nod. We wait, let the machine pick it up.

It's a woman's voice. "Henry Oliver?"

"Missy Holloway, from across the lake," I whisper to Emmy, as if we could be overheard. "You know her?"

She nods, listening carefully.

"Normally, I wouldn't call you, since you've been such an a-hole, but Doc and I got in a huge fight, and he just left, and he's maybe coming over there, since I told him about you, and he keeps his .45 in the glove box of the Durango, in case you care, so if you're there, you might want to leave. That's all."

Emmy and I make big eyes at each other, and I start laughing. "Oh, damn. The boathouse?" I say. "I have a nice warm bottle of Merlot."

We gather ourselves, we dress quickly, we step from the house into the dark night, and my heart is leaping. Her hand is soft in mine, and despite this new and laughable peril, despite all the things we still need to say, everything, I think, is deeply good.

Tillie leaps

The lake road is empty in the twilight except for a dark sedan parked down the road from the house. There's a tall man in a baseball cap looking for something in the trunk, but he waves and smiles a golden smile as I drive past, and just that little kindness elevates me. I am trying to screw my bravery up tight, afraid that Gavin is done with me. I drive into Portland and park in the one handicapped spot outside the club, trying to act as if I do this sort of thing every day. The growing dark is kind, hiding me as I transfer into my chair. I wonder what the hell I'm doing, wonder why I would ever want to leave the easy rooms of my home. I haven't seen Gavin since the other night, since I skidded down her stairs, away from whatever truth she might make me see. I don't think she's expecting me to come to the show tonight, but something in me, something fierce and proud, wants to try and try and try again.

I pay the cover charge and let the burly bouncer hold the door for me. The club is dimly lit and crowded and loud. Women are tightly packed, and I roll my way through at waist-height, feeling small. I hate crowds because I can't travel through unnoticed, though iron-ically I'm largely unseen. I roll toward the bar as women step out of my way in surprise, and realize how foolish I was in thinking I could find her easily in this overfull room.

There is a mash of women at the bar, and I'm not sure which way to turn. The stage is lit and full of sound equipment, but otherwise empty, so I guess I'm not too late. I am a middle-aged, in-bed-by-ten, historically straight woman in a loud room full of young, proud, cool-looking kids, and my discomfort is becom-ing a physical thing itching at my skin. I maneuver slowly, and finally I see her, sitting at a table with friends down near the front. I'm anxious and suddenly terribly shy. She didn't know I was coming. Maybe she has a date. Maybe she decided I have run through my usefulness. The list of vulnerabilities runs long-winded through my mind.

I wheel close and come up beside her as she's laughing with her friends. I hear the joy in that sound, even over the loud hum around me. She looks lean and strong in her T-shirt, totally at ease, drinking a pint of what looks like porter, and when she turns and sees me, her eyes wide with surprise, all my fears feel completely founded.

I open my mouth, then close it again quickly. I duck my head, I can't help it, and turn to go. I cannot do this. How could I think I could do this? She grabs my arm just as I'm turning away, and crouches down close beside me.

"Tillie!" she says loud over the crowd. "I didn't know you would come, I—" She shakes her head and her eyes, those quick eyes, suddenly flash with pain. "I'm so sorry," she says, and her hands are on my arm, my face is too hot. "I'm really sorry if I screwed up. I really, really am."

I shake my head and try to smile. "You don't have to apologize. I overreacted." Because really, why should I care whether it was raining or not that night? Why does it matter? Emmy lost control, she didn't mean to—it was simply a mistake, an accident. I lick my lips and glance at the table of her friends, now watching us. "Is it okay that I'm here?"

"Yes, yes, please," she says, and leans her head close, resting her forehead lightly on mine. I love her for doing that. I raise my hand to her cheek and feel her breath rush out quick. "Thank you," she whispers. "Thank you for coming."

I nod, and she leads me back to the table. She introduces me to her three friends, whose names are spoken and forgotten, and they all start talking to me at once, and I feel lighter, more welcomed at the party. A black-aproned server comes around—short-haired, thick-waisted, tattooed to her wrists—and I watch her put her hand on Gavin's shoulder, casually. She looks like she could bench-press me, but when she turns my way, her smile is sparkly bright and I feel oddly flattered.

"White wine?" I ask.

She shrugs. "We'll see. Backup choice?"

I shrug back. "Nothing's coming to mind."

The woman smiles and everyone laughs and Gavin says, "Put it on my card, please," and slips her hand into mine, high on my thigh. I feel a buzz through my jeans, just with that slight touch. The lights grow dimmer and the crowd softens. I feel Gavin lean toward me as we all turn toward the stage.

"You look fantastic," she says. "I haven't been able to stop thinking about you."

I smile at her and she kisses me, and it's suddenly so easy and I'm glad I came. A woman in soft brown pants and a black tank top comes on stage carrying a guitar. Her face is soft and kind, and her smile is shy.

"Wow," she says into the mike. "Full house. Damn, I love this town."

The women around me holler and cheer and I squeeze Gavin's hand. The black-aproned server reappears at my side, kneeling, an unlit cigarette precarious behind her very-pierced ear, holding a full wine glass and a charming grin. I thank her and she winks at me, stepping away as the singer on stage starts to play.

The room is hushed as the first chords tremble around us, the full house respectfully silent. I don't know this folk singer; I didn't recognize her name and can't remember it now, but I'm richly entranced by the crowd's response as much as anything. She begins hesitantly, as if she's remembering how to do this. She warms, she plays, she sings, and some parts are so beautiful it hurts, as if every heart in the room were dreaming the same earthly dreams. Why is it that we all feel so stuck when we have this much power between us?

Her lyrics swim like poetry around me, and I sip my wine, one hand in Gavin's. I feel like I'm spiraling upward on some gust of wind, as if the energy in the room itself is building inside me. Is this what an audience does? Combine with the music and create a new, more magical thing? My mind wanders and I find myself thinking of my art. Does having an audience enhance the work, give it further life? Or can each painting, each song, stand on its own without being seen or heard or known? It's good to be asking questions again, in my own life, even if I'm afraid of some of the answers.

After I've finished my glass of wine, another singer joins the first on stage. The second woman is older, rounder, more deeply etched. Her voice is rich and smoky, and the two guitars together weave sadness and wanting and hope around us like warmth from a distant sun. I look at Gavin's face, looking so much younger and fresher than I ever remember being. Her silver earrings catch the light, and she gives me a perfect, golden smile, and in my mind I hear Walter Cronkite's steady, reliable voice say, "And that's the way it is," while Emmy sets the table for dinner, and Butch taps his foot against mine.

"I'm sorry," I whisper harshly to Gavin's open face. "I have to go now. I have to go home." I turn and thread my way around tables, rolling quickly to the door as the urgency leaps in my chest. I'm almost at my car when she catches up to me, startled.

"Why do you keep running away?" she cries. "What happened?"

Her face is lit by streetlights, and her hurt radiates. "I'm sorry," I say again. "I can't explain. It isn't you, I promise."

Gavin laughs dryly and holds her arms wide in supplication to the streetlights. "Tillie, I don't know what I'm doing wrong here, except maybe trying to date someone who isn't all that into dating me."

"I'm sorry, you haven't done anything wrong. Right now, I promise, I just have to get home, I just have to check something." I don't know why it's so hard for me to say my worry out loud. Maybe I'm trying to keep it far-fetched and unbelievable. Because if I told her I think I saw my sister's stalker outside our house, Gavin would believe me instantly.

She kneels down on the concrete beside me, and when she gets close, I think maybe she's right, maybe it is just another excuse to run away from her. Pain washes through my body like a rainstorm, and my whole chest feels cracked open—raw and vulnerable. I need to get back home.

"When I'm around you, I feel like I'm where I'm supposed to be." She shrugs her shoulders, sits back on her heels. "You make me want to grow in my garden. Dig my hands into clay. Make soup and watch the rain. Tillie," she sighs.

"I want that too," I say, and I'm surprised the words are steady. "I do, I think. But you have to be patient with me, please. I'm sorry. Can I see you tomorrow?"

She nods and opens the car door for me to get in. My heart is pounding, overwhelmed as I am by the wine, by the crowd, by the music, by this woman I'm afraid I'm losing, by the urgency of *Hurry, hurry* in my skin.

I reach through the window and grab her hand. "I do want this, I want to try," I whisper, and feel her nod. And then I'm backing out and reaching for my cell phone at the same time and the worry is building greater still, whispering, *Faster, faster, get home now.*

Eve leaps

I wake to a whisper in my ear and look up to see Addie sitting beside me on the bed, shaking me gently.

"Oh," I say. "I was just dreaming about you. You were at your mother's orphanage." I don't tell her the building was crumbling around her as she watched her mother leave, that in the dream, her eyes were deeply and darkly haunted. Now, awake, she looks wide eyed and frightened.

"What is it, dear? Did you have a bad dream? Were you night-walking again?" The moon is bright, streaming long fingers of light through my window and onto her raven-black hair.

"Ms. Eve, Ms. Eve, someone's here, there's a man here. We have to go." She's whispering and I watch her mouth move before the words really land in my ear.

"What man? Where? Did you see him? Where's Emmy?"

She shakes her head and her nightgown trembles. Poor Mrs. Anderson trembles too, clenched against her stomach. Tillie helped Addie paint on eyes, since the last plastic one fell off, and now the doll looks comically wide eyed and surprised.

"I didn't see him, I felt him. And I smelled him. No one else is home. Please let's just go."

Her urgency is real enough to awaken a surge of excitement in my chest. I'm reminded of frightened daughters at midnight, insistent in their belief of witches and cages and hatchways under beds.

I sit up, feeling my head swim a little, and let my feet feel for my slippers. My body is back to being mostly my own now since that little bout at the hospital, but I can't move as fast and I tire easily. My vision is still a little wonky, but mostly better. Addie brings my robe and helps me into the sleeves.

"Where should we go?" I whisper, and my voice crackles with enthusiasm. "I'm not supposed to drive yet. Is Henry home, do you think? I'm sure he is."

"No, I think we should go to the boathouse. And then I'll go find Henry."

"Wait, child, I have to use the bathroom. Old ladies get excited easily!" She waits for me on the bed while I do my business. In the dark of the bathroom mirror, my hair is wild around my head. "Oh my," I whisper to my own smiling reflection. "You're a sight!" I slide my feet back to where Addie stands with her doll, and take her warm hand in mine. "Let's away!" I whisper loudly, and we tiptoe down the hall.

The house is dark and still around us. The moon is bright enough to see by, and I gently squeeze Addie's hand as we sneak down the stairs. This is much better than sleeping, I think. I can feel the worry sliding off her in waves and want to reassure her, somehow, without stoking the misapprehension.

"What did he feel like?" I ask. "What did he smell like?"

Her wide brown eyes find mine in the dark. "Like rust in the pipes. Like a bad luck metal charm. Like smoking cigarettes."

"Goodness, you'll be a writer yet!" I whisper back. At the bottom of the stairs, I see my prescription bottles laid out where the day nurse left them. Nice girl—she's a birdwatcher, she says, so I think we'll get on fine. We tiptoe down the hall to the back door, stopping to listen now and then. *Nothing, nothing, nothing.*

We step outside onto the porch, and my soul leaps at the bigness of the moon. "Look at that, child! It's full tonight!" The yard is bathed in cold white light and I leave my slippers on the wooden slats so I can walk barefoot in the grass. Addie is pulling me toward the lake, but I have to stop halfway down.

"Look," I say again, lifting my chin to bathe in her full-bodied, beatific light. I feel my breath expanding in my chest, filling so much of me. It's warm out still, and gently quiet. My feet are cool in the grass, but I feel magnificently alive. I spread my arms out like open wings, willing to accept whatever benevolence is bestowed. I wonder how much I am seeing right now, and how much I'm not seeing.

"Ms. Eve, hurry," Addie says, and I turn to her in the moonlight.

"Oh, you were made for this," I say, and she reaches up to the bear amulet at her chest. "You have so many wonderful things waiting for you in your life!" I feel warm and deeply held, reverent. "I love you, granddaughter," I say, touching her shoulder.

"Please!" she says, and my forehead wrinkles. Oh, I never mean to make them worry!

"Okay, okay," I say, and she hustles me through the moonlight, down the damp grass to the pebbled shore. The boathouse casts shadows by our feet and the lake sparkles in the moonlight. The water is so still that even the brightest stars are reflected on her surface.

"You go on inside," she says quietly, patting my hand. "I'll go run and get Henry."

"Sure, sure," I say. "You do that." I watch her run off in her nightgown towards Henry's cabin, the doll slinging back and forth at her side. I wonder if maybe I should have stopped her, but I'm sure she'll come back if no one's there.

I hear voices from the boathouse behind me, and push open the door to find Henry and Emmy heaped like kittens on pillows inside, whispering by lantern light. They both have half-empty wine glasses and dopey grins and I think, *Oh, goodness, they've gone and done it!*

I put my hands on my hips, and try to look stern. "You look like royalty there. Leaving us up at the house to battle nightmares all by ourselves."

Henry looks sheepish, his blond hair wildly happy. Emmy smiles dreamily, and I'm suddenly so glad for her that my heart melts.

"Isn't Tillie back yet?" she asks, and I shake my head no. She's wearing a necklace I haven't seen before. The black stone seems to swirl like water in the light from the lantern. I point to my own neck and give her a thumbs up.

"Where's Addie?" Henry asks.

"Oh, she ran up to your cabin to get you. She thought someone was in the house with us." I pat the side of Will's boat like an old friend. "And did you see that moon?" I say. "Goodness me."

"Mother?" Emmy says, sitting up. "Did you say someone was in the house?"

"No, no, Addie thought someone was. She said she felt him. Said she smelled cigarettes. I walked through the house with her, no one's there."

Henry bites his lip. "Could be Doc, but he wouldn't..."

Emmy nods, all business. "I'll go," she says. "I'll go get Addie. Doc doesn't want to castrate *me*. Henry, you stay put with Mother, and Mother, don't go wandering off anywhere, you hear?"

"Aye, aye, cap'n," I say, and give her my best salute. She bends down and lands a peck on my check as she passes by.

"Where's my cell?" she murmurs, patting her hip pocket. "Must've left it. Henry?"

"We're fine, Em. Just go find the kid." He smiles at her and I want to reach my hand out to touch the energy flying between them.

I tromp over to the pile of pillows and sit beside Henry, leaning into his strong arm, stealing his glass of wine. "Eve, you really shouldn't—" but I'm already sipping the rich red wine. It makes my toes warm.

"You two are lovely together," I say, and he looks surprised. I drop my voice to its lowest register and furrow my eyebrows at him. "It's about time," I whisper, and he covers his mouth to keep a laugh of surprise from spilling out. All my loves, and how lucky I am.

Emerson leaps

The moon is splendid tonight, Mother was right. I stand on Henry's rocky shore and turn to marvel at Looking Lake, so calm behind me. Everything is quiet and there's no wind, though I can see wisps of cloud traveling high. *Why don't I spend more time doing this?* Being outside at night, so serene, with moonlight calmly bathing my face. I take a breath, listen to the beat of my heart. I can still smell Henry on my skin, the musky soap that Mother must have given him last Christmas. My skin feels electrified remembering his touch.

I walk through his stone garden, listening to the quiet around me. Henry's cabin is as dark as we left it, and I think maybe Addie went through the gate back to the big house, or is circling back to the boathouse. I consider calling for her, but the night is so peaceful and still that I don't want to interrupt. I stop at the weathered cedar pergola, lean into it, let my head rest against it.

"Will," I whisper, and I know I'm a little drunk, and it's only the moon that hears me, but I say it anyway. "I love you. I miss you so much. You can let me be now. I'm not as mad anymore." The warm and the quiet nestle around me in the dark, and the moon whispers, *Beautiful, beautiful.* I reach a hand to my pearl necklace and hold and hold. "Darling," I breathe, "I forgive you for leaving me."

My exhale is deep and good. I turn toward the gate, I take one step, and then a muffled whumping sound thrums into my bones. *What? What?* Henry's house is softly lit now, and my body is tense, listening. I lift my chin to watch the crying birds dash into the air overhead, pausing to stand and listen to the crackle and hum before I realize: *Fire, it's fire, Henry's cabin is on fire.* His front room, fifteen paces in front of me, is backlit now, and there the outline of a girl, my girl, my Addie. I unfreeze, I leap, I run, and trip on the pressure washer cord and hose, still plugged in—*Goddamn, Henry!*—and slam hard, face-first into packed earth. I scramble to my feet and barrel through the cabin door.

She's inside by the workbench, standing so still, so carefully. Her shocked eyes meet mine, then look back to where Butch Henley stands in the bedroom doorway. He looks tall and strangely stunning, as I imagine the devil looks, and frighteningly vacant eyed. He's talking, just talking, mumbling some argument to himself. "It isn't so much that, but you have to admit, you're watching something big fucking happening, I don't think you really have any idea," he puzzles on, and Addie stands, watches. *Why is she just standing there?* The fire is growing louder, a rolling crackle building like the tide. The room is already too hot as the adjacent bedroom starts to burn, and my body screams *Get out, get out, get away!* I feel a wash of panic slide through me, and my voice feels stuck in my throat. I step in front of Addie, shielding her.

"Run to the boathouse," I whisper hoarsely. "Go get Henry. Call 911." I can feel her breathing behind me, not moving.

The fire behind Butch grows wickedly, filling the tiny bedroom where I'd opened so much of myself to Henry. Butch swings the door shut to bar the fire, and shakes his hand, blowing into his palm. In his other hand, he holds Henry's can of varnish.

"Shouldn't touch the doorknobs, now!" he yells between mumbles, and I have a distinct vision of ragged men on street corners, minds bent by meth and mental illness. Butch starts dumping varnish onto Henry's old couch, painting a spotty line into the kitchen. My heart pounds in my throat. A bedroom window shatters and I jump.

"I heard you with that man, Emmy. The one with the black hat. I saw you through the window." He watches me from the kitchen while smoke seeps insidiously under the closed bedroom door and thickens overhead. "You shouldn't have done that to me. I was ready to fix everything with you!"

I turn to Addie, grab her shoulders, shake her. Her eyes are big and cold with shock. "Come on, I can't carry you! Move!"

I push her toward the door, watching Butch snap his silver lighter open to light his cigarette, and his eyes lock onto mine. He smiles a terrible smile and drops the lighter. Blue fire leaps to life as the spilled varnish catches, and the air looks rich and oily around him.

The fire is burning through the bedroom door, and long fingers of flame are reaching to kiss the front room's ceiling. I see all of this in exquisite focus, as if time itself has slowed down. Smoke makes my eyes water and I hear Addie cough beside me. *How is he still standing there like that?* I push her out the cabin door and toward the garden. Butch is in the kitchen, singing loudly around his cigarette, some punk anthem from the '80s.

"Run, Addie!" I say, and this time she does, barreling down toward the water.

The front room is filling with smoke now as the fire spreads. My shoulders jump as more glass breaks. I stand in the cabin door, trying to look in.

"Butch!" I yell, "Get out of there!" I cough around the black smoke and strain to see his outline in the kitchen. He's still in there, singing.

"Henry!" I hear, faintly. "Henry! Emmy! Are you in here?" A voice is calling from inside, so slight. I squint my eyes, my face sweating in the doorway. The smoke makes my throat chafe and burn. Distantly, I can hear Henry hollering from behind me, but I don't care, can't possibly care.

"Who's there?" I yell. "Who's there? Goddamn it, shut up!" I scream at Butch. "For the love of your mother, shut up!" He stands in the kitchen, moving his hands while he sings, staring exquisitely at the ceiling as the countertops around him burn.

"Henry? Are you in here?" *Oh my God, it's my sister. My baby sister.*

"Tillie!" I scream. "Where are you? Get out of there!" The hallway, she must be in the hallway, she must have come in the front door by the driveway. Surely the bathroom is burning now, which means the hallway is too. I step over the entry back into the cabin, but it's too hot, and the smoke is terrible—I drop to my knees, blinking and squinting and coughing. Then Henry is pulling me out into the night. "Tillie!" I scream. "Tillie!"

The roof is on fire now. The workbench is burning. I can hear sirens, and Henry saying my name, trying to drag me further back.

"No!" I scream. "Goddamn it, no! She's in there. Get them out, Henry! She's in there! She's in there!"

Addie leaps

Ms. Eve is in the rowboat named *Daisy*, tied to the dock, calling to me.

"We're safe on the lake, Addie! Come on, honey, I can't much row this thing myself!"

I know I'm supposed to stay with her, but I can't. I turn and run, back to the burning cabin, back to where Henry is holding Mrs. Worthy on the ground. She's yelling and the cabin burns, everything burns. The roof is full of fire now, and the sirens are very loud. I can see the flashing light from the firetrucks as they light up the hedge between the houses. I run to the thing Henry calls the pergola and grab on, not daring to go any farther. Even standing here, it's awfully hot and smoky.

Mrs. Worthy pushes Henry away and she's kicking him now and he's yelling. She kicks him a good one on the chin and his head snaps back and she's up quick because she's a fast runner too, running back to the fire. She must be trying to get to the man inside, the rusty metal one.

Henry lifts his face from the dirt, and I see there's blood dripping from his nose. He starts to push himself up, and I leap forward to grab him and hold him down. I don't know why, I just do it. The air around us is burning hot, and the smell is strong and sharp, not at all like a campfire.

I put my arms around Henry's head and lay my head on top of his. His breathing is hard and fast. I watch Mrs. Worthy run to the bright-yellow power washer from earlier today, and lift the wand.

"How do I turn this on?" she screams, and then she finds the switch.

"Squeeze the trigger for it to run! Squeeze hard!" Henry is still trying to stand even as he yells at her, and I'm holding him down. The firemen are calling to each other on the other side of the cabin, and one hustles around and starts yelling our way.

Mrs. Worthy points the trigger at the door of the cabin and squeezes. Water shoots out in a big rush and white steam rises up fast like a science project. She is yelling and spraying, stepping forward into the doorway, and I start crying. I can't help it. She's lit like magic by the moon, by the fire. Little pieces of burnt something are falling everywhere like snow, and I watch them land in her hair. Her face is different, tight like a spring that's about to break, and she's yelling, yelling.

Then a big gruff man in yellow is pulling on me and Henry, telling us to get back, get away, and both of us look at the fireman in surprise, because what does he know? Another fireman is running toward Mrs. Worthy, but she's walking into that doorway, that burning doorway, and there's no way he can get there in time. I hit the fireman's strong hands away from me, and Henry calls "Emmy, Emmy!" calling for her to come back because it's no use, she can't go in there now. But she does, following the strong stream of water as steam rises all around her.

I'm lifted off the ground, carried. I beat at the man's back, but he's running me down to the lakeshore. I cry, I scream at him, "She's inside! Go get her!"

"Stay here with your grandma, kid," he says, dumping me on the dock. "It's spreading."

Ms. Eve is still in the little rowboat, her robe bunched up on her lap, barefoot, and she looks so small and scared it makes my crying stop. When the grown-ups are scared, you have to pull yourself up tall. This I know. I step into the rocking boat and sit beside her on the bench, tightly holding her hand. My stomach hurts with worry, but I'm glad for the hurt this time.

"Why did she go in?" Ms. Eve chirps, my grandmother chickadee, and she's seen the whole thing. From the boat, we can see the cabin directly.

"To save him," I say. "I don't know why."

Henry is by the pergola yelling at a firewoman, and hoses are being unrolled, and there are people everywhere. And then a fireman with an air tank on his back trips back out the cabin door and falls down in surprise—even though I don't think firemen are supposed to fall—because two smudged people are dragging themselves out the burning door. Black smoke curls up and around and it's hard to see from where we sit, hard to see anything. The ambulance men have stretchers and block everything, and the police are there, and the firemen spray the roof and the hedges, and it goes on forever. Ms. Eve and I are huddled together, rocking gently, and I'm as scared as I've ever been of anything. I can't stop seeing his eyes—the rusty-metal man's with the gum—the way they held on to me, the way I couldn't even move.

"Mrs. Anderson!" I say, suddenly remembering. "I forgot her in there! I left her behind!"

Ms. Eve pulls me closer and I can't see anymore as the crying fills my everything, just fills my everything. I think maybe I should pray, but I can't remember how. I look up, finally, and the moon has moved across the sky, still brightly lighting us all as if it were all the same to her, as if to the big out-there, none of it matters anyway.

Nine

Henry resolves

The late morning sun is warm on my face as I stare, swollen-eyed. I sit on the ground, unmoving, relishing the little stony sharpness beneath me. The charred black remains of my cabin stand behind the yellow tape like a testament to something I don't understand. *The cabin that once was*, I think. *That which was previously cabin.* I hear Will's quick, rich tone in my head: *Call it whatever you want, chief. It doesn't care.*

The wood-framed building burned like good seasoned tinder, like it had found its true vocation. I helped my father build that cabin, lakeside visit after visit: camping upshore in the giant, far-flung darkness, burning my tongue eating hot fish from tinfoil, hammering 16-penny nails into spruce boards with my quick, smart, kid hands. Today—now—parts of walls still stand, bleakly; sodden black humps all that's left of my rocky life there. I feel the sun tease sweat down my temples, but I cannot move, mesmerized as I am by the thick and complete wrenching of my heart.

I hear the gate open and close, hear Addie's quiet padding feet. She kneels down beside me and I know she sees my stony resolve, my unshaved chin, the damp on my cheeks. I know and I can't make it easier, can't reach out to where she's at. I hear her quiet exhale of breath as she scoots closer to me, joining me in silent examination of the wreckage. After a moment, she puts her hand on my arm and I reach over, pulling her close. We sit together in the dirt, and the sound of her breathing reminds me that I am still breathing too. Addie's like a small and powerful star to me, so amazing because she doesn't know she has such a mighty pull.

"Ms. Eve says you finally slept last night. She says your snoring was like music to fly away on."

I laugh unexpectedly. "Like music, huh? Never heard that before."

"She says to tell you Jack White and—his wife? The flower?"

"Lily, I think?"

"Jack and Lily White are picking up from the hospital, and it's time for you to come back home soon."

I feel something heavy spring onto my chest, just for a moment. "But I thought I was going to pick them up?"

Addie shrugs and we sit and stare some more. She's right, it is good that I finally slept last night. And really, it's good to get the help too. After the ambulances left, I called Matt Vincent, who came to stay with Eve and Addie while I went to the hospital. I didn't know how to be everywhere at once, didn't know how to be everything to everybody this time.

But now, a day and some later, having finally slept dreamlessly and wandered my way into late morning light, having sat with the charred remains after the investigators left, having leaned my head against Eve's own forehead in fear and agony, having wept a little, just a little, I slowly, softly, begin to feel better.

"Addie, I like sitting with you," I whisper into her silky child's hair.

"Me too," she says. "Come on." She pulls my hand and we stand up. My knees pop and she laughs brightly. I never realized before how much parents must get from their children; really, I thought it was just the other way around.

"I talked to my mom on the phone," Addie says, opening the gate for us, turning back to give me a fine white smile. "She's happy. She talked to me. But she's still tired, I guess."

"Give her time," I say, wiping my hand over my mouth.

"She says Captain Mike is coming and he has a good something for me, she thinks. I could hear the happy in her voice, even. I think she might have told me, if I'd pestered."

"But you didn't pester? That's probably good."

"She gets tired," she says again.

We're in the yard now, heading toward the house, and when I look up, I see Emerson standing on the porch, watching us come. She looks a little thinner, a little paler, but beautiful still in such simple ways. She raises her hand in a small wave, and my heart leaps into my throat. I have to stop walking just so my legs will keep me upright. I feel vitally connected to her and grateful as an acolyte. I remember watching her from the ground as my nose bled extravagantly, my limbs heavy as ancient, unmoveable stone. Watching her bully her way past smoke and flame for reasons I didn't then understand.

Emmy smiles and says, "I think your bruises are worse today than yesterday. Well, darker, anyway."

"And may you never give me a black eye again, lady."

"May you never again give me cause," she says. She coughs deeply and reaches for the porch rail to steady herself, and I reach for her elbow. She waves me off. "I'm fine," she says, "fine. Take me to see?"

I nod Addie toward the house. I can hear voices inside, muted laughter. Our moon-round, black-haired girl runs to the porch door as we watch.

Emmy turns back to me. "Michael's coming this afternoon." I smile at her and she adds, softly, "It'll be good to see him."

I take her hand and lead her down the porch steps, back down the path I'd just come, back to the garden gate between our properties. We pass through and she stops, stares. I cross an arm behind her back, down low, and feel her lean a heavy sigh into me.

"I'm so sorry, Henry," she says. "So sorry for you."

The garden paths, the deliberate stones, the cedar pergola and life-saving bench are all untouched, as if unbothered by such a thing as fire, but the place where the cabin stood is a black and lifeless mess.

I rub a hand across my bruised face, bite my chapped lips. "Eve said the investigators were all business. She said they found him pretty quick. You talked to the detectives at the hospital, right?"

Emmy turns and leans her head against my quick heartbeat. I wrap my hands around her back and shut my eyes, letting something go a little.

"Are you sorry you lost the pearl?" I ask. We didn't discover this until the hospital, but it wasn't much of a surprise the black pearl was gone, with that delicate chain and all.

"Makes me sad," she says. "But maybe I only needed it for a little while? Magical thinking, I'm sure."

I consider that, the thought of Will sending a talisman. Magical thinking or not, the idea gives me pause, and I smile in the direction of the pergola.

"Thank you for staying with us yesterday," she murmurs. "It could have been so much worse. We were lucky."

Yesterday I wandered between their beds hourly, held two sets of hands lined with similar black deltas of soot, waited through coughing fits, lifted cups of water, spread balm on dry lips. No intubation, no oxygen chambers, thank God. Scrapes, small burns, singed hair—miraculous, really. After the detective left, Emmy was chatty, triumphant. Tillie was quiet and distant, and I found myself spending more bedside time with her.

"I came home," she said. "I felt *compelled* to come home. Do you know that feeling, Henry? That *have-to* feeling?" And whether I believe in such things or not, her quiet vehemence was compelling in itself.

"On some level, I must have recognized him, although it took me a while to realize. And then when I came home, I pulled into your driveway before I even knew what was wrong. Why would I do that, Henry? Go to your house instead of my own? And then when I saw fire from your bedroom window, I thought you were inside."

I sat in the hospital with Tillie in the late afternoon light, listening to a story that would later get refined, become apocryphal, if never anecdotal; listening to it before it's been edited, listening to her tear-streaked amazement, squeezing her hand. I have felt many things for many women in my life, but Tillie in that moment felt deep as ancient earth to me, like loving the very soil I'd sprung from, like digging my toes into the safe and warm and letting it cradle me like a sacred stone. *She went inside for me.*

"I was in your hallway, and the walls were burning, there was just enough room for me, and I got hung up on that stupid braided rug in the entry. I couldn't go forward and I couldn't go back. And I heard singing, can you believe it? I thought you were in the shower singing, and you didn't even know your house was burning down around you. I called for you! I called!

"And when it got hard to breathe, I left the chair and crawled, but I couldn't get through, and I couldn't see, just heard your goddamn singing. I went back to the chair, I yanked that fucking rug out from under the wheels, and pushed it in front of me. I crawled on it, pushed and crawled. And then that man—goddamn that man! Lord, he surprised me! He reached down like he wanted to pick me up and dance, and his clothes were burning; his watch looked like it was burned into his arm, Henry! And I heard the cabin like it was sighing, like it was crying. My eyes were stinging shut and just as he reached for me a hurricane of water—water so violent I thought it was murder itself!—it blasted him backward, back into the kitchen, pushed him up against the burning cabinets. I was pulled and dragged, and the rug was burning but I didn't care anymore, because I could feel the cool on my head, on my cheeks, and I could breathe, Henry, I could breathe…"

Back in my garden, Emmy squeezes my waist, and I land my lips on her temple, just over the little scar.

"The fire investigator said it's a damn fine thing I had concrete floors. Tillie wouldn't have gotten out if she'd been crawling over burning carpet."

I feel her breathe into me, wonder what she thinks about saving Tillie's life, maybe for a second time.

"What are you going to do, then?" she asks. "You have plans to rebuild? Maybe go a little bigger this time?"

I shake my head and shrug. "I haven't decided yet. I called my dad back East, at his sister's. He's sad to hear about it. He loved this place. He told me he's been paying on a policy for years, and I didn't even know it. It's not much, but it's something. It's a nice surprise."

I imagine she's thinking, *What kind of an adult doesn't know he has insurance?* and then I think, *Well, my kind, I guess,* and then I think, *Well, I don't have to be that way.*

"Caciitua, " I say. "I have no idea what I'm doing. "

"Your little Japanese maple's gone," she says, then stops to cough. "And all your things. Your art. The things you love."

"Most of that's here," I say, motioning to the sweeping stone garden, "and there," I say, nodding toward her big white house. "And here," I say, turning my face to hers.

Emerson's voice is low and still. "You know you can stay with us, as long as you want. I mean," she says, her bright blue eyes like a promise of sweet rain to come. "I mean, I want you to stay with us, while you rebuild. Will you?"

"You'll get tired of me," I say, letting my lips rise into a smile.

"Yes, and you'll get tired of me too, I'm sure," she says, returning the smile. I kiss her softly and feel her fingers run tenderly on my cheek.

"We need you, Henry," she whispers. "I need you, just a little."

"Okay," I whisper back. "Okay." And it is, and it will be, cabin or no cabin, and how blessed I am by these astonishing elements, these women that love me and shelter me and challenge me so.

Emmy turns toward home and I follow, stopping, momentarily, to lay the lightest of kisses on my fingertips and raise my hand skyward, my own private benediction to whatever it is that somehow cradles us all.

Tillie resolves

The house is full of noise and joyful fuss, and I find my pensive self needing a little solitude. Emerson's friends are still in the kitchen with Mother, and Addie is hopping around like a bright-tailed comet. The rental wheelchair is big and heavy, and I just want to be rid of it. Mother was prompting me to look at new ultralight chairs online, but it's too much to think about right now. I roll heavily into my studio, banging the oversized wheel into the doorframe glumly, like new shoes three sizes too big.

I hoist myself from the chair onto the futon and lean my back against the wall. The exertion makes me cough hard enough to make my ribs ache.

A knock on my door and Emerson comes in, holding my phone. "You left this, and it keeps ringing."

I nod at her and she tosses it to me. Gavin's been calling. *Good*, I think, and feel a tiny smile pulling at the corners of my mouth. I look up; my sister's still standing there, watching me.

"You okay?" I ask, lips tight with caution.

She sighs, rubs a hand through her hair, closes her eyes, hands on hips. "There's just so much to do. I'm tired."

"We did just get out of the hospital. I was wondering if you're allowed to get tired. That's a lot to live up to."

"Meaning what, exactly?" she asks, folding her arms.

I sigh, then laugh, which turns into a cough. "Why do you think everything I say is a criticism? I just don't have that much free time, Emmy, to keep thinking of ways to insult you."

Her eyes narrow and my phone rings in my hand. It's Gavin again, and my heart flutters gladly. I put the phone on vibrate and look back at my sister. "I meant it as a compliment," I say. "A lot to live up to because you have such high standards. For yourself, for everyone else. I always assume I'm not measuring up." My head is resting against the window sill, and I reach my arms up and grab the sill to stretch. Despite the heavy wheeziness in my chest and the scrapes on my arms, I feel good and solid.

"Don't worry, I don't measure up either," she says, looking out the window toward the lake. Then she looks back at me and says, "You have such strong arms. I've always been jealous of your arms."

I start to say, *You try dragging yourself around all these years*, but stop myself. I hate how sharp I get with her and resolve to try and do it differently. I drop my hands into my lap and look at them. "Thank you," I say, and sigh. "And thanks for saving my life. Again."

She's quiet, distant, and I want to ask her so many things. Feeling her arm on my back as she dragged us out of that suffocating nightmare, every inch of scraped-up skin screaming to live. Sick on adrenaline, seeing her sooty face on the other stretcher under an oxygen mask like my own, clamped so sister-hard together they had to pry our hands apart. And through all of it, Gavin's out-of-place voice saying, *No rain that night, dry roads*, like a litany, a horrible accusation.

Emerson lowers herself down onto the futon beside me, and we sit in silence for a while. I can hear Henry's rumbly voice and Addie's quick feet. The house feels vibrantly alive around our quiet, like we're in some separate, time-bound pocket.

"Mother seems to be feeling better, have you noticed?" I say. "More with it?"

Emmy turns her head to look at me, then pulls her knees up close to her chest. "I didn't save your life that night, Tillie. You saved mine. And you don't even know it."

My heart is pounding like a quick and sudden earthquake, and I want to say, *What? What?* even though I can hear her perfectly well.

"What do you mean?" I ask softly, and we both stop to listen to the sound of Henry laughing in the kitchen.

"Mother and Father were in New York with the Henleys, you remember? And we didn't go because we still had school."

"I'd just had my birthday," I say. Seventeenth birthday, it was. "You gave me *Goodbye Yellow Brick Road*, and Father wouldn't let me go to the Grateful Dead show at the Coliseum."

"And I'd broken it off with Butch. He'd just found out his scholarship was under review because of the morality charges. You were at your friend Wendy's for a sleepover, and I was home alone."

Emerson's voice is even and careful, but I can hear the emotion at the edges of her words. Tears jump into my eyes, and I don't even know why. "I don't remember that," I say.

"Butch came to the house and I let him in. I was scared not to. I thought maybe I could calm him down if I just talked to him." She's staring at her entwined hands, and I can see her lips trembling.

"He was so terrible, and I was so scared, Tillie. He kept yelling that I'd ruined his life, that I owed him, that I needed to fix it. He was like a different person."

She clears her throat, spots of color high on her pale cheeks. "He broke my lip open with his class ring. This," she says, tapping the small white scar on her temple, "this is from the corner of the glass-topped table."

"Not the accident?"

"No. Tillie, I hardly got a bruise from that and you..." she trails off, and I feel my breath hitch in my throat. "I remember lying on Mother's new orange shag and looking at him standing over me while the blood ran down my face. I thought he was going to kill me. I think he would have hurt me badly at least."

"What stopped him?"

"You did, Tillie. You called home. The phone rang, and I said it's probably Mother and Father calling from New York to check on me, even though it's late back East. It was you. You wanted to come home."

"I don't remember that. I don't remember much of any of it."

"So I told him I had to go get you. I just grabbed the keys to my car and walked out the door. My heart was pounding, and I could hear his feet on the gravel behind me. I saw the blood on my face in the rearview mirror, saw him standing by his car."

"It wasn't raining, was it?"

Emmy looks surprised. "Raining? No, it was a nice spring night, you know? Your friend lived pretty far out of town, out in the country, and any other night I'd have been cursing you for making me pick you up."

"I didn't like to drive," I murmur.

"No, you never did," she says. "I didn't come to the door because I didn't want your friend or her mom to see me, so I just honked. It was dark, and you couldn't really see my face. I'd cleaned up with my handkerchief some.

"He'd followed me there, and I didn't know it. I drove back toward home, because I didn't know where else to go, and I thought if you were with me he wouldn't... it was so dark, there weren't lights out there then, and almost no other cars on the road. The moon was bright, though. It was almost full, I think. And then I saw headlights behind us, getting closer. I sped up and he sped up, and you asked me what the hell was going on, and you were yelling for me to slow down, but I couldn't, he was right on top of us.

"I saw the road turn up ahead and I tried, I tried to make that turn. The tires were so loud! I remember the smell of burning rubber. We crashed through the barrier and down the embankment into that field. I remember we rolled and rolled. My door was smashed. The windshield was shattered. I crawled out the window, and when I looked up, he was standing on the road. I could see his silhouette in the light from his headlights. The moon was behind him, and he was just watching. I would never have left you, Tillie, if he hadn't left. I would have stayed."

"I know," I say. "I believe you."

"I watched him walk back to his Mustang and drive slowly away in the dark. I was so scared, Tillie—you were covered in blood and broken glass, and all I could see was from the waist up, the car was just crumpled around you. I called to you, but you were unconscious. I knew you weren't dead because you kept making little sounds. I didn't know what to do, and when I saw the lights from that farmhouse, I started running. I got a side ache but I didn't stop. I ran across the field in the moonlight."

"Why did I want to come home?" I ask, suddenly feeling like that's important.

"I don't know why. I didn't ask and you didn't say. I didn't care why. But if you hadn't called…I don't know what would have happened to me, what he would've done." I reach over and take her hand, and I can scarcely see the tears on her cheeks for the damp in my own eyes.

"I have never stopped hating myself for what I did to you, Tillie. Never. I always tried so hard to take care of you, and instead I do this!" She motions to my legs and then hits her hand on the futon, her face crumpled with tears.

I reach my arms for her and pull her close as she whispers, *I'm so sorry, I'm so sorry*, into my strong and earthen chest. I rest my cheek against her bent head, holding her and loving her with all my might. Thirty-two years since the accident I thought was caused only by wet roads, and when have I ever thought of the pain it's caused her? How do we manage this life, any of us, and why is it so goddamned hard for us to connect with each other when that's really the thing we need most?

"Listen to me, listen," I whisper. "I am proud of you for what you did, standing up to him and standing up to Father. I think you were unbelievably brave, and not even twenty years old yet. I would forgive you, Emmy, if there was something to forgive, but I don't think you did anything wrong, and I don't think anyone could have handled it better. Well," I add, "maybe you could have told me sooner, since I barely remember."

She raises her head, looks at me with gentle eyes. "I couldn't," she says. "You understand that I couldn't."

"Last night, Emmy—no, two nights ago—you came back into Henry's cabin to get me. Here I thought I was saving him and nearly got the both of us killed. I owe you my life. Well, you and his rag rug."

"No," she says, shaking her head. "Can't we just call it even?"

"Okay," I say, "We're even."

We lean against each other for a long time, listening to the laughter from the kitchen, and I feel soft as a clay riverbank with her in my arms. I think of the other night, think of Butch singing while his shirt burned. I imagine him standing on a country road by a broken barrier, watching the tires spin on a crushed car, and try to imagine what sort of personality disorder would do that to a man. On the ride home from the hospital, Lily White kept asking questions about the fire, and neither Emmy nor I had much to say. I understand more now about why she's kept the story to herself for so long, holding her dark and painful secrets in private counsel.

Her body is warm against mine, and I feel unbelievably safe.

"Emmy," I say, and she tilts her chin toward me, listening like I matter. "Despite what it looks like, I'm still whole."

"Yes," she says, "anyone can see that. You are. I think I am too."

I nod slowly and together we sit in peace, whole as we are, as we were meant to be, probably, needing nothing else but goodness and warmth and light, a little rainfall, and good solid earth in which to deepen and thrive.

Eve resolves

My home is full of laughter again, and I feel like I'm floating. Emmy seems calm but cheerful, and Henry looks like he could lift boulders. I've put him to work peeling and slicing potatoes for the big dinner tonight, and Addie is working on a card for

Michael. She sits at the table with big paper and colored markers, carefully drawing bright fish in concentric circles. I wonder how much of her mother's artistic eye she has, and the thought pleases me immensely. So many ways she will find to express herself in this lifetime.

Emerson is on the phone in the great room, talking some business, I'm sure. I've already sent the young day nurse home, telling her I feel fit as a fiddle, and I do. Oh, I'm getting tired, and an afternoon nap will be in order, but I'm up and cooking, humming to the children. Looking at us all, you'd never know I was so recently out of the hospital, or that Henry's cabin had burned to the ground, with all of his things too. But then again, I never was a delicate lady, and he never was a things kind of man.

"Do we really need all these potatoes, you think?"

"Oh, yes," I tell him. "We certainly do. Everyone wants second helpings of my scalloped potatoes. Addie, honey, when you're done with your card, will you pick out napkins for the table?"

She nods without looking up, and I'm glad to see her so comfortable with me. I wonder how she's feeling about Michael's visit and this whoever he's bringing along. I think back to Emmy's first day here with her, how surprised we all were, and now look at us together.

The doorbell rings and I get flustered, thinking Michael's come early, and wipe my hands on a damp dish towel before hustling to the door. It's the co-op Gavin to see Tillie, and I usher her in joyfully. She kisses my cheek, hands me fresh tomatoes and an embarrassingly large cucumber.

"From my garden," she says. "They're organic."

"Of course they are, dear," I say, patting her arm. "They always are with women like you!"

Her laugh is plum bright and fills the kitchen as we step in.

"Henry, honey, do you know each other? Of course you do, what was I thinking? I'll just go get Tillie."

I pat Addie's shoulder on my way to Tillie's studio and knock lightly before opening the door. Tillie is in her rental chair over by the half-finished painting of women.

"Your Gavin's here," I say. "What's wrong?" Her face is pale and puffy from crying, and I cross over to where she sits.

Tillie shakes her head. "Nothing's wrong, Mother. Everything's just close to the surface today."

I pull the stool up close beside her and look into her earth-tone eyes, greenish now from the crying. "You've been through the wringer; I'm not surprised. I'm glad to see you've been talking to Emmy."

Her face is a question and I wave my hand. "Oh, I can always tell with you two, but you know, it's good to travel apart sometimes and come together again. As much as I loved to travel with your father, I also loved the coming home. You always had so much to tell me!"

My strong and tan daughter has gray in her hair now, and crow's feet that echo mine, her father's hazel eyes, my mother's love of the earth, and still I see her ponytail-young, pulling a red wagon neighbor to neighbor for a newspaper drive, her rocket pop dripping down her fingers. Or soaking in her skin-tight jeans and leaving the bathtub blue. Or arguing with Adam, tear streaked, after Walter Cronkite's report on My Lai.

"Henry's good for her," she says, and I guess she's talking about Emmy. "He's powerful in a different sort of way than what she's used to."

"More levelheaded too. The Henley boy was unbalanced; I thought so then. He should have been in a mental asylum."

"Mother, I don't think they call them that anymore. And being a sociopath is probably different than being mentally ill. Will was bipolar—but we called it manic then, remember? And usually he did well on his medication, right? Do you think he should have been committed?"

"Of course not." I sigh and rest my hand on her long brown hair. "I think we're all a little crazy," I whisper. "We're all mostly just doing the best we can."

Tillie looks at her painting of the reverent women, watching something unpainted in the middle of the circle. She reaches her hand out as if to brush something away that isn't there.

"You gave me my first set of oils," she says, and I nod.

"Well, you wouldn't even leave your room that summer. I had to give you something to do." I remember her always in bed or sitting at the window, so silent, so newly broken. How often I had to fly away from where she'd been planted so she wouldn't see my own broken heart. Mothers don't ever recover from their children's pain. Not ever.

"I wonder if I would have found it any other way. My art, I mean. I don't know if I've ever really thought of that before."

I rub my hand on her strong back and think how good it is to make peace with ourselves. Such bravery!

"I don't want to finish it," Tillie says, nodding at the canvas. "Do you think it's okay to leave something unfinished and call it good?"

"Well," I say, "I think it depends on your reasons."

"Nothing I could paint would do it justice," she says. "It feels so big to me. There isn't enough talent or luck in the world for what I'm trying to say. Like trying to write the name of God. Like it's more honorable not to try."

"I think you would know what's best for you, honey. And speaking of what's best for you, Gavin's still waiting in the kitchen."

"Oh," she says, as if she's forgotten, then blushes boldly in front of me.

"I love you more than you can even imagine," I say brightly, and plant kisses all over her earthen cheek. She laughs and pushes me away and rolls to the door. I stay on the stool, feeling warm and light and happy, as if I could just float away. I can hear the girls' laughter from the kitchen, can see sunlight sparkle freely down on Looking Lake.

I walk over to Tillie's futon and lie down, spreading my arms wide to my sides, like wings. How I used to love to travel; I loved skyrides and chairlifts and funiculars. First-class flights everywhere, and once a fifteen-minute biplane ride that left me red-cheeked and grinning all day.

And now my body is old; she's wearing out on me. But my mind, my spirit! I feel like I'm still seventeen, drinking Cokes with my girlfriends, tossing my chin away from serious Adam Foster. I could never have guessed at this life of mine. I'd like to think I've always sought joy, newness, opportunity, always been willing to fly on a moment's notice. And if my daughters are different than I am, then what of it? They are lovely and smart and capable, different from me in so many ways, but that's nothing to mourn. I rather suppose our differences are something to celebrate.

I think of Tillie alone in her room after the accident, how I couldn't even bear it. So many things I didn't know then; so many things I ran from. I failed my daughter then. Both of them, when they needed me.

And I think of Henry's rowboat in the darkness, the fire blazing wild, the moonlight all around. I watched my eldest daughter walk into fire, felt my heart stop cold, felt the tethered panic of powerlessness. I thought it was sacrifice. I thought it was penitence, hers or my own I couldn't say, because maybe as mothers we always feel punished, responsible. And if I could have flown away at that moment, disappeared entirely into that bright-moon night and left that dreadful scene behind? I wouldn't have, and I didn't. In my own small way, I stayed, stood fast, did it better.

Tears push from my eyes and I curl over and into myself, just for a minute, to rest. Tillie's studio is warm and bright, nestling me. I think of how the stroke frightened me at first—this betrayal of my once-loyal body—but now it's only deepened my resolve. I'm not ready to leave this world. I still have lifetimes ahead of me, and no frailty, no mental gaps, no faltering power will take that from me. I can soar through a year in a moment, by lying in the grass with the bluebirds, or humming a lullaby to Addie, my lovely child. My daughters look at me with pity sometimes, now creeping through the last decades of my life.

Don't they know it could be gone for any of us, at any moment? Don't they know there is a world of possibility around them, always, always?

"Travel with your own light, girls," I whisper to my folded hands the words I used to whisper in their ears at bedtime. "And you'll never be in darkness long."

Emerson resolves

I finished the potatoes for Mother so she could have her nap. I found her curled like a child in Tillie's studio and felt flush with love, covering her with a thin blanket. And when I came out, Tillie said Michael had called, they'd landed at PDX, and were on their way to a rental car.

Now I am pacing—I can't help it—and Addie is furiously illustrating a story she's written. Tillie and Gavin are in the garden, and bruise-faced Henry is off doing some sort of Henry chore, shovel in hand. I do appreciate a man that likes his alone time, same as I. I stand bent-armed and aimless in the kitchen and drink strong coffee like it's the last I'll ever have. I have so many things to do, and I can concentrate on none of them.

My chest aches from deep smoke, and I know my eyes are still bloodshot. Yesterday at the hospital, I could think only of the fire, playing and replaying the scenes in my head, but doing that awful thing we do—that *what if* thing. What if I hadn't heard her? What if I had, but had done nothing? What if and why and what if again.

One of the detectives kept alluding to the fact that I knew this man was dangerous, suspected he was following me, was fairly certain he'd broken into my home, but had done nothing.

I said, "It's fairly obvious he was decompensating rapidly, and do you honestly think a restraining order would stop a man who was willing to set himself on fire?"

But that was yesterday, and today I just feel exhilarated from the other night and wrenched clean from my conversation with Tillie, like a wet cloth squeezed dry.

It isn't lost on me that without this almost-tragedy, it's almost certain we would not have spoken of the accident. I wouldn't have, anyway. Why is it I waited so long to tell her what she didn't know? The pain of telling was nothing compared to the pain of holding it so tightly. I think of Henry telling me about Will. How long he's held that from me. How many times he's glanced my way in the past ten years, gauging, biting his tongue. Did he expect me to blame him for the suicide? There is only one man I've ever blamed for that, and my anger at Will, my turning away from the memory of him, only injured me. It does no good to snub the dead. I've tried.

I think of Henry's soft eyes and stubbled chin, think of his mouth on the corner of mine, the rush of heat through my body. And Will, my Will, did he feel those things too? I feel waves of conflicting emotion when I let my mind flow there, to thoughts of them. And I have so many questions! These two men I've loved, I imagine them loving each other. The thought of Will's hands on Henry's strong, bare chest, the two of them standing chin to chin, thigh to thigh...I feel sudden heat spring to my cheeks and step quickly across the kitchen, as if trying to step away from my own daydreaming blush.

I glance over and Addie is watching me, crayon poised above the paper. She bends her head back to her work, and I rub my hand on the back of my neck, rinse out the coffee pot, and measure out more of the freshly ground coffee. My son is coming home today, home to me. My stormy black-haired Michael, as brilliant and cunning as his father, as vulnerable and darkly barricaded as I can be. He is distant to me, and I miss him terribly. No child can possibly understand how easily and completely they're able to wrench the ones that love them most. And yet he's only ever been a mirror of us, of Will and me. At least that's all I've ever seen.

"Addie?" I say, and watch her crayon stop on the page, though her eyes don't rise. "Tell me about Captain Mike? What do you think of him?"

Her forehead creases like it's an odd question, and I suppose it is. She plays with the black crayon, rolling it on the table between her fingers.

"He's good," she says, in her careful tempo. "He visits. He brings me red hot candy and takes us out to dinner. He smokes too much. He is very kind and he makes me laugh." She starts coloring again, and I think she's done. I'm turning away when she says, "What do you think of him?"

I look at my hands resting on the burnt orange counter. I remember the way he curled into me, our new son, wedged between Will and me, the feel of his toes on my belly, his fat fist resting on his cheek, sleeping through our silent amazement.

"I think well of him," I say, and I'm glad my back is turned so she can't see the trembling sadness as it tumbles through me.

"You should tell him," Addie says, and my sudden smile is broad. "Maybe he would like to know."

I'm opening my mouth to speak when I hear the sound of a car in the drive. I look through the kitchen window quickly and see the rental sedan parking beside my Lexus. I thought I would rush out, but I can't, I can't. I turn to where Addie sits at the table, thinking maybe she will leap to the door, but neither of us move. All we can do is look at each other. We hear doors slam, footsteps on gravel, soft voices, and then Henry calling a hello.

I take a deep breath and watch Addie do the same. I reach out to her, wordlessly, and she scrapes her chair back, stands, walks over, takes my hand. There is a world of possibility, I think, every time we—any of us, all of us—are brave enough to walk toward it. Her small hand is warm in mine and we smile small smiles together.

"Okay, then," I whisper, and we go to the door.

Michael is standing with Henry, smiling and nodding, talking. Laughing about Henry's bruises, I imagine. He stops and turns to us as we walk down the porch steps. Tillie and Gavin are there too, standing with a Native woman, a sparkling-bright stranger.

"Michael," I say, quietly. I walk to where he stands and put both my hands on the forever wind-roughened cheeks of my fisherman son. "Sometimes I forget how much you look like your father," I say. "You're beautiful. I've missed you so much."

"Mom," he says, pulling my hands from his face. "Stop. You're leaking." But his cheeks rise in a smile, and he lets me hug him close.

"Hey, Addie," he says, motioning to her bone necklace. "Spirit Bear." He crouches down, hugging her at her height. "Hey, it's been okay here, right?"

She nods and he stands, looking around at all of us.

"I have someone for you to meet," he says, and we turn to the woman.

She is maybe in her late forties, but it's hard for me to say, short and broad and well-dressed, beaming widely. Her black satin hair is pulled back and she looks comfortable, casual, as serene as new-fallen snow. Her hands are crossed at her waist, and I'm surprised to notice she's wearing a silver Fendi watch I'd considered buying myself. I feel like kicking myself for being surprised; me and my stupid assumptions.

"Hello, Addie," she says warmly, and it's a pleasure to hear someone else speak in that careful and distinctive way. "I'm Ruth," she says. "I'm your Aunt Ruth."

I feel Addie's hand in mine again, but tight this time. She stands a little behind me, and I feel her shake her head, a slow no.

"My Aunt Ruth's dead," she says quietly. "She died in the earthquake at the orphanage, with the others. Mama dreams her ghost sometimes."

"We were young," the woman says, and her voice is calm and clean. "I was six when I was adopted. Your mother, Leah, she's only one year older. My parents—the Andersons, they're good, kind people—but they couldn't adopt two girls, they couldn't take us both."

I can feel Addie close beside me, as if we're vitally connected somehow. I pull her in front of me, put my arms around her, put my face close to her cheek, and nod my head, *Yes, yes.*

"I didn't ever know what happened to her. I assumed she'd been adopted too. Every time I did something new with my family, I imagined she was doing the same somewhere with her new family. But it broke my heart to be away from her." There are tears in her strong eyes now, and we all stand, watching, listening. Her soft words have a calming effect, and I feel bundled inside, banked by snowdrifts.

"Your friend Michael found me," she says and smiles at him. "He brought me back to Leah. Never did I think, not ever in this lifetime...Do you know why you have your name?"

Addie shakes her head no, but she's listening raptly, and warming, I can tell.

"When we were girls," Ruth says, "Leah and I used to pretend we were sister queens. I remember dragging my blanket around behind me like a cape and getting wound up in the metal legs of the bed. I was Queen Adelaide. I thought it was the most beautiful name I'd ever heard. And I was right," she says. "It still is."

Her words land into the silence between them and it's a frozen moment, no one moving, no one tipping the scales, all of us waiting.

"Aunt Ruth?" Addie says finally, so quietly it's like a breath on my arm. "Aunt Ruth. Would you like to come inside?"

She leads her aunt inside, and everyone follows but Henry and me. I step to him, clutch his arm, and watch them, this clan, walk into my home. Watch Gavin push Tillie up the ramp. Watch Michael wipe his boots outside the door. My heart feels too big right now, and my mind makes slow circles of disbelief.

"What do you think about that, huh?" he says, stepping back so he can look me in the eye. "How did he find her? She looks just like Addie, I think. That's so cool."

He leans against his shovel handle, looking handsome and smudged.

"Digging up rocks again?" I ask, because I don't want to talk about her right now. Not casually, not like this.

"I tried, Em. I looked through it all but I couldn't find your pearl. I'll go back later if you want, maybe use a rake."

"You aren't supposed to cross the yellow tape," I say, shaking my head. I had no idea that's what he was doing, such an act of kindness for me. He is so beautiful in his body it's magnetic to be near him, knowing I can touch him however I choose.

"Don't hug me," he says. "Look, I've already gotten soot on your arm."

I wrap my arms around his waist anyway and lean against his warm, granite chest.

"Thank you for trying," I say. "But I don't need it. He isn't lost to me."

"I was thinking," Henry says brightly, tapping his shovel on the gravel. "I have some ideas, for the rebuild. I was thinking of a water feature for the garden. Like a fountain, maybe?"

I pat his chest softly. "How about you think about living quarters first?"

The kitchen is full when we go in. Mother is awake now and flitting around, talking to everyone at once. Ruth sits with Addie at the table, speaking softly. I see Michael in the hallway looking at the photographs on the wall. Henry lets my hand go, and I walk to him, my cloudy son.

"Mom," he says, without looking at me. "Are you living here now? I'm glad if you are. This is a better house for you."

This is the house where he found his father, in Henry's yard. There are oceans of things I want to say and questions I want to ask, but I don't know how. I'm afraid anything I do will drive away my mercurial child.

"I'm thinking of selling the other house," I say carefully, watching him intently. "It's what your father asked me to do."

Michael turns from the pictures, his dark brown eyes examining me squarely. "He did? Well then, you should sell it."

His almost-black hair is curly, scruffy, and he smells like cigarettes. So toughened now. I think of him carefully bent over the piano, twelve-year-old fingers long and lean on the keys, practicing his lesson in private, always so serious. He used to buy me flowers for my birthday, and iron his own shirts before dances, and win school awards without telling us. How is it he ever traveled so far from me? Became so coarse?

I take a deep breath, feeling my lungs rasp still, and put my hand on his arm. I'm resolved to ask him, no matter what.

"Is she yours, Michael?"

"Mom, no. You mean Addie? No. Did you think she was?" His brow tightens and I drop my arm, thinking his anger will storm out at me now.

"I—I didn't know. I thought it was possible, yes."

"No, Mom. I would tell you if I—goddamn, I would never do that to you." He turns to me, grabs my forearms, and I think, *Now it comes, now*.

"Mom. I would never do that to you, do you hear me? If I ever have a kid, God help me, I'll tell you, okay? I wouldn't take that away from you. My kids would need you. You could teach them about...stock portfolios and wine and cashmere."

This makes me laugh, as it's meant to, and I'm not sure if what I feel is relief or disappointment. "Okay, okay," I say. "You'll tell me."

"But family isn't just what you're born into, Mom. You know that." He rubs a hand on the back of his neck in a gesture I recognize as my own.

"I worked with Paul out of Dutch Harbor, back in the day. He was a good deckhand, but rough. Worked hard, played hard. We met Leah when she was serving drinks at our favorite bar, and they were inseparable. Felt like we played years worth of three-man cribbage and spades, listening to Christmas shout-outs from family to family on the radio. She was funny, and smart, and he wanted to get married before the baby came but they didn't get the chance.

"We were pulling up crab in a storm, running on almost no sleep. He slipped on the deck and got crushed under a heavy pot. I saw it happen, but couldn't get over there fast enough. I just wanted to help Leah. I wanted to do something. So I help, I stay in touch. Addie's a great kid. Paul would be proud."

"I'm proud," I say, and Michael's eyes flash at me, dark as his father's. "I'm proud of you."

He puts his hand on my shoulder, gently, then takes it away. "So that's the story," he says and bites his lip. "I'm really sorry for Henry, his house. I didn't hear the details yet, so maybe later? I'm glad you're okay though, all of you." He sighs deeply, and I want to hug him and hold him close. "I'm not gonna lie, Mom. It's tough to be here."

"I know," I barely say. "I know, honey. And I'm so glad you're here." He lets me squeeze his hand, then he pulls away.

"I'm going to go make myself useful, okay?"

He walks from the hallway back into the kitchen and calls loudly to Mother. "Grandma! I'm taking you home with me. I could use your help on deck!"

"Why?" she calls back. "You need a new captain?"

I lean my shoulder against the wall, just to watch them all. Addie is not my granddaughter, and it changes nothing. I love her as my own. Tillie catches my eye as her cute Gavin lays a lively hand on her shoulder. My sister, my mother, my son. My Henry. My love for them is elemental. I did not expect this in my life, and I have to wonder, again, what else I've been missing.

I walk through the kitchen, past everyone's industry, walk through the great room, past the formal dining table with color-ful tableware. I pull a volume of poetry from a shelf and slip my shoes off on the way. The tan leather sofa is soft and wide, wait-ing. I lay myself down and listen to the buzz of family nearby.

A clatter of flatware, and I look up to see Henry's bruised face gaping at me.

"Emerson? Are you okay? What are you doing?"

Everyone stops and looks at me from the open kitchen.

"I'm fine," I say. "I'm resting. If any of you has a problem with that, please do let me know."

I smile like we have a secret and his eyes flash. My body feels warm, just to see him across the room. He will sleep in my bed tonight. And after that, I don't know. Don't need to know.

I set my book on my chest and close my eyes, just for a minute, to let my brimming feelings wash through me. In my mind, I see a long line of people standing on drought-hardened, cracked earth. The sky is cloudless blue; the sun is bright, baking down on my succession of people: My father with a suitcase in each hand. My mother in her fur, then again in a bright headscarf, car keys in hand, then again older, smaller, white haired. My baby sister young, standing still and upright in her Brownie uniform, eyes closed. My sister again, strong chin raised, sixteen and powerful. Again, but diminished, now legless in her chair. The line rolls on and on, each person I love in all the ways I remember them, all the times I've known them, standing in silence, in shut-eyed separateness. My husband, my son, myself—even myself—so closed off, far away. No one speaks, no one even reaches out to touch. Why am I seeing all of us this way?

I remember suddenly the stormy afternoon with the psychic, Tillie's errand. *You see truth when others are blind*, she said. *Let go the control. Be generous with your gifts.* And something of Tillie's: *Bring them to life with rain.* Was that right?

"Let's all just love each other," I whisper and feel Henry sit on the couch beside my hip. He takes my hand but I don't open my eyes.

I imagine the deep-blue sky darkening, and when the first raindrops fall on their faces, the people flinch, squint, wake their faces into surprised smiles. The rain falls harder and eyes open, faces turn upward, even mine. All these people I love, and all of us thinking we're doing it wrong, that we aren't good enough or loveable enough or anything enough. The baked earth eases, softens, begins to sprout green. The line loosens, my people step away, see each other, speak and smile and laugh and hug, our young selves with our old selves, all of us together. As if it were that easy. As if we all could just wake up and be brave and not hurt each other anymore and get what we need.

"Henry," I whisper. "Henry."

"I know," he whispers back. "I know, it's all so big. You're lovely, and I'm going to miss her too."

Addie is going to leave us, I know, and I think of a thousand lakes I would swim across to keep that from hurting as it's going to. In my mind, I let the rain fall. Welcome it, even. *Be of forgiveness*, Addie whispers, as the psychic did. *Yes*, I answer. *Yes and yes and yes.*

Addie resolves

I did not know things like this could happen to people like me. My Aunt Ruth is beautiful like Mama, and she keeps smiling her big and snowy smile at me like we have a secret. I show her everything. I show her my room and the place where Mrs. Worthy's present was hiding and the garden I help with and the gate I found. I show her the burned-up cabin and watch her face become still like the blue heron stands. It is good to see someone else's face like my own face.

I take her down to the lakeshore, and we stand on the rocks, watching a fast boat go by in the middle of the lake. The waves come after the boat is gone, late like thunder, and I watch Henry's rowboat, *Daisy*, go up and down.

"Would you like to go for a row around the lake?" I offer, but Aunt Ruth laughs and hugs me close.

"No, thank you," she says. "Another time."

We walk to the end of the Worthy's dock and sit cross-legged at the end. The sun is warm and I could dangle my feet in but

I don't. I watch her face instead, watch the way she shines like sunlight on snowbanks.

"Your mother misses you terribly, Addie," she says, and I don't say anything, just look at my hands in my lap. But what I'm thinking is, *I'm not so sure.*

"Leah loves you. She talks about you more than anything."

I grab on to my Spirit Bear amulet, Mama's most precious thing. *Then why did she want to leave?* I'm thinking. *Why did she do that?*

"When the phone rang, after all these years, I felt a hundred different ways at once. When I saw her, I cried, we both cried. Not just because of all those feelings, but because I could see the hard parts too. My beautiful, strong sister, smart and wise, with such pain inside. A solitary nomad."

"Like a bear," I say. "Or the fox or the wolf. If they lived in the city, in an apartment."

I didn't mean to be funny, but Aunt Ruth laughs, so I guess it was funny. I smile and keep my eyes on the too-bright lake. Aunt Ruth talks like she's used to talking to kids.

"Yes, like that," she says. She stops and takes a breath like she's thinking hard. "I have two sons, your cousins. They're teenagers. They still think everything I do is about them. It's true that some things are about them, but not everything.

"And my husband makes the same mistake sometimes. He's a doctor, a surgeon. I teach at the university. We are educated people. And still he thinks everything I do is about him. So maybe that is human nature?

"I will tell you, since maybe you do not know. Your mother has a chemical imbalance that makes it hard for the good feelings to win out over the bad feelings. She's taking medicine now that will help, and she's seeing someone regularly who she can talk to about her feelings."

"She can talk to me about her feelings," I say, knowing I'm interrupting.

"Addie, it's different. Let her take her grown-up problems to other grown-ups. That's how it's supposed to be. I'm sorry she placed some of this burden on you, but sometimes the bad feelings take our good judgment away."

I don't have anything to say, even though I have a hundred things to say.

"We don't know who our parents were, Addie, and your mother has been alone for a long time. I found some good people, my husband's people. My husband is Sugpiaq. The rushing-ocean-waters people. They have welcomed me as true family. We live in the city, but summer with them in a village near Homer. My sons are there now."

I turn to her open face, her kind eyes. "Is it fish camp?" I barely say.

"Yes," she laughs. "Your mother told me how much you loved the Yup'ik camp. Some things will be different, some will be the same. I'd like for you to join us there while she gets well. Come stay with us. Leah can visit. You will both be welcomed."

My Aunt Ruth puts her arm around me, and I lean against her. I almost feel like crying, but the feelings are bigger than that. It's a feeling like being alone and then suddenly not being alone. And you didn't even realize how alone you were until you aren't anymore. Mama and I have been alone for a long time. Now maybe we aren't.

"Help me up, niece," she says, and touches her head gently to mine. "Let's go see if we can be helpful."

We nearly run into Henry at the back porch door, who's come looking for us. Captain Mike is on the porch smoking a cancer-causing cigarette and talking on his phone. He winks at me, like he does, and we go inside. The table I set looks very important, and Tillie's co-op friend is putting fresh-cut flowers into a vase, and there are a hundred different smells to enjoy. It's very early in the evening, but I guess we're eating now.

I wash my hands then sit down beside Aunt Ruth. She has stayed very close to me, and it feels nice. The grown-ups are all laughing and talking at once. Mrs. Worthy is happy and warm like bathwater, and she and Henry keep touching each other's arms. He's always looked at her like his eyes are opening to a secret, but only partway, like his hidden gate. Now he looks at her with eyes wide open, and she looks back. He is like a giant boulder I want to climb on to watch the sky. He feels that good to me.

And Tillie moves her hands like fine musical instruments, like the symphony we saw. She is the willow tree, protecting me. We've laid in the grass and painted quietly and dug in the earth and cried. I have to look at my water glass for a minute because I will be leaving soon, and my heart feels full-moon big, too big for my body to hold.

Ms. Eve is laughing with Henry like they have a special joke, and she isn't wearing any shoes, I notice. Her white hair is sticking up in back perfectly from her nap. She is my chickadee friend. I think of pulling her across the grass at night, under the bright moon. How she stopped to stare at the sky, like a child would, like I would. I think of her falling, her body a limp bird. I will never forget the sound of her hitting the ground, and how the white fairy fluff just kept floating by and the sky stayed forever blue. I don't know why we love people that will leave us, but I guess we just keep doing it anyway.

Everyone sits, finally, and wine is poured, but not for me, and Ruth is telling a funny story about a professor at her school. And then she tells everyone that Mama just won a juried art competition for her beads, which I didn't even know. And then all the grown-ups are telling stories, and Captain Mike has his arm on the back of my chair, and he's texting someone with his phone. He is very busy and I know it's hard for him to be here.

I watch Mrs. Worthy and I watch him and they don't really seem to notice each other. It makes me sad. I take small, delicious bites of food and watch them. I think if my son were home after a long time, I would want to sit near him and touch his arm and listen to everything he has to say. I think I would wrap safe magic powers around him, even if he doesn't know it. But then I think maybe she is doing that, very secretly, so he doesn't get angry, and I smile at her because now we have that secret and I understand how she's keeping him safe.

Mike leans back and wipes his mouth and says, "Well, she didn't even know to look. It's true that adoption records are private, but death certificates are a matter of public record. Leah thought Ruth had died in Seward, but there was no record. All I did was hire a good investigator who did the rest."

Ruth is nodding and smiling. "And there are reunion websites online. I've been looking for years. I didn't even know our last name. My parents are lovely people; they were trying to protect me. I used to think perhaps it was a dream I'd invented, this sister of mine."

"It must be amazing," Tillie says, "to find her after this long. In a sense, it's almost like finding yourself."

Ruth nods slowly, and I'm proud to see how they watch her and listen so respectfully.

"Identity is so vital to us all…" she says and my mind wanders.

I watch Tillie's friend eat just the vegetables and think about what we've lost. I lost what I thought was my regular life, and now that I've gotten used to this, I'm going to lose it too. Tillie lost her legs but found other things, she says. Mrs. Worthy lost her husband and her son, even though he's sitting with her now. Henry lost his mom and dad both, even though one is still alive. My favorite, Ms. Eve, lost her husband and some of her hair.

She sees me watching and offers me more potatoes, with just her hands. I shake my head no so I don't interrupt.

Then I resolve to think about what we found instead. Well, Mrs. Worthy found she likes this house better, and Tillie found a nice friend that I saw her kiss in the garden, and Henry found out he's allowed to love Mrs. Worthy, and Ms. Eve and I found each other. And Aunt Ruth found me.

My fork drops too heavy from my hand, and everyone stops talking to look at me. "Your hat, Henry."

"My hat?" he says.

"Your black 'Best Friends Forever' hat?"

"My black Blond From Fargo hat?"

"It burned up," I say, and he nods. "And your present that we found," I say, pointing at Mrs. Worthy, even though pointing is bad and I forgot.

"My pearl," she says. "From Will." Then coughs.

"It burned up. And your wheelchair," I say to Tillie.

"It burned up," she says trying to sound like me, but kindly, not mean.

"And Mrs. Anderson!" I say. "Her too!" I feel excited, like I'm figuring something out.

"Mrs. Anderson?" Aunt Ruth says. "But I'm Mrs. Anderson."

"My doll," I say. "She died in the fire. You're Mrs. Anderson?"

"Ruth Anderson. I kept my name when I married."

Everyone sits in silence for a minute, trying to figure out what that means. Maybe it means nothing, maybe it's just funny, like how life is funny sometimes.

"They were all presents, weren't they?" I ask, trying to think. The hat and the necklace and Mrs. Anderson and probably Tillie's fancy wheelchair, although I'm not sure about that one.

Ms. Eve opens her arms wide towards everyone. "These are the gifts that matter, I think. The ones worth keeping."

"Ms. Eve, you didn't lose anything in the fire, did you?"

"Oh, I'm not much for things, Addie," she says, light as air. "We knew the Henleys well, a long time ago. Adam was very fond of Karl. And there was a time when Emerson Foster was too. Maybe he lost his way. Maybe his compass was broken from the start. But his life had value, just as each of our lives do."

She picks up her wine glass, and all the adults do the same. I've seen toasts before but never been in one. Mike nudges me and I pick up my water glass.

"To our lives, that we each may live them to the fullest."

We all clink glasses, and the smile is so wide on my face I can barely make it stop. Then there are more toasts, because it seems like everybody has something important to say. Then Henry says it's time for me to read my moon report. I get that nervous feeling in my throat, but I stand up anyway.

"Moon Facts," I say, and my paper shakes in my hands. "By Addie Long." I'm nervous to feel all of them watching me.

I explain how the moon orbits the earth and has no atmosphere and no water, which of course they should already know. I tell them the moon's gravity is why we have tides, even in big lakes, not just oceans. I tell them about how other planets have moons too, some bigger than our earth even, so maybe moon shouldn't just mean small. And I tell them about fresh water oysters taken into labs, still timing their movement with the moon, even when they can't see her light, and then pause for a minute to let them all think about that amazing thing. I tell them all kinds of things and show them the illustrations I made, which are not half as good as the pictures I can see in my mind. Everything I tell them is very factual and true, so I don't know why I start crying, I just don't know why. I keep crying and talking, talking and crying, and no one is trying to stop me.

I am standing and thinking of being sick on the bathroom floor and Tillie crawling to me. Thinking of Ms. Eve in the moonlight, and needing to run so fast, when she wanted to gaze at the moon, and how do we take care of all these people that need our help? How do I take care of Mama from here and how will I take care of these grown-ups when I'm there? And what if Mrs. Ruth Anderson changes her mind or leaves or gets tired of us? I stop talking but nobody moves.

Henry says, "Is it over?" and I shake my head no, feeling my lips shake and not able to stop them.

"We're listening," he says, then he stands up beside me and puts his hand on my shoulder, so I can lean against him if I want. His arm is strong and safe and I want to stay there forever.

"It isn't hard to imagine human beings one day living on the moon," I say, my voice still shaking. "But for now it is good to admire her from earth and let her shine for us at night. In this author's opinion, people need the moon, even if they don't always remember they do." I look up at everyone's expecting faces. "The end."

"Bravo!" Mike yells and everyone claps and cheers. I didn't know they would like it so much, or maybe they just like me that much. Then Mike gets up to smoke and Tillie is smiling at her friend and Henry gives me a squeeze then looks for Mrs. Worthy's eyes and Ms. Eve is clearing plates. Aunt Ruth sits and watches me still.

"You did well," she says. "Come here."

She opens her arms, and I walk to her and feel her wrap warm and soft around me. I will take this Aunt Ruth, my new Mrs. Anderson. I will make something special of my life, like Ms. Eve said, and be my fullest like the moon. I don't think I'm the Spirit Bear for this family, but maybe Mama is, even from far away, because she sort of sent me to them, in a way. I will come again and visit, I hope more than anything. I will help Mama the best I can. I will listen for the old stories and help write the new ones.

"Yes," Aunt Ruth whispers in our hug.

"Yes," I whisper back. There is so much for me, for all of us, and I will be brave and go looking for it. *Yes.*

About the Author

The Gifts We Keep is Katie Grindeland's first novel and select participant of the 2016 Multnomah County Library Writers Project. Katie grew up outside Seattle, Washington, and has lived in Portland, Oregon, for most of her adult life. When she is not working as a 911/Police/Fire dispatcher, she enjoys hiking, cooking, and watching *The Office* on repeat with her two teenagers.

Acknowledgments

In addition to the talented staff at Ooligan Press, I want to extend my deepest thanks to the Multnomah County Library and their Library Writers Project for the opportunity to get this novel out of a dusty binder and into the hands of their wonderful readers. I especially want to thank my librarian spirit guide, Alison Kastner, for being such an enthusiastic champion of this project, and for further convincing me librarians are secretly angels.

Ooligan Press

Ooligan Press is a student-run publishing house rooted in the rich literary culture of the Pacific Northwest. Founded in 2001 as part of Portland State University's Department of English, Ooligan is dedicated to the art and craft of publishing. Students pursuing master's degrees in book publishing staff the press in an apprenticeship program under the guidance of a core faculty of publishing professionals.

Project Manager
Emily Frantz

Project Team
Bryn Kristi
Rachel Palmer
Nada Sewiden
Julie Collins
Kimberley Scofield
Maegan O'Brion

Acquisitions
Ari Mathae
Taylor Thompson

Design
Jenny Kimura
Kristen Ludwigsen

Digital
Kaitlin Barnes

Editing
Hilary Louth
Emma Hovley
Elise Hitchings
Monique Vieu
Kelly Hogan
Brennah Hale
Scott MacDonald
Esa Grisby
Meagan Nolan
Megan Huddleston
Marina Garcia
Hanna Ziegler
Des Hewson
Jennifer Guiher
Jessica DeBolt

Marketing
Sydney Kiest

Social Media
Sadie Verville
Katie Fairchild